CINDERELLA'S ONE-NIGHT BABY

MICHELLE SMART

AWAKENED IN HER ENEMY'S PALAZZO

KIM LAWRENCE

MILLS & BOON

First published in Great Britain 2024
by Mills & Boon, an imprint of HarperCollins*Publishers* Ltd,
1 London Bridge Street, London, SE1 9GF

www.harpercollins.co.uk

HarperCollins*Publishers*, Macken House, 39/40 Mayor Street Upper,
Dublin 1, D01 C9W8, Ireland

Cinderella's One-Night Baby © 2024 Michelle Smart

Awakened in Her Enemy's Palazzo © 2024 Kim Lawrence

ISBN: 978-0-263-31994-1

02/24

Michelle Smart's love affair with books started when she was a baby and would cuddle them in her cot. A voracious reader of all genres, she found her love of romance established when she stumbled across her first Mills & Boon book at the age of twelve. She's been reading them—and writing them—ever since. Michelle lives in Northamptonshire, England, with her husband and two young Smarties.

Kim Lawrence lives on a farm in Anglesey with her university lecturer husband, assorted pets who arrived as strays and never left, and sometimes one or both of her boomerang sons. When she's not writing she loves to be outdoors gardening, or walking on one of the beaches for which the island is famous—along with being the place where Prince William and Catherine made their first home!

CINDERELLA'S ONE-NIGHT BABY

MICHELLE SMART

MILLS & BOON

CHAPTER ONE

THE BORDERS BETWEEN the tiny principality of Monte Cleure and the countries it was sandwiched between, France and Spain, had, for generations, been lax. A wave of your passport at a bored border guard or a facial recognition scan had been considered the height of security. As the principality was considered to be Monaco on steroids and awash with millionaires and billionaires taking sanctuary in its low tax regime, this laxness, along with its notoriously lazy, corrupt police force meant it also attracted the more unscrupulous, namely drugs, arms and people traffickers who found Monte Cleure the perfect place to launder their dirty money.

This shameful attitude to law and order came to an abrupt end when its internationally loathed monarch and ruler, King Dominic, met an untimely end in a racing accident and his sister, Catalina, reluctantly took the throne. One of her first acts on being crowned Queen a couple of years before was to crack down on the criminals who used her beautiful land for their nefarious enterprises. Which meant tightening controls at the borders. Within months of Catalina taking the throne, the borders were strengthened and mandatory retraining given. Any guard suspected of corruption was sacked and new recruits taken on. One of those new recruits was Gabrielle Breton.

A year into the job and Gabrielle still loved it. It wasn't

the path she'd intended to take in life, but she'd determined to make the best of it. No two days were the same. For sure, most days were routine but on days like today, when a tip-off had come in that a luxury car was being used to smuggle a million euros of cocaine into the principality from Spain, the excitement would swell inside her. She always made sure to hide it, of course. Gabrielle took pride in her professionalism, a pride that had seen her immediate supervisor recently encourage her to apply for a promotion. It was something she was still carefully considering. Gabrielle rarely did anything without careful consideration.

The main problem with the luxury car tip-off was that luxury cars accounted for roughly seventy per cent of the vehicles that passed the border. If you didn't have pots of cash there was little point in visiting. Fortunately extra information had been provided. The car in question was a brand-new model and would be driven by a man and a woman.

With barely an hour to go until her shift finished, Gabrielle and her team had thoroughly searched nine cars, X-rayed three of them to be certain, and found nothing. The other team had also come up with zilch. And so it was that when a futuristic-looking sports car that looked as if it had been driven straight out of the factory approached the border, a man behind the wheel, a woman beside him, both teams willed it to join their lanes. Gabrielle's team won, and it was her turn to take the lead on it.

Waving the driver of the gleaming machine with Spanish number plates into a bay, she waited until it had parked and then indicated to the driver to wind his window down.

A darkly handsome, black-haired man with a thick designer beard duly obliged.

'Passports, please,' she said politely in Spanish.

'I am already on your system,' the man replied with more

than a hint of impatience. 'I am entitled to use facial recognition.'

She vaguely recognised him, was quite certain this was a face she'd seen when on facial recognition duty and possibly in the media too. But that made no difference to the job in hand.

'I asked for your passports.'

Strong jaw clenching, long fingers with short, buffed nails handed them over. 'Is there a problem?'

She opened the first passport. 'We shall find out shortly, Mr... Morato.' Andrés Javier Morato. Spanish national. Recently turned thirty-three.

Gabrielle glanced at his passenger before opening the second passport. Sophia Maribel Morato. Spanish national. Thirty-five. 'What is your purpose for visiting Monte Cleure?'

'What is the purpose of asking that?'

'The purpose is for my job, sir.'

Lips that could only be described as sensuous tightened in a scowl. 'I have property and business interests here. I put a *lot* of money into your economy.'

She resisted yawning. 'Congratulations. The purpose of your visit?'

'The purpose of this particular visit, *miss*...' the *miss* had a nice dismissive ring to it '...is tonight's party at the palace. I am a friend and invited guest of your Queen.'

'Lucky you.' She swore half the people crossing the border that day were attending Queen Catalina's party. Gabrielle would have happily sold one of her kidneys for an invitation to be under the same roof as the woman she idolised, but as that was as likely to happen as Gabrielle growing a second head, she kept her tone disinterested and professional. 'And if you want to address me, it's *officer*. Are you concealing any illegal drugs of any quantity on your person or in your vehicle, or any other goods that run contrary to the laws of Monte Cleure?'

He gave her the kind of look she'd expect to receive if asking whether he ate pet goldfish straight from the bowl.

'No,' he said tightly. 'I have nothing illegal in my possession or anything I need to declare. Are we done? Only, we're already running late. I have a team of people due at my apartment in twenty minutes to prepare Sophia and myself for the Queen's party.'

'I'm afraid we are not done yet, sir, and namedropping the Queen isn't going to make the process go any faster. Please step out of the car. Both of you.'

Eyes almost as black as his hair and beard lasered with fury onto her. 'Do you know who I am?'

That old chestnut. Nearly as common and as tedious as the *I put a lot of money into your economy* one. 'I'm sure you are very important, sir, but I have a job to do and I need you to comply.'

The man's wife, who'd been silently observing, tapped his wrist with the hand her huge diamond engagement ring and thick wedding band resided on, and made a gesture with her head before pressing something on the door. It lifted up like something from a sci-fi movie.

With a put-upon sigh, Andrés followed suit, unfolding what turned out to be an incredibly tall, muscular body from the car. His wife was much smaller, only a few inches taller than Gabrielle, although the heels she wore made her appear statuesque.

'Stand behind the line, please.' Gabrielle pointed where she needed them to go, just a couple of feet from the bay the car was parked in. Sophia didn't need telling twice. Andrés though, folded his arms across his broad chest, pecs flexing beneath the black shirt. The sleeves were rolled to the elbows, revealing a sleeve tattoo on his left arm that, at first glance, looked surprisingly tasteful.

'Why?'

'We need to search your car and regulations don't allow us to do that until you're behind the line.' She indicated her two colleagues and the sniffer dog waiting patiently for the go ahead.

Varying forms of anger and outrage contorted the handsome face. 'How long is this going to take?'

'It will take as long as it takes.'

'I need you to fast track it.'

'I'm afraid your friend the Queen dislikes it when we cut corners. Now stand behind the line, *sir*.'

For a moment she thought it quite possible that his head would explode.

A year ago, Gabrielle would have found it intimidating having a man twice her size staring down at her with such arrogant loathing. She could practically read what he was thinking: *No one told Andrés Morato what to do! Car searches were for the hoi polloi, not for someone as important as him!*

'It's your own time you're wasting,' she helpfully reminded him.

Nostrils on the patrician nose flared. Chiselled jaw clenched hard enough to grind wheat. And then he saw sense, walking backwards three steps without removing his 'I'm going to make you pay for this inconvenience' gaze from her.

'Thank you for your co-operation, sir.'

'If you damage it in any way, officer, you will pay for the repairs.'

'Don't worry, sir, the money you put into my country's economy means we can afford it.'

Andrés stared at the diminutive woman politely bossing him around and politely using his words as weapons back at him, and the fury that had been curdling his stomach all week grew. 'What are you hoping to find?'

Her response was to squeeze her hands into latex gloves and pretend not to hear him. But she had heard, of that he was certain.

Andrés was not used to being ignored. He was not used to being bossed around. He was used to deferment. His family was the only exception to this, and it was only because of his sister that he'd dragged himself out of bed that morning instead of catching up on all the sleep he'd missed in recent weeks thanks to the legal letter that had rocked the foundations of his world. The last thing he wanted was to socialise with hundreds of people.

His good friend and business partner on a number of ventures, the king consort, would have understood if he'd cancelled. Sophia would have sulked until Christmas. This was a day she'd been hugely looking forward to, and so, Andrés had done his best to keep his bad mood to himself. He thought he'd been successful, right until his helicopter landed in Barcelona and he'd got behind the wheel of his brand-new toy.

Sophia had put her seatbelt on and faced him. 'We don't have to go to the party if you don't want.'

He'd glared at her. 'You could have said that before we left Seville.'

'I was hoping you'd cheer up. I haven't seen you in a month. The least you can do is pretend to be happy at spending time with me.'

He'd put the car into gear without another word and had ignored her every effort at conversation since. That the traffic had been heavy, stopping and starting at will and refusing to part like the Red Sea at his command had only added to the foulness of his mood. The hope that actually getting behind the wheel would lift his mood had been a false one. Should have taken the helicopter all the way into Monte Cleure. He'd be already in his apartment brooding that he'd have to leave it shortly and fake gregariousness for the evening, not having to deal with a jobsworth border guard.

In his best sarcastic voice, he addressed the border guard again. 'You must be searching for something, so what is it? Drugs? Counterfeit handbags? A litter of puppies?'

'If I find puppies, sir, then I will personally use this on you.' She patted the bulge at her hip, the expression on her face making it impossible to tell if she was joking or not.

'Is that a gun or a taser?' Sophia asked, finally joining in.

'A taser.'

'Can I use it on him?'

'If it was at my discretion then gladly, but I'm afraid it's against regulations and more than my job's worth, miss.' She crouched down and ran her hands beneath the wheel arch. She was so short she didn't have to crouch very far.

'That's a shame,' Sophia mused.

The guard, or *officer* as she preferred to be addressed, still examining the wheel arch, said over her shoulder to Sophia, 'I believe if you search the dark web, you can purchase your own. If in doubt about how to use it, just aim and press.'

Sophia laughed. 'I will certainly keep that in mind for the next time he embarrasses me by throwing his weight around.'

The officer's face didn't even flicker. 'I couldn't possibly comment.'

Andrés looked between the two women and the darkness eating at him flickered.

He was being gratuitously rude, he realised. He'd spent the day letting his sister take the brunt of his foul mood and now he was throwing his weight around with a border guard and behaving like a self-entitled brat. As bureaucratic as the officer was being, she was only doing her job.

Inhaling deeply, he held his hands up and attempted a facial expression that wasn't a glare. 'Okay, okay, I get it, I'm behaving like an ass who deserves to be tasered.'

The officer, who'd moved onto the next wheel arch, almost smiled. Her lips, Andrés observed, were only a touch away from being too big for the rest of her face. If they weren't set a normal distance beneath her rather squashed nose he would assume she'd had them enhanced like so many women liked to do in this day and age.

Hers was an interesting face. Even more interesting; not a scrap of makeup on it. A smear of oil down the right cheekbone though. Slightly frizzy dark brown hair scraped into the kind of ponytail he hadn't seen on a female since his childhood. Absolutely no way to tell what was hidden beneath the severe, masculine uniform of dark blue shirt and trousers and polished black steel-capped boots.

His phone vibrated in his pocket. It was his lawyer. This was the call he'd been waiting for, the call that could either shift the darkness or push him further into it.

Forgetting all about the pocket-sized officer's interesting face and nondescript body, he moved away from Sophia to answer it.

Although Gabrielle was in no way intimidated by the man, she found herself breathing a little easier when Andrés turned his back and walked away to take his call. He wasn't intimidating but *unnerving*, she decided.

His wife though, was the complete opposite, and quickly struck up conversation. In no time at all, she was telling Gabrielle all about the boutique she owned and designed the clothing for, which explained the gorgeous floaty dress she was wearing, and how she didn't particularly like leaving Seville but when it came to a party with royalty then who was she to refuse?

It was rare that someone whose ultra-expensive car was being subjected to a forced search was friendly and chatty. Usually they behaved like Sophia's husband and sulked like small children. Gabrielle was an expert on small children. Even when face down on the floor having a temper tantrum because you had the temerity to say no to them, they were easier to deal with than entitled billionaires of either sex. One thing life had taught Gabrielle, long before she'd become a border guard, was that rich people were a law to themselves. This billionaire, Sophia Morato, was a refreshing change, even if she did make Gabrielle feel like a moon eclipsed by the sun. It wasn't just her slender beauty, but her vivaciousness and the ease she so clearly felt in her own skin. It was an ease Gabrielle envied. In truth, it would be easy to envy everything about Sophia Morato…with the exception of her arrogant husband. Imagine having to deal with that rude, entitled attitude every day. Having the looks and physique of a Greek god in no way mitigated that.

He really was gorgeous though, and as he pocketed his phone and walked back to his wife, Gabrielle had to stop her eyes from wandering to him for another gawp and concentrate on her search of the car's bonnet. Not only was gawping unprofessional but he was a married man.

'How are you getting on?' he asked Gabrielle in a much lighter tone than he'd used before.

'So far, so good.'

'Do you think it will take much longer?' No sign of impatience. Whatever his conversation had been about, it had definitely had a positive effect on him. Maybe he'd lost a billion euros and just learned it had been found down the back of a sofa. Gabrielle had lost ten Monte Cleure dollars recently and had cheered right up when she found it in the back pocket of her jeans.

'Depends if we find anything.' The longer the search had gone on, the more inclined she'd been to call the whole thing off and send the Moratos on their way. She would bet her salary they had nothing illegal stashed in it. Gizmo, the sniffer dog, hadn't reacted at all. But she had a job to do, a job where cutting corners was forbidden, and the search would be completed with the thoroughness demanded.

Bonnet done with, Gabrielle opened the tiny boot. It contained a mandatory breakdown kit and nothing else. Gizmo had a good sniff but, again, nothing.

Suppressing a sigh, she carefully lifted the boot's luxury floor carpet and opened the hatch beneath it. With practised ease, she removed the spare tyre.

'They get the smallest person on the team to do the heavy lifting?'

She flicked her gaze to the Spaniard. His arms were folded loosely across his chest, a half-smile on his face and a thick black eyebrow raised.

'I'm fitter than I look.'

'So I see.'

Although he was only making an observation, something fluttered deep in the pit of Gabrielle's stomach.

'Do you work out?'

'Only if you count lifting spare tyres as working out—being a single mother and holding down a job doesn't leave much time for gym memberships.'

She had no idea why she'd just mentioned being a mother.

Sophia did an exaggerated double-take. 'You have a child? How old?'

Although Gabrielle knew there was little danger in talking about Lucas, especially with people whose paths she would never cross outside this border, her stomach still tightened. Time had only eased the terror that had cloaked her in the days and weeks and months after bringing Lucas home, not eradicated it completely. 'Four,' she answered with practised steadiness.

'You must have been young.'

'Nineteen.'

'And you're a single mother?'

'It's just me and Lucas.' And that's exactly how it had to stay. It was far too dangerous for Gabrielle to entertain anything else.

'That must be tough.'

She could have no idea. 'Sometimes.'

'Do you get much help?'

'My mother helps as much as she can—Lucas is spending the weekend with her and my brother, which is great for all of them.' Even if it meant Gabrielle returning to her apartment and physically hurting at Lucas's absence.

Closing the boot lid, she patted it gently. 'We're all done here.'

Gizmo hadn't reacted to the spare tyre. The car was clean.

'We can go?' Andrés asked.

'Once you've inspected your vehicle for any damage we might have accidentally caused and signed the form for it.'

He immediately crossed the yellow line to join her and looked at his watch.

Unable to resist, she adopted an innocent voice and said, 'Do you have to be somewhere, sir?'

Andrés snapped his attention back to the officer. It was

the barely suppressed humour flitting across the interesting face that had been mostly deadpan throughout the ordeal she'd put him through that brought a short burst of laughter from his mouth. Raising an eyebrow, he said with mock seriousness, 'I don't know if you're aware but we are expected at the palace for the Queen's birthday party.'

Dark brown eyes widened in mock surprise. 'You should have mentioned it.' Then, pillowy lips tugging at the corners, she indicated the stone building that housed the Monte Cleure border staff's administrative offices. 'I'll make it as quick as I can for you. I'll start on the form. If you find damage, take a photo of it. If there isn't any, all I'll need is your signature and… Are you okay, miss?'

It took Andrés a beat to realise she'd turned her focus to Sophia. Following her gaze he saw she'd covered her hand with her mouth.

'Feel sick,' she mumbled, doubling over. 'Bathroom?'

The officer sprang into action and hurried her off into the administrative office. Andrés watched them disappear inside, perplexed that his sister, who'd been perfectly normal up to that point had, without any warning or build-up or hints that anything was wrong, suddenly declared a need to vomit.

Not having the strongest of stomachs when it came to illness, Andrés decided to leave the officer to deal with her, and inspect his car. After close examination, he headed inside and found the officer at a desk behind a computer.

'No damage,' he confirmed. 'How's Sophia?'

She looked up at him and grimaced. 'I've given her some water but she didn't want me to stay in the bathroom…' Her words tailed off as Sophia came in through an internal door and flopped onto a visitor chair.

Running the back of a hand dramatically over her forehead, she said, 'Andrés, I feel awful. I don't think I can make it to the party.'

He stared at her with narrowed eyes. His sister had always been a terrible actress and this over-the-top performance reminded him of when she would try to convince their mother she was too ill for school.

'I was sick twice,' she insisted into the silence, then lowered her voice and weakened it to add, 'Can you imagine if I gave the Queen an illness? On her birthday?'

He could laugh at the irony. All day he'd been like a bear with a sore head wishing to be hit by a meteor to get out of having to attend the damned party, but since receiving the excellent news from his lawyer, his mood had done a one-eighty. Now, just as he was looking forward to a night of celebrating his life not being upended after all and partying without any press intrusion, his plus one was bailing on him.

Andrés continued studying Sophia. She didn't look ill. Not in the slightest. But, he reminded himself, this was a party she'd almost cried when he asked if she wanted to go with him, a party she'd spent two months designing and creating a dress to wear for. Why would she pretend illness for something she'd been so excited about?

With a twinge of guilt for assuming she was faking, he said, 'I'll get Rich to collect us.' Rich was his helicopter pilot. The building of his Monte Cleure apartment had its own helipad. If he'd got Rich to fly them straight here all this hassle would have been avoided.

'Oh, you must go still.'

He raised both eyebrows at this uncharacteristic selflessness.

'We've travelled all this way,' she insisted. 'And it would be rude for you to cancel at such short notice. This is the

Queen of Monte Cleure we're talking about. Her husband's one of your business partners.'

'If you don't come then I will be the only person without a plus one,' he pointed out. 'The meet-and-greet part starts in two hours. The women I know who could take your place would never make it in time.' Well, there were some women who could make it, but they were women who would assume his invitation was just a short step to a marriage proposal.

Sophia's gaze drifted to the officer who'd been quietly completing the form for them to sign. Andrés followed her gaze then looked back to his sister, his brow creasing in a silent question that was answered with a subtle nod. He looked again at the officer and tried to imagine her in a ball gown. His imagination completely failed him but...

There was real merit to Sophia's silently delivered suggestion. *Real* merit.

Gabrielle had been following the conversation in the same way she followed Lucas's inane chatter when he was describing in exact detail the plot of his favourite cartoon: with one ear. It was only as she was printing off the form that would let the Moratos leave and signalled the end of her work shift that the silence suddenly became loaded.

She looked from one Morato to the other. Both were sizing her up as if she were a prize cow about to be sold off to market.

Comprehension dawned. Her mouth fell open. 'You cannot be serious?'

CHAPTER TWO

IT TURNED OUT the Moratos were completely serious. They wanted Gabrielle to take Sophia's place as Andrés's guest for the Queen's birthday party. The same Queen Gabrielle positively *idolised*. The same Queen she'd lined the streets to see, with Lucas in his buggy, and cheered for when she'd passed them in her coronation procession. The same Queen who'd enacted laws that had made Gabrielle feel a little safer.

Visions of princesses in fairy-tale dresses dancing with handsome princes in swallowtail suits floated in her mind, of delicious food, champagne and…

'I can't go,' she said, shaking off the longing and bringing herself back down to earth. 'I don't know you and I have nothing to wear.'

'You can wear my dress,' Sophia said.

When Gabrielle realised she wasn't joking, she burst out laughing. 'You're taller and skinnier than me!'

'Not by much. There's a team at the apartment waiting to turn me into a princess for the night and make any last-minute alterations to my dress.' Her eyes narrowed as she studied Gabrielle's physique. 'The hem will obviously have to be adjusted and a little work needed around the bust and hips but it's doable in the timeframe.'

Cheeks burning at the scrutiny, she wailed, 'I can't!'

Sophia arched a brow. 'Do you have a better offer for the evening? Your son is with your mother, your work shift is over…what better way to spend a Saturday night than at the party of the decade?'

Gabrielle was fighting hard not to give hope and excitement air. It had been well over four years since she'd been on a proper night out.

The circumstances around Lucas's conception had compelled her to distance herself from her friends. By the time he was born she'd managed to alienate all of them with her refusal to discuss the father and absolute refusal to include them in anything to do with the pregnancy or birth. She still felt terrible about it, terrible for hurting the tight-knit group she'd grown up with, but she'd had no choice. The risks had been too great.

Since she'd brought Lucas home, one evening had been much the same as the next. Saturday evenings had ceased to have any meaning. Tonight, with Lucas at her brother's, Gabrielle's grand plan had involved a long bath and an action movie too old for Lucas to watch. There was no spare cash for her to go out and party even if she had friends left to party with.

'You don't even know my name,' she felt compelled to remind them *and* herself, because this whole idea was bonkers, and that they were taking it seriously only proved the Moratos themselves were bonkers and she shouldn't even be entertaining the idea, no matter how her heart soared at the thought of it.

Andrés, who'd been a silent observer propped against the wall up to this point, stretched his neck. 'What *is* your name?'

'Gabrielle. And I only know your name because the two of you and your car matched the profile of a pair of drug smugglers.'

The hint of a smile played on his lips. 'Gabrielle, if you attend the party with me, you will be sparing me from social humiliation and saving the palace staff an enormous headache—by now, the tables for the banquet will have been laid and the places set—'

'But I don't *know* you,' she interrupted. 'I can't go off with a stranger even if it is to the palace! For all I know, you two are the Spanish Bonnie and Clyde and planning to lure me to my death… No offence,' she hastened to add when she realised she'd just accused them of being notorious criminals.

The hint of a smile widened. 'None taken. You are right to be cautious.' In two easy strides he was resting a butt cheek on her desk and leaning across to look her in the eye. 'Gabrielle, I can assure you of your safety. There is a team of people waiting to transform Sophia into a princess at my apartment—they can transform *you* into that princess. My driver will take us there and when the party has finished, deliver you to your home. You will not have to spend any time alone with me. We will be chaperoned at all times.'

Oh, but she was torn. Situations like this only happened in the movies, and it would be much easier to think logically if her airwaves hadn't suddenly become deluged with the delicious scent she'd caught a trace of when Andrés first entered the office. Not only did the man have the face and physique of a Greek God but smelt much as she imagined one would too. Some people really did have everything, and as she gazed into his black eyes, the image of the dancing princesses and handsome princes floated back into her mind and longing refilled her soaring heart. Gabrielle hadn't even attended her own senior school graduation; had missed out on all the glitz and glamour and excitement because her sister had been in no state to be left alone.

Eloise had been broken by a man whose life was every bit as glamorous and as self-centred as Andrés Morato's.

'Andrés is a gentleman. I trust him to take care of you and to make your experience at the Queen's party one to remember for the rest of your life,' Sophia said gently, and it was with a burn of embarrassment that Gabrielle realised she'd briefly tuned out that she was in the room too. Sophia must be one trusting woman to encourage her husband to take another woman to a party as his plus one…

It suddenly became clear why they were asking this of her.

Sophia didn't have to worry about her husband making a move on plain old Gabrielle Breton and Andrés didn't have to worry about temptation. Eloise was the beauty of the Breton family. Gabrielle wasn't attractive enough to be a threat to the Moratos' marriage.

'Think of the story you will have to tell your son when he's older,' Andrés coaxed. 'The story of the night his mother went to the Queen's birthday party and dined and danced with royalty like a princess.'

Even more longing swelled in her chest. The minute Fran, her old best friend from school had turned eighteen, she'd bagged herself a part-time job amongst the palace's waiting staff and had regaled their old gang with tales of the fanciest food imaginable and a palace more spectacular than the public could imagine.

To actually attend one of those parties as a guest…

Striving to keep her professional face in place, she looked into Andrés's black eyes, so hypnotic that even if he wasn't married she'd be having to fight to stop herself from falling into them. 'If I agree…'

He nodded encouragingly, smugness already spreading over his handsome face at what would have been, to his mind, a foregone conclusion.

'*If* I agree then which Andrés Morato will I be accompanying? The spoilt brat or the less spoilt brat? Because if it's the spoilt brat I think I'll give it a miss.'

The smugness evaporated. His expression could only be described as gobsmacked.

The moment Gabrielle agreed to the outrageous suggestion, things moved terrifyingly fast. Refusing the Moratos' offer to drive her to their apartment—not only was it quicker for her to cycle but the back seat of their car was so cramped that even little old her would struggle to fit in it—she allowed herself to be talked into going straight to their apartment rather than returning to her own for essentials. Everything she needed, they assured her, would be provided.

A ten-minute bike ride later, during which she called her mother to check in on Lucas and fill her in on everything, and Gabrielle looked at the huge gold doors of the Imperium, one of Monte Cleure's most magnificent apartment blocks, and shook her head in wonder. She'd cycled past this building twice a day, four days a week for the last year, passed it numerous times in the twenty-two years before that, and never had it crossed her mind that one day she would be invited inside.

A man in a professional suit appeared like an apparition. 'Ms Breton?'

She nodded. No point asking how he knew. Her uniform was a dead giveaway. At least this meant Andrés hadn't changed his mind. It had been patently obvious from his shocked reaction to her calling him a spoilt brat that no one had called him anything insulting in a long, long time, and though he'd broken the stunned silence with laughter, she'd wondered if she'd arrive at his apartment and be given a curt note and a banning order forbidding her from entering the building.

'I'm Bernard, the Imperium's concierge. Allow Pierre to take your bicycle. I will show you to Mr Morato's apartment. He arrived three minutes ago.'

She assumed Pierre was the gangly teenager standing behind him. 'Thank you... Where will you put my bike?'

'It will be kept in storage until you or Mr Morato request it.'

'You will look after it, won't you?' she asked the teenager anxiously. She couldn't afford a replacement.

After assurances were made, Gabrielle was swept into a gorgeous atrium that reminded her of the seven-star hotel casino she'd briefly worked weekends at as a croupier when she turned eighteen. Her border guard uniform made her feel decidedly unsophisticated and out of place, and she self-consciously smoothed the strands of hair that had come loose from her ponytail and tried not to tread so heavily in her clumpy boots. Not that her own clothes would make her feel any less frumpy and out of place.

Led into a mirrored elevator with sink-your-toes-in maroon carpet and an armchair for the lazy, and which had two non-emergency buttons: up and down, Bernard doffed his hat again as the door closed on her. A short, silent ride later and the door slid open into a small room with marble floors, a small marble desk and one door. Next to the door was a security box. It was while she was peering at the box wondering which button she needed to press that the door opened.

Andrés, shirt buttons undone revealing a muscular chest with a healthy smattering of black hair covering it, greeted her with a dazzling smile that revealed dazzlingly white, straight teeth and an outstretched hand. 'I was afraid you might have changed your mind. Forgive my state of undress but my tailor is about to make last-minute adjustments to my tuxedo.'

Not knowing where to put her eyes, aware of heated colour staining her cheeks, it took a beat longer than was polite to realise she was supposed to shake the outstretched hand. Painfully aware her own hands were filthy with oil and grime, the need for speed meaning she'd bypassed her usual end-of-shift hand-wash, Gabrielle gave it the quickest, lightest shake she could get away with. Except Andrés had other ideas, firmly wrapping his fingers around it and clasping his other hand to it, flooding skin that hadn't been cold with tingling warmth. His hands were so big compared to hers that it was like being engulfed by an oversized bear. 'Thank you for agreeing to this. I am in your debt.'

Releasing her hand with the same nonchalance with which he'd clasped it, he stepped to one side and waved a hand for her to enter. 'Please, come in.'

Absently rubbing her still-tingling hand, Gabrielle entered an apartment that made her feel so insignificant and self-conscious that if the door hadn't closed behind her, she'd have bolted.

She'd been born in Monte Cleure. The district she'd been raised in and still lived in was a tiny dot in the landscape, an anomaly compared to the grandeur the rest of their citizens lived in. Her district was protected from the bulldozers for redevelopment only because it provided the staff who worked on the yachts, in the hotels, in the penthouses, in the palace, kept law and order, and nursed people when they were sick. She'd spent her whole life in the principality she called home and she had never, until this moment, entered the home of someone outside her own district.

Too busy gawping at the gorgeous living space she'd been

ushered into that in itself was twice the size of her whole apartment, taking in the multiple high sash windows, the luxurious furnishings and exquisite modern art works, she failed to notice Sophia until she was right in front of her. 'Let me introduce you to your team,' she said, taking Gabrielle's hand.

'One minute,' Andrés interrupted. 'The NDA needs to be signed first.'

That would be the non-disclosure agreement briefly discussed as they left the border force office. And *discussed* was a loose term for Andrés calling out as he strode to his car that he'd have one drawn up and ready for her to sign when she arrived at his apartment.

A pencil-thin man in a business suit appeared, seemingly from nowhere, and handed her a tablet. 'Input your details, then read the contents and sign.'

'I need to get on. Any problems, Gino can handle it,' Andrés said before disappearing through an archway.

More than a little dazed, Gabrielle did as Gino, who she assumed was Andrés's lawyer, instructed. Her details inputted, the agreement itself appeared on the screen. The language used was clear enough. Signing meant she promised not to disclose any personal details about Andrés, his home or any conversation she was privy to with him and any guest at the party, including any conversations overheard. Compared to the NDA Eloise had been tricked into signing, it wasn't particularly onerous and didn't forbid Gabrielle from talking about the party itself. Also, the reasons for signing it were completely different to Eloise's situation, so she swallowed her misgivings and signed the box indicated with her finger.

No sooner had she passed the tablet back to the lawyer than Sophia snatched hold of Gabrielle's hand and dragged her off through the same tall, wide arch Andrés had vanished through. It led into a small corridor with three doors. She opened the furthest one, plunging Gabrielle into the most stunning bedroom she'd ever seen. More than a bedroom. More like the suites found in Monte Cleure's finest hotels used exclusively by their wealthiest guests, but with a real feminine tone to it. The huge sleigh bed only took a fraction of the space. Waiting for her were five ultra-stylish women.

'Ladies,' said Sophia, 'meet Gabrielle. I need you to work your magic on her.'

For a good minute, the five women did nothing but stare critically at her. And then they swooped.

First she was ushered into an ultra-modern bathroom with a walk-in shower you could party in.

'Shampoo your hair and then use this,' the tallest of the women said, pressing a small tube into her hand. 'Keep it in for two minutes before rinsing. When you're showered, wrap your wet hair in a towel for no longer than thirty seconds. Time is of the essence—be finished in ten minutes. Make sure to use the nail brush.'

Showering orders given, the women left the bathroom.

Gabrielle stripped her uniform off and stepped under the square shower head that gave the illusion of floating off the ceiling. It was so large it could comfortably shower water on two people, and as she made that observation, an image floated in her head of Andrés standing beneath the spray, the chest she'd had that glimpse of completely bare…

Flustered at the unwanted image, flustered too at the hot, sticky feeling in the base of her abdomen, she quickly turned her attention to the digital screen inbuilt into the tiles that had an array of symbols and temperature readings on it. Not having the faintest idea what she was doing, she tentatively pressed the largest symbol, a circle, on the top left corner. In less than a second, water set at the perfect temperature cascaded over her.

Resolutely *not* thinking of the married Andrés or his naked chest, she popped the shampoo lid. It had the most delicious scent she'd ever smelt and felt like silk on her hands. If she didn't have *time is of the essence* playing on a loop in her head, she'd have washed it twice just for the pleasure. Instead she moved onto the tube, which turned out to be an anti-frizz deep conditioner. Normally only able to afford the cheapest conditioner, she happily coated her hair with it, and then, while waiting for it to do its thing, sniffed the four varieties of decidedly feminine shower gels. The first was so delicious, reminding her of lilies in bloom, that she came close to swooning. She scrubbed every inch of her body with it.

Hair and body clean and rinsed, she reluctantly pressed the circle symbol again and the cascade stopped.

Oh, well, she told herself as she wrapped the warmest, biggest, fluffiest towel around her body, at least she had a story to share with Lucas; the day mama had a taster of how the elitist of society's elite lived.

Teeth brushed, oversized fluffy robe on, she stepped back into the bedroom and found it transformed into something that resembled a beauty parlour, the dressing table chair pulled back, hair styling products and a vast array of makeup and brushes lined up and ready for use.

Sophia, sitting on the corner sofa talking to a woman with a tape measure in hand, turned her face to Gabrielle with a smile and, for that brief moment, Gabrielle found herself ashamed to meet Sophia's eye; ashamed because if she could peer into Gabrielle's mind she'd find in it that brief fantasy of Sophia's husband naked.

At least it had been unbidden and she'd cut the imagery off practically the moment it formed, Gabrielle tried to comfort herself. Tried. Because unbidden or not, it had been *her* brain that conjured the image, and though she'd steadfastly refused to allow it to form again, it made her feel terrible to know she'd betrayed this nice woman with her imagination. As far as Gabrielle was concerned, the moment a couple committed themselves, that made them off-limits, even in the mind. Marriage made that commitment sacred. Or it should.

Before Lucas, marriage was something she'd assumed would be in her future. Meet a nice man, fall in love and settle down. But the commitment of marriage meant two becoming one, a unity of complete openness and the baring of souls. For Lucas's sake, she could not risk opening her soul to anyone. The consequences of it all going wrong— and many marriages *did* go wrong—were too great.

Returning Sophia's smile, the shame in Gabrielle's chest lifted.

It had been a mental blip, that was all. When they got to the palace, it would be Queen Catalina, and the party itself that would take all her attention, not the man she was accompanying as a favour.

Andrés was sprawled on a sofa sipping bourbon, flicking through the television channels and telling himself that checking his watch every twenty seconds wouldn't make the stylists working on Gabrielle work any quicker. They had a lot of work to do with her. That wasn't a criticism, just an observation. Andrés and Sophia hadn't been born into money. He remembered well the life they'd had before weekly manicures and pedicures and thrice weekly trims became routine. That life had been one of scrimping and saving. He remembered walking to school in shoes too tight around the toes and seeing flash cars zoom by and thinking, *One day I'll drive a car like that.* He would see men in tailored suits made of the finest material and think, *One day I'll wear clothes like that.* And he would see his father return home after a long day at work to a wife who worked equally long hours, the pair of them barely able to conceal their contempt of the other, and think, *There will never come a day that I marry.* By the age of thirteen, he'd been firm in his mind about this. When he grew up, he would be rich and happy and travel the world wearing the best clothes and live exactly as he pleased, single for ever. Which meant no children. His parents were proof that children were a tie you could not escape. Children with someone you detested was a recipe for a lifetime of misery and to Andrés's mind, life was too short to spend it being miserable. If his parents wanted to spend the rest of their lives stuck together, even though their children had both long flown the family nest and the wealth Andrés shared freely with them meant they had the means to escape each other and forge new lives apart, then that was their business.

His last-minute date for the evening had the right idea. He'd seen the tightening of her mouth when Sophia had asked about her son, and guessed the relationship with the son's father had broken down and she'd sensibly decided to live apart from him. Better than making her child live in a war zone? He didn't know. His parents' marriage had been very much a verbal war zone but as a child, he'd been terrified of them splitting up. Divorce had loomed large in his mind from the day he'd first learned what it meant.

The good thing now was that the whole mess with his ex, Susi, was over. These were things he need never worry about again, and he made a mental note to call his doctor first thing and get a vasectomy arranged. It was time. He would not put himself through that again. He'd known in his heart that her child couldn't be his—he was far too careful of accidents to let that happen—but still there had been that cold spark of fear that an accident *had* happened. If the tests had proved the child to be his then he would have felt obliged to tie his life to a woman who had more sides than a hexagon.

He wondered why the father of Gabrielle's child wasn't on the scene before dismissing the thought as none of his business. She'd been very young to have a child in this day and age though. Again, not a criticism, just an observation. Andrés did not appreciate people casting judgement on his life and so made sure not to cast judgement on theirs. Her judgement on him, calling him a spoilt brat, had been deserved. His bad mood had led to him behaving atrociously, but what had shocked him had been Gabrielle's willingness to call him out on it. Only Sophia ever did that, and that was only because she was his big sister and thought it her duty.

He poured himself another bourbon—just a small one—and allowed himself a look at the time. They needed to leave in four minutes if they were going to make it to the palace before the banquet started. He'd accepted that they would miss the initial champagne reception meet-and-greet but so long as they were there in time to take their designated seats then all would…

Voices sounded, breaking through his thoughts. The team had finished with his last-minute date.

Tipping his bourbon down his throat, he rose to his feet at the same moment the most ravishing woman he'd ever set eyes on appeared through the archway.

CHAPTER THREE

GABRIELLE KNEW THE shoes Sophia had coaxed her into wearing were perfect for the dress, mainly because the heels meant they didn't need to take much of the hem up. The problem was, she hadn't worn heels since those horrid casino days, and trying to walk in them with anything like elegance was a battle she feared she would lose, and so it was that she joined Andrés in the living area of his magnificent apartment with Sophia walking behind her softly chanting, 'One foot in front of the other, one foot in front of the other,' and mentally praying not to fall flat on her face. So intense was her concentration that at first the figure rising from the far sofa was nothing but a blur in her vision. It wasn't until her heart made a powerful thump that her eyes focused.

She actually felt her lungs close up and push the air out.

It took a long beat for Andrés to recognise the ravishing woman who'd appeared under the archway with Sophia as the oil-stained bossy border guard of the unflattering uniform and masculine boots. An even longer beat for him to close his mouth.

It was Sophia who broke the silence. 'Well?' she demanded, pointing her finger at Gabrielle. 'What do you think?'

Her words brought Andrés round from his temporary

paralysis. 'I think,' he said drily, focusing on Sophia as he strode over to them, 'that you look and sound very well for someone with a sickness bug.'

'I'm feeling much better,' she said cheerfully. 'Too late to change the arrangements back to what they were though. Now tell us what you think of Gabrielle's transformation. Doesn't she look divine?'

He found he had to snatch a breath before letting his gaze fall back on his last-minute date.

It must be the starkness in the difference between the woman who had disappeared to be made over and the woman who'd returned that had caused his paralysis, he figured. The contrast was astounding. The woman standing in front of him, blushing beautifully under the weight of his scrutiny, was wearing an elegant deep blue velvet dress that swept over one shoulder and beneath the other. Flaring gracefully at the hips, it pooled in a small train behind her. Her hair was loose; thicker, glossier and longer than he'd envisaged and fell like waves down to the swell of her breasts. He would never have guessed the utilitarian uniform concealed a perfect curvy body, or guessed that a shimmer of makeup could make an interesting face come alive and turn into something beautiful.

The only thing missing was jewellery. She wore not a scrap of it. About to suggest Sophia lend her some of her own, he looked even closer and realised Gabrielle didn't need jewellery after all. She sparkled perfectly without it.

'The team have done an amazing job,' he agreed. He'd known the team he'd brought in for Sophia could make anyone look a million dollars but this was incredible. He would have to pay them a bonus. 'No one would guess from looking at her that she works as a border guard.'

'Excuse me,' the woman in question said archly, 'but I am here, you know.'

Sophia was immediately contrite. 'I'm sorry, Gabrielle. I'm just incredibly excited for you.'

The pillowy lips covered in a sheen of red lipstick tugged into a smile. 'Apology accepted.' Then dark brown eyes accentuated by subtle, smoky makeup, locked onto his. 'As for you, Mr Morato, please remember that I am a human being and treat me as such.'

If she hadn't delivered her warning—and it was a warning—with a dry wryness, he would have taken offence at the implication that he would treat her as less than human if not reminded.

He'd have taken offence when the truth was Gabrielle was right, just as she'd been right to call him out earlier as a spoilt brat. She was setting her stall out early on how she expected to be treated and he could only respect her for it, respect her honesty; an honesty missing from the yes-men and -women he surrounded himself with. He'd been thinking about that when getting ready that evening and the tailor he'd used since he'd first earned enough to buy a fitted suit had been his usual deferential self. Because he hadn't always been deferential. When Andrés had first stepped into his tailor's shop over a decade ago, he'd been treated with politeness but there had been no reverence. That had only come about as his wealth and power had increased. It had happened in tiny increments, and not just with his tailor but everyone, staff, friends, acquaintances and lovers. They'd become nodding dogs only saying what they thought he wanted to hear.

Staring down into eyes that stared back with actual challenge and which grew more stunning the more he looked, he gave a half smile. 'Any more instructions before we leave,

Miss Breton? Or is it enough that I promise not to act like a spoilt brat and promise to treat you as a human?'

Her cheeks sucked in as if she were suppressing laughter. 'A promise to give me a crash course in palace etiquette on the drive there would be helpful.'

Sophia waved them off.

After seeing Gabrielle into the limousine, Andrés turned to his sister and hissed, 'You were damned well faking that illness. Don't deny it.'

She gave a beatific smile. 'I can deny whatever I like. What *you* can't deny is the spark between you. She's great.'

He glared at her.

'Andrés, she made you laugh. After the last couple of weeks you've had, you deserve some fun, and something tells me you'll have a lot more fun with Gabrielle than with me.'

If time wasn't so tight, he'd give his interfering sister a piece of his mind. He settled on another glare.

She waved cheerfully.

Setting off, he scrutinised the woman his sister had manipulated into taking as his replacement. Was she in on Sophia's Machiavellian plot? While he'd been learning from his lawyer that the world as he knew it hadn't ended after all, Sophia and Gabrielle had been chatting away like old friends.

It was the lack of guile in the returning stare, followed by her, 'Well come on then, palace etiquette. Unless you want me to embarrass you, tell me *everything*,' that sealed it for him.

'If in doubt, watch what I do and copy me, and you're going to make the muscles in your neck stiff if you don't relax.'

Gabrielle, who'd been listening intently to Andrés's rapidly delivered condensed palace etiquette tutorial, gave a surprised snigger. 'How can I relax in this thing? I'm frightened to touch anything in case I leave a mark.'

The car they were being chauffeured to the palace in was of a breed she was so used to seeing in the principality that she never even registered them other than to hope the gleaming monsters didn't knock her off her bicycle. The interior was as vast as she'd expected, smelling of leather and so shiny and sparkly that she could easily imagine being beamed up into space in it.

In answer, Andrés spread his hands and shrugged. 'It is a car, not a museum. Any marks will be cleaned.'

She'd never known people could live in such spotless fashion. His apartment had been just as immaculate as his car, not a speck of dust on any of the polished surfaces. No doubt he had a hidden army of minions emerging to spot clean the second a crumb was dropped. Andrés was immaculate too, from the perfectly quiffed black hair and the perfectly groomed thick black eyebrows to the perfectly trimmed thick black beard. Even his nails were buffed and trimmed to perfection. She'd guess no one had ever thought it necessary to order him to use a nail brush to scrub grime out from them. But then, she doubted he'd ever done a physical day's work in his life. She wondered if he worked out with people hovering beside him to wipe any sweat that dared pop out on his forehead.

There was a clear glass partition between them and the driver, but it had still been a relief that Andrés had kept close to the car door, legs stretched out, clearly making an effort to ensure distance and appear unthreatening despite his huge frame. What was less a relief was having to make a conscious effort not to stare at him. This was on top of dealing with the shame of her reaction to seeing him in his tuxedo. It had been a physical reaction her brain had had no control over and the only excuse she could come up with was that any woman would have looked at Andrés Morato filling a black tuxedo with a velvet lapel and sighed with pleasure. She guessed Sophia was too inured to the sight to bother sighing, not even an admiring glance of appreciation. Her attention had been all on Gabrielle, and it had been Gabrielle to whom she'd given the biggest embrace goodbye. Her lips had hardly grazed her husband's cheek when she'd seen them off into the limo. But then, Sophia was as beautiful as Andrés was handsome. She must be really secure in their marriage not to have any qualms about him spending the evening with another woman, even if that woman was a plain border guard with a small child, who needed an army of people working in tandem to make her presentable.

'What are you going to say when people ask why you're attending the party with someone who isn't your wife?'

His forehead creased with confusion. 'What are you talking about?'

'Sophia.'

His face contorted with what could only be described as grossed-out horror. 'Sophia isn't my wife. Sophia is my *sister.*'

Her heart slammed into her ribs. 'Your sister?'

'My sister.'

'But your surnames...'

The horror was replaced with disbelief. 'You speak my language better than most native speakers and deal with my compatriots every day at your border, and you don't know Spanish women keep their own names when they marry?'

'I...' Gabrielle tried to think coherently through the blood pounding in her brain. It hadn't occurred to her that the

Moratos were anything but husband and wife. 'I've never really thought about it, and Sophia wears a wedding ring.'

'That's because she *is* married. Her husband's in New Zealand on business—he's a wine dealer. A simple internet search will confirm that I have no wife or partner, and for the avoidance of doubt, I have no intention of ever marrying.' His black stare bored into her. 'Is this a problem for you?'

'No, of course not,' she lied, even though she wasn't exactly sure why it was a lie. Nothing had changed as far as the party went. This wasn't a real date. She was still Sophia's substitute, accompanying Andrés only because there hadn't been time for him to arrange someone more fitting. 'I just thought you were married, that's all. It doesn't change anything.'

He held her stare another moment before giving a short, sharp nod. 'Good. Because we have arrived.'

Gabrielle blinked her gaze away from him—it was unnerving how staring into those black eyes made her feel all aflutter—and saw they were driving through the palace's famous arched gate built high into the ancient stone perimeter wall.

The car stopped and two members of the palace staff appeared and opened their respective doors for them.

Out on the gravelled stone of the huge courtyard, Gabrielle breathed the fresh sea air—the palace was built in the rocky shores of the Mediterranean overlooking its own private bay—deep into her lungs and took a moment to compose herself by taking in her surroundings. Her heartbeat was strangely erratic.

Andrés observed Gabrielle's stare fix on the huge fountain with the three marble horses rising majestically out of the water in the centre of the courtyard before her gaze lifted to take in the palace itself.

Now that he'd got over the ick factor of Gabrielle thinking he was married to his own sister, he found himself considering her reaction to it. It had put to rest the lingering doubt that she'd been a willing participant in his sister's matchmaking scheme. She'd been clearly mortified at having made the wrong assumption but he sensed something more than embarrassment had heated her cheeks enough to warm an igloo. Intriguing...

The last of the day's sun was landing like microscopic jewels over her oval face and one bare shoulder, and when she turned her face to him and her oversized lips tugged into a hesitant small smile, the strangest frisson raced through his blood to imagine if those lips were as soft and pliant as they appeared.

One of the palace guards waiting for them cleared his throat loudly, snapping Andrés back to the present.

Shaking the strange frisson away, he indicated for Gabrielle to follow him to the main door.

As they were the last guests to arrive and he'd called ahead to notify the officials of the change to his plus one, they got through the security part quickly, and then they were led inside the palace itself. Having visited it a number of times since Catalina had taken the throne, Andrés's familiarity with the route they were taking and the lavishness of his own lifestyle meant the opulence of the palace was something he barely noticed. As such, when they followed the palace officials escorting them into a long, wide corridor, he'd taken a handful of steps over its deep blue carpet before he noticed that Gabrielle had dropped back.

Not just dropped back. She'd stopped walking altogether, her chin lifted and neck craning slowly about her, dark brown eyes wide with wonder as she soaked in the majesty surrounding them.

He strode back to her. 'I appreciate that this is your first time here but we have four minutes to take our seats before the banquet starts.'

Andrés's deeply masculine voice cut through Gabrielle's almost panicked stupor.

Never in her wildest dreams had she imagined she would one day find herself on the threshold of the famed Portrait Gallery, where the painted images of every single one of Monte Cleure's monarchs through the centuries lined the high walls. To be here, in the flesh, seconds away from sharing four walls with Queen Catalina...

The excitement and nerves churning in her stomach had become so violent that she could easily vomit over the deep blue carpet running the corridor's length.

She blinked vigorously, snatched as much air as she could get into her tight lungs, and met Andrés's black stare.

Surprisingly, sympathetic amusement tugged at his sensuous lips. 'The first time is always overwhelming.'

'Even for you?' She couldn't imagine this arrogant, confident man feeling overwhelmed by anything.

He raised his eyebrows pointedly. 'I don't come from money, Gabrielle. I remember well the feeling I had in my stomach when I first joined this world. I was certain that people would take one look at me and judge me an imposter.'

She took in the immaculately groomed features of this devastatingly handsome man and the way his tuxedo wrapped around his fabulous body as if tuxedos had been designed with Andrés Morato in mind, and just could not imagine him ever doubting himself or his place in this world. 'How did you do it?'

'By telling myself that I could. I made a determined effort not to let my body language show my fear.'

'It worked?'

He raised a shoulder nonchalantly. 'We're here right now aren't we? And it can work for you too. You have an excellent poker face—'

'Do I?'

The way Gabrielle's face had scrunched up in disbelief amused Andrés. 'I spent the time you were searching my car wondering if you really were going to taser me.'

Her pillowy lips quirked. 'I was tempted.'

'I did wonder,' he said drily. 'And I would have deserved it. If you feel nerves getting the better of you, all you have to do is remember to breathe, hold your head high and put your poker face on.'

She considered this for a moment then sniffed through her slightly squished nose, lifted her chin and adopted a glazed expression like something out of a zombie movie. 'Like this?'

'That's not quite the poker face I remember,' he murmured, stifling a laugh.

Her cheeks sucked in as they'd done earlier when he'd suspected she was stifling her own laughter. 'I didn't even know I *had* a poker face.'

'You'll find it if you need it.' He held the crook of his arm out to her. 'Hold on to me for support and remember that you have nothing to fear. I promised my sister that I would take care of you and I never make promises I can't keep.'

Heart suddenly thumping again, Gabrielle hesitated a moment, not even knowing *why* she was hesitating when all he was doing was offering the support she needed, then slipped her hand as loosely as she could through his elbow. She fixed her gaze forwards, lifted her chin and tried to tune out the size of his bicep flexing against her fingers.

'Big breath,' he commanded.

She obeyed and was rewarded with a huge dose of his

scent deep in her lungs. The only upside to that was her lungs gratefully opened up to receive the scent so she supposed being able to breathe semi-properly again was kind of a win, even if her heart was now smashing against her ribcage.

At the door of the busy banquet room, which Gabrielle was only able to get a tiny glimpse into, stood a makeshift archway elaborately decorated with roses. A photographer materialised.

'I'm afraid we're already late,' Andrés told him smoothly.

'The champagne reception has only just finished,' the photographer informed them. 'There is time before everyone takes their seats if we work quickly.'

Andrés's black stare landed on Gabrielle. She watched him deliberate in ultra-quick time then nod his assent.

In seconds, Gabrielle was taking her position beside Andrés under the arch.

'Closer together,' the photographer commanded.

All the breaths she'd managed to get back into her lungs rushed out of her when Andrés's arm slid behind her back and a giant hand rested on her hip.

Her heart thumped painfully against her already bruised ribcage, and she swallowed hard, as aware of the heat emanating from Andrés's huge frame pressed so tightly into her side as she was of the butterflies suddenly loose in her stomach. It took far more effort than should come naturally to bring a smile to her face.

The camera clicked, but there was no merciful release from Andrés's touch for he rested his hand on her lower back and steered her through the door into the banquet room.

Hundreds and hundreds of people dressed in the finest clothes money could buy were taking their seats. It wasn't until Gabrielle, trying valiantly to pretend that she wasn't in the slightest bit affected by Andrés's hand on her back, caught a glimpse of her heroine at the long top table that overlooked the dozens of round tables that she realised she'd completely forgotten all about the reason for the party.

'Did you just *squeal*?' Andrés asked in a low, astounded voice.

'I'm sorry,' she whispered, practically bouncing in excitement. 'I couldn't help it. I just spotted the Queen.'

Making a concerted effort not to look in the Queen's direction again so as not to embarrass herself again, Gabrielle flickered her eyes over the other guests and found herself having to clamp her lips together to stop another squeal escaping at all the faces she recognised. Anyone would recognise them. In this elaborately decorated banquet room, where light from gold and crystal chandeliers bounced off the oak floor and the beautifully laid tables, she recognised prime ministers and presidents, the bosses of multi-billion-dollar businesses, leading influencers and other faces she couldn't put a job or name to but whose faces were known around the world. Many of them were looking at her too, their faces drawn first to Andrés and then to his date, their expressions those of people trying to work out who she was. She wondered if any of the couples whose cars she'd searched earlier would recognise her now, in all Sophia's finery, and decided not. For some of them it was because they were too important in their own minds to look at the hoi polloi long enough for their faces to register, for the others it was just a stretch of the imagination too far. She wouldn't have believed it herself if it wasn't actually happening to her.

'Are you remembering to breathe?' Andrés enquired once they'd taken their seats, speaking close to Gabrielle's ear so only she could hear. The tip of his nose brushed against the strands of her hair and he suddenly found his senses filled with the contrasting scents of the musky perfume she'd chosen to spray herself with and the sweet shampoo she'd washed her hair with. *Dios*, the combination was temptation itself.

She nodded rigidly and after a beat turned to him. 'How's my poker face going?'

Her latest attempt reminded him of the victim of a zombie movie playing dead so they wouldn't get bitten. It was both amusing and yet strangely touching, and he reminded himself that this was Gabrielle's first foray into his world and that she'd had only hours to mentally prepare herself for it. He'd spent his entire life preparing for his first foray into this world.

'Terribly.' Keeping his voice low, he added, 'Just remember, every person in this room, including your Queen, has the same bodily functions as you and me.'

Her mouth dropped open in faux outrage and she leaned in closer to hiss, 'I do not want to think of Queen Catalina's bodily functions, thank you very much! I prefer to think of her as a mythical creature spreading goodwill and hope amongst her subjects, so do not ruin my illusions by humanising her for me.'

Staring into dark brown eyes dancing with amusement, Andrés caught another waft of her perfume. It was a familiar scent but the way it reacted to Gabrielle's skin...

Something stirred inside him, a tightening, a flicker of heat that was only partially broken a beat later when the waiting staff descended. They filled the smallest of the crystal glasses set out before them, little bigger than his thumb, with amber liquid.

Gabrielle picked hers up and sniffed it gingerly. It smelt sweet. Safe. Because sniffing the sweet liquid meant she wasn't inhaling the scent of Andrés.

She could still feel the tiny quivering tendrils that had formed at the roots of her hair when he'd spoken into her ear. Still feel the whisper of his warm breath on her lobe.

'It's the pre-banquet drink; a form of sherry,' he explained. 'In a moment we will all stand and drink the first toast to the Queen's health.'

No sooner had he spoken than a glass was tapped.

Chairs scraped back as all the guests got to their feet. Gabrielle rose in time with Andrés, completely forgetting that heeled shoes reacted differently to being stood up in than clumpy boots. Losing her balance, she swung her arm out, instinctively grabbed his hand and swayed into him.

CHAPTER FOUR

IF ANDRÉS WASN'T so strong Gabrielle would have sent them both sprawling. As it was, he was not only strong but had superb reflexes and instincts. Long, warm fingers wrapped around Gabrielle's and squeezed, the solid muscle of the shoulder her cheek landed on not giving way an inch.

Heart pounding wildly, wholly aware that the tip of her breast was squashed into his forearm and mortified at how close she'd come to embarrassing them both, she took a deep breath and adjusted her stance.

It frightened her how badly her hand wanted to stay in his, frightened her even more that when she pulled it free her hand refused to make a quick release, their fingers drifting apart like a caress.

The whole thing lasted seconds. It felt like for ever.

'Sorry,' she whispered.

'Don't be,' he murmured.

The toast to the Queen's health was made. The whooshing of blood in Gabrielle's ears drowned it out completely.

She didn't dare look at Andrés. Not a part of her didn't tingle. How she hadn't spilled her drink everywhere was a mystery she would never solve but she gladly drank it in one swallow when the command was given. Not strong enough to burn but potent enough to take the edge off her nerves. It barely touched the tingles.

She was only having them because, outside of work, she was starved for adult company and, she could admit, more than a little lonely, so was it really a surprise that she should develop an attraction to the first reasonably handsome man to stray in her path?

She nearly laughed out loud at the understatement of her thoughts. *Reasonably* handsome? Andrés would give Zeus an inferiority complex.

What she needed to do, Gabrielle decided, was accept that she was attracted to Andrés, accept that learning he wasn't actually married had accelerated it, and park it. Enjoy the party that she was the luckiest woman in Monte Cleure to be attending and enjoy the company of her handsome date on what wasn't a real date in the real sense because if it was, she wouldn't have agreed to it and he certainly wouldn't have suggested it. Glamorous men like Andrés Morato liked glamorous women with matching glamorous lives, not ordinary, squat border guards. You didn't live in the principality of Monte Cleure your entire life without learning that. Once the evening was over, she would never see him again. He'd forget about her in days. Probably hours. Most likely by the time his car had turned around after dropping her home.

And she'd return to the beautiful boy she'd given her life to protect, and forget all about him.

Andrés swallowed his pre-dinner drink and turned his attention to Gabrielle. Not that his attention had left her. Awareness was thrumming through him at a rate he could scarcely believe, and all because she'd stumbled into him and grabbed his hand for support and the soft swell of her breast had pressed against his arm, accelerating the awareness that had already been building.

Something in the way she was holding herself and the

way her teeth were sinking into her bottom lip made him think the awareness wasn't entirely one-sided.

As they retook their seats, the waiting staff arrived with the bread rolls. Andrés cut straight into his, slathered one half with a pat of butter, and took a huge bite. It had been a long day and he'd hardly eaten. He was ravenous.

Taking another huge bite, he watched Gabrielle butter her own roll and idly wondered if her golden skin matched it for soft smoothness. Wondered what it tasted like…

Her face turned to his and she casually—too casually?—asked, 'Which wine should I have? White or red?'

He spread another pat of butter on the other half of his roll. 'Whichever you like.'

'But I don't really like wine,' she confessed, making a face that matched her dislike of it. 'Some friends and I shared a bottle years ago—it tasted like drain cleaner.'

The way she said it made him want to laugh. 'I am sure you will find the wine here infinitely more palatable.'

'I hope that's the case because I don't really think it's the done thing for guests to be sick over the silk tablecloths.' And then, with a gleam of amusement, her delightful pillowy lips closed over her own roll.

Grinning at her irreverence, he nodded at the approaching wine servers. 'It's time to decide.'

She swallowed her mouthful and pulled another face. 'I'll let you decide, and if it's horrible and I'm sick, you can take the blame.'

Andrés didn't know if it was the face she'd pulled or what she'd said or how she'd said it, but the laughter he'd been holding back escaped.

His sister had been right. Gabrielle had made him laugh earlier and she was making him laugh now. He had a feeling that even if the legal issues with Susi hadn't been resolved earlier that day, Gabrielle's company would still have lightened the tightness that lived in his chest during those torrid weeks, because he was feeling lighter than he'd done in a long, long time.

Choosing red for them both, he watched Gabrielle sniff hers suspiciously like she'd done with the pre-dinner drink.

'If you don't like it, we'll get something else brought over for you,' he assured her.

Her nose wrinkled. 'It doesn't smell offensive.'

'I should hope not,' he observed, smothering another laugh. Raising his glass, he held it out to her. *'Salud.'*

She tapped her glass to it. *'Santé.'*

Her lips pulled in as she swirled the red liquid around her mouth before taking another, larger, drink.

'More palatable than the drain cleaner?' he asked, even though the wonder in her eyes already told him the answer.

She swallowed another sip and shook her head. 'That is…' She put her glass on the table and pinched her forefingers and thumbs together into circles.

Gabrielle's tongue was rhapsodising. She'd never known wine could be so smooth. It was easily the most delicious thing she had ever tasted…right up until the scallops with crispy pancetta were served…and then a lemon sorbet palate cleanser…

She was in heaven! She demolished every last morsel, delighted to have her attention and senses filled with the wonderful aroma and taste of food rather than Andrés. Not that she'd tasted him of course, and she quickly drank some wine to counter the thrill that zinged through her to wonder what his lips tasted of.

By enthusiastically concentrating on the fabulous food, Gabrielle was able to push any Andrés effect away and just enjoy herself as she'd already determined to do, and she quickly relaxed into the meal and her surroundings. She would have been happy to just listen in on the conversations washing around her but Andrés made sure to include her in it all. It didn't escape her attention that he instinctively seemed to know which subjects, like the German stock market, meant nothing to her and leaned his head close to hers to give a quick, discreet summary under his breath. While those discreet summaries kept recharging the Andrés effect, she was touched and grateful for his consideration. Her short time working at the casino that boasted the highest percentage of the world's billionaires in its membership had taught her that many men in his situation wouldn't care if their date could keep up with the conversation, never mind go out of their way to include her in it. They'd be too puffed up with the sound of their own voices to even care.

'So what is it you do?' the forty-something white-blonde lady sitting on the other side of Andrés asked Gabrielle in English after the third course had been cleared away and the table conversation had come to a natural break.

Gabrielle, who'd just dropped the velvet place setting with her name embroidered in gold thread into her clutch bag and was pondering how to pilfer her personalised place menu, shot her gaze to Andrés with a sinking dread in her stomach.

How did he want her to handle this? She didn't want to lie—she'd told so many lies since the pregnancy that if heaven existed she'd be barred from entering—but she didn't want to embarrass him either.

His eyes caught hers before the faintest of smiles played on his lips and he said in perfect English, 'Gabrielle is a border guard.'

Only by the skin of her teeth did she stop her mouth dropping open. The last thing she'd expected was for Andrés to tell the truth, not because she assumed he was a natural born liar but because she'd assumed he would think it beneath him to admit he'd brought along a nobody to an event with the world's elite.

Another assumption she'd got wrong.

The woman slapped his arm. 'You are such a tease, Andrés.'

'I'm not teasing. Gabrielle stopped my car at the Spanish border earlier and searched it for drugs.' He lifted his glass to his mouth. 'Gabrielle will confirm it,' he added before dropping her a wink that made her stomach dip.

'It is true,' she piped up, speaking carefully as her English wasn't as fluent as her Spanish. 'I work as border guard. Andrés fitted the…' She grasped for the translation of *profile* but came up blank. '…details we were given of a drug smuggler bringing cocaine over the border. I am here only because Sophia fell ill. I am the substitute.'

The woman pouted. 'Oh, you're as bad as he is.'

Gabrielle met Andrés's stare. The conspiratorial crinkling of his eyes and flash of perfect teeth made her stomach dip again even more powerfully, as did the frankly shocking realisation that she could perfectly read in his expression that he found the blonde woman ridiculous.

He moved a touch closer to her and, switching back to Spanish, murmured, 'You wait, Lucida will spend the rest of the evening trying to get to the bottom of who you really are.'

'Lucida? She was named after a *font*?'

Surprise lit his face and then he gave such a deep throated rumble of laughter that everyone surrounding them whipped their stares to him.

It was laughter that, despite the tight control she was keeping over her reactions to him, made Gabrielle's heart swell.

He moved his face even closer and dropped his voice even lower. 'Legend has it that she changed it from Lucinda. Someone told her it sounded classier.'

'I take it that someone was having a joke?'

'I believe that is a fair assumption.'

Luckily their next course arrived, saving either of them from having to explain what it was that had them both laughing and saving Gabrielle from the effects of Andrés's breath whispering against her temple.

A large sip of wine in an attempt to mute the awareness whooshing around her body, and then she popped a crispy potato ball with the fluffiest inside into her mouth. That was better, even if she was acutely aware of the closeness of his thigh under the table. Still, she told herself, a bit of internal discomfort was nothing when she was eating food fit for a princess and drinking wine that Zeus himself would have declared all the superlatives. And thinking of Zeus, Gabrielle was starting to understand that there was far more to Andrés than his devastating looks. He wore his arrogance like a cloak but he wasn't a snob and actually had a sense of humour, something she would never have believed five hours ago. With the crispiest pork crackling in the whole world dissolving on her tongue, all she could think was that for this one night, she was the luckiest woman in the world. To think she'd thought the highlight of her evening would be a bath!

'Can I ask you something personal?' he asked as the last of the crackling dissolved into nothing.

The old internal alarm system went off. Choosing her words carefully, she said, 'You can ask but I might choose not to answer.'

'That is fair. I'm just wondering why you do the work you do.'

She narrowed her eyes to scrutinise him, wondering where this was leading. 'That is a strange way to phrase it.'

His broad shoulders rose as he drank some of his wine. 'See, this is why I'm asking. You are clearly educated. You speak three languages…'

'French is my native language and all Monte Cleure children are taught English and Spanish at school,' she interjected. 'It is nothing special.'

'You speak my language as well as I do and your English is excellent.'

She felt her cheeks flush with pleasure at the compliment. Spanish had always come easily to her but English was *hard*.

'You must have studied hard to be as proficient as you are at them,' he continued. 'Then there is the way you speak, your knowledge of fonts.' He pulled an amazed face. 'Come on, who knows about fonts?'

'I do. You do.'

'I know about fonts because I own Janson Media.'

'The TV company?'

'We also publish newspapers and magazines.' He named a few that made her eyes widen. 'When I buy into a company I want to know everything about it.'

'And that meant learning about *fonts*?'

He grinned. 'I can be obsessive. Also, it was the first major company I bought into—they were struggling to transition into the digital age and the shares were going cheap enough to entice me. I'm now the majority shareholder. Funnily enough, I'm currently going through the process of buying a Japanese publishing company. I've wanted to break into the Asian market for a long time and this is the first real viable option for me, but going back to you, Gabrielle, you are an intelligent woman. I cannot believe a career as a border guard is what you dreamed for yourself.'

And she couldn't believe he'd tapped into her so easily. She couldn't decide if it was terrifying or enthralling, knew only that the beats of her heart were racing at a canter. 'It isn't what I dreamed of doing,' she agreed, forcing herself to speak calmly. Just because Andrés had picked up on certain things about her in the short space of time they'd spent together did not mean he could actually read her mind. 'But then, I never imagined I would have a child at nineteen.'

'What career did you dream of?'

'Publishing. Books,' she hastened to clarify, not wanting him to think she was only saying it because he'd mentioned he owned a media company and was in the process of buying another. 'I had a place at a university in England to study English Literature lined up.'

Andrés was impressed. He could never understand people who were content to limit their horizons to the places of their birth. 'Publishing is wide ranging. What did you want to do within it?'

'I hadn't decided. I just liked the idea of being absorbed into the world of words. I was going to do my degree and then see where it led me. My mother is a reader. We never had much money but there were always books at home. You could open one and be transported to any place in time anywhere in the world.'

'What stopped you pursuing your dream?'

She pulled a 'duh' face. 'I told you, I had a baby. I couldn't go to university in another country with a baby in tow. It just wasn't feasible even if I could have afforded it, and Monte Cleure doesn't have a university, and there is no point in me bewailing it because I made my choice and that choice was Lucas. I won't lie, being a border guard isn't the career I once dreamed of but it's a living and one I'm proud of, and it has a career ladder I can climb as Lucas gets older and becomes less dependent on me.'

'I'm not criticising you,' he said, noting the defensiveness in the rapidity of her speech. 'Being a parent means making sacrifices and I have nothing but admiration for the people who are prepared to make them.'

Something flickered in her eyes, an emotion he couldn't discern but which strangely tugged at his chest. Gabrielle had been so young when she'd had her child that he could only imagine the other sacrifices she'd had to make. 'I know you said it was just you and Lucas but is his father on the scene?'

The colour that suffused her face was so different to the colour it had turned when she'd learned that Sophia wasn't his wife that he immediately regretted asking. 'That is none of my business. I apologise. Forget I asked.'

She had a long drink of her water. 'No, it's okay. And no, he isn't on the scene at all. It's been just me and Lucas since the day I brought him home.' The pillowy lips he was finding it harder and harder not to fantasise about the taste and feel of curved into a smile that didn't quite meet her eyes. 'And as we're speaking of Lucas, does your jacket have an inside pocket?'

Her change of subject threw him. 'Why do you ask?'

'I want to sneak my place menu out as a memento for him but the bag Sophia lent me is so small I'm scared I'll damage it.'

Gabrielle held her breath as she waited for him to respond, and she mentally kicked herself for not giving him the pat response she'd honed over the years to explain The Bastard's absence to the curious, which consisted of Lucas's father being a tourist she'd had a brief fling with and that he'd given her a fake number and so she'd never been able to tell him of their son. She'd repeated the lie so many times it came naturally to her. What wasn't natural was her tongue's refusal to repeat that lie to Andrés.

After what felt like an age in which the black stare she was finding increasingly hypnotic bored into her, the sides of his eyes crinkled. A giant hand reached across her empty plate. The sleeves of his jacket and shirt pulled back, revealing the fine dark hair covering his arm and the base of his sleeve tattoo. A place deep and low between her legs pulsed. A moment later her place menu was swallowed into the mysterious confines of Andrés dinner jacket.

'If I get thrown in the dungeon for theft, I will expect you to plead my case for me,' he said in the lighter tone of their earlier conversation.

'I will get down on my knees before my Queen and beg for your mercy,' she agreed, laughing at both the absurdity and the relief that came with the complete change of subject.

Over the next two courses, Gabrielle stuck to water while they ate and chatted. She was making herself ration the wine. She drank alcohol so rarely that the last thing she wanted was to get drunk and make a fool of herself. Besides, she didn't need alcohol. She was high enough on the buzz being induced by the whole evening and, she had to admit, the buzz that came from being the sole focus of Andrés's attention.

Something was happening inside her, butterflies multiplying and growing in wing strength, but so long as she didn't look at him too hard or let his scent seep into her airwaves and so long as she completely tuned out the closeness of his body next to hers and didn't look at his arm—she had no idea why she should react to an *arm* of all things—she was able to temper the Andrés effect and just enjoy talking to him. But temper it only slightly. She doubted there was a woman alive who wouldn't react to being in close proximity to such a rampantly masculine man whom even Zeus would be jealous of.

She could scarcely believe that the arrogant, entitled jerk who'd practically had a tantrum at having his car searched was someone she actually liked. She would never have believed such a man could be so easy to talk to or that she could be so enthralled listening to his tales. He was only ten years older than her but had lived, truly *lived*, enough to have five decades on her.

To learn he'd founded his multi-billion business empire out of nothing blew her mind.

'I thought you were just trying to calm my nerves when you said you didn't come from money,' she confessed after he'd explained how he'd signed himself up for a distance-learning business degree whilst still studying at school *and* worked weekends as a barista and how, once he'd saved twenty thousand euros by the age of twenty, he'd invested it in two start-up companies founded by school friends which had both struck gold.

'I *was* trying to calm you,' he said with the sensuous smile that had made her stomach dip more times than she could count that evening. 'But it also happened to be the truth.'

'Where do you get your *drive* from?' she marvelled. The hours he worked, the relentless travel…

She liked that he didn't give her a pat answer. Liked that he considered the question before answering. 'It's something that has always been in me. It runs in my family—Sophia has the same drive. Our parents are both hard workers but the money they earned was hardly enough to keep the wolves from the door. I always wanted to be rich and so I made it happen.'

'Does that always happen for you?' she asked, fascinated. 'Do you always get what you want?'

Gabrielle suddenly found herself holding her breath as his face drew closer to hers. The swirl in his hypnotic black eyes deepened and pulsed as the sensuous lips her eyes were increasingly drawn to parted. *'Always.'*

CHAPTER FIVE

THE REST OF the party attendees had ceased to exist for Andrés.

The longer the meal went on, the more he was reminded of long ago years, when he'd been too young for any lover to expect anything but fun from him, before he'd found himself approaching relationships wondering when he would be forced to end it. He'd learned to be forthright, firmly stating at the outset that he would never settle down or marry and while they always—*always*—reacted with a nonchalant shrug, each of them managed to convince themselves that they would be the one to change him, to make him fall in love. As if love even existed beyond the bonds forged by blood! His parents had believed they loved each other once but before their children reached double digits had become incapable of holding a conversation without dripping poison into it.

The moment marriage was hinted at, he ended it. Same as when lovers 'accidentally' left their toothbrush in his bathroom. Experience had taught him that ignoring those hints and letting things drag on until boredom kicked in meant a messy disentanglement. None had been messier than with Susi, the woman responsible for the dark cloud that had hung over him these last weeks.

The call from his lawyer had lifted that cloud. Having

Gabrielle as his date for the evening had blown the last of it away completely.

Other than her relative youth, Gabrielle was nothing like those young, carefree lovers of his early twenties, but there was something about her that reminded him of that time, before life had made him so cynical, a time before he'd become jaded with humans in general. A time when he'd woken each day enthusiastic for what lay ahead.

He'd known she was different from his usual dates and lovers when he'd agreed with Sophia's suggestion that Gabrielle be her substitute for the evening. The fact of her child had sold it for him. A woman with her own life and responsibilities and who lived in such a vastly different world to his wouldn't view him with long-term grasping eyes. When the evening had begun, Gabrielle hadn't wanted or expected anything from Andrés other than to be delivered safely home at the end of it.

And now…?

Call him arrogant but Andrés knew when a woman was attracted to him. It was all the little signs and Gabrielle was displaying them in abundance. What made it more erotic though, was his certainty that she was unaware of the signals she was giving. She couldn't know that her beautiful dark brown eyes had melted into a bar of the most luxurious of chocolate or that her body was subtly leaning towards him, or that her face was constantly tilted to his.

He was coming to think Gabrielle might just be the most interesting and intriguing woman he'd ever spent time with. She had that rare combination of seriousness and intelligence coupled with a mischievous joy of the absurd that was sexy in its own right, and when the sixth course was cleared away, he put his elbow on the table, rested his chin on his closed fist and drank her in some more. She was *extraordinary*.

Taking a sip of what was only her second glass of wine, she studied him meditatively before putting her own elbow on the table and resting her chin on the palm of her hand. Her hair spilled over her shoulder. 'Can I ask *you* something personal?'

'I think that is only fair but the same rules apply.'

She smiled slowly. 'Of course.'

The heat in his veins thickened some more. Their faces were only inches from each other...

'Why were you in such a bad mood earlier?'

'I didn't think you'd noticed,' he jested even as his heart sank. Andrés had hoped to get through this evening without having to think about the nightmare he'd just been through.

'Don't worry,' she jested back, 'it wasn't particularly obvious.'

He grinned ruefully and studied her with the same meditation with which she'd studied him. For a moment he debated whether or not to enforce the 'choosing not to answer' clause they'd already agreed on. 'I've been embroiled in a paternity battle.'

A dark brown eyebrow arched.

'A woman I dated briefly for a month last year got in touch a few weeks ago and told me I was the father of her child.'

'And were you—are you—the father?'

He shook his head emphatically. 'No. I knew the child couldn't be mine. It wasn't possible. A DNA test confirmed it. My lawyer called me with the results when you were searching my car.'

She moved her hand from her chin, sitting back a little

from him, and rubbed her arm. 'Was it the thought of being a father that put you in such a foul temper?'

'No… Yes. But not for the reasons you think.'

Her eyebrow arched again. 'You can read my mind?'

'Unfortunately all the riches in the world doesn't bestow that power.' He grabbed the back of his neck and wished that he could read her mind. It was one thing discussing these matters dispassionately with his legal team but Gabrielle had a child she was raising without the father's involvement. For all that she refused to *bewail* the choices she'd made, he didn't imagine life was easy for her.

'Gabrielle, I like children—I'm godfather to my cousin's sons and I very much enjoy the time I spend with them— but I don't want to get married or be stuck with a long-term partner, and having children means I would be stuck in a potentially toxic relationship. I couldn't be like Lucas's father. I would want to be there every day for my child, just as my father was for me, but my parents' marriage is toxic and I have never wanted that for myself.' He drained his wine and shook his head. 'I can barely remember a time when they didn't hate each other but they stayed together for mine and Sophia's sake and now I think they enjoy hating each other so much that they stay together out of spite.'

'That sounds horrible but there's no reason any marriage you made would go the same way.' She shrugged her shoulders lightly. 'My parents' marriage was happy.'

'Was?'

Sadness clouded her stare. 'My father died when I was ten. Sepsis.'

He gave a grim shake of his head. 'I'm sorry,' he said, meaning it. Divorce had been Andrés's biggest fear at that age. He couldn't begin to imagine how he'd have coped if either of his parents had died, and a sharp pang sliced his chest to think how much he'd neglected them in recent years. It wasn't deliberate, merely that all his business interests meant there weren't enough hours in the day for anything other than business.

'Thank you. It's been thirteen years but I still miss him. My mother does too. Losing him devastated her.' Her shoulders rose again and she softly added, 'Not all marriages end in acrimony.'

They were words he'd heard before, from countless lovers. Usually they sent alarm bells clanging and sent Andrés heading swiftly to the nearest exit, but on this occasion he sensed they came from a thoughtful place, not a self-serving one.

'I know that but when you've lived through a toxic marriage, life is too short to take the risk. If Susi's child had been mine I have no doubt it would have turned toxic between us quickly.'

'How can you be so certain?'

'She took a baseball bat to my Maserati when I ended things. She smashed all the windows and the bonnet. She was trying to smash her way into the garage to get to the other cars when my security apprehended her.'

Gabrielle's eyes had widened, shock ringing loud and clear. 'After you'd been together only a month?'

'Yes. And it was never serious. I saw her maybe five times in that month.'

'That is not someone who sounds stable.'

'Exactly. It is why I ended things with her. I was getting some serious bad vibes. When she told me I was the father, I knew she was lying. I am scrupulous about contraception.'

'That poor baby,' she said with a hint of distress.

'Don't worry about the baby,' he assured her. Not even Sophia, the only person outside his legal team he'd confided the situation to, had mentioned any concerns for Susi's child. 'I've had business dealings with Susi's father and I spoke to him and Grace, Susi's mother, when she first made the claims. They know their daughter needs help and they've promised me they will give it to her.'

Her features relaxed at this. Putting her chin back on her hand, she murmured with more of that husky softness, 'That's good. And good of you to think to do that.'

Andrés actually felt his chest expand. Why a woman he'd known barely a quarter of a day's opinion mattered he couldn't begin to explain but there were a lot of things about this woman and the things he was confiding and the way he was reacting to her that couldn't be rationalised.

At that moment, a server reached between them to lay the plates of their seventh and penultimate course down, and Andrés experienced a stab of resentment at being prevented from looking at Gabrielle for all of ten seconds.

It was her eyes he realised a few moments later when they each lifted a spoonful of warm lemon tart to their mouths and their gazes were drawn back together. They were so expressive and warm and open that it was impossible for a man to look into them and not feel the urge to spill his soul…

Incapable of pulling her stare away from Andrés, Gabrielle inhaled the scent of her beautifully presented individual tart that smelt as if the lemons had been picked only minutes ago and thought that as beautiful as its aroma was, it could never smell as good as him. Nothing could.

Muting the Andrés effect had become impossible. The constant fluttering in her chest and the churning sick-like feeling in her stomach had grown so strong it was a struggle to swallow the dessert that tasted as good as its scent promised.

Would he be having such a stark effect on her if she'd let her brother fix her up with his friends like he'd pestered over the years? Hadn't he told her more times than she could count that committing herself to a life of celibacy went against every human instinct and craving?

Gabrielle's deep, abiding love for Lucas and profound terror of losing him had allowed her to ignore her brother's wisdom. And besides, how, she'd asked herself, could she miss something she'd never had?

It was pointless to wonder. That the Andrés effect was strong was one of only two certainties she had because she knew she wasn't imagining that the attraction was mutual. She was inexperienced but not naive. With every passing minute she could feel the charge between them growing, a thought that thrilled and terrified her in equal measure.

She'd made a promise. A vow. No relationships. Just her and Lucas. The risks of giving herself to a man were just too strong.

But Andrés's heaven-sent scent and the pull of those sensuous lips…

'Tell me about your life,' Andrés said once the coffees had been poured and they'd both demolished a delicate *petit four* each.

He could watch Gabrielle talk for ever. There was something about the way her mouth and face moved when she spoke that fascinated him. A deep thrum pulsed relentlessly through his thickened veins to imagine what those oversized lips would feel like crushed against his mouth.

As if she could sense the direction of his thoughts, her fingers flew to her mouth and rubbed gently against it. He was quite sure she was unaware of doing it.

'What do you want to know?'

'I don't know... What is a typical day in the life of Gabrielle Breton?'

'I suppose a typical working day starts with early morning cartoons and breakfast, then a fight with Lucas over wearing more than a pair of pants, then I drop him either at nursery or if my shift's over the weekend at my mother's, and work until my shift finishes and then collect him, go back home to throw something together for dinner, kick a ball about in the park—my brother has taught Lucas the joy of soccer and I'm now required to be the goalkeeper and have balls kicked at my face every day—and then I wrestle him into his pyjamas, read him a story and then bed.' Her nose wrinkled and then her mesmerising eyes gleamed. 'I bet it's very different to a typical day in the life of Andrés Morato.'

'Just a little bit,' he admitted with a laugh, thinking of the few times his godsons had talked him into playing soccer with them. Another sharp pang pulled at his chest to remember he hadn't seen them since Christmas.

Gabrielle's oh-so-interesting, beautiful face lit up with a mischievous smile. 'Yours is a life of glamour and travel while mine is a life of domestic drudgery and the vain hope on a work shift of actually catching some smug billionaire with a large haul of drugs.'

'Am I still included in your smug billionaire hit list?'

Her delicious pillowy lips pursed in pretend concentration before she grinned. 'I think we can safely let you go back to using facial recognition. After all, you're a very busy and important man who pumps a lot of money into my country's economy. I would hate to delay you on your important business.'

He adopted a deliberately smug expression. 'Now you are thinking in the correct way.'

'One evening with a billionaire and I'm already corrupted.' Amusement dancing in her eyes, she lazily brought her coffee cup to her mouth. 'By the time you take me home I'll be stamping my feet at the unfairness of not having my own staff to help with all the chores.'

'To *help* with the chores?' He shook his head in faux disappointment. 'If you are going to employ staff it is to do the chores for you.'

Her left eyebrow rose and wriggled. '*All* the chores?'

He raised his right eyebrow in imitation. 'I am a very busy and important man.'

She put her cup and saucer back on the table without breaking the lock of their eyes. 'I'm surprised you haven't already mentioned that.'

'Modesty forbade it.'

'I would say you should give classes in modesty but your time is precious. I bet you don't even have time to make yourself a snack when you're hungry.'

'I poured my own bourbon while I waited for you to finish getting ready earlier. Does that count?'

Her laughter whooshed through his ears and seeped into his veins. Gabrielle's laughter was the definition of sexy.

'When was the last time you did your own laundry?' she challenged teasingly.

'What is laundry?' he joked, to more of that glorious laughter.

'The last time you dusted?'

He wondered if she was aware of the lock of hair she was winding around her finger. 'I have a vague idea of where the cleaning items are stored in all of my homes if that counts?'

Gabrielle was laughing so hard that she didn't hear the call for the final toast of the evening to the Queen. It was only as fresh champagne flutes were delivered to their table and everyone around them started rising to their feet that she realised what was happening and followed suit.

'If you stumble again, you are more than welcome to fall into me,' Andrés's deep voice murmured close to her ear.

Blood whooshed straight to her brain, its strength making her sway on her feet.

As with the first toast, Gabrielle didn't hear a single word. It was impossible with the roaring in her head. It didn't help that Andrés's arm was brushed against hers. Or was it her arm brushed against his...?

There had been no mistaking the suggestive undertone in his words. No mistaking the first verbal acknowledgement of the attraction that had seen them spend the vast majority of the banquet ignoring everyone around them, and her cheeks heated to realise she'd been flirting with him. Teasing him. Completely wrapped up with him. The signals she must have been giving out...

Oh, God, did this mean he thought...?

Her breaths were short and her legs decidedly shaky when she retook her seat, and she edged her chair away from his, taking a moment to breathe and collect herself by checking her phone for any messages. Her mother had sent her a picture of Lucas sleeping in Romeo's arms.

That helped hugely. A picture of her cherubic son was just the tonic she needed to counter the heady thickness in her veins and the smashing of her heart against her ribs.

She'd just responded with a melting heart emoji when an arm slid around the back of her chair and the sleeve of Andrés's tuxedo tickled against her neck. Before she could think to react, a warm cheek pressed against hers and the soft bristles of Andrés's beard were grazing against her skin.

All the air flew out of her lungs while simultaneously

her pelvis flamed and contracted, warmth gushing through her like a tsunami.

'That has to be your brother,' he said, peering at her screen. 'He looks just like you. And is that your son?'

Gabrielle had to swallow the moisture that had flooded her mouth. All she could manage was a short nod.

'He's beautiful,' he observed huskily.

Suddenly she found she didn't dare move a muscle. When she did manage a response, her voice sounded distant, like it belonged to someone else. 'I like to think so too.'

Mercifully, an official called for everyone's attention and announced the party would be moving to the ballroom.

At least she thought it was merciful timing until the tip of Andrés's nose dragged along her cheekbone, the sleeve of his arm slid in reverse and then the heat of his face against hers and the heat of his body was gone.

How was it possible to be both relieved and internally screaming in disappointment at the same time and over the same thing?

There was still a little champagne left from the toast in her flute, and she knocked it back before summoning the courage to meet Andrés's stare.

He'd already risen, his black stare penetrating down at her.

The dip in her stomach was so powerful it would have knocked her off her feet if she'd been standing.

Without saying a word, he extended a giant hand to her.

With no knowledge of allowing them to do so, her trembling fingers reached out to take it. Long fingers wrapped around them and then Gabrielle was being gently helped to her feet, which was just as well as her legs had turned to wobbly water.

Upright, gazing into Andrés's face, as aware of the inherent masculinity that breathed in his huge frame as she'd ever been, more aware of her own contrasting femininity than she'd ever been before, aware her cheeks were drenched in hot colour, for one thrilling, terrifying moment, time ceased.

And then air forced its way into her lungs and her head cleared enough for her to regain enough sense to move back a little, just enough to stop the heat of his body penetrating her in the same way his hypnotic eyes were. It made no difference. The cells of her body were still straining towards him. Her effort to remove her hand from his clasp was a failure too, her fingers absolutely refusing to cooperate.

'What comes next?' she asked in a voice that still sounded like it belonged to someone else, then felt more hot colour suffuse her cheeks at how her question could be interpreted and almost tripped over her own tongue to add, 'I mean with the party.'

The black eyes gleamed and the lips she kept fighting to stop herself from imagining kissing quirked at the sides. 'Dancing and cocktails.' With another gleam of his eyes, he released her hand and held the crook of his arm out. 'Shall we?'

Feeling like she'd slipped into a dream, Gabrielle slipped her hand into it, just as she'd done over four hours earlier. Except, those few hours earlier her legs had been shaking with excitement, her physical awareness of Andrés in its infancy.

If she'd known how quickly and deeply that awareness would mushroom, she'd have pretended to have caught Sophia's bug.

But she couldn't have known. Couldn't have *imagined*.

Nothing could happen, she told herself desperately as her senses were once again filled entirely with Andrés. So filled were they as they joined the exodus from the banquet room to the ballroom that she barely registered the French actor they passed whose posters she'd plastered all over her teenage bedroom or noticed when she was within arm's reach of the Queen.

If you stumble again, you are more than welcome to fall into me.

Those words had let the Genie out of the bottle, and Gabrielle quivered inside to remember the suggestiveness of his undertone and the seductive sensuousness that had laced it.

Until he'd said those words she'd been fully aware of the growing attraction between them, of course she had, as aware as she'd ever been of anything in her life, but she'd been able to contain it by the skin of her teeth. Saying those words, bringing it out into the open for the first time...

And then that caress of his cheek against hers. She didn't think she could have reacted more strongly if he'd kissed her, which was the wrong thing to think as now she was thinking about his sensuous lips again and her pelvis was contracting painfully... No, not painfully. The ache deep within her wasn't pain.

The myriad of waiting staff now carried trays of tall cocktail glasses filled to the brim with colourful liquid, and Gabrielle gladly helped herself to a pink one and drank deeply through its straw. So wrapped up were her thoughts on Andrés that she barely tasted it, and whatever alcohol it contained did nothing to help.

Unexpected help though, came from two couples of around Andrés's age who beetled over to them. Before she knew what was happening, Gabrielle had been forced to disentangle her hand from his elbow so they could both be enveloped in embraces and air kisses. The banter and familiarity amongst them made it obvious that these were his friends, not just acquaintances, and when names of introduction were thrown at her, she was too busy alternating between the relief of being part of a pack and no longer the sole focus of Andrés's attention, and longing for him to steer her away to a private table for two to listen properly.

Heaven help her, as desperately as she knew nothing could happen between them, already she wanted time to reverse back to the banquet and those magical hours when it had felt like she and Andrés were the only two people in the world. Back to those magical hours before he'd let the Genie out and Gabrielle had realised just how much danger she was in.

CHAPTER SIX

THE ATMOSPHERE IN the ballroom was dramatically different to the formality of the banquet room. The room itself was twice its size and positively oozed glamour, the disco music pumping out and the effects of multiple disco balls hanging from the impossibly high ceiling giving it a real retro vibe.

An abundance of round tables encircled the sprawling dance floor, and when the group bagged one as a base, Gabrielle copied the other women in throwing her clutch bag onto it then helped herself to another pink cocktail. She was sure her tongue should be rhapsodising about it as it had done with the wine but her tastebuds seemed to have gone on strike.

The dance floor was already half filled with people shaking their moves and she gladly followed the women of their newly formed group onto it, leaving the men to continue whatever they were discussing.

She sensed Andrés's gaze following her every step.

It took all her willpower not to look back at him.

The physical space away from him was just what she needed and, in the company of women who were clearly on a mission to party the night away, she made sure to position herself with her back to the tables. After forcefully reminding herself that she would never again be invited to dance in the palace ballroom, she danced like she hadn't danced since she was an adolescent. Which wasn't hard as she hadn't actually danced at all since she was eighteen and had found Eloise collapsed in distress in the family bathroom on the night of what should have been Gabrielle's prom.

Ignoring the ache in her feet, which were practically begging for mercy from the elegant heels she'd forced them in, she threw herself into the music. Her body was desperate for an outlet for all the Andrés induced feelings ravaging her, and the music did its best to oblige, but it wasn't enough. Every beat of every song, she could feel his eyes on her. With every wriggle of her hips and every wave of her hands in the air came a fight not to turn around and seek him out. So desperately in tune was she to him that the whump of her heart told her of his approach long before her head whipped around to confirm it.

He'd removed his dinner jacket and bow tie. Undone the top two buttons of his shirt.

She tried to pretend his appearance on the dance floor meant nothing, she really tried, but she could no more stop her eyes from finding his than she could stop the beats of her ragged heart. Could no more stop her body gravitating to him than she could stop her lungs from working. Could no more stop the flames from flickering low in her abdomen at the sight of his chest hair where his shirt had opened than she could stop her name being Gabrielle Jeanne Breton.

As in the banquet, the world around them seemed to disintegrate. The ravishing blonde who Gabrielle had been dancing beside and who'd made sure Gabrielle, the outsider, was kept within their group and included in the funky dance moves she led, became blurred.

Gaze intent on her, snake hips swaying, he rested a hand loosely on her hip. His other hand captured hers. Or did her hand capture his?

A new track came on.

Eyes fused, they began to move.

The party continued around them, periphery extras in their private dance for two.

The ache in her feet had disappeared. If she didn't have Andrés anchoring her to the dance floor she felt she might have floated to the ceiling.

Another track played. Slower in tempo. Much slower.

They slowed down with it.

The hand at her hip slid around her waist and pulled her closer.

Andrés blew the stale air in his lungs out slowly. The weighty beats of his heart rippled through his entire being.

His shirt acted as the barrier between the skin on his back and Gabrielle's hand but he could feel the burn of her touch as strongly as if he were naked. He kept catching wafts of the delightful scents that had tantalised him throughout the banquet. The urge to bury his nose into the top of her head and inhale her shampoo deeply into his lungs was becoming torture to deny himself.

The deep thrums of awareness zinging through his veins and over his skin were growing too, increasing with every sway to the music.

The flickers of arousal were fighting to burn into flames.

He needed to do something to distract him from the effects of the sexy creature he was dancing with before he lost the fight. The sensible thing would be to remove himself from the situation, leave the dance floor and give himself a few moments for the arousal to simmer back to a manageable level.

Andrés had never chosen the sensible option in his life.

'How are you enjoying the party?' he murmured.

'Very well, thank you.' She answered with such politeness that he moved his head back a little so he could look down at her face. The Gabrielle Breton who'd been at his side the entire evening had been many things towards him but polite was not one of them. He didn't count her efforts at politeness when she'd searched his car as the underlying bite had negated it. Her lack of deference was one of the many things he liked about her.

Oh, yes, he liked this woman, and not just because he found her the sexiest creature to walk this earth. He liked her humour. Liked her intelligence. Liked her compassion. Liked her commitment. Liked her straight talking. Liked her enthusiasm for food. Liked the pulse in her eyes whenever their gazes locked together. Liked that when he'd snaked his way to her on the dance floor she'd looked at him as if he were the only man in the world.

She was holding herself stiffly, her gaze fixed over his shoulder making it impossible to read her expression.

'Glad you came?'

'Yes,' she replied with the same politeness. 'Thank you for inviting me.'

'It has been my pleasure.'

Another slow song began to play.

The crowd around them continued to mushroom. The floor space they had to call their own continued to shrink, forcing their bodies even closer.

The swell of her breasts crushed into his chest. A rush of awareness strong enough to fell a horse thickened his loins. If they hadn't been so closely entwined he would have missed the hitch of Gabrielle's breath, missed the shudder that ran the length of her body, missed the almost imperceptible tightening of her fingers on his back.

'I mean it,' he murmured, finally giving into temptation

and rubbing his nose into her hair. The strands felt like silk. 'Having you as my date has been a delight, Gabrielle.'

Dios, this woman *did* something to him.

Gabrielle's head was still spinning with the blood that had rushed to it at the first crush of their bodies. Pressed so tightly against the hardness of Andrés's torso, his breaths dancing into the roots of her hair, the musky heat of his skin and cologne dancing in her airwaves and their bodies swaying in time together, it was all she could do to keep her legs upright, never mind push him away so she could run.

Because she should run. This was madness. Dancing with him like this was madness. She was feeding the ravenous butterflies in her belly and stoking the flames of a desire that could never be given air.

But her body was begging her to press even closer. Her breasts were as sensitised as she'd ever imagined they could be and pleading to be crushed tighter into his chest, the skin on her back aching to feel the hand making slow circular motions against it without the barrier of her dress.

That same hand moved lower to caress her bottom.

Impulse overcame reason and she turned her face to the opened part of his shirt and rubbed her nose against his exposed throat and breathed him in.

The musk of Andrés's cologne and another underlying scent…the scent of his skin…filled her airwaves at the same moment she became aware of the hardness pressing against her abdomen. The thrill that rushed through her was so strong it knocked the air from her lungs and infected every cell in her body with pulsing heat. For one heady, tantalising moment she ground herself into the hardness only to come to her senses with a shock that had her yanking herself out of his arms.

Her cheeks burning at her own wantonness, she met his

hooded stare and somehow managed to speak through the raggedness of her breaths. 'I need air.'

Terrified to look at him a moment longer, Gabrielle span around and slipped her way through the pulsing dance floor to escape.

Andrés watched Gabrielle disappear into the crowd with his heart thumping wildly.

Dios, he could hardly breathe through the desire blazing through him, but he filled his lungs and then, uncaring of the dancing couples he had to push out of his way, set off after her.

He'd just cleared the dance floor when she vanished through the opened French doors that led out into the palace gardens.

Following her lead, he stepped out into the quieter, warm sweet air.

Only a handful of other people were out there, sitting on the benches of the perimeter patio…and then he spotted her in the distance, shoes in hand, treading over the immaculate lawn to the nineteenth century gazebo that looked like a miniature castle in its own right, her path lit by tiny nightlights and the stars high in the night sky twinkling down on her.

He descended the steps and stepped onto the grass.

His stride being twice the length of hers, he made an effort to slow his pace and give her a little of the space she needed.

He was closing in on her when she sank onto one of the marble benches. He was out of her eye line but she must have sensed his approach for she turned her face to him before he'd put his foot onto the first of the gazebo's steps.

She'd done the same on the dance floor he remembered. Sensed his approach.

Propping himself against a pillar a good distance from her, Andrés studied her without speaking. Just as she'd sensed his approach, he sensed that he should wait until Gabrielle was ready to break the silence.

It felt like it took for ever before her quiet voice cut through the still night. 'I'm sorry for running out on you like that.'

'I frightened you?'

She swallowed and then shook her head slowly. 'I frightened myself. Andrés...' Her voice caught but she didn't drop her stare from his. 'This isn't *me*. I don't... I don't do this.'

He didn't need her to explain what *this* was. They were both adults. Adults sharing the strongest chemistry it was possible to be caught in.

He took a deep breath, hating to vocalise the question he knew he must ask. 'Do you want me to get my driver to take you home?'

Gabrielle got to her feet and took a step towards him before she even realised what she was doing.

Until he'd asked the question she would have said yes: take me home. She'd escaped into the palace gardens to cool her overheated body and get air that was fresh enough to clear her mind enough to think rationally into her lungs.

Except no matter how rationally she tried to think, the only thing to race around in her mind was how thrilling it had felt to be crushed against Andrés...and how badly she longed to be crushed against him again. Not just to be crushed against him but to bury her face in his strong throat and feel the warmth of his skin against her and refill her lungs with his scent and experience the pleasure of his hands caressing her in all the places she'd never been touched.

She drifted closer and gazed up at him.

His jaw was clenched, magnificent body tensed.

Without the extra inches the shoes gave her, he seemed even taller and broader. Even more virile.

She leaned her face closer to his, closer to the magnetic darkness of Andrés's black eyes and unthinkingly lifted a hand to touch his face.

Moving with a stealth-like grace no man of his size should possess, he caught her hand mid-air and snatched the other too, holding them firmly as he brought his face even closer to hers.

Gabrielle could feel herself falling into the hypnotic swirl, couldn't have broken the lock of their gazes if she tried... Didn't *want* to break the lock.

Releasing a hand to grip her hip and maintain the few inches of air separating their bodies, he pressed the tip of his nose to hers. 'Do you want my driver to take you home?' he repeated hoarsely. 'If you want to leave then all you have to do is say. I will step away from you and call my driver to collect you and see you safely back to your apartment.' His breathing became heavier, each word whispering against the delicate skin of her sensitised lips. 'What do you say, Gabrielle? Do you want me to make that call?'

The alternative went unspoken. Nothing more needed to be said.

Skimming her fingers up his arm, she placed her palm on his chest. He sucked in a breath. His grip on her hip tightened. The thuds of his heartbeat perfectly matched the thuds of her own.

In a brief moment of clarity she realised that the alternative wouldn't mean breaking the promise she'd made to herself when she'd brought Lucas home. Andrés was a strictly short-term relationship man. He wouldn't want more than she could give, and all she could give him was one night. It was all she could give to herself.

This was meant to be, she realised, staring even deeper into his eyes. It had been from the start. If she'd known he was single, she would have refused point blank to attend the party with him, would have spent the night alone in her tiny apartment unaware that he held the key to unlocking all the desires she'd kept buried so deep for Lucas's sake that she'd hardly been aware they existed.

For this one night she could put those desires first, and do so with the sexiest man to roam the earth, the man who had the power to turn her to liquid without even touching her.

A man who wouldn't want anything more from her.

She moved her face closer. Their lips brushed like feathers. The heat of his breath filled her senses.

The butterflies in her belly had grown so big the beat of their wings had become at one with the beats of her heart. She was barely aware of her hand sliding up from his chest to cup the back of his strong neck, not until she felt the scorch of their flesh connecting. The thrill of Andrés's fingers biting deeper into her hips sent a tiny moan escaping in the moment their mouths fused together, and then she was caught in a kiss so deep and sensuous that the last thought before she lost the last of her mind was that Andrés's kisses tasted of hedonistic heaven.

Nerve endings on fire, Gabrielle dug the tips of her fingers through the soft bristles of his hair, and melted into the most passionate and thrilling moment of her entire life. The first slide of his tongue against her own sent a fireball of desire screaming through her, and she held onto him tightly as the dance of their mouths deepened into a hunger that had every cell in her body begging for more.

Laughter close by echoed in the night air and penetrated the sensual vortex Andrés had fallen into.

With a muttered curse, he broke away from the woman

who, with one hungry kiss, had fully aroused him in a way he'd never experienced before.

This went bone deep. Marrow deep. Hunger fuelling hunger.

The feel of those pillowy lips against his and that sweet tongue in his mouth...

Smothering a groan, he took a step away from the temptation that was Gabrielle, muttered another curse and dragged air into his lungs.

What the hell was he doing?

They were in the Monte Cleure palace garden. Anyone could see them. He needed to get control of himself.

Another lungful of air and he let himself look at Gabrielle.

The expression on her dazed face perfectly matched the torture he was experiencing.

He'd never known lust could grip so swiftly. So completely.

With another groan, he closed the gap he'd only just created and hooked an arm around her waist.

'You never answered my question,' he said, his words harsher than he'd intended. The depth of the attraction between them was a life-force of its own but he would not take advantage of her if any trace of the doubts and fears that had seen her run from the ball room still existed.

Her gaze locked onto his. A hand flew to his chest. Fingers pinched at the silk of his shirt. Her breasts were rising and falling in rapid motion.

He found himself holding his breath as he waited for her to respond.

The pillowy lips parted. 'I don't want to leave without you.'

Still gazing into her desire-filled dark brown depths, he

breathed in deeply, his relief at her softly delivered words close to overwhelming.

What magic ran in Gabrielle's veins? he wondered. Her beauty grew every time he looked at her but the world was overrun with beautiful women. If he was being dispassionate, he would say there was nothing special about her. No goodly reason on earth that one kiss with her, one simple connection of their mouths, the aperitif of courtship, should blow his mind so badly.

No goodly reason that he felt he would combust if he didn't get one more taste of that potent magic.

But then her pillowy lips parted again and closed in on his, and he realised dispassion had already gone to hell when it came to this woman.

Their lips melded together for one long, lingering kiss that roused his senses completely.

Breaking the kiss, he gripped the hand still locked against his chest and rubbed his nose into her soft cheek. 'Let's get out of here.'

Detouring only to collect Gabrielle's bag and Andrés's dinner jacket and bowtie, they slipped out of the palace, hands clasped together, without saying goodbye to anyone. It was a rudeness that wouldn't go unnoticed but Andrés didn't care. Let them say what they wanted. They could add it to the rudeness he'd displayed when he'd given his entire attention to Gabrielle during the banquet.

He took a deep breath. It had been many years since his guts had been filled with such nerves and excitement.

His driver crunched his car over the palace courtyard. By unspoken agreement, they were going to Andrés's apartment.

In the back of the car, he took a moment to breathe before looking again at Gabrielle.

Her wide-eyed stare was already fixed on him, her body twisted to face him. The silence was so total he could hear the shallowness of her breaths.

Dios, he'd never known his heart could beat so hard.

Without speaking, he pressed the button that darkened the dividing glass, giving them complete privacy. Only dim lights illuminated them.

He leaned closer to her and put a hand on her thigh. She visibly trembled.

Eyes locked on hers, he slowly, slowly gathered the velvet of her dress up to her trembling knee.

'It has been a long time since you were with a man?' he guessed quietly, splaying his hand over the soft skin of her naked thigh. It took all his control not to grip it tightly.

Something he couldn't read flickered in her eyes before she nodded.

He brought his face closer to hers. He had to swallow the moisture that had filled his mouth to speak again. 'We don't have to do anything you don't want. We don't have to do anything at all.' Although if he never got another taste of those beautiful pillowy lips he had a feeling a part of him might just well die…

Instead of saying anything, she palmed his jaw. The pads of her fingers dug into his cheek as she brought her mouth to his for a featherlight caress.

She pulled away to look into his eyes again before bringing her lips back to his for a harder, more substantial kiss and then, with the softest moan, her lips parted, her tongue danced into his mouth and the spark caught.

Mouths locked, they devoured each other. Every sweep of Gabrielle's tongue against his sent fire to his loins and fed the hunger…fed it but left him ravenous.

Laying her down so she was flat on her back, the velvet

skirt of her dress bunched around her hips, one knee raised, a bare foot pressed against his thigh, the other trailing on the car floor, he dragged his fingers over the most succulent thigh imaginable. The mew of arousal that sounded from her throat fed his own rock-hard arousal. Covering her with his body, he kissed her again.

A vague awareness that they would arrive at his apartment shortly echoed in the back of his head, and he broke the lock of their mouths for another look at the beauty that captivated him more with every stare.

She lifted her hand to run her fingers through his hair. The desire blazing on her face was like nothing he'd seen before. It was there in the slash of colour high on her cheeks and the heavy-lidded, drugged dilation in her eyes.

One more taste, he promised himself. Just one more taste and then he would help her sit up, straighten the skirt of her dress, and control his ardour until they reached his apartment.

Maybe he would have been able to make good on his mental promise of just *one more taste* if, when he crushed his mouth back to hers, his fingers hadn't crept further up her thigh and clasped onto a bottom so plump and peachy that every cell in his body shot to electrified attention.

It was possible that he would still have been able to break away if she hadn't raised her pelvis and, with another of those soft mews, hooked her leg around him.

Keeping their mouths fused together, Andrés lifted himself slightly, giving just the space needed to bring his hand around to Gabrielle's pelvis. He cupped it whole. *Dios*, the *heat*…

The moment Andrés put his hand to her pubis, Gabrielle lost the last of any inhibitions she had left. With one touch, the ache that had been slowly growing as the evening had gone on turned into an acute delicious pain begging for something, *something*. Moaning into his mouth, she twisted her body so both her legs wrapped around him, and ground into his hand. When his fingers dipped under her knickers and cupped her without any barrier, the sensations were so good and so powerful that all she could do was rock into his hand in the urgent need for that something. She was barely conscious of fighting with the button and zip of his trousers until his giant hand abandoned the source of her pleasure to cover hers and free his arousal.

She sucked in a breath as he curled her fingers over the pulsing hot length before his hand dove back between her legs, aware only that Andrés's grunts as she gripped his erection and made the movements that turned his grunts into groans were as exciting and thrilling as what his hand was doing to her.

Groans turned into shallow breaths, their mouths touching but hardly moving. The urgency for that *something* grew, and she gazed into his glazed eyes, silently pleading with him to…

He shifted the angle of his hand so a finger slid inside her sticky heat and his palm cupped harder to her pubis. She gasped at the pleasure and reflexively tightened her grip on his erection as she ground against his palm and then she felt it, the release of the coil that had wound tighter and tighter inside her and spasm after spasm of the most intense pleasure imaginable flooded her and turned the world around her into flickering white light.

CHAPTER SEVEN

IT WAS ONLY the beauty of Gabrielle's face lighting up in shocked wonder as she lost control that stopped Andrés giving in to his own release. It caught him in his own shocked wonder.

He'd come so close. So damn close.

When she had finally stilled and the only movement was in the dazed eyes ringing at him, he inhaled deeply to bring about the final bit of control needed, and kissed her gently.

He thought Gabrielle's climax might just be the most beautiful and erotic thing he had ever witnessed.

Somehow managing to trap his erection in the tight confines of his underwear, he pulled the zip of his trousers up as light filtered through the car's tinted windows.

'We are here,' he told her huskily.

She blinked, raised her head and then let it flop back onto the seat. Her chest rose as she took a long breath.

'Are you okay?' he asked, lightly tracing the back of his finger over her cheek.

Her pillowy lips attempted a smile. 'A bit shaky.'

He shifted to free Gabrielle's leg trapped between him and the car seat. 'Good shaky or bad shaky?'

Her next smile was a little more convincing and came with a short laugh. 'Good shaky…' She pressed her thighs together and twisted so both her feet dropped to the floor. 'I think.'

'Do you need me to carry you inside?' he half jested.

This time, her smile pulled across her whole face. 'What, like a *real* princess?'

He couldn't explain why this touched him as it did, but he had to fight to keep the lightness in his tone. 'Just like a real princess.'

The car came to a stop.

She held a hand out. 'I think I'm good to walk but I could do with your help sitting up.'

He took hold of it and grazed a kiss to the tip of her fingers then pulled her upright.

Between them, they tugged the skirt of her dress back down to her ankles—pretty ankles, he noted—before Andrés slid her shoes back onto her feet.

'Now I am a real princess,' Gabrielle teased as the door opened.

Only when he turned his back to her so he could unfold himself out was she able to take the moment to properly compose herself without his watchful stare on her before swinging her legs out of the car, taking Andrés's hand and joining him in the Imperium's private underground car park.

If he didn't have such tight hold of her hand she thought it possible her shaky legs really would have given way.

She had never imagined...never *dreamed*...that pleasure could be so intense. That a climax could leave you feeling like your bones had melted.

And if she'd thought about it, she wouldn't have dreamed that she could behave in such a wanton way and not feel an ounce of shame...but that was part of the Andrés effect, she realised. It wasn't just that he wore his sexuality like a second skin but the look that pulsed in his hypnotic eyes, the sense that this was a man who embraced all the sensual pleasures life had to offer...and as she thought this, the spent flame deep in her pelvis flickered back to life at the sensual discoveries that lay ahead of her.

She wished she could tell him that she'd just experienced her first ever climax but feared it would lead to a conversation she mustn't have. She'd already proven herself incapable of lying to him and...

Oh, just stop thinking!

Stepping into the elevator Andrés guided her to, she met his stare as the doors closed around them.

To think they hadn't even made it into his apartment yet...

A burst of laughter came from nowhere, and she wrapped her arms around his waist and gazed up at Andrés's devastatingly handsome face.

He squeezed her bottom. 'Are you going to share the joke?'

'There is no joke. I just felt like laughing.' Gabrielle lifted herself onto her toes and kissed him.

No point in analysing what had just happened to her. She'd made the choice to embrace the Andrés effect and it was more potent than she could have dreamed, but just as with everything else that had happened to her that evening, come the morning the magic would go pop and she would return to her real life. Nothing like this would ever happen to her again.

No point either, in worrying that she was already finding Andrés's kisses headily addictive.

The elevator door slid open.

She hadn't even felt it move.

Happily slipping her hand into his, she stepped into a different welcome room to the one she'd arrived at via the

atrium and as a far more elaborate door to the other welcome room swung open, an unexpected thought made her
heart lurch and rooted her feet to the floor.

'What's wrong?' Andrés asked.

'Sophia.' Gabrielle didn't think she could look the Spanish woman in the eye. It was one thing approving—*suggesting*—a border guard accompany her brother to a party
as a last-minute substitute, quite another for the brother to
bring that same border guard home.

He coaxed her over the threshold. 'You have nothing to
worry about. She's flown back to Seville.'

A man who looked to be around the fifty mark and who
was wearing a monogrammed black polo shirt with *AM*
embroidered into it materialised. Andrés acknowledged
him with a nod then held his arms back so the man could
remove his dinner jacket for him, all the while continuing
their conversation, saying, 'She messaged earlier. Said she
was bored being stuck in the apartment on her own and
wanted to sleep in her own bed. Thank you, Michael,' he
added in English to the man Gabrielle assumed was some
kind of butler. 'You can finish for the evening now.'

The man bowed his head. 'Goodnight, sir.'

'Goodnight, Michael.'

As if by magic, the man disappeared as unobtrusively as
he'd appeared, although Gabrielle thought she might have
had a better idea of the direction he'd taken if her stare
hadn't been glued to Andrés.

Suddenly she felt very much aware that it was only the
two of them and for the first time experienced a frisson of
nerves, nerves that increased when he took her hand and
led her through a different door to the one she'd taken earlier. It was a kitchen. A kitchen so startling in its contrast

to her own tiny cooking space that all she could do was shake her head in awe.

'Champagne?' Andrés asked.

'Sure you can manage without your butler to do it for you?' she teased.

That was better. He'd sensed the stillness of his apartment working to feed Gabrielle's nerves. Her teasing already felt familiar. Felt good.

'I'm sure I can work it out,' he said with wry self-deprecation, then opened the fridge. This one was full of food. Closing it, he opened the adjacent one and was greeted with rows and rows of white wine, rosé and champagne. Selecting a bottle of Louis Roederer, he opened cupboards in the search of champagne flutes.

'You don't know your way around your own kitchen?' she said with a splutter of laughter as he opened the third cupboard.

He grinned sheepishly. 'I keep spirits and glasses in the bar in the living room that I help myself to whenever the mood takes me. That is the extent of my domesticity. I'm afraid I wasn't exaggerating the lengths I go to avoid chores.'

'Is champagne a Michael job?'

'It isn't an Andrés job.'

She arched an unimpressed eyebrow. 'If you refer to yourself in the third person again, I'm going home.'

'Andrés would never refer to himself in the third person.'

Feeling ridiculously pleased at Gabrielle's sniggers at this, he opened the door that led into a pantry and found a shelf full of crystal champagne flutes.

He was even more ridiculously pleased to return to the kitchen and find Gabrielle had hoisted herself onto the marble island and kicked her shoes off.

With a wink, he worked the cork and in one quick move, it popped.

'Hidden talents. I'm impressed.' She laughed.

He blew her a kiss then poured them both a glass. When he handed Gabrielle her flute, he kissed her for real, a short, hard, hungry kiss that flooded him with heat.

Dios, what was she doing to him?

Who the hell cared? Tonight was turning into the best night of his life and he wasn't prepared to waste another minute of it by thinking.

He raised his flute. *'Salud.'*

'Santé.'

Flutes clinked together, they drank.

Champagne fizzing on his tongue, Andrés stood before her and drank the whole of her in. With the bright kitchen lights bathing her, he would expect to find the imperfections that the clever lighting of the palace shadowed, but all he found was her beauty enhanced. She was breathtaking.

He traced the pads of his fingers over her cheek. *'Tu es belle,'* he murmured.

Her chest rose slowly and then she expelled the breath with a sigh of pleasure. 'I didn't know you spoke my language.'

He hovered his hand. *'Un peu.'* A little. His chest swelling, he drank her beauty in some more then plucked the flute from her hold and placed it with his own on the island before putting his hands to her slim waist. 'Let's share a bath.'

Her eyes widened but she didn't object.

He pressed a light kiss to her irresistible lips and whispered, 'I am not in any rush, *ma belle*. Let's make the whole night count.'

Despite the heated arousal that had infected every cell of his body, Andrés wanted to make the most of every minute he had with this woman. He wanted to know her intimately... In every possible way.

Gabrielle experienced a moment of weightlessness as she was lifted off the island. Once her feet were on the ground, Andrés moved his hands from her waist, expertly picked up their flutes with one hand and reached for the champagne bottle with the other.

His eyes gleamed as he beckoned for her to follow him.

She allowed herself only a moment's hesitation before making her feet move.

She wasn't actually sure why she hadn't just said no to the suggestion of sharing a bath. She'd had the opportunity. A fear of seeming gauche and unsophisticated? No, it couldn't be that. He already knew she didn't have a sophisticated bone in her body.

She could still say no. Tell him the truth.

But how could she admit that she was terrified as she'd never been naked in front of a man before? She couldn't. As with her never having climaxed before, it would only lead to questions she couldn't answer.

But she wished she could. Wished she could tell him the truth about everything...

Stop thinking, Gabrielle!

Yes. Stop thinking. She'd known the night would involve them taking all their clothes off but she'd assumed it would be in a bedroom with the lights out.

Oh, help, what if her naked body turned him off? Could that happen?

Oh, shut up, brain!

Falling into step beside him, she finally quietened her brain and treaded over carpet her bare feet practically cried with joy to be walking on.

He pushed a door open with his elbow and Gabrielle

found herself in a bathroom of such size and opulence that her mouth fell open.

And she'd thought the bathroom she'd showered in earlier was amazing.

Stepping over the colourful mosaic floor, she slowly took in the clean white tiles of the high walls and the embellished gold architrave, and then her gaze drifted back down to the enormous walk-in shower—twice the size at least of the one she'd showered in earlier—at the far end before finally resting on the long, sunken bath.

The lights dimmed, bathing the entire room in a romantic golden hue.

She snatched a breath before allowing her gaze to fall on Andrés.

He was watching her with an expression that set her heart pounding all over again.

'Do you need to call Michael to show you how to work the bath?' she said teasingly, needing to break the silence she knew her own nerves had created.

He stared pointedly at her before turning to a keypad built into the wall and pressing a button on it. Less than a second later and streaming water gushed out of dozens of hidden internal faucets. Next, he poured a liberal amount of bubble bath into it and immediately the most mouth-watering scent filled the air.

'See?' he said, his tone serious. 'Andrés can run a bath.'

Mirth bubbled up in her in the same way the bubbles foaming in the bath were rising. 'Very impressive,' she said with a snigger.

Smirking, he dropped a wink. 'I like to think so.' Then, without missing a beat, his fingers went to the buttons of his shirt. In moments, he'd shrugged it off. He let it drop to the floor and moved his hand to the button of his trousers.

Gabrielle's mouth ran dry. She'd caught a glimpse of his naked chest when she'd first arrived at his apartment, had touched the contours of it over his shirt but even so…

Nothing could have prepared her for the raw beauty of it. Every inch, from the deep olive hue of his skin to the dark hair that covered from the band of his trousers up over the washboard stomach and smattered over his defined pecs… beautiful. And his *arms*… They were a work of art in their own right, even without the sexy sleeve tattoo.

He watched her ogling and grinned. 'You like what you see?'

She tried to affect nonchalance. 'It's…quite pleasing.'

His eyes glittered knowingly. In one fell swoop, he pulled his trousers and underwear down and stepped out of them, taking his black socks with them.

The mouth that had become so arid the Sahara would have felt sorry for it suddenly flooded with moisture.

Fully, unashamedly naked, Andrés's body transcended beauty. This was masculinity in its purest form, a feat even Michelangelo would have struggled to replicate even when considering he'd have had to greatly reduce the size of a certain aroused appendage so as not to fall foul of obscenity laws, and it came to her in a flash why she hadn't objected to sharing a bath with him.

The thought was too thrilling to refuse.

He stepped to her.

Her abdomen contracted.

'Turn around,' he ordered huskily.

Legs suddenly trembling again, she obeyed.

Warm hands clasped her arms. Warm breath danced into her hair. His erection jutted into her back. 'Lift your arms.'

Closing her eyes, resisting the strong yearning to lean back into him, she again obeyed.

He pinched the tiny hidden zipper that ran beneath her armpit and tugged it down slowly all the way to where it met the skirt of her dress. Then he brought his hand to her shoulder and pinched the dress where it swept over it, and brushed it down her arm. The top part of her dress folded in a swoop to her waist, exposing her naked breasts.

Her whole body was trembling.

Giant hands cupped her breasts.

She could no longer stop herself from swaying back into him. His fingers gently squeezed, capturing her nipples.

The sensations were so intense that she moaned and arched her back, pushing her chest forwards in a wordless plea for more.

His breathing deepened and he groaned into her hair. '*Tu es si belle*, Gabrielle. So beautiful.'

She could have wept when his hands abandoned her breasts to palm gently over her stomach to where her dress had fallen to. Still breathing heavily into her hair, he found the clasp at her waist. There was a rip as he grew impatient at the fiddliness of it and tore at it, and then heavy velvet pooled at her feet.

His erection now a thick rock pressed into her back, he pinched the sides of her panties and tugged them down her hips. A sudden impatience to be as naked as him had Gabrielle take over and wiggle them down her legs and kick them off.

His hand caught hold of hers and twisted her to face him.

The look on his face would have blown away any of the shyness she'd expected to feel at being naked in front of a man for the first time. But there hadn't been any shyness since he'd taken her breasts in his hands and held them so reverentially. Only arousal. An arousal that deepened at the hooded hunger in his stare.

Impulse had her close her lips around a flat, brown nipple. He groaned and clasped her bottom, pulling her flush against him. His arousal stabbed into her belly and before she could even think about what she was doing, she dropped to her knees and kissed the tip.

Andrés could hardly draw breath. His feet were ground to the floor, refusing to cooperate with his brain's command to step back, to reset things to the slow seduction he'd...

She took him in her mouth.

Holy...

She drew her lips back slowly then, keeping his length clasped in her hand, looked up at him with those deeply beautiful eyes and, almost shyly said, 'Do you like this?'

He had to swallow to speak. 'Yes, but, Gabrielle...'

His intention to tell her to stop, that he was already too close to the edge, dissolved when those pillowy lips enclosed around him again.

Holy, holy...

With a growl, he clasped her head with all the gentleness he could muster, withdrew from her mouth, then reached down, scooped hold of her waist and lifted her into his arms.

Then, without a word, he carried her to his bedroom and practically threw her onto the bed.

Gabrielle gazed at the man roughly parting her thighs and dazedly thought, *I've caused this. I've done this to him.*

Just as he was to blame for turning her entire body into a molten pool of hot, sticky desire, she was to blame for the pulsing black eyes and aroused tension etched on his face.

His erection jutting against her pubis, he snatched her hands and pressed them either side of her head.

Breathing heavily, jaw clenched, he gazed down at her.

'Kiss me,' she breathed.

He closed his eyes tightly and then they locked back onto

hers. And then his mouth swooped for a kiss so savage in its passion that at the first fusion of their lips, Gabrielle found herself lost in the sensation that was Andrés, and it was the most incredible sensation in the world.

There was something almost unleashed in his kisses and the graze of his tongue as he touched and tasted every inch of her, a sense that he wanted to bite his way through her skin and burrow himself inside.

This was Andrés stripped back to his animalistic, masculine essence and it was the most hedonistic, mind-blowing pleasure imaginable.

Every suck and caress of her breasts added to the exquisite agony. Every drag of his fingers over her thighs and belly stoked the fire, releasing the animalistic feminine essence she hadn't even guessed lived inside her. When he buried his face between her legs, she grabbed his hair and urged him on, begging and pleading until her second climax ripped through her and her pleas became cries of bliss.

This time though, there was no time to luxuriate in the sensations because the spasms had hardly abated when his giant body covered her and his mouth connected with hers for another bone-melting kiss. With his arousal pressed against her pleading folds, she instinctively spread her thighs further apart and raised her pelvis.

She gasped at the first push of his arousal inside her heat.

This was it, she thought wildly. *The point of no return.*

She had never wanted anything more in the whole of her life.

'Protection,' he groaned, even as he pushed a little deeper. 'We need…'

Swearing, he pulled out of her, stretched out an arm and yanked his bedside drawer open.

Gabrielle barely had the time to be grateful for Andrés

finding sense for them both when he'd sheathed himself and he was back exactly where she wanted him to be.

With one hand clenched in hers, the other gripping her hip, with one long thrust he buried himself deep inside her.

The shock made Gabrielle suck in a breath and freeze.

Had that been *pain*?

Andrés had stopped moving. She could feel the thumps of his heart against her breast. Had it hurt him too...? But then he pulled back almost to the tip and with a groan of what could only be pleasure, drove back inside her.

Oh, that was better. Much better.

He lifted his head and kissed her.

By the fourth thrust, she'd adjusted to the newness and the sensation of being completely filled.

By the sixth thrust she'd stopped counting.

Arms and legs wrapped tightly around him, she closed her eyes and submitted to the burning flames of the passion scorching them both.

Andrés would never have believed something could feel so good. So damn incredible.

Incredible.

Dios, she was so *tight*...

Release hung tantalisingly close but he wanted to make this last as long as he could and experience every one of Gabrielle's soft cries of pleasure, to feel her nails dig into his skin, to be inside her as one with her...

Her hold on him tightened, her moans deepening, and he sensed her climax building.

Needing to watch, he placed a lingering kiss to her lips then raised himself onto his elbows, adjusting the lock of their groins to increase the friction she needed.

With drugged-like movements, her head moved from side to side, pillowy lips parting, colour rising on her cheeks and then she was clinging to him, her back arching and then her eyes flew open and he felt the most powerful thickening around him, pulling him deeper and deeper until he could hold on no more and the pleasure of release saturated him in vivid, powerful colour.

CHAPTER EIGHT

IT WAS FOUR A.M. and they'd finally made it to the bath.

After making love a second time, the water had gone cold so Andrés had run them a fresh one and lit candles so their only illumination was the soft romantic glow of candlelight. It suited Gabrielle's mood completely.

Sipping at yet another flute of champagne—they were on their second bottle—she gazed at the gorgeous face of the man who had taken her to such dizzying heights and sighed.

His foot pressed against her hip. Both of them were stretched out, facing each other, legs entwined. 'Are you okay?'

She smiled at his concern. 'Very okay, thank you. Just thinking I don't want this night to end.' Then, in case he thought she was suggesting something, added, 'Real life awaits me, but it isn't here yet so let's just enjoy the time we have left and I'll try to catch up on sleep before Maman and Romeo bring Lucas back.'

The face he pulled made her smile widen. '*Romeo?* Your brother is called *Romeo*?'

She giggled softly. 'I know. I told you, my mother's a reader. She went through a Shakespeare phase when she was pregnant with him.'

'What phase was she going through when she was pregnant with you?'

Her giggle turned into a snigger. 'I have no idea—my dad had put his foot down by the time I was born and insisted on normal names.'

'You are one of how many?'

'Three,' she replied, glad he'd phrased the question in a way that meant her answer wouldn't turn the conversation onto darker territory. 'I'm the youngest.'

'The baby of the family like me.'

She prodded his thigh with her toe. 'I bet you hated being the baby.'

Andrés breathed through the tightening of his chest. He'd never known anyone to get him the way Gabrielle instinctively seemed to. If he didn't know better he would think she had a conduit to his brain. 'Loathed it,' he admitted.

Her teeth flashed. 'Knew it.'

'How?'

She shrugged. One of her breasts crested above the inches-deep bath foam, giving him a tantalising glimpse of its succulent perfection. 'I don't know. I just can't imagine you being happy being coddled and petted and told you were too young to do the things your big sister was allowed to do.'

'When I was small, my grandmother always used to pinch my cheek when she visited and tell me what a cute little boy I was.' He grunted at the memory. 'I hated being babied. The worst was when Sophia was old enough to be left in charge of me. She took an evil delight in bossing me around.'

'Did you put up with it?'

'What do you think?'

Her eyes narrowed in contemplation. 'I think you probably took an evil delight in winding her up.'

He grinned at her astuteness. 'And you? No, let me guess…' Narrowing his own eyes in contemplation, he said, 'No one babied you.'

Her eyes flashed with surprise. 'How did you guess?'

'You haven't got a spoilt bone in your body.' And what a body it was, he thought, his loins stirring just to remember what lay beneath the thick bath foam.

The dress Gabrielle had worn that night had displayed her curves to perfection but he'd been prepared for the signs of birth. They would have made no difference to him—to Andrés, the stretchmarks of the belly and thighs, and the loosening of the flesh of the breasts that came with birth should be worn as a badge of honour for the giving of life— but Gabrielle had none of them. Her breasts were plump and succulent, her belly and thighs toned, not even a silvery sliver of a stretchmark on them.

Had her young age when having her son protected her from those effects? he wondered. He was no expert, had only a vague memory of his mother's stretch-marked body from the days she'd sunbathed in a bikini in their tiny garden when he'd been growing up to go on, so what did he know?

Still, it was strange. Surely childbirth should leave some form of mark on the body?

'Romeo's five years older than me and was always too busy knocking a ball about with his friends to pay much attention to me,' she said, breaking through his thoughts. 'He's always looked out for me though.'

'He looks out for your son?'

'As much as he can. He works on an oil rig, six weeks on, two weeks off. His girlfriend lives in Cadiz so when he's off he splits his time between us and her.'

'And your other... You never said if it was a brother or sister.'

Sadness flitted over her face and she looked away, draining her champagne before answering. 'A sister. Eloise. If I'd been born a week earlier we would have been in the same school year.'

'I went to school with identical twins born four minutes apart. Sergio told everyone who would listen that he was the eldest.'

She smiled at the anecdote but the sadness remained. 'Eloise was never like that.'

By the time Gabrielle started school, she'd already known in the instinctive way that children just knew things that Eloise needed protecting.

'Enough talk,' she declared.

A thick black eyebrow rose. 'Oh?'

Tonight was the first night Gabrielle had taken for herself since bringing Lucas home, a memory she knew she would treasure for the rest of her life. To bring Eloise into it when just saying her name made her heart weep...

Foam clinging to parts of her, she got to her knees and sloshed through the water to straddle Andrés's lap. Emptying the last of the second champagne bottle into their flutes, she clinked hers to his and drank it in one go. Aroused amusement on his face, Andrés followed suit.

Both flutes empty, she placed them next to the empty bottles on the low fitted cupboard that ran behind where his head rested, then placed her hands on his chest and leaned her face down to his.

She was drunk she realised, drunk on alcohol and drunk on Andrés.

Holding his cheeks, she kissed him deeply, and welcomed the glorious sensations that roared to life with the fusion of their mouths and tongues, sensations strong enough to drive out all thought and give them the moment for what it was. Pleasure.

For the first time Gabrielle really understood what she'd

committed to missing when she'd committed herself to a lifetime of celibacy.

Intimacy and pleasure. All the things most people her age took for granted.

And emotional connection.

It was the latter she suspected she would feel the most bereft to leave when she walked out of this apartment.

Whether the desire consuming her would have sparked to life with anyone else was pointless in trying to guess, but she knew in her heart that the magical alchemy that had enveloped them so completely was a one-off, and she would take every ounce of the pleasure and connection they could share with each other until the time came to say goodbye, because she would never have any of this again.

That time was speeding towards them.

Dragging her mouth over the bristles of Andrés's beard, she slipped her fingers around his head to clasp his skull and lifted herself so he could take a breast into his mouth.

Hands trailing up and down her spine, his hungry mouth and tongue working their magic, Gabrielle threw her head back and lost herself to the heady sensations. The burn deep in her core pulsed strongly, and she ground herself against the hard thick length of Andrés's arousal, her body instinctively seeking the hedonistic sensations of relief only he could provide, and it was without any conscious thought whatsoever that she lifted herself enough to sink down on his length.

'God... Gabrielle...' The last conscious part of Andrés tried to cut through...*holy Dios*...the pleasure of being completely bare inside her...and he'd thought the pleasure he'd found with her already had been the pinnacle... When her glazed eyes met his and thick spasms gripped him as her beautiful mouth parted to release the cries of her climax, he only just held on to that last wisp of consciousness to lift her off him.

He caught the confusion on her face before her eyes glittered, and, still straddling his lap, she wrapped her fingers around his arousal and brought him to his own climax.

Gabrielle's eyes flickered open to early sunlight. Andrés's arm was hooked around her belly, a leg draped over her thigh, his breathing deep and rhythmic.

There was a dull ache pounding in her head. It had nothing on the heavy pounding in her chest.

She looked at her watch. Seven thirty a.m.

Tears prickled her eyes.

The night was over. It was time to go.

Carefully moving his arm off her, she slid away from his leg and sat up. The throbbing in her head even more acute, she looked around the vast room for something to cover herself.

A black towelling robe hung on the back of a door. She padded gingerly to it and slipped it on.

It smelled of Andrés. Its size drowned her.

Her chest filling, she crept out of the bedroom and into the bathroom opposite.

Her dress was neatly folded on a chair she barely remembered seeing before, shoes and clutch bag beside it. Andrés's discarded clothes, the champagne bottle and flutes had all vanished. The bathroom was as sparkling as it had been when she'd first set foot in it.

It was as if what they'd shared in there had never happened.

But it *had* happened, she thought, a sad smile pulling on her lips to remember just how amazing it had been.

She pulled the heavy velvet up to her waist, blinking more tears away.

Only when she'd put her arm through the sleeve and zipped the dress up did she allow herself to look in the full-length mirror. Her reflection shocked her. She'd expected to look different, that what she and Andrés had shared would have marked her in some obvious way, but it was still her face looking back at her.

She felt different. Changed.

Changed or not, she had her real life to return to where nothing had changed.

After several long breaths Gabrielle ran her fingers through her hair in an attempt to tidy it and noticed there was a gaping hole at the side of the dress where Andrés had ripped the clasp. A tear finally sprang free. She hastily wiped it away.

She supposed a touch of melancholy was to be expected after the night she'd just experienced.

Picking up her shoes and the clutch bag, she left the bathroom and padded back to Andrés's bedroom. Heart now thumping violently as the time to say goodbye drew near she pushed the door open.

Her heart sighed. He was still deep in sleep.

With another sigh, she took the whole room in properly for the first time, committing the dark blue fitted wardrobes and side boards, and velvet blue soft furnishings dominated by the huge bed to her memory.

It was a beautifully modern room she acknowledged with a deep pang, and that was the bed she'd given her virginity in, given it to a man she wished with all her heart...

She closed her eyes and forced her thoughts to where they should be, not to a place they should never go. Lucas was her priority. His safety and happiness were all that mattered.

Tiptoeing to Andrés, she carefully leaned over and placed a gentle kiss to his cheek.

His eyes sprang open.

He blinked a number of times before rolling onto his back. Patting the space next to him, his voice was thick with sleep. 'You're going?'

More choked than she'd imagined she'd be when she'd agreed to stay the night with him, she nodded, and perched her bottom on the bed.

He reached for her hand. 'I would drive you home...'

She threaded her fingers through his. 'You're probably over the limit.' Make that definitely.

His grin was rueful if pained. 'I think there's been an explosion in my head.'

She started to laugh but it hurt her own head too much. 'And mine.'

'It was worth it.' An intensity came into his stare. 'I had a great night, Gabrielle.'

She squeezed his fingers. 'Me too.'

It had been the best night of her life.

'Michael will give you a lift and arrange for your bike and things to be brought to you.'

'Thank you.' Leaning down, she kissed his mouth. 'Thank you for everything.'

Her intention to move away was scuppered when he caught the back of her head and kissed her so deeply and thoroughly that for a moment she didn't even feel her poorly head.

Grinning, he rested back on the pillow and hooked an arm above his head. Stretching his body quite clearly showed the delineation of his erection beneath the light grey silk bedsheet covering him to his waist.

'Sure you can't stay for a while longer?' he coaxed knowingly.

This time she did laugh, even as desire pulsed heavily

inside her. Planting one last kiss to his mouth, she dragged herself back to her feet and shuffled to the door where she turned to face him one last time and blew him a kiss.

He pressed it to his lips and blew her a kiss back.

It was mid-morning when Andrés finally threw the covers off and dragged himself out of bed.

What a night.

Donning his robe, he laughed under his breath at just how fantastic the whole night had been. There was a very good chance he wouldn't kill his sister for manipulating him into it after all. An internal stop button when drinking meant he hadn't suffered many hangovers in his life but of the few he'd had, this was the only one that felt good. Even better, Gabrielle had left without any drama or hints about seeing him again. They'd both known exactly what the night was and that had been enough for them both. Still, he had to admit that if she hadn't needed to return home to her son, he'd have coaxed her into staying in bed with him. *Dios*, just to remember how fantastic the sex had been was enough to make him hard…

A mark on the light grey under-sheet suddenly caught his eye.

Pulling away the crumpled heap of silk sheets partially covering it, he looked a little more closely.

It was blood.

A shiny, futuristic car approached the border. Gabrielle's heart jumped. It was an automatic reaction that had occurred every time a car that vaguely looked the same as Andrés's arrived at the principality over the last five days. None of them had been his and nor was this one. The system that registered every non-domiciled person in the principality, and which she had access to as part of her job, showed he'd left Monte Cleure late on Sunday evening.

She wondered where he was. What he was doing…

An idle fantasy drifted into her vision of riding her bicycle in a floaty summer dress and a huge shiny car pulling to a stop beside her, and the window rolling down and…

'Gabrielle?'

Her colleague's voice pulled her out of her daydream.

'Sorry,' she muttered. 'I was miles away.'

Remi peered closely at her. 'Who is he?'

'What?'

'It's got to be a man. You've been smiling to yourself and falling away into your own little world all week.'

Mortified, aware she was blushing, Gabrielle shook her head. 'It's no one.'

Mercifully, three cars joined the manual passport check line and she was able to escape Remi's prying, but even as she made a concerted effort to get on with the job, her colleague's words rang continually in her ears.

Gabrielle had known all those years ago from the way Eloise kept smiling to herself that her sister had fallen for someone. It seemed that no time passed from those early dreamy smiles before she fell into the pure, deep love that would destroy her.

She wasn't Eloise, Gabrielle reminded herself. Of course she'd fallen for Andrés, but it was a chemical thing, a lust thing involving the body and not the heart. One precious night of hedonism. It was over and now she needed to gently push him into the treasured memories part of her mind and stop his occupancy of it.

The Thursday morning traffic rush was over when Andrés left his Barcelona office complex and got straight into the waiting car. A short drive and he'd be in his helicopter and on his way to Monte Cleure. That was the plan until he stepped out of the car at his airfield and the hot mid-morning sun beamed down on him. The last few months had been so busy that he couldn't remember the last time he'd fed vitamin D straight into his flesh.

'You take the helicopter, I'm going to drive,' he impulsively told his entourage. He'd only driven the newest addition to his fleet of cars once and as it was currently being stored in the hangar here and he had the rest of the day free from meetings, why not take advantage of the freedom?

The shocked eyes of his PA, bodyguard and lawyer zipped to him before they all bustled into the helicopter. He could imagine what they'd be saying. Andrés hadn't driven himself on a working day in a decade. His trip to Monte Cleure was business. He had an early morning meeting with Nathaniel and the lawyers the next day to thrash out the final details of their latest joint business venture.

The roads to Monte Cleure were clearer than the last time he'd made this journey and, shades on and the music turned up loud, he put the roof down to enjoy the feel of warm air flying through his hair.

He thought back to the last time he'd made this journey, almost three weeks ago, and how his preoccupation with the paternity case had ruined what could have been a fun drive with his sister. Sophia had called him the evening after the party brimming with excitement and curiosity about how things had gone with Gabrielle. Andrés had taken great delight in not satisfying any of it other than to confirm that no, he hadn't made plans to see her again. His sister's disappointment at this had been palpable. She couldn't understand that the night with Gabrielle had been as perfect for its ending as it had been for the night itself. He had no wish to pursue a short-term fling with her and ruin that perfection with an inevitably bitter end and he'd sensed it was the same for Gabrielle. Their night together had been one of a kind, a memory to be treasured.

Traffic slowed to a crawl. He'd reached the queue for the border.

He wondered if Gabrielle was working. It was a thought that had floated in and out of his mind since getting in the car, although obviously had played no part at all in his impulsive decision to drive.

Smoothing his hair back, he cruised into the facial recognition line. As he inched forwards, he noted a car being searched but none of the staff undertaking it were Gabrielle.

Now at the front of the queue, he looked into the camera. A light went green, the barrier lifted and he crossed the border.

Gabrielle logged onto the system. Quickly checking that no one in the administration office was paying her any attention, she clicked the link that listed all the cars and every non-domiciled visitor currently in the principality. Having spent yesterday afternoon processing a drug-trafficker caught with methamphetamines in his wheel hubs, liaising with the police and then hurrying off to collect Lucas from nursery, this was her first opportunity to check since early yesterday morning. She had twenty-four hours' worth of data to scroll through and exactly ten minutes until her shift started to do it in.

It took two minutes until the name she'd been both praying and dreading to see appeared.

He was here. Finally. After four days of diligently checking the system whenever she could for his name, Andrés had passed the border at around the time she'd been in the processing unit carefully testing, weighing and recording the drug stash. Unless he'd since left the principality by helicopter, which the system was always a little slower to update, he was still here.

The nausea that had been rolling in her stomach for days on end rose up her throat. She covered her mouth and closed her eyes, willing it to pass.

'Is everything okay, Gabrielle?'

She opened her eyes to the concerned gaze of the shift manager. 'I'm sorry, I know this is terrible timing but I need to go.'

Her manager's stare became meditative as she waited for an explanation.

'Please?' Gabrielle whispered. She wouldn't lie and say she was ill—the sickness in her stomach was wholly fear. 'It's a personal matter. I wouldn't do this if it wasn't important.'

Eventually there was a nod. 'I'll get cover for you.'

She exhaled her relief. 'Thank you.'

'Is there anything I can do to help?'

Fighting tears, she sucked in a breath and shook her head. No one could help her with what she needed to do.

CHAPTER NINE

THE CONTRACTS OF his new business venture with Nathaniel signed, his stomach filled with the exquisite food served by the palace's talented chefs over a late lunch, Andrés peered out of the car window at Monte Cleure's bustling pristine streets, tuned out the talk between the staff travelling with him, and contemplated the rest of the day that lay ahead of him. Two video conferences, one for the forthcoming Janson Media AGM and one with the acquisition team in Japan for his buyout of a cutting-edge Manga publishing company that had, in the last twenty-four hours, hit unexpected roadblocks. Hopefully it would all be sorted before he left for the evening get-together at the private members' club. By rights, he should take a date with him, should already have organised one. It was a task he'd kept putting off and now it was too late to get anything organised. That was okay. He didn't mind that all the others in the group he was meeting with would be paired up, and the great thing about Club Giroud was that it was no gentleman's club—rich, successful women were equally drawn to it. Andrés had met three previous lovers in Club Giroud's various incarnations across Europe. It was about time he found himself another lover. Tonight would be an excellent place to start.

His mind drifted to Gabrielle. It had drifted to her numerous times since their night together. Numerous times he'd been tempted to get in contact and offer to fly her out to him because, *Dios*, his veins still thrummed from their lovemaking. Nights were the worst. He couldn't seem to stop his mind from reliving the pleasure they'd shared which only ramped up the thrumming in his veins that no amount of self-care seemed able to alleviate.

But just as he'd resisted reaching out to fly her to him, so too would he resist calling to see what her plans for the evening were…

A small figure hunched on the doorstep of the rear entry into his apartment building pulled him sharply from his thoughts. Craning his head back, the position of the car as it turned into the underground car park made it impossible to see for certain but that didn't stop his hand hitting the intercom and Andrés commanding his driver to stop.

Gabrielle had watched so many chauffeur-driven cars come and go from the Imperium's underground car park that she'd lost count. Once they were swallowed inside it, the guarded doors closed and she had no chance of following. All she could do was sit there and hope Andrés went in or out before she had to collect Lucas, and pray that he noticed her. If he didn't or time ran away from her then she'd leave a message with the concierge for him to call her. She hoped it didn't come to that. What she had to tell him needed to be done in person.

Time almost had run away from her when the enormous Range Rover came to an abrupt halt at the halfway point of its turn into the car park. Her heart and legs kicked into gear before her brain did, pumping wildly as she hurried to it, and so it was that when he emerged from the back, everything she'd spent the past days going over in her head dissolved.

The reality of Andrés in the flesh after nearly three weeks of memory came as a powerful shock.

Dressed in a clearly bespoke dark grey suit, everything about him was so much more than she'd remembered, from his height and breadth—he towered over her—to the dark olive hue of his skin and the blackness of his hair, even the depth of his voice when he warmly said, 'This is a pleasant surprise. Are you here to see me?'

Her senses overwhelmed with the man who'd haunted her waking and sleeping dreams since she'd left his bed, Gabrielle nodded.

'You should have waited in the atrium. It's far more comfortable.'

She had to swallow to loosen her vocal cords. 'I was afraid I'd miss you.' The concierge—not Bernard this time—and the other staff member had taken one look at her work uniform and wrinkled their noses in unison. They'd been spectacularly unhelpful. One had called the apartment and spoken to Michael to establish that Andrés wasn't in but refused to assist in any other way, including a refusal to let Gabrielle speak to Michael herself and at least know if Andrés was planning to return to his apartment that day.

The fizzing bolt that had shot through Andrés to realise that it really was Gabrielle on the step slipped away as he took in the pallor of her skin and the nervous, almost frightened energy she vibrated with.

Folding his arms slowly across his chest, he looked at her more closely. 'What's wrong?'

'Can we go somewhere private, please? I need to talk to you about something.'

His concern growing, he indicated the open door of his car. 'Get in.'

He followed her into it. The last time they'd shared the back of a car together, it had been only the two of them. This time his PA, lawyer and PA's assistant were with them, all pretending it was perfectly normal for a frazzled young woman in a border guard uniform and clumpy boots to join them, a pretence they kept up when the car was parked moments later in Andrés's designated bay and maintained in the elevator ride to his penthouse. Inside, they disappeared to his offices to get back onto the phone with the team in Japan while he led Gabrielle into the main living room, the beats of his heart now painful weighty thumps.

In all his imaginings—and of course he'd had idle fantasies about running into Gabrielle again, passing her in the street, spotting her from the window of a restaurant, sometimes riding her bicycle, always with her hair loose, an irreverent laugh that only she knew the meaning behind a whisper away from escaping her pillowy lips. He'd imagined her double take when she spotted him, the smile that would spread across her face, the knowing look that would pass between them...

He'd never imagined those pillowy lips could be pulled so thin or that hair scraped back in a neat ponytail could conversely be messy and unkempt. She was holding herself so rigidly a jolt would snap her in half. Something was clearly wrong and he hoped like hell it wasn't anything to do with her son. In the few idle hours he'd had since his last visit to Monte Cleure he'd researched the principality's social system and learned that citizens were entitled to only the most basic health care.

Finally alone, he was about to ask again what the matter was when her dark eyes suddenly locked onto his. 'I'm pregnant.'

Her words landed like a cold punch in his guts that spread like ice straight into his brain.

Gabrielle watched the colour drain from Andrés's face. She watched the emotions flicker over his handsome features in slow motion, incomprehension slowly morphing into stunned disbelief and then back into incomprehension.

'That isn't possible,' he dragged out hoarsely.

She forced herself to maintain eye contact. 'I took two tests on Monday.'

She'd known even before she was a day late that something was happening to her. She'd buried her head in the sand for two days, telling herself that swollen, tingly breasts this close to her period was nothing to worry about, then spent three further days hitting the toilet at increasingly frequent intervals, desperately waiting for blood to appear.

His colour was slowly returning, the incomprehension of his stare slowly dissipating as his clever brain began to turn and his eyes narrowed.

'It's yours,' she confirmed before he could voice the cynical thoughts she could see rotating in his mind.

A moment passed between them, a flash where she could see into his thoughts and knew he was remembering the bath they'd shared, when she'd lost all control of herself and sank onto him without protection.

Her cheeks flamed and pelvis contracted, just as they did every time she made herself remember that moment. Had it happened then, even though he'd lifted her off him? That was the question she'd tortured herself with. The hour or so before they'd finally passed out wrapped in each other's arms was still a potted blur of hedonistic champagne-fuelled memories.

How could she have been so reckless and irresponsible?

And how could she be standing only feet away from him with her heart thrashing so wildly and an increasingly desperate yearn to throw herself into his arms and beg him to tell her everything would be okay?

Feelings like this were dangerous.

Once Andrés accepted he was the father he'd want to be involved. He'd said as much at the party, that the reason he didn't want children was because he'd want to be there every day for them, therefore binding him and the child's mother for life. It was being bound to a woman for life he found so repellent and the reason his acceptance of paternity would only come with cast iron proof. Gabrielle accepted this and had prepared herself for it. What she hadn't anticipated was all the emotions swelling in her at being with him again.

Only by bringing Lucas to the forefront of her mind, just as she'd done every time she'd felt the panic starting to rise and consume her, was she able to clamp down on the swell and dredge the words she'd rehearsed for this moment. Her little boy had suffered too much in his short life already without the only mother he'd ever known falling apart. Gabrielle remembered all too clearly how her mother had fallen apart when her father died and could never put Lucas through anything like that.

'I know this is a shock for you and that you're not going to take my word that the baby's yours,' she said as calmly as she could manage. 'I accept that you will want to wait until it's born and a DNA test can be done before acknowledging paternity, but this baby *is* yours. I don't have a lawyer but I will comply with any test your legal team asks of me so long as it isn't harmful to the baby.'

She had to swallow bile to force the last words out. 'I also want to make it clear that there is no way I'm going to have an abortion.'

The mannequin called Andrés who'd listened to her pre-prepared speech without moving so much as a facial muscle came to life. The narrowed eyes glittered, the handsome face darkening as he moved towards her.

Gripping her arms in an effort to control her trembles,

Gabrielle tried not to feel guilty for her assumption that he would want her to take the easy way out. The one thing she knew about rich men was their belief that cash made all problems go away. Lucas's father had offered cash for a termination and while the only thing Andrés had in common with The Bastard was his wealth—even his arrogance was of a different hue—she would not take the risk. Better she be upfront and say an abortion was not on the cards than experience the pain of him suggesting it, even if it was an eminently sensible suggestion. Sensible or not, Gabrielle could never do that, a notion that had crystalised when she'd walked Lucas to the beach an hour after the tests had both proved positive and she'd looked at his little hand clutched so trustingly in hers and imagined the little hands forming inside her.

Little hands created by the most passionate and wonderful night of her life, and as she gazed into Andrés's glittering eyes, she had to hold herself even more tightly as the fear of his denouncing of her and the life they'd created together grew even stronger.

Whatever Andrés had intended to say to her was forgotten by a loud rap on the door behind her. The woman who'd been in the car with him burst into the room waving a phone, closely followed by the other two from the car, one of whom she now recognised as the lawyer who'd drafted the non-disclosure agreement.

'Sorry to interrupt,' the woman said, thrusting the phone into Andrés's hand, 'but Kaito will be calling in one minute. You need to talk to him—he's learned that members of the board are trying to kill the deal.'

The curse that flew from Andrés's mouth made the woman's eyes widen in shock. Even the men looked taken aback.

Only Gabrielle knew the curse wasn't aimed at the deal

being killed but at herself and the situation she'd just hit him with.

The phone rang in his hand.

Nostrils flaring, jaw tight, he looked at it before his eyes pinned back on Gabrielle.

'Take the call,' she said, almost weak with relief at the timely interruption.

He held her stare for a few more loaded moments before jerking a nod and putting the phone to his ear. 'Kaito? What the hell is going on?'

With one more hard stare at Gabrielle, he disappeared from the living room flanked by his minions.

Dragging his legs to the bar, Andrés poured himself three fingers of bourbon and downed it. Then he poured himself another hefty measure, drank half, and had another read of the note Gabrielle had left for him.

Dear Andrés,
    Sorry for leaving but I need to collect Lucas from nursery. My mother's taking him to France tomorrow for a few days if you want to talk things through? Will understand if you'd rather go through your legal team.
    Gabrielle

Head spinning, he went over her spiel again. Remembered the way she'd held herself. Her fear. Her bravery... The way she'd spoken to him as if they hadn't shared the most unbelievably perfect night together.

All her assumptions.

He took another large drink and sloshed it around his teeth, thinking hard through his spinning head for the reason his initial gut reaction had been that it was impossible for Gabrielle to be pregnant.

A tap on the door that connected the living room with the offices brought him back in the room.

His PA peered in. 'The team in Japan agree with Kaito— you're needed in Tokyo or the deal will be lost. Lara's arranging the flight slots now—we should get you in the air within the hour.'

She disappeared without expecting a response. She didn't expect a response because it was unthinkable that Andrés would do anything but fly to Japan to salvage a deal he'd long coveted and which he'd already spent millions in legal fees and other sundries on.

He threw the rest of the bourbon down his throat and headed to his offices.

An air of efficiency pervaded the room, laptops and tablets being packed into briefcases, translation apps being updated. His closest staff were well used to crossing continents without any notice. It was why he paid them such hefty salaries. That and their uncanny business acumen.

'I'm not going.'

They all looked at him with a variant of the look they'd given when he'd announced he'd drive himself into Monte Cleure.

'I'm taking the weekend off.'

His PA was the first to speak. 'But... Kaito said...'

'I don't care. The three of you go and do the best you can to save the deal. I've got something much more important to deal with.'

Gabrielle put her mug of hot chocolate on the small pine coffee table, turned the television on with the remote and, exhausted, sank onto the sofa.

She flicked through the channels looking for something to catch her eye but all the titles were a blur.

She knew the sensible thing would be to go to bed even though it was much earlier than her usual bedtime but the thought of lying down and being alone with her thoughts...

All her thoughts made her want to cry.

Selecting the comforting familiarity of an action film she'd watched so many times she could recite the words, Gabrielle cuddled a cushion to her belly, snuggled down and tried to lose herself in it.

She'd thought telling Andrés would be a relief after the dread she'd carried all these days, but if anything she felt worse. Being with Andrés in the flesh, in all his physicality... She could still feel the longing that had gripped her, the ache deep in her bones...

She hadn't expected it to be that strong. That intense.

Maybe it was for the best that things would be handled through his lawyers until paternity was confirmed to his satisfaction. It would give her the time she needed to really get a handle on the emotions thrashing through her. She'd left the ball in his court about talking things through but held little hope that—

There was a knock on her door.

Startled, she lifted her head and looked at her watch. Eight p.m. She rarely had unannounced visitors during the day never mind in the evening.

The second knock shifted her off the sofa.

She put her eye to the spyhole. Her heart thumped so hard she reared back.

It was Andrés.

Andrés had lifted his fist to rap on the door for a third time when he heard the distinctive click of a door being unlocked.

Gabrielle's shocked face appeared.

His chest tightening, he took her in, the faded jeans, the loose white top that had slipped off a shoulder reminding him of the dress she'd dazzled him in at the party, the thick dark hair worn loose but no neater than it had been earlier, the bare feet with the pretty painted toenails.

Dark brown eyes wide with apprehension, her voice was shaky as she whispered, 'What are you doing here?'

'You have to ask?' he said tersely. 'Are you going to let me in?'

Top teeth slicing into her bottom lip, she looked over her shoulder and then back at him with a pained shake of her head. 'Lucas is in bed. Let's talk tomorrow after my mum's collected him or we can—'

'We talk now.' Gabrielle had delivered her bombshell news four hours ago. In the intervening hours he'd likely destroyed the Japanese buyout, a setback to his Asia expansion plans that should not be underestimated, and likely destroyed the flooring of his apartment with all his pacing as he'd put his runaway thoughts into order. The thought of waiting one more minute was intolerable.

'He's a really light sleeper, and this isn't something he should overhear.'

Andrés leaned forwards and pitched his voice as low as it would go, enunciating every word so there could be no misunderstanding. 'If you don't let me in right now, I will file a report with the authorities that you are passing someone else's child off as your own.'

CHAPTER TEN

BLACK SPOTS FILLED Gabrielle's vision.

Hot, rabid blood filled her head.

A deep voice that brooked no argument echoed in her ears. 'Last chance, Gabrielle. Let me in.'

The world was swimming around her.

Only the image of her son, tucked up in his bed, enabled her feet to move.

Andrés knew from Gabrielle's ashen face that he'd put the pieces of the jigsaw together correctly, all the thoughts that had raced through his mind as he'd paced his apartment, impressions of their night together coalescing and solidifying into the only possible explanation.

He stepped into a narrow entrance hall with a bicycle hung on the wall and closed the door behind him. One glance in the open-plan living space was all it took to take in the small kitchen area and the small dining table that separated it from the living area, which consisted of a small sofa, an armchair, a television, a high book case crammed with well-thumbed paperbacks, and a large box crammed with toys. The whole living area could fit in his main Monte Cleure bathroom. Like the building the apartment was homed in, everything was old but clean and well looked after, little touches lifting it into something cosy and inviting. It reminded him of his childhood apartment.

All this he processed without conscious thought, his attention fully taken with the woman pregnant with his child, who was now standing against a freestanding fridge looking like she was about to collapse.

'Why don't you sit down?' he suggested curtly.

'Who's that man, Mummy?'

A small, tousle-haired child in too-short superhero pyjamas had appeared from the corridor to the side of the living area.

It was the waking version of the sleeping child he'd seen on the screen of Gabrielle's phone at the party.

The boy's appearance brought Gabrielle to life. She dove to him quicker than a sprinter at the sound of a starting gun and scooped him into her arms.

'You should be asleep,' she scolded, holding him tightly and smothering his cheek with kisses.

He wriggled and looked over her shoulder at Andrés. 'A noise woke me. Who is he, Mummy?'

'I'm Andrés,' he said in French with a wave, doing his best to appear non-threatening to the child who was clearly unsettled at the strange man in his apartment. He had to think of the correct French to add, 'I'm a friend of your mother's.'

Dark brown eyes narrowed with suspicion at Andrés before he put a palm to Gabrielle's cheek. 'Why is he here?'

'To see me,' she answered, shifting his weight to her hip.

'Why?'

'Because he's a friend, and friends sometimes like to visit each other. Your friends from nursery come to play with you, don't they?'

He considered this. 'Are you going to play a game with him?'

'No. He'll be leaving in a few minutes. Come on, let's get you back to bed.'

As she started walking, the boy put his face on Gabrielle's shoulder then lifted it again to look at Andrés. 'Goodnight,' he said before his thumb disappeared into his mouth.

Andrés would have thought he was too choked to smile but he managed to raise one for this little boy. 'Goodnight, Lucas. It was nice to meet you.'

Gabrielle tucked Lucas under his duvet and kissed his forehead. 'Goodnight, my sweet.'

His big trusting eyes held hers. 'Mummy, is that man my daddy?'

How she held back the tears at this question she would never know. Lucas had only asked about his father once, shortly after he'd started nursery. She'd truthfully told him that his daddy lived in another country, and had been filled with gratitude that he'd asked no more. More questions would come one day. Until a few minutes ago she'd thought the worst thing would be still not knowing how to answer them. Now terror had struck her heart that she might not be the one to answer them at all, and she had to concentrate with everything not to let the fresh swimming in her head sink her.

'No,' she whispered.

How did Andrés know? How was it possible that he'd discovered the truth?

It *wasn't* possible.

Lucas's skinny arms hooked around her neck. 'Can I have another story?'

She kissed his nose and swallowed back tears. 'It's late and you need to get some sleep. I'll read you one in the morning.'

He smacked a kiss to her lips.

After a dozen more kisses and a dozen '*I love you*'s, Gabrielle left her son on the cusp of sleep and gently closed his door.

Hand pressed to her racing heart, the sickness churning in her stomach making the nausea from telling Andrés about the pregnancy seem like a tepid test run, she lifted her chin and straightened her spine.

As terrified as she'd ever been in her life but filled with all the fight that had enabled her to get through these last four years, she found Andrés examining the photos displayed on the walls of the living section.

Andrés turned his head to her. 'I'm sorry for waking him.'

Lucas's appearance had dampened much of the angst and fury that had propelled him to Gabrielle's apartment.

Guilt lay heavily in him, a guilt that had been steadily growing while he waited for Gabrielle to put the boy to bed and his attention had become increasingly captured by her photographs. The walls were crammed with them, ranging from her childhood to the present day, plenty of full family pictures from when her father, a smiling man Gabrielle bore a strong resemblance to, had been alive, going as far back as her parents' wedding day. All the most recent ones featured Lucas, starting from when he could have only been days old. Most were of him with Gabrielle, but there were some too of him with the woman he already recognised as Gabrielle's mother and a couple of others with the man he recognised as her brother.

He kept going back to one particular picture of the three Breton children sitting in descending age order like a caterpillar, Gabrielle barely a toddler, and comparing it to one of the most recent Lucas pictures. The resemblance between Lucas and the other Bretons was obvious but with Gabrielle's brother, the resemblance was unmistakable. Lucas could be his doppelgänger.

The longer he'd looked at the pictures, the harder the pulse in his temple had throbbed. A hazy memory kept playing in his mind of the cloud of sadness that had enveloped Gabrielle during that brief mention of her sister when they'd been sharing a bath. She'd blinked the sadness away and replaced it with a seduction so hedonistic he'd been closer than he'd ever been in his life to saying to hell with the need for protection.

The irony of her being pregnant despite his self-denial was strong.

It had been the seductive hedonism he'd lived over in his mind since, forgetting that brief cloud, and now that cloud was all he could see.

There was a steely determination in the dark eyes locked on him which carried into her walk as she strode to stand before him. She pitched her voice low but strength resonated in it. 'Andrés, you need to leave. We can't talk with Lucas around, you must see that.'

He thought of the way the little boy had palmed Gabrielle's cheek, and the pulse in his temple beat harder than ever. As much as he wanted to shake answers out of the woman pregnant with his child, that little boy sleeping his innocent sleep had burrowed into his conscience.

Breathing heavily, he rubbed the back of his neck. 'What time is your mother collecting him tomorrow?'

'At eight.'

'I'll be here for nine.'

She closed her eyes. 'Thank you.'

Keeping a few paces behind him, she walked him to the door.

Once he'd crossed the threshold, she called his name.

He turned back to her.

The steel in her eyes blazed stronger than ever. 'I don't know what you think you know, but Lucas *is* my son, and there is nothing I wouldn't do to protect him, so don't you ever threaten me with him again.'

A lump lodged in his throat. He thought again of the small boy in the too-small superhero pyjamas palming Gabrielle's cheek. The love and trust in that gesture.

He thought too, of the undeniable familial similarity between them. The photos crammed all over her walls.

And then he looked more closely into the steely eyes and for the flash of a moment was transported back in time. It wasn't steel ringing at him but fire. The fierceness of Gabrielle's love for her son was the same fierce love for their children that had kept his parents together when it would have been better for them to go their separate ways.

He understood in that flash of a moment that Gabrielle really would do anything to protect Lucas and that that same fierce love would be used to protect the child developing inside her.

His child. Their child.

His heart twisted.

'Gabrielle, I give you my word that I will never make such a threat again. Lucas is your son, I can see that.' Holding her stare, he dropped his voice to a murmur. 'But you and I both know you didn't give birth to him.'

Gabrielle climbed into the back of the car feeling as wretched and sick as she'd ever felt, a sensation not helped by the scent of Andrés's cologne diving straight into her bloodstream and making her pulse surge before her bottom had even made contact with the leather seat.

It shouldn't be like this, she thought miserably. Not only

was Andrés far richer and far more powerful than The Bastard, but somehow he knew the truth about Lucas. He had the power to destroy her entire world. It shouldn't be possible that she could still feel so drawn to him and that she should be so acutely aware of the muscular tanned arms and the sleeve tattoo on display in the khaki polo shirt he was wearing. It was disconcerting to find him wearing smart tan shorts too. She'd assumed he only owned suits and tuxedos. Or was this all just her fevered mind going into overdrive after a night of tossing and turning?

He nodded a greeting to her. 'Did Lucas and your mother get away okay?'

She could hardly work her throat to answer. 'Yes.'

This was the second year in a row her mother had taken Lucas to France and waving goodbye had been just as bittersweet for Gabrielle as it had been last year. Bitter because being in the apartment without him felt like she'd had a limb removed. Sweet because the bond between grandma and grandson was so strong. They might not have much in the way of riches but one thing Lucas had been raised with was an abundance of love.

She cleared her throat. 'Where are we going?' Andrés's driver had headed off in the wrong direction to his apartment.

'Somewhere neutral.'

'Why neutral?'

'Because I suspect the conversation we're going to have will be difficult for us both.'

Her stomach dropped.

Breathing deeply, she gazed out of the window and ordered herself not to panic.

She could laugh. She'd told herself not to panic at least every ten seconds since Andrés had left her apartment. It frightened her how much she wanted to trust the sincerity she'd seen in his eyes when he'd sworn never to use Lucas as a threat again, but even if she could trust it, there was nothing to stop him carrying out his threat to report her to the authorities. She had everything she needed to back up her lies to them—and she would lie to the Queen of Monte Cleure herself if the alternative meant losing Lucas—but if they ordered a DNA test all the lies and documents supporting them would come to nothing.

How did Andrés know? That was another thing she couldn't get over. The secret had been kept tight for four years.

'We are here,' he said, breaking through her rabid thoughts.

Somewhere neutral turned out to be the harbour.

They walked in silence down the jetty to a gleaming yacht, one of the biggest docked there.

'Is this yours?' she asked, unable to imagine Andrés bothering to invest his money on a superyacht she doubted his workaholic lifestyle gave him the time to enjoy.

'Yes.'

'Then how can it be neutral?'

'Because I've not spent any time on it since the day I took delivery of it.'

'Seriously?'

He raised a broad shoulder. 'Sophia went on and on at me until I gave in and bought it. You can blame her for the interior decoration. All my family enjoy using it. The rest of the time it's chartered out. It was pure luck that it was docked in Barcelona.'

Climbing the steps that had been lowered for them, the professional crew greeted them with glasses of freshly squeezed orange juice.

The interior decoration was tastefully extravagant and Gabrielle easily imagined the rich colours and plush furnishings coming from Sophia's creative imagination. If her stomach wasn't so tight and cramped with nerves of what was going to come, her mouth would be open in stunned appreciation at yet more evidence of how the super wealthy lived.

This yacht that had to have cost around the hundred million mark, had essentially been bought as a gift for Andrés's family to enjoy.

By the time they'd settled on the sprawling sun deck with an array of breakfast food and fruit and drinks laid out for them, the captain had already set sail and the harbour was a speck in the distance behind them.

Nibbling on a chocolate brioche roll, Gabrielle tried to regulate her breathing, a feat not made easy with Andrés sitting across the table from her nursing a coffee. She hadn't thought to bring sunglasses with her and with his eyes hidden behind a pair of aviators that perfectly suited him, she felt strangely exposed. At least she'd changed from her faithful jeans into her only summer dress, a floaty, modest thigh length cream creation that dipped in a V to skim her cleavage and matched perfectly with her ballet shoes. It had been a last-minute panicking change made after Lucas and her mother had driven away that she couldn't explain any more than she could explain the application of mascara and lip gloss and the extra conditioner used to defrizz her hair.

Armour, she told herself. It was going to be hard enough getting through the day without feeling like a bag lady, especially when pitted against the dark masculine perfection that was Andrés.

How could someone grow more beautiful each time you set eyes on them?

'How did you know about Lucas?' she asked when she couldn't bear another second of the loaded silence. All her emotions had coiled so tightly that she could feel them trying to break free. She *had* to keep herself together.

Andrés put his coffee on the table and stretched his neck. It had been a long night, his overloaded brain making way for sleep in snatches, memories of their night together colliding with thoughts of the future he'd never wanted.

His life as he knew it was over.

Gabrielle was carrying his child.

He'd be tied to her for ever.

Amidst all the turmoil of his thoughts was the indisputable fact that she was passing off someone else's child as her own, and until he knew for certain that Lucas hadn't been snatched from his real mother, coming up with a game plan for their own child was out of the question.

The visit to Gabrielle's apartment had given him a good idea of who the child really belonged to but he needed it confirmed, needed to hear all the reasons why.

One look at her ashen face when she'd climbed into his car and the grim determination to drag all the answers from her that he'd set off with had melted away.

To see the wry, determined, intelligent, fun woman he'd spent the best night of his life with in such clear turmoil and distress did something to him. It was similar to how he used to feel when growing up at Sophia's distress, as if her distress was his distress. To have similar feelings...similar but far more acute...for Gabrielle had been disconcerting in the extreme. It had knocked him off his stride.

Up here on the sun deck, with the rising sun landing like jewels on Gabrielle's skin just as the setting sun had done the night of the party, his tastebuds tingled to remember the sweetness of that skin, his fingers tingled to remember its smooth, soft texture, his loins tingled to remember the sweet, hedonistic perfection of their night together, and the questions had melted even further away.

And now her quietly delivered question had pulled him back to the here and now.

'It was an educated guess but your reaction confirmed it,' he said tightly.

A line appeared in her forehead and she shook her head. 'But… How could you guess something like that?'

'There was a smear of blood on my sheets.'

Her eyes widened, colour saturating her face.

'I assumed at the time that it was menstrual blood and that you must have started your period.' As his hangover had worn off and the haziness of the night cleared, Andrés had been glad of that stain. They'd used protection but they'd been careless. Gabrielle starting her period had put any worries about their carelessness to bed.

He'd never been in the slightest bit careless before that night. Not ever.

That she'd conceived that night meant the chances of it being menstrual blood was reduced to practically zero, and as soon as that fact lodged in his brain, it brought fresh insight to everything else, including the lack of physical evidence that she'd carried or given birth to a child. That there was not a single photo of Gabrielle pregnant on her walls had only added weight to this.

'You were a virgin.'

Dark eyes swimming with unshed tears, pretty chin wobbling, her nod was barely perceptible.

His chest sharpened to remember the gasp she'd made when he'd entered her for the first time. That gasp hadn't been the shock of pleasure like he'd experienced but the shock of pain. If he'd known he'd have been gentle with her, so, so gentle.

'Is he your sister's?'

Her lips clamped together but the widening of her eyes let him know he'd hit the mark.

'He's obviously a Breton,' he said. 'There are many photos of Eloise displayed on your walls but none with him.' No photos of Eloise at all after Lucas's birth...

Blinking frantically, she got unsteadily to her feet and staggered to the railing, holding it tightly as she stared out over the endless sea.

Andrés stood beside her, waiting for her to speak, the sharpening of his chest a physical pain to witness the great gulps of air she was taking in.

He hated that this was so necessary.

Eventually, she said, 'Lucas *is* mine. I'm named as his mother on his birth certificate. He's been mine since he took his first breath.'

'Tell me what happened.'

Her voice caught. 'I can't.'

'I can't help if you don't tell me.'

'I don't need help.'

'Gabrielle, you only agreed to accompany me as my date that night because it was the perfect storm of timing for you.' Andrés spoke slowly, his words forming as they formulated in his mind. 'Lucas was with your mother and you'd been offered an invitation to the party of the century with a man you believed to be happily married, all arranged with his wife's urging. If you'd had the slightest idea of what would happen between us, you would have refused to be my date and no amount of bribery or coaxing would have caused you to change your mind. Am I wrong?'

Eyes now locked on his, she shook her head.

'If Lucas is legally yours then how is it that something—or someone—has frightened you into hiding away?'

'Not hiding,' she refuted. 'I have a job. Lucas goes to nursery and will be starting school in a few months. We do all the normal things that normal people do.'

'You were a twenty-three-year-old virgin,' he pointed out bluntly. 'That is not normal, not for a woman as sensual as you. Your life revolves entirely around Lucas. Everything you do is for him.'

'It's called being a mother.'

'It's called hiding from intimacy.'

Gabrielle looked back out over the calming sea and filled her lungs with the salty air. What was the point in fighting it any more?

Andrés already knew the bare bones of the truth. To entrust the rest of it to him…

She'd entrusted her virginity to him. She'd given the whole of herself to him that night and he'd given the whole of himself to her.

She'd told him about their baby expecting him to denounce her and refuse to accept paternity until he had cast iron proof but he believed her. He'd questioned *how* she could be pregnant but he hadn't questioned his paternity. He'd accepted her at her word.

He could have taken his suspicions about Lucas straight to the authorities. His power meant they would have taken his suspicions seriously. The truth and his power could easily find Gabrielle in the situation of losing both her children. He could gain sole custody of their child and never have to bother with the thing he wanted the least—being tied to a woman for the rest of his life.

Just as on some basic level he must trust her, so too, she realised, did she trust him because as all the thoughts of what he could do swirled in her mind, a certainty grew in her that he would never do them.

She took possibly the deepest breath of her life and said, 'Lucas's father is a nasty, evil, rich bastard, and if his name is ever made public, he will have him taken from me.'

CHAPTER ELEVEN

GABRIELLE EXHALED. She'd said it. She'd rubbed the lamp and let the Genie out. And as she made that exhale, she heard Andrés take a sharp intake of breath.

Fixing her gaze on the horizon, she said, 'You need to understand what Eloise was like to understand it all. You see, she was always different. Her brain never worked the same as other people's. Monte Cleure has terrible mental health provisions—it was worse when we were ruled by King Dominic and his father before him, but I honestly think all the provisions in the world wouldn't have helped. Her brain was just wired differently, like there was something missing in it, if that makes sense? She was the sweetest, most loving person you could meet but she just couldn't process her emotions—the slightest thing would upset her and send her into a spiral of screams and tears and self-harm. When our father died she had to be hospitalised until she wasn't a danger to herself any more.' She closed her eyes, remembering how her mother too had fallen apart at the seams at the agony of losing her soul mate.

'She was so beautiful,' she continued quietly. 'Men always looked twice at her but The Bastard was the first man *she* ever noticed, and she was so excited for her first date. I imagined a sweet teenager but instead this man in his thirties wearing typical rich man yachting clothes turned up.

It was obvious to me that he thought he was living danger-ously by inviting a girl from Monte Cleure's poor district on a date. Most people sensed Eloise's vulnerabilities but I didn't trust that he'd picked up on them so I made sure he knew she had certain issues and that he needed to treat her kindly. He treated her so kindly that when she fell pregnant, he dumped her on the spot and wanted nothing to do with her or the baby. He told her she was unfit to be a mother and demanded she abort it.'

She felt Andrés stiffen.

'I had to threaten him with the press to make him take responsibility, but he gave her a wedge of hush money and tricked her into signing a contract forbidding her from ever making contact with him again or naming him as the fa-ther with the penalty for breaking it being that he'd take custody of the baby he didn't even want and force her to repay the money.'

At this, Andrés hissed a particularly crude curse under his breath.

'Yes, he is,' Gabrielle agreed. 'That bastard's treatment of her and his rejection of their child broke her, and she spiralled. She stopped eating, never left the apartment, her health deteriorated… I deferred university to care for her because we didn't dare leave her alone, and then on one of her lucid days, she sat down with me and Maman and told us she loved her baby too much to put it at risk of being a mother to it and that she wanted me to have it. She wouldn't listen to reason or take no for an answer, and worked herself up into such a state…' She squeezed her eyes shut to drive out the image of her beautiful sister screaming and hitting herself. 'What else could I do but agree?'

'Couldn't your mother have…?'

'Eloise wanted it to be me. She was adamant. She knew I

wouldn't be allowed to adopt the baby because of my age—you have to be twenty-five to adopt in Monte Cleure, even if it's a family member and even with the consent of the mother—so it had to be made out that the baby was mine. She was insistent.'

'But why not your mother?'

'Because I was her protector and she trusted me more than anyone. Our mother took our father's death very badly and when Eloise fell apart over it too, it was me and Romeo who got her the help she needed because our mother couldn't even get out of bed.'

Andrés felt sick. Hadn't Gabrielle said her father died when she was ten? What a burden for a child of that age to endure. When he'd been that age and terrified of his parents' divorcing, he'd never had to fear losing one of them let alone both of them.

'So you agreed to pass the baby as yours.'

'I had to. No one outside the immediate family knew Eloise was pregnant. We told a few reliable gossips that I'd got pregnant after a fling with a tourist and they reliably spread the word. I started stuffing cushions under my clothes to mimic pregnancy… Honestly, I look back and wonder how I could have done it but it felt vitally necessary at the time, and my agreement calmed her. She stopped self-harming and started eating. Started showering again. When she was eight months gone, we did a moonlight flit to France so none of the neighbours saw that the wrong sister was pregnant, and rented a house close to a maternity hospital. When Eloise gave her details, she gave my name. We looked enough alike that my passport was accepted as identification.'

With fresh tears welling, Gabrielle took a moment to compose herself, only to jolt as warm fingers pressed lightly on her hand, an unspoken gesture of comfort that made her aching heart swell and gave her the strength to continue.

Turning her hand so their fingers threaded together, she took a deep breath and said, 'The birth went reasonably well. There were complications but she coped better than I could have hoped, and, Andrés, I swear to you she was happy, really happy, and completely smitten with him. She chose Lucas's name, changed his first nappy and when we returned to the house two days later to continue her recovery, she gave him to me. By then I was comfortable with the idea of being named as his mother but I fully expected we would all go home together and raise the baby between the three of us.'

'What happened?' The gentle squeeze of his fingers told her he'd already guessed what came next.

'She developed an infection.' Unthinkingly, Gabrielle rested her head against his arm, and dropped her voice. 'She didn't tell us that she was feeling unwell, just said that she was tired. She hid it so well and by the time we realised there was something wrong it was too late. We called for an ambulance and she was admitted to hospital but there was nothing they could do for her.'

The fingers threaded through hers tightened but he didn't speak.

'She slipped away from us.' A tear fell down her cheek. 'And the thing I remember most clearly is how peaceful she looked. Eloise suppressed her worst instincts for months to get Lucas safely into this world and then she let go.'

And with that, Gabrielle let go too, the tears she'd hardly been aware of holding back unleashing in a flood as the coil holding all her emotions tightly in place snapped.

Wiping her face frantically was futile, the blinding waterfall pouring down her cheeks an impossible force, but still she tried to stem the flow, right until strong arms wrapped around her and she found herself crying into Andrés's rock hard chest.

Oh, that wonderful familiar scent...

It only made her cry harder.

How could it be so familiar when all they'd spent was one night together? How could it be so *comforting*?

He held her tightly, mouth pressed into the top of her head, hands stroking her back, whispering words of comfort that she couldn't hear through the sound of her own blubbing but which acted like salve to her wounded heart.

Andrés had dealt with many feminine tears throughout the years but this was the first time each sob had landed like a blow to his own heart.

The burden of release, he guessed. Gabrielle had been carrying her secret and the pain of her sister's death for a very long time.

It took a long time for the tears to run dry and for Gabrielle to rub her cheek into his sodden chest and sigh. Making no effort to let go of him, her voice stronger, she said, 'Lucas was six months old when we ran into his father on the promenade. He was outside dining with a woman and saw us out walking. He came over, looking to all the world like he was admiring the sleeping baby in the pram, and he said with a great big smile on his face that he'd heard my "retard sister" had died.'

Andrés flinched.

'He used that cruel, nasty, *foul* language against a woman whose only crime had been to love him,' Gabrielle continued, angrily impassioned, 'and then he looked at Lucas, his own flesh and blood, and said that my son looked very peaceful and that it would be a real shame if someone opened their fat mouth and had him taken away.'

Knowing there was a real chance he was going to erupt with the fury her words had triggered in him, Andrés snatched at one part of her sentence to focus his attention on. 'When he said, "my son", who was he referring to? You or him?'

'Me. He must have been keeping tabs on us because he knew I was passing myself as Lucas's mother.'

He had to grit his teeth to ask the next question. 'Have you seen him since?'

'No, but since then I've kept tabs on *him*, and I get the feeling he's been avoiding Monte Cleure since Catalina came to the throne, probably because of all the changes she's making. He couldn't have been invited to her party as he was hosting a shooting weekend at his English estate that weekend. That's how I knew it was safe to go with you.'

'So he's English?'

'I never said that.'

'But he has an English estate that he holds shooting weekends at so will be easy to find.'

'Don't you *dare*,' she said, lifting her face from his chest to look up at him with horror.

'I can deal with this for you,' he said tightly, holding onto his temper by a thread, *only* holding onto it because even amidst the rage flowing through his veins he knew the person he wanted to direct all the rage at wasn't the beautiful woman imploring him with her eyes. 'Give me his name.'

'No.'

'The man is a bully. I have dealt with many bullies in my time.'

'No! You can't. Please, leave things be. I don't want any more of his money and I will not risk Lucas for anything. It would kill me to lose him, so please, please promise you won't do or say anything or have any contact with that man, *please*.'

So many emotions were contained in those beautiful dark brown eyes another blow smashed into his already bruised chest and the fury ebbed to a simmer.

How big a heart could one woman have? Gabrielle could be filled with bitterness for the cards life had dealt her, could resent the child she'd been emotionally blackmailed into raising as her own at the expense of the future she'd planned for herself, but instead, and without an ounce of self-pity, she'd taken her nephew into her heart and loved and protected him as fiercely as if she'd carried him himself.

He'd thought he'd known the night of the party that Gabrielle was a one-off but he'd had no idea of the extent of it.

She was incredible.

Palming her cheek, he brought his face down to hers, close enough to catch the faint trace of her scent... *Dios*, that scent intoxicated him. It was the scent that had underlined the perfume she'd worn that night, the sweet, unique scent of Gabrielle.

Staring intently into her eyes, he said, 'It took a lot for you to put your trust in me and share what you did, and I will do nothing to abuse it.'

Her chest and shoulders rose and then she dealt another blow to his heart by attempting to smile. 'What I told you about my mother...please don't think she was a bad mother,' she whispered, her eyes once again pleading. 'She wasn't. It's just that my father's death came as a huge shock to her. They were devoted to each other.'

'And a shock to you too, I would imagine,' he pointed out softly.

'Of course it did but I had Romeo to lean on and he had me.'

You were ten, he resisted from saying.

Gabrielle was an emotionally intelligent woman. If she'd

forgiven her mother for falling apart when she needed her most then who was he to criticise?

'You'll see when you meet her,' she said. 'She's a very sweet and loving woman, and she's a brilliant grandmother to Lucas, and she'll be a brilliant grandmother to our baby too.'

Our baby.

Two words to make his guts clench…but not as tightly as they'd done a day ago. Not when his gaze was locked on the dark chocolate swirls of Gabrielle's heavenly eyes and those pillowy lips, so ripe for kissing, were moving ever closer to his…

Or was it his lips moving closer to hers?

Dios, how was it possible to ache so badly for someone? Was it because she was carrying his child that he felt so many damned feelings for this woman? That she touched him in a way no one had ever done before?

But the ache for her had started long ago…

Gabrielle felt purged. For the first time since bringing Lucas home, she'd shared the sacrifice her beautiful sister had made for the love of her child, and sharing it had been cathartic. Necessity meant Eloise's love for her son had to be hidden from the world, a secret kept between the three surviving Bretons and the man who didn't want him, a secret kept tightly, the circumstances of his birth never discussed even amongst themselves. And she'd shared too, the one secret she'd kept entirely to herself, deciding it was better her family didn't know because of the hurt it would cause them—the threat The Bastard had made to her. She'd shared it with the man who'd fathered her own child, a man she knew would never reject the life growing inside her, and as she gazed at Andrés, her senses opened up to him like the petals of a flower opening to the sun and she found herself falling into the eyes that had hypnotised her from the very first look.

Their faces were so close she could see the individual bristles of his thick beard, fill her lungs with the divine scent she'd gone to bed every night since their night together playing like a phantom into her airwaves. The sensitive tips of her breasts were barely a whisper away from touching the hard chest she'd been crushed against for comfort only minutes before, and now she could feel them stir in a tingle of anticipation and need, desire awakening and trickling with a steady relentlessness through her veins.

Their lips brushed in the lightest of caresses. The fingers pressed against her cheek tightened.

Her senses filling with the heat of Andrés's breath, she closed her eyes...

The unexpected loud ring of a phone cut through the air.

Eyes flew open and locked back together.

The phone continued to ring.

An instant later, they pulled apart, Gabrielle's heart hammering so loudly it was a drum in her ears.

It frightened her how much she wanted him. Terrified her how comforting it had been to just...*submit* herself and let him give her the comfort she hadn't even known she needed until he'd held her so tightly.

And it frightened her to see the hunger in his eyes. Frightened her because it fed her own.

Andrés took a visible deep breath before pulling the phone from his back pocket. When he saw who the caller was, he came back to life with a curse.

Eyes on Gabrielle, he put it to his ear. 'I told you not to disturb me unless it was life or death.'

His face darkened as he listened to the caller but then something changed, his eyes narrowing. 'Hold on,' he said curtly before covering the mouthpiece and asking Gabrielle, 'When is your mother bringing Lucas back?'

'Tuesday.'

He nodded and spoke again to the caller. 'Coordinate with the captain and get the helicopter to me.'

Disconnecting the call, he rubbed the back of his neck and breathed deeply through his nose before meeting her stare. 'We're going to Japan.'

Thrown by the *we*, she stared at him without comprehension.

'The deal I told you about is hanging by a thread,' he explained tersely. 'I need to be there but I also need to be here with you. I cannot magic myself into two places so you will have to come with me.'

It took a good few moments to realise he was serious. 'I can't. I'm working tomorrow, and—'

'Gabrielle, you are having my child. You will never have to work again.'

Her mouth fell open.

'We need to talk seriously about our future and how we're going to play things, but whatever it holds for you and me, you are the mother of my child and that means your life changes as of now.'

She shook her head in disbelief. 'I'm only weeks pregnant. *Anything* could happen.'

'Yes,' he agreed. 'Anything could happen but that doesn't mean it will, and I will not have you spending the pregnancy living in a cramped apartment when I can provide you with the home of your dreams and everything you need. We have a lot to discuss, *ma belle*, and with Lucas safe with your mother, now is the perfect opportunity to discuss them.'

'I can't just fly to the other side of the world on a whim!'

'Why not?' he challenged.

'Because…' She closed her eyes and took a deep breath. 'You're asking me to trust that when I lose my job—and I guarantee that flying to Japan with you instead of turning up to work will be considered gross misconduct—that you'll… Andrés, it's hard enough making ends meet as it is. I can't afford to miss my mortgage payments.'

Warm hands captured her cheeks.

Opening her eyes she found herself trapped again in Andrés's black stare. 'You trusted me with the truth about Lucas,' he said, his voice containing the same intensity as his eyes. 'Trust that I am not Lucas's father and that when I give my word, I never go back on it. Come to Japan with me, *ma belle*. I swear you will not suffer for it. You will never suffer any form of deprivation again.'

Gabrielle had never flown before, not by helicopter or plane, so to use both modes of transport within an hour of each other blew her mind. It blew it almost as much as agreeing to go to Japan with him.

Within two hours of Andrés receiving the call, they'd been helicoptered off his yacht, flown to his apartment, driven to her apartment to get her passport and an overnight bag she rammed the first items of clothing to hand in, driven back to his apartment, then helicoptered to an airport in Barcelona where they bypassed what she assumed would be the usual security checks at an airport to be ushered onto a plane so luxurious she actually wondered if she'd fallen into a dream. Only the butterflies in her stomach, fluttering their wings in time to the beats of her heart, convinced her this was real.

That and Andrés's cologne.

While she'd been chauffeured to her apartment, he'd showered and changed into a business suit. She'd been stuck in confined spaces with him smelling good enough to eat ever since, and now she was destined to spend twelve hours with him confined in a space with no escape.

It should not be a thought that sent thrills racing through her veins, just as her lips shouldn't still tingle from that brief caress and just as her stare shouldn't be locked on his face watching every second of the call he'd been on since they arrived at the airfield and which hadn't let up even when he sank onto the plush leather seat opposite hers. The concentration lines on his forehead and the polite curtness of his tone reminded her of how big a deal this deal was to him. One of the biggest deals of his life...

He should have flown to Japan yesterday to deal with it. Instead he'd come to her.

He could have taken his suspicions about Lucas to the authorities. Instead he'd come to her.

Instead of concentrating fully on his important call, his stare kept locking onto hers.

As the plane taxied down the runway, her heart swelled with an emotion so powerful that for a moment she couldn't breathe, and she closed her eyes, trying desperately to swallow it all away.

Andrés watched Gabrielle close her eyes and struggle for breath, and abruptly ended the call with his finance director.

How could he concentrate on business when the most beautiful woman in the world was directly in his line of sight and the thrills from the connection of their lips were still as vivid as if it had happened only moments ago?

Dios, he could still taste her breath. He breathed it in with every inhalation.

Her chest rose, breasts straining beneath the fabric of her dress and, even as awareness strained his every sinew, he had the sense to remember this was her first time on a plane.

Switching seats to the one beside her, he took hold of her hand and held it tightly.

Her eyes flew back open.

Leaning into her, he said, 'You have *nothing* to be frightened of. Pilots are some of the most highly trained professionals out there. You are safer on a plane than you are on the roads.'

Something flickered on her face, something that set a jolt of pure emotion into his heart.

He'd had no idea hearts could bruise so easily. The story about her sister had been close to unbearable to hear but the bruises had all come from the blows of Gabrielle's tears. Now, each beat, he felt it, like he'd never done before. Just to look at her bruised him in ways he could never explain.

Just to look at her was to want her.

Gabrielle had become so lost in the black depths of Andrés's eyes that she didn't even notice they'd taken off until her stomach dipped from the plane, much like the dips to her stomach he induced.

His phone had saved them before. Saved her.

There was nothing to save her now from the lips she'd dreamed about every night since their one night together closing in on her.

As hard as she'd tried these last weeks to lock Andrés and the joy they'd discovered in each other's arms into her memory box, it had been impossible and after the whirlwind of the last twenty-four hours, she felt like she was walking on quicksand, the body that had clung to the joy fighting with the brain that knew all the feelings sweeping and clinging to that body were dangerous...

But when their lips met, the quicksand deepened and she was helpless to do anything but sink into it.

CHAPTER TWELVE

ANDRÉS LED GABRIELLE into the plane's bedroom, far beyond caring what was happening in Japan or anywhere. He was beyond thinking.

From the burning daze in her eyes, she was gripped by the same fever.

As soon as the door closed behind them, their mouths and limbs fused back together in one ravenous moan. Hungry lips parted, tongues plunging and exploring, and in no time at all Gabrielle's legs were wrapped around his waist and he was carrying her to the bed.

Dios, he'd dreamed of this for so long.

All those nights, Gabrielle and the night they'd shared together haunting him.

Clothes were stripped and flung without care.

Both fully naked, Gabrielle on her back, chest rising and falling rapidly, cheeks flushed…he soaked in every inch, taking in the changes pregnancy had already made, changes that would be imperceptible to anyone else.

Desire as strong as he'd ever felt gripped him at the same time his chest tightened to a sharp point. That was his baby developing in her softly rounded stomach. The swelling of her breasts was the pregnancy preparing her body for the gift of life.

She'd never looked more beautiful.

Climbing between her legs, he pushed her thighs back and kissed her with a savagery she matched with her own.

She writhed against him, nails scraping over his back as she groped for his buttocks, her breaths hot and ragged, urging his possession.

His arousal guiding itself to the heat of her femininity, he drove into her.

Dios, he came *this* close to losing it with that first thrust.

He'd thought he'd remembered the intensity of the brief pleasure of being inside Gabrielle completely bare but this was something else.

Gabrielle had lost herself to the quicksand. Every cell and nerve ending burned at the feel of Andrés's huge body covering her and possessing her.

If this was madness then she gave herself to it willingly, throwing off the shackles of her fears for the hedonistic connection that felt as necessary as breathing.

Gabrielle's moans of pleasure fell like nectar into Andrés's ears and fed the fever gripping him. This went beyond *everything* and he was having to fight to hold on, fighting and fighting until her moans shallowed and he felt the thickening around him. Thrusting himself so deep inside her he didn't know where he ended and she began, he shouted out her name and climaxed with enough force to shatter himself into atoms.

Tokyo was the most fascinating place Gabrielle could have dreamed of, and considering she was completely thrown by being in a completely different time zone, everything happening to her felt much like a waking dream. It had done since she'd fallen back under Andrés's spell on his plane.

They'd spent the whole flight in that bed. All talk about their future, the very reason for her accompanying him, had been forgotten as they'd made love, dozed, made love and dozed until time had run out.

Andrés had been locked in perpetual meetings to thrash out the deal's stumbling blocks ever since.

While he'd tried to salvage the deal that meant so much to him, Gabrielle toured Tokyo's streets with the French-speaking guide he'd arranged to keep her company and act as translator, with the thrums of their lovemaking beating strongly inside her.

She couldn't get over how clean the city was. She'd thought Monte Cleure was clean but here it was so spotless it all looked brand new. In complete contrast to the seem-ingly chaotic roads they'd travelled to their hotel on, the pedestrian areas were sprawling and orderly, the high-rises dominating the skyline making her feel buffeted and safe.

Everything about Tokyo seemed busy, busy, busy but she never felt that she had to rush. An air of politeness pervaded the city and she wished she had more time to spend here and explore. If Andrés pulled the deal off then he would become a frequent visitor to the city.

Who would he bring with him the next time he came?

It was a thought she quickly pushed aside. They were hav-ing a baby together; their lives would always be entwined, but she wasn't foolish enough to expect anything more, not with the memory of her sister's desolation at The Bastard's cruel treatment so fresh in her mind.

Eloise's pure heart had fallen madly in love and it had been smashed into pieces.

Andrés would never treat Gabrielle the way Eloise had been treated but that didn't mean she shouldn't tread care-fully with him. Treading on quicksand with lust when that lust would come to a natural end was one thing. Planning a future where their lives were entwined around their child was another thing.

Imagining a future, a real future, with a man who didn't do future was for fools.

After two backbreaking days, the deal was ninety per cent assured.

Confident his team could take it from there, Andrés took Gabrielle to one of Tokyo's hidden gems, a Kaiseki restaurant set in a quiet residential area.

Their table overlooked a tranquil secret garden, an abundance of sweet-scented flowers in full bloom. Gabrielle outshone its beauty.

Ravishing in a pretty black kimono-style dress with red lilies embroidered onto it that she'd bought earlier, one look had been enough to steal his breath, just as she'd stolen it that first night.

Just as she did every time he looked at her.

'What time do we have to leave?' she asked, attempting to grip a matsutake mushroom with her chopsticks. Andrés had offered to ask for cutlery but, determined to master it, she'd refused.

To his deep regret, this was the first meal other than breakfast they'd been able to share together. Negotiations over the deal had been more fraught than even he'd anticipated, the cultural differences as difficult to navigate as the main business issues. He'd returned to the hotel both nights mentally drained but still intending to discuss the issues he'd insisted Gabrielle accompany him here to discuss, only to take one look at her and find all thoughts escaping his mind.

'Early in the morning. With the time difference and the flight times, we'll be back in Monte Cleure with time for you to rest before your mother brings Lucas home.'

She shook her head. 'How do you cope with it all? I've only just got over the flight over and adjusted to being in a different time zone, and now we have to go back. You do this kind of travelling constantly. Doesn't it exhaust you?'

'I can sleep anywhere and never suffered from jet lag so it's never been an issue for me,' he dismissed with a shrug. 'But I'm going to make changes to my schedule now that we're having a baby. All this travelling across continents isn't right with a child. Children need stability.'

Her thoughtful gaze settled on him. 'If our baby's raised with a father who spends a great deal of time travelling then that will be his or her normal. That will be stable.'

'Not in the way I want and it is for this reason that I think we should live together.'

Andrés didn't know who was more disarmed at his choice of words, himself who hadn't meant for it to come out like that, or Gabrielle who almost choked on a bonito flake.

Luckily a drink of water was enough for her to catch her breath, and he explained his thinking before his mis-choice of words could root. 'I grew up with parents who hated the sight of each other but being together as a family was important to me. Like you, I only want what's best for our child, and I want them to grow up knowing that if they wake in the night with a terror, that their mother and father are both there for them, and I think the best way of doing that is if I buy a property to use as our main home where we can each have our own wing and lead our own lives but still be under the same roof.'

He watched her intelligent eyes process this.

'You can choose where we live. It can be Monte Cleure if you wish. Wherever you choose, this arrangement will allow us both to keep our independence and once this...' He had to swallow a sudden lump in his throat. '...thing between us fades away, we will be in a position to parent as friends, if not lovers.' His eyes glittered as he added, 'I will be honest with you, Gabrielle, *ma belle*, I am in no hurry for that to happen. What we have between us is pretty damn incredible.'

Gabrielle's heart was beating fast, and she drank some more of her iced water in an attempt to calm herself.

This *thing*.

What a horrible way to describe something so beautiful.

But that was Andrés, she accepted painfully. He did not do emotional commitment to anyone that was not blood.

It was nothing she didn't already know. More importantly, it was nothing she didn't want for herself. When their sexual relationship ended, her heart would be perfectly intact.

For all her internal reasoning, it took effort to make her voice temperate. 'I had both my parents for the first ten years of my life and I will be for ever grateful for that, but if they'd never lived together, that would have been my normal and I wouldn't have known any different.'

'I want to be there, Gabrielle. Why do you think I've been so intent *not* to have children? It's because I've always known how I would feel. The thought of my child growing up under a different roof to me and living with a man who is not me is intolerable.'

'I can put your mind at rest on the second part. I have no intention of living with anyone.'

His black eyes glimmered. 'I'm not *anyone*. I'm the father of your child.'

'And you're not proposing that I live with you in that way, but I don't imagine many other people will understand it. What do you think will happen if Lucas's father learns about us?'

'I can protect you both from that man.'

'Maybe you can, I don't know, but either way, this…' She scrambled to put her thoughts into order. 'It's a good, logical idea.' She had to admit that. In many ways it was the perfect solution for two people who shied away from real relationships. 'But I have Lucas to think of, and not just because of his father. He's used to it being just the two of us. He needs to get to know you, and you need to get to know him, and until I know he's comfortable with you I can't even entertain the idea of us sharing a house.'

'I will get to know him and work on building his trust.'

'That's great but there has to be boundaries. He can't know that you and I are lovers, and if all goes well with the two of you and we get that house you talked about, you can't bring women to it. That part of your life will have to be separate. I will not have him confused or upset for anything. He's been through too much as it is.'

He raised his wine glass. 'I can accept those terms.'

Gabrielle clinked her grape Ramune to it, managing a tight smile, proud that she'd been able to give her conditions without her voice cracking.

This really was the perfect solution. Other than Lucas's emotional security, there was not one good reason to dislike it, not when it gave them both everything they needed and, more importantly, provided the children with the stability that all children deserved, and she couldn't understand why her stomach was twisting so tightly.

Andrés thanked the waitress who'd appeared to clear their table in preparation for the next course, and drank the last of his wine.

Gabrielle had agreed—in a roundabout way—to his eminently sensible proposal. Her only reservations were also eminently sensible. He should be delighted, thrilled that he'd judged correctly that the headiness of the chemistry they currently shared wouldn't cloud her thinking and compel her to ask for more than he wanted to give.

He should be feeling euphoric that they'd organised everything so neatly, not feeling flattened.

Gabrielle had assumed Andrés's Spanish home would be palatial. She'd severely underestimated. There, in the heart of the city, set back off a wide road with wide pavements lined with orange trees, a beautiful three storey townhouse that dominated the entire area.

If she was overawed, she thought Lucas's eyes were at risk of popping out.

Where the architecture of the house had a gothic feel, the interior was sleek and modern with distinctive Spanish touches. Three living rooms. *Three.* Two dining rooms. *Two dining rooms!* A study that also doubled as a library. A games room. A cinema room. All except the latter with high, frescoed ceilings and late afternoon light pouring in at all angles. Each bedroom had its own adjoining bathroom.

Then there was the grounds, a perfect oasis of beauty surrounded by a perimeter of huge trees that gave the illusion of being in the middle of nowhere.

They toured it all, Lucas clutching her hand, even more intimidated than he'd been when they'd spent the day in Andrés's apartment last weekend.

For a month they'd been working on getting Lucas comfortable with Andrés. This hadn't been helped by the amount of travelling Andrés had done, their time together coming in fits and spurts. His intention was that by the time the baby came, he'd have moved his head offices to wherever she decided they would set up home together and be under the same roof as her at least eighty per cent of the time. One place he'd asked her to consider was Seville, the city he called home, and so she'd agreed to bring Lucas for a weekend there. Andrés had cleared his entire diary for them, and invited his family over, including his godsons in the hope that seeing other children comfortable with him would help Lucas learn he wasn't a bogeyman.

But it wasn't just the travelling that had stopped Andrés and Lucas from bonding. The simple truth was Lucas distrusted him, and no amount of toys as bribes or rides in a helicopter could get him to view Andrés with anything less than suspicion. As a result, Gabrielle had refused Andrés's offer of renting a home for them until she deemed the time right for him to buy them the house he'd spoken of. His presence in their life had unsettled her little boy enough without ripping him from the cosy apartment that had been their home his entire life, the deposit for it paid with the last of The Bastard's hush money.

Her brother, spectacularly useless at emotional stuff but excellent with practical stuff, had insisted on paying the small mortgage until she'd been in a position to go out to work; his way of playing his part, and she intended to offer it to him when she moved out.

She still couldn't get over having the luxury of being able to let it out rent free. Without her knowledge, Andrés had paid the mortgage off. For the first time in her life, Gabrielle had money to burn, all thanks to Andrés and the money he'd deposited into her account, also without her knowledge. She'd begged her colleagues' forgiveness for skipping to Japan and parted on good terms with them, her mother had accepted the situation with a stoic grace, and for the first time in almost five years, the future she'd once wanted for herself looked possible. More than once, Andrés had mentioned her doing the degree she'd always wanted.

Really, she should be buzzing that her future was brighter

than she'd ever imagined it could be, but for a reason she couldn't discern, a kernel of fear still beat in her chest.

She would wait until the baby had been born before making any decisions about her personal future. As it was, there was too much in her head to think beyond the next day. Everything in her head was wrapped around Andrés and it frightened her how completely he occupied her mind. It frightened her even more how much she missed him when he was away.

Those nights in Japan had spoilt her because she'd never known nights could be lonely.

She'd have to get used to lonely nights permanently once he'd bored of her, a thought she steadfastly refused to allow to set in, and as the sun went down on her first night in Seville and her exhausted child fell asleep in his ice-cream, her pulse quickened to think that after five days of no physical contact, they could be together.

'Let me carry him up,' Andrés said, carefully lifting Lucas from his seat.

He opened his eyes, and immediately looked over Andrés's shoulder for her, but instead of reaching for her when his eyes found her, rested his head back on Andrés and relaxed.

Only once Andrés had laid him on the king-size bed of the room he'd been appointed for the weekend, did their eyes meet in silent wonder at this huge leap in progress.

'I'm going to take a shower and get to bed myself,' Andrés said, throwing her completely.

'Oh. Okay,' she said, simply because she couldn't think of anything else to say.

A faint smile played on his lips. 'Goodnight, Lucas. Sweet dreams.'

He slipped out of the room leaving Gabrielle bewildered and disconcerted that he didn't wish her a goodnight too.

The staff having already unpacked their possessions for them, it was for once an easy matter to get her usually wriggling child into his pyjamas. Lucas was simply too exhausted from the lateness of the hour, the travelling and excitement of the day to be anything other than compliant, no energy to even wriggle at the sight of the toothbrush aiming for his mouth.

He was asleep before she'd read two pages to him.

Kissing his forehead, she whispered, 'I love you,' before creeping out of his room and into her own adjoining one.

Oh, well, she thought moodily as she closed the door, if Andrés was going to bed then she might as well too. And at least her room was fit for a princess and had a television because she didn't feel in the least bit sleepy.

And at least she had her own beautiful bathroom, and when she stood under the powerful shower head she tried not to let the panic nibbling at her heart take root, only to find that actively trying not to let the panic take root had the opposite effect.

Was he boring of her *already*? Was that really possible when he called her every night? When he pulled her into his arms the second they were alone, which admittedly wasn't enough for either of their liking.

The emotions rising in her chest threatening to erupt, she wrestled her pyjama shorts and vest top on, and brushed her teeth harder than she'd ever done before stomping back into the bedroom...

Andrés was in her bed.

Her mouth fell open. 'What are you doing?'

He threw the bedsheets off him. He was naked, and fully erect. 'Thinking about you.'

'But...' She could hardly think let alone speak under the weight of her relief. 'I thought you were going to bed.'

His eyes gleamed wickedly. 'I didn't say whose bed I was going to.' He gripped his arousal. 'Going to join me?'

Unconsciously, she cupped her breast, even as she shook her head. 'I...' She swallowed the moisture that had flooded her mouth. 'I can't.'

He nodded at the tablet on the bedside table. 'Turn that on.'

'What?'

'It's a monitor. If he wakes, it will alert you.'

She pressed the biggest of the buttons. Immediately the screen filled with an image of Lucas sleeping.

'Touch the screen.'

She did so. The screen went blank.

'Now it is set to sound activation.' His voice thickened and his movements over his excitement strengthened. 'Take your clothes off.'

Now fully locked in the sexual haze Andrés was exuding, Gabrielle pulled her vest top up and over her head.

He groaned.

A surge of heady power rushed through her at the effect she was having on him, and she stepped back. Cupping a breast and rubbing a thumb over the erect nipple, she dipped her other hand beneath the band of her pyjama shorts and touched the core of her own arousal.

'Let me see,' he begged.

Now it was her turn to smile wickedly. Squeezing her breast, she continued to pleasure herself, all the while relishing and feeding off the effect it was having on him.

'Do you do that to yourself at night when you're alone?' he whispered.

She answered with a lascivious smile and pulled her shorts down.

'I do,' he said hoarsely, eyes glazed, his hand now a blur, the tip of his excitement glistening. 'Every night when I get into my lonely bed, I close my eyes and think of you naked. I imagine touching you and being inside you…it is all I think about.'

He crooked a finger at her.

The burn of desire now so strong she could hardly walk, her legs obeyed his wordless command.

In seconds he had her flat on her back.

Seconds later he was inside her and the burn blazed into a flame that scorched them both.

Early dawn light was filtering through the curtains when, with a strangled moan, Andrés climaxed.

For the longest time they did nothing but lie there, holding each other tightly, hearts beating in rhythm as they caught their breath.

How was it possible for his desire for Gabrielle to keep strengthening the way it did?

He'd never felt such reluctance to leave a bed before.

He gave Gabrielle one last kiss and pulled the sheets off him.

He was already counting the hours down until they would be together again.

Gabrielle watched Andrés slip silently out of the bedroom and closed her eyes in an effort to control the emotions swelling in her chest.

The bed already felt empty without him.

She already felt empty without him.

CHAPTER THIRTEEN

ANDRÉS FELT A tug on his shorts and looked down to find Lucas gazing up at him.

'Andrés, can I go in the pool with Raul?'

'Have you asked your mummy?'

He shook his head.

'Then we should go and ask her.'

Lucas slipped his hand into Andrés's.

Trying hard not to show his shock at this unsolicited trusting gesture, he put his beer on the table and walked across the lawn to where Gabrielle and Sophia were sprawled out on two of the many sun loungers spread around the pool, deep in conversation.

Gabrielle wasn't quick enough to hide her surprise at seeing Lucas's hand in Andrés's.

Was that good surprise or bad surprise? He couldn't judge. There was something about Gabrielle's mood that day that struck him as off. Not that *she* was being off. No, it wasn't that, more a melancholy? No, not that either. He couldn't think what the little glimpses into the distance as if she were lost in thought and then the blink back to the present and the usual smile lifting on her face he kept catching meant.

'Lucas wants to go for a swim,' he told her.

She looked at her son. 'Okay, but put your T-shirt back on.'

'But…'

'No arguing. You'll burn your shoulders. Where did you put your armbands?'

He ran off to get them.

Gabrielle's gaze turned to Andrés. 'Looks like you're starting to win him over,' she murmured.

He raised his eyebrows and crossed his fingers.

She grinned but before she could say anything further, Lucas came charging back with the armbands, closely followed by Andrés's godson Raul who had a unicorn rubber ring around his waist. The two boys being a similar age had hit it off in the way only small children could, becoming instant best friends.

Lucas gave the armbands to Andrés to put on for him. 'Will you come in too?' he asked shyly.

He couldn't have been more moved if the boy had embraced him.

Swallowing, he tapped the boy's snub little nose. 'Sure. But no splashing me.'

Minutes later shrieks of laughter filled the pool area as the two small boys mercilessly splashed water over Andrés, who splashed them back with equal ruthlessness. Gabrielle watched it all with a huge smile on her face and a huge fist in her heart.

Bringing him to Seville and the relaxed atmosphere of it all was having the effect they'd both hoped for and now, finally, she could see the Andrés effect working its magic on her son.

Which meant that soon he would broach the subject of them all moving in together as one big family in two separate wings.

'Something on your mind?'

Sophia's voice broke through her thoughts.

Bringing her smile back, glad she'd put her sunglasses on, she said, 'Just thinking how great it is to see Lucas having fun.'

'Andrés has always been good with children.'

This was the first time Sophia had mentioned her brother since they'd sat down together twenty minutes ago. Instead, their chat had been Gabrielle filling her in on the party, a valiant attempt made to remember the names of the people they'd been sat at the table with, and not making it sound as if she'd been so wrapped up in Sophia's brother that she'd forgotten to beg an introduction to the Queen she idolised and completely failed to soak in the full magic of the evening.

She'd been wrapped in an entirely different magic. She was still wrapped in it, had enveloped herself so tightly in it that, despite her efforts to kid herself that Andrés's magic only reached her loins, the desolation she'd felt when he'd left her bed that morning proved she was becoming vulnerable.

One day he would leave her bed for good. She had to be prepared for that, especially now that Lucas was taking him into his heart.

'You know, I hoped this would happen.'

Broken out of yet another reverie, Gabrielle again forced her attention to Sophia. 'Hoped what?'

'That you and Andrés would get together.'

'It isn't like… Hold on, did you say you *hoped* we would get together?'

Sophia smiled. 'My brother has been a selfish asshole for too long. Do you know this is the first time he's had the whole family over since he bought this place? He needs a woman like you, someone straight talking and who will call him out when he needs it, not those insipid women who cling to his every word and bore him in seconds. It's easy to say you're never going to marry or settle down when you only involve yourself with women you can picture yourself breaking up with.'

Stunned, her heart beating fast—too fast—something finally became clear. 'You faked your sickness.'

'I did,' Sophia admitted without an ounce of shame. 'You were just so unimpressed with him, it was hilarious, *and* you amused him, I saw it, and I saw the look you gave each other. I'm a big believer in trusting my gut—remind me to tell you how I met my husband—and my gut was telling me loud and clear that you had the potential to be perfect for him. You can say thank you to my gut when his ring's on your finger.'

Before Gabrielle could tell Sophia that was never going to happen, the Spanish woman's voice dropped. 'Uh oh, our parents have arrived. Andrés has told you about them?'

'Only that they have a toxic marriage.'

'He thinks it's toxic. I've come to think it's funny. It's like getting a ringside seat to the Punch and Judy show for free, but without the violence. Come on, I'll introduce you to them.'

The party Andrés had organised intending it to be a lunchtime affair spread into the evening. His staff were as excellent and efficient as always, bringing out an endless supply of food and ensuring the garden bar was always fully stocked. After an especially vigorous game of football in which Andrés, Lucas, Raul and Gabrielle made a team against his father, Mateo his other godson, Mateo's father and Sophia's husband, and thrashed them eight nil—Gabrielle made a surprisingly effective goalkeeper—the happy, exhausted children were sent to bed in Lucas's room and the champagne was opened.

Music piped through the garden speakers, they pulled chairs into an informal circle and everything was great, the most fun he'd had with his family since he could remember, and then his parents, who'd kept their sniping at each other down to pointed barbs and muttered insults, spoiled the relaxed atmosphere by having a stand-up blazing row that ended with his mother storming inside and his father rolling his eyes at anyone who would look at him.

A hand covered his. 'Are you okay?'

He locked onto Gabrielle's eyes and felt much of the poison witnessing that charade had induced drain away. 'I'm good.'

Her lips curved in sympathy. 'That was quite the performance.'

'That is one way to describe it.'

'It's strange how Sophia finds their behaviour funny but you find it toxic.'

'She finds it funny now but she hated it as much as I did when we were kids.'

'Maybe her own marriage gave her a change of perspective.'

He grunted.

'Have to admit, I'm leaning to the Sophia side.'

A black eyebrow shot up. Gabrielle shrugged. Having observed his parents together that day, she understood where Andrés was coming from but as an outsider, she didn't think it was all bad. 'The impression I get is that they seem very close. Maybe arguing is their language with each other. Everyone else just seems to roll with it.' She shrugged again. 'I don't know, I've only just met them, and as we're speaking of your family, you never told me Sophia faked her illness for the party.' She strove to keep her voice casual as she said this.

The more she'd thought about it, the more Gabrielle thought she should have guessed, but then how could she have? Who faked illness to shoehorn a stranger to take your place at a royal party? To Gabrielle, Sophia had been just another rich woman used to the world revolving around her, albeit an unusually nice one.

Now she thought she understood Sophia's thinking. Sophia was happily married. Her brother had had a succession of affairs with the same breed of women, none of whom made him happy because he'd chosen those women deliberately. She'd spotted her chance to foist someone different on him, someone who, in her words, had the *potential to be perfect for him*, and had taken it.

It was those words… Every time she thought of them, the weight in her stomach grew.

There was a flash of surprise and then comprehension and a low chuckle. 'She gave you a straight answer on that?'

'Yes.'

'That's more than I got when I confronted her. By the time we left for the palace I knew but she refused to admit it outright. My sister is a law unto herself.' His black eyes gleamed. 'You know she will take credit for the baby when we tell them?' Which would have to be soon as it wouldn't be long before Gabrielle was visibly showing. They'd agreed to wait until after the weekend before sharing the news with his family.

From the corner of his eyes, Andrés spotted his mother come back outside. Usually this would not be something he thought twice about but with Gabrielle's observations about his parents still fresh, he turned to watch her. It was only because he was actively watching that he noticed her trail her fingers over the back of his father's neck as she retook her seat next to him. If he hadn't been observing them so closely, he would have missed his father reach back to squeeze her hand.

The hairs on Andrés's arm lifted.

He closed his eyes. When he reopened them, he noticed his mother had already started an animated conversation with one of his cousins but that her right foot was pressed against his father's left foot.

'Andrés?'

His heart began to pound.

'Andrés?'

Slowly turning his head, he met Gabrielle's concerned stare and suddenly found it impossible to look away. The thoughts churning in his head were as impossible to comprehend as the emotions smashing into his chest.

Andrés had always kept his head down when his parents argued, normally escaping to another room until the storm fully passed, not wanting to be forced to see their hatred for each other as well as hear it. It felt like he'd done that for his entire life.

How many other small intimacies had he missed over the years? And as he wondered this, the realisation came that although he'd lived with them, he hadn't lived their marriage. He'd never worked the hours the two of them had during his childhood and still not earned enough to meet the bills.

Was it any wonder they'd taken the stress and exhaustion out on each other?

The stress from their lives had gone and now they liked to bicker and argue for fun or out of habit, but whatever their reason...

So what?

In his loathing of the toxic nature of their marriage, he'd

missed the love that underpinned it and was their marriage's foundation.

Sophia had been raised in the same household. She hadn't replicated their marriage. Sophia was happy.

Gazing into the eyes of the bravest, fiercest, sexiest woman in the world, eyes containing an ocean of emotions directed at *him*, his own future suddenly became clear.

'When will we see Andrés again?' Lucas asked as she went to switch his light off.

'Soon.'

'Can we go for another sleepover at his house?'

'I'm sure that can be arranged.'

'Will Raul be there?'

'I don't know. We can ask. Now go to sleep.'

After another kiss to his forehead, she trundled back to the living area of her apartment that, after the glorious weekend in Seville, felt claustrophobic.

Or maybe it was her thoughts making her feel that way.

No sooner had she curled on her sofa than her phone rang.

She closed her eyes before answering it. Andrés had the uncanny ability to know exactly when the right time to call was.

Before Seville, she'd lived for his calls. In the three days since he'd dropped her home, she'd come to dread them, dreaded the direction the conversation would take. His business must be keeping him extra busy because so far he'd failed to mention the home she'd more or less promised to move into with him once he'd won Lucas over. But he would. Soon. She could feel it in her bones.

The quicksand was fastening around her. She'd felt its weight in Seville when she'd wanted to cry when he'd left her bed, felt it tighten as the miracle they'd been waiting for of Lucas accepting Andrés had come into being, and then start to pull her down with the words of Sophia continually floating in her ear.

You had the potential to be perfect for him.

Being without him after those wonderful days in Seville...

She needed to end things now, before she found herself stuck in the quicksand for ever.

Before she had her heart broken in the way she'd seen a broken heart destroy those she loved so dear.

'Gabrielle, *ma belle*,' he sang once she'd answered. 'How has your day been?'

Trying to inject life into her voice, she filled him in.

Once he'd given the potted highlights of his own day, to which she tried valiantly to make appropriate responses, he said, 'I will be flying back late tomorrow afternoon. Come to the apartment? I'll do dinner. There's much we need to talk about.'

The thump of dread that banged into her chest winded her.

'Bring Lucas with you,' he added. 'I'll get the spare room made up for him.' Loud voices echoed in the background. He muttered a curse before saying, 'I'm sorry but I need to go. I'll have my driver collect you for seven. Goodnight, *ma belle*. Think of me.'

The line disconnected.

Sleep took a long time to come that night.

Andrés entered the London skyscraper that had once been considered an architectural marvel but now looked sad and pathetic in comparison to the Gherkin, the Shard and the like crowding it out of existence, and was escorted to the elevator and up to the fifteenth floor. The elevator too, had seen better days. He briefly wondered if his antipathy to the building was in part caused by his antipathy to its owner.

His escort took him into a large reception room and announced him to one of the receptionists, who made the call.

A door opened and Gregory Jameson appeared, striding towards him with his hand outstretched.

Smiling with his teeth, Andrés shook the hand vigorously and followed him into the office, signing to his bodyguard, who'd spent the past two weeks twiddling his thumbs, to stay in the reception room.

'I have to say, it is an absolute pleasure to meet you,' Gregory said as he took a seat on one of his plush office sofas.

Andrés took the opposite sofa, laid his briefcase flat beside him and hooked an ankle to a thigh. 'Believe me, the pleasure is all mine.'

A secretary bustled in with coffee, pastries and water. Once she'd left, Gregory said, 'So, to business. I understand you want to discuss a proposal that could make us both a heck of a lot of money.'

Andrés picked up a chocolate croissant without bothering to use a plate, and took a huge bite out of it. 'Actually,' he said after swallowing, 'it's a proposal that, if you accept, will protect the wealth you already have.'

Thirty minutes later, Andrés put the pre-prepared and freshly signed documents back into his briefcase and got to his feet. Sweeping the crumbs that had fallen over his suit from the pastries he'd consumed onto the floor, making sure to scatter them in all directions, he extended a hand.

Gregory looked at it much as a lamb conscious of its fate would look at the knife about to slaughter it.

Andrés kept his steely gaze fixed on the spineless coward and his hand extended until Gregory's tremulous fingers reached over.

When Andrés strode out of the office, Gregory was rocking with his closed hand loosely tucked under an armpit debating through the throbbing pain whether what he needed to call for first was a hand doctor or a bucket of ice.

CHAPTER FOURTEEN

IT WAS WITH a pounding heart that Gabrielle entered Andrés's apartment.

'No Lucas?' he asked, swooping in for a quick, hungry kiss which she wasn't quick enough to duck out of the way of and which made her heart both sigh with the pleasure of it and sink to the pit of her stomach to know it was the last real kiss they would share.

She kicked her ballet shoes off and followed him through the reception room and into the main living area. 'I got my mother to babysit.'

His eyes narrowed slightly before he shrugged and lifted a folder from the table. 'Maybe it is for the best. It means we can talk while we eat. The chef is preparing steak for us.'

Carrying the folder into the dining room, he put it on the table next to the place setting with the glass of iced water already poured, then pulled out Gabrielle's chair.

She sat, trying not to look at the surplus place setting with the glass of milk. It made her heart hurt.

Andrés had a large drink of the red wine already poured to accompany his meal, and nodded at the folder. 'Open that.'

Certain it would contain house details, she opened the lip.

'Start with the top document.'

She had to read it three times for it to make sense. Or,

rather, for her brain to comprehend what she understood on the first read but which the violent thrashing of her heart pumping hot blood swimming in her head made impossible to digest.

'Gregory has signed away all rights to Lucas,' he explained into the ringing silence. 'I have bought a majority shareholding in his company. If he makes one move out of line then I sell for a loss and destroy him. The country estate he is so proud of is owned by the company, ergo it is now owned by me. I have put a loaded gun to his head but I have left it for you and your family to decide if you want me to pull the trigger.'

She could only stare at him, hardly able to believe her eyes or ears. Hardly able to dare.

'I know you were worried about the consequences of my involvement in this, but once I'd gathered and dissected all the information about him and got my legal team—who are all bound by confidentiality so please don't worry about them—onto it, I knew I could make my move without any penalty to you or to Lucas.' His eyes were shining. 'This has freed you, Gabrielle. He can never do anything to hurt you or your family again.'

It took a long time for her to whisper, 'Why didn't you tell me you were doing this?'

The shine dimmed a fraction but his gaze remained steady. 'I was trying to clear a burden that has laid heavily in you for far too long before I asked you to marry me.'

Gabrielle was almost stunned into silence. 'You... You want to *marry* me?'

'Not only that but I want to adopt Lucas too.'

Now she really was too stunned to respond.

'This is the point where you're supposed to say something.' His tone was teasing but she detected a slight edge to it.

She had to swallow hard to make her weak vocal cords work. 'But we're not going to marry. We're going to move in together and live in separate wings and lead independent lives.'

'I have had a change of perspective about things,' he explained slowly. 'It was the party. My parents' arguing.' He shook his head and drank some more of his wine. 'What you said…it made me look, and for the first time I saw their marriage clearly. Everything they've been through and all the hardships they suffered. Those circumstances…we will never have to go through what they have. Our marriage doesn't have to be like theirs.'

It came to Gabrielle in a flash that he was serious, and as that penetrated she was transported back to the palace when she'd been dancing in his arms, terrified of the feelings sweeping through her, telling herself that she should run.

She *had* run… But she'd run in the wrong direction. She should have run all the way out of the palace.

She'd run only far enough for him to catch her.

Scrambling to her feet, all the dread and fear she'd been carrying inside her leapt up her throat as a loud, *'No.'*

For the beat of a moment Andrés thought he'd misheard her. 'No?'

'No. I don't want to marry you. I'm grateful—so grateful—for what you've done freeing us from that man, but I can't marry you.'

He looked at her carefully, taking in the wildness of her stare.

A pulse throbbed in the side of his head. None of this was going at all as he'd envisaged.

Andrés had returned to Monte Cleure with the same lightness in his chest being with Gabrielle had induced at the palace. The future he'd seen so clearly in Seville had only brightened, the certainty that he was taking the right path, the certainty not just of his feelings but of hers too.

The passion. The tenderness. The emotions he'd glimpsed when she'd looked at him before she could blink them away.

What he hadn't paid attention to was the duller tone of her voice in all their calls since Seville. If he'd not been so intent on his quest to free her from the English monster, he would have paid better attention to it.

And if he'd not been so intent on giving her the document that had freed her, he'd have paid better attention to her closed-off body language when she'd entered his apartment, and her failure to bring Lucas.

'Why not?'

He detected movement in the doorway. Michael bringing their dinner to them.

'Leave us,' he commanded, not taking his eyes off Gabrielle.

The door closed.

Those few seconds of distraction had given her time to compose herself for her tone was a fraction calmer. 'Marriage is unnecessary. We both know that. I appreciate that Lucas has accepted you and that we can move in together, but I think it best we abide by the original agreement and live as individuals with separate living accommodation raising our baby as one. I'm glad you recognise your parents' marriage isn't as toxic as you've always thought but that—'

'Oh, it is,' he interrupted, holding tightly onto the emotions rising like a cobra in his chest. 'Incredibly toxic, and not the kind of marriage I would wish for any child to suffer, but it is their marriage and for whatever reason it works for them. My epiphany, if you can call it that, is understanding that it is *their* marriage. Not mine. Not one you and I would have. We were already committing our lives together as parents but things have—'

Now Gabrielle was the one to interrupt, the panic clawing at her chest scratching deeper with each passing second. 'I'm abiding by our agreement—it's you who's trying to change it. I don't want to get married, so please respect that and let's put an end to this conversation. In fact, I think it best I go home and we discuss all the other issues another time.'

She'd moved only two paces from the table when he said, 'You still haven't given me a reason.'

She closed her eyes and fought for breath. 'I don't have to give you a reason.'

'Agreed, but it would be courteous seeing as you're throwing my proposal back in my face. Your silence about me adopting Lucas is very telling too.'

Something inside her snapped and she spun back around to face him. 'Why are you *being* like this? We had every-thing arranged and now all this? You don't even *want* to marry me.'

His face darkened. Arms slowly folding across his chest, he said in a silky tone, 'Making assumptions again? You did that when you told me of the pregnancy. You assumed I either wouldn't want you to keep it—you can have no idea how offensive I found that assumption—and assumed I would force DNA tests.'

'Can you blame me for that?' she cried.

'I was honest with you about the circumstances with Susi and they were nothing like our circumstances.' His tone hardened. 'You assumed the worst of me then and you're assuming the worst of me now.'

She took a deep breath, trying her hardest to fight her insides from unravelling. 'Andrés, if it wasn't for the baby, you wouldn't even be entertaining the idea of marriage.'

'Only because without the baby there would be no you and I, but there *is* a baby, and there is a you and I, and there is a little boy crying out for a father.'

Andrés watched the anger ignite in her eyes. 'Don't bring Lucas into this,' she said fiercely.

'Why not when you've spent years hiding behind him?' he sneered.

'Now you're the one being offensive. You know—'

'I know that you were a twenty-three-year-old virgin with no intention of ever forming a serious relationship and you used Lucas's father as a means to justify it.' Pressing his hands on the table, he rose to his feet. 'Those means have now gone. He is no longer a threat to you. There is noth-ing—*nothing*—to stop you from committing yourself prop-erly to me.'

'Other than I don't want to. You're so damn arrogant, thinking you can spring this on me and that I'll just bow down to your will.'

'If it's arrogance to believe your feelings run as deep as mine do then yes, I'm arrogant. Look me in the eye and tell me you don't have feelings for me,' he demanded. 'Look me in the eye and tell me you're not feeling everything I feel for you.'

She turned her face away.

He slammed his palm onto the table. 'God in heaven, Gabrielle, what are you so frightened of? Or are you just being blind? Don't you get it? There hasn't been anyone else for me since the moment you pulled my car over, now look me in the eyes and tell me you're not in love with me. If you can do that, then I will let you go and never mention marriage again.'

Gabrielle's stomach was rolling so violently she feared she'd be sick, images flashing, her distraught sister on the floor of the bathroom, her mother turning her pillow sodden with tears, all the damage, so much damage, that came when hearts were broken into pieces.

It took all the strength she possessed to step back to the table and meet his stare.

She could hardly make her throat move let alone hold his stare to truthfully croak, 'I left Lucas at home tonight because I was going to tell you that *this thing* between us...' Her throat caught. 'Is over.'

The clenching of his jaw was the only hint of emotion to pass his face.

And then he smiled cruelly. 'That is not what I asked of you, Gabrielle. I asked you to deny that you're in love with me, but you can't do it can you? You can't deny your feelings.'

It was the flicker in her eyes before she staggered to the door that convinced Andrés he'd had the truth all along. Gabrielle was running scared.

'I never thought I would say this, Gabrielle, but you're a coward.'

Her back stiffened.

'You, the bravest person I have ever met in my life, a damned *coward*,' he snarled. 'All this time I thought it was me putting up the barriers in our relationship but they came from you too, and it's you who can't bear to let them down and see the truth. Love *terrifies* you. All these years, hiding behind your son... You only gave yourself to me because you thought I wouldn't want anything more from you than one night and now you want to throw away something that you know in your heart is beautiful and pure because you're too scared to put yourself on the line. So go on, coward, run away to your lonely bed and find something else to hide behind, but don't expect me to wait for you. I grant you your wish. Separate lives. You and I...this thing...it's over.'

Gabrielle only realised she'd left her ballet slippers behind when she found herself in the Imperium's car park barefoot. She didn't even remember getting into Andrés's elevator.

The lights that should automatically switch on at any motion within the car park stayed off. The only illumination came from what her dazed mind assumed were emergency lights because none of the exits opened.

Banging on the main doors the cars went in and out of proved futile. The duty guards, appointed to stop the public gaining access to some of the world's most expensive cars were missing.

Restless, nauseous, desperate for fresh air, even more desperate not to think, she prowled the car park looking for another means of escape.

'I'm sorry to tell you, sir, but she seems to have vanished.'

Only moments, mere seconds, after Gabrielle left the dining room, Andrés had gathered his wits about him to give the order for her to be driven home.

'How can she just vanish?' he demanded icily.

'I don't know, sir.'

'Well don't just stand there,' he roared, furious at this time wasting. 'Go and find her.'

It was on Gabrielle's fifth circuit of the cavernous car park that her eyes finally skimmed the one car she'd been studiously avoiding.

Her feet stopped walking.

Her stare fell back on the car that had started it all.

Her eyes swam.

If this car had taken the different line, she wouldn't be standing here. The other team would have processed it. She would never have set eyes on Andrés.

The bones in her legs weakening, she pressed a hand to her swollen stomach.

If Andrés had taken the different line, the little life inside her wouldn't be there. She wouldn't be there. She would be in her apartment watching a movie she'd seen a hundred times or reading a book she'd read a dozen times. She would be thinking of going to bed soon and resting enough for her work shift.

She would be oblivious to the bliss that could be found in the arms of someone you loved.

She closed her eyes and swayed.

The elevator door pinged open.

Andrés stepped into the car park. He'd searched every inch of his apartment. The Imperium's security cameras had proved she hadn't left through the atrium. An eagle-eyed security guard had spotted the slight figure pacing the car park but a problem with the electrics, which the maintenance crew were at that moment working on, had affected the main lights and meant the figure was impossible to see clearly.

He'd known though, and he strode to the woman who'd stopped pacing and now stood motionless in front of his car.

'Are you so stubborn that you would rather stay in the dark in a locked underground car park than come back up to the apartment and leave another way?' His relief at finding her mixed with the fury still pumping through his blood at her cowardice.

Her head turned slowly to him.

Even with the minimal lighting he could see the pallor of her skin.

'Do you want to stay here all night?' he demanded.

Her throat moved.

He turned his face from her. It made his guts shred to even look at her. 'Come on,' he said tersely. 'The concierge has arranged for a car to take you home.'

After three paces he realised she still hadn't moved from her spot.

Her expression was stark. 'Do you love me?'

'If that wasn't made clear to you, then yes, I love you, and now that you've ripped out another piece of my scalp, can we get out of here?'

He set off again to the elevator.

'Andrés, I'm scared.'

Now he was the one to freeze.

'I've seen what love can do. I've lived it. I watched my mother waste away through the pain of losing my father, and Eloise...'

His heart caught in his throat. Turning slowly, he found himself caught in the dark brown eyes brimming with tears.

A wave of shame drove through him. He'd backed her into a corner and like a frightened kitten she'd come out fighting.

Rubbing her eyes, she said, 'You were wrong, you know. It isn't love I'm frightened of. It's losing it.

'I've always been the strong one. Eloise saw it, it's why she was so insistent that I be Lucas's mother, but I never asked or wanted to be the strong one. It was a role I was given and I've never had any choice but to live up to it for everyone else's sake, and then you...'

She drew in a long breath and whispered, 'You make me feel vulnerable.' She swallowed. 'It's not something I've felt before and... Andrés, it's terrifying.'

'Enough,' he said hoarsely, his legs unlocking themselves

to stride to her. Hauling her into his arms, he pressed a long kiss to the top of her head. 'Enough.'

After a moment's hesitation, Gabrielle's arms wrapped around and she held him as tightly as he held her.

He exhaled his deep relief into her sweet-smelling hair. 'No more explanations. I love you, Gabrielle. With everything I have. I fell in love with you when you were dressed as a princess and I've loved you ever since. You are everything to me and I swear that if you put your heart and your trust in me, I will never abuse it. You don't have to be the strong one any more. Just be you, because it's you I love, you with all your strength and all your vulnerabilities, and I swear I will never let you down.'

A shudder ran through Gabrielle, so powerful she had to cling even tighter to him. When it had passed, she lifted her head to gaze up at the handsome face of the man who had stolen her heart without even trying.

Bathed in clarity, she palmed his bearded cheek.

'I love *you*,' she breathed. 'I fell in love with you when I was dressed as a princess and I've never stopped. You are everything to me, and there is nothing I want more than to marry you.'

'Ah, Gabrielle, *ma belle*,' he groaned, and then his mouth claimed hers and Gabrielle found herself bathed in the warmth of a love so deep and sincere that the last of her fears evaporated.

EPILOGUE

THE PRIEST POURED the blessed water over baby Eloise's head. To neither of her parents' surprise, she carried on sleeping, blissfully unaware of the occasion that made her the centre of attention. At eight months old, Eloise was a happy little lump who epitomised the saying of sleeping like a baby.

Once the Christening had finished, Gabrielle, Andrés, the proud godparents and the family and friends there to witness the event stepped out of the pretty church into the pretty grounds and the warm Seville sunshine.

Lucas, who'd been sat with Gabrielle's mother and brother during the service, bounded over to his parents. Having finished his first year of school, he considered himself too big to be carried any more, but, thankfully, not too big to hold his mummy and daddy's hands, and his hand was swallowed straight into Andrés's.

'Can Raul and I play football when we get home, Daddy?'

'After we've eaten.'

Everyone, the priest included, was going back to their home to continue the celebrations.

'Will you play with us?'

'Only if I can be on your team.'

Lucas turned to Gabrielle. 'Will you be goalkeeper?'

'In this dress and these shoes?' she teased. 'Ask Aunty

Sophia. She was telling me only yesterday how much she loves football.'

He went running off to his favourite—and only—aunty.

Moments later, amused daggers were being thrown at Gabrielle who grinned and turned to greet Queen Catalina and her husband, Nathaniel, who'd come over to admire baby Eloise.

One day she would get used to calling her heroine a personal friend. One day.

Soon, the official photographer was calling everyone together.

Passing Eloise to Andrés, she slipped an arm around him and held Lucas's hand with the other.

'Have I told you how sexy you look in that dress?' Andrés murmured into her ear while everyone gathered and jostled around them.

She fixed him with her primmest look and slipped her hand beneath the tail of his suit jacket to pinch his bottom.

He grinned and, holding the baby firmly, kissed her.

The photographer caught the moment where their mouths pulled apart but their eyes were intimately locked together. In that picture, Lucas was beaming widely at the camera and baby Eloise's dark eyes had opened, her face a picture of contentment.

Both Gabrielle and Andrés carried a copy of it in their wallets for the rest of their lives.

* * * * *

AWAKENED IN HER ENEMY'S PALAZZO

KIM LAWRENCE

MILLS & BOON

For Dan, thanks for stepping in last minute!

CHAPTER ONE

THEO STOOD BY the glass wall, hands thrust deep into his pockets, presenting a perfect patrician profile to the four other men in the boardroom. Theo thought very little, if at all, about his profile. He had his faults, as he would be the first to acknowledge—though not apologise for—but vanity was not one of them, despite the fact that even his most severe critics agreed he had plenty to be vain about.

Being six feet four, and blessed with an impressively athletic physique that impeccable tailoring did nothing to disguise, ensured that Theo was an attention-grabbing figure in any setting. Combined with his physical presence he possessed razor-sharp instincts and a reputation for forensic attention to detail that meant no one came into any meeting where he was present unprepared.

Today, his normal ability to focus on detail was not functioning at full capacity. He wasn't absorbing more than one word in three—a circumstance which was obvious to those around him. But although a few subtly raised eyebrows and loaded glances were exchanged between the nervous-looking suited figures delivering expensive advice to him, none of them mentioned the fact that their target audience appeared to be supremely uninterested in it.

The current speaker paused, losing his thread as he

found himself no longer speaking to a pair of broad shoulders but instead to a pair of jet-black eyes, obsidian-dark and inscrutable. He straightened up in his seat, exhaling slightly as the tall Italian, hands thrust deep in the pockets of his tailored suit trousers, turned back to his appraisal of the panoramic view, his expression set in a scowl of irritation.

The irritation was aimed at himself. Theo hated the fact that his thoughts were all over the place. Although that was not strictly true. He knew exactly where they were—in Tuscany.

An image of the palazzo where he had grown up floated into his head and he pushed it away—but not before he had seen himself as a child, laying flowers on his mother's grave, his tears falling onto the dry, dusty ground as he swore to hate his father for ever.

He pressed his fingertips to his temple, where a blue vein beat, as he stared out, seeing for the first time the rain that had been falling for the last half-hour.

Was it raining in Tuscany as Salvatore was being laid to rest in the family crypt beside his late wife? Or was the sun shining as the great and the good of Italian society, and also the not so good, dressed in designer black listened to the priest lie about what a good man his father had been?

He'd thought that once too. He had worshipped the man. And then he had discovered the truth. He'd been thirteen years old at the time, still in his black funeral suit, hiding in a cupboard to cry the tears he had held in during his mother's funeral because his mother had not liked him to cry. It had made her unhappy.

'Why are you not going to your father's funeral?' Cleo had asked as he'd left her apartment that morning.

The scantily clad luscious redhead had been lazily curious, and not judgemental or particularly surprised when he had not responded to her question while she carefully reapplied her red lipstick.

That was what made Cleo a perfect companion for him. Along with her voracious sexual appetite, she was fine with his silences and didn't make any demands.

Hadn't made demands, he silently corrected in his head.

He had reached the door when that situation had changed—when she had voiced the fatal words that had brought him back into the room.

'So, where do we go from here, darling?'

His response had been short and to the point. Other people equated honesty with cruelty, but not Theo. He believed the truth was just the truth; it was not emotive, just fact.

'Nowhere,' he'd told her.

It had ended neatly, the way he liked things—neat, simple and uncomplicated by messy emotions. It was a pity... Cleo was beautiful, desirable, and until *that* question had been exactly the sort of female he was attracted to. A talented, successful woman, as single-minded and as ambitious as he was, with a life that was separate from his. It had been a positive that they did not share friends or opinions. She was not interested in going anywhere with him outside the bedroom or the occasional photo opportunity public event.

There had been a time when he had been concerned that some sort of chemistry with a woman might at some point cause him to overrule his decision that marriage was not for him.

His concern had been misplaced.

If it had been going to happen, he reasoned, it would have done so by now. He had had plenty of *chemistry* with women, but none of it had made him lose his mind enough to forget that nothing lasted for ever—certainly not sexual attraction. And what else kept two people together? Except perhaps laziness and a lack of options.

To Theo's way of thinking there were two sorts of marriage: those that ended in messy divorce and those that continued in lies.

The former was, to his mind—while messy and expensive—infinitely preferable. But then he had had a front row seat for the latter. To the world, his parents' marriage had been perfect—but it had been an act they had perpetuated to disguise their mutual misery.

A shaft of sunlight had appeared through the clouds when he finally turned back to the room full of lawyers. He scanned them, the seemingly relaxed stance of his tall, rangy frame in contrast to the expectant tension emanating from the group.

'I want to sell.'

His simple words were greeted by a stunned silence and collective dropped jaws.

'Sell...?' one of the lawyers queried tentatively.

'Some land, you mean?' another interrupted, with a smile that suggested he was more in tune with the way the mind of a financial genius who had made his fortune in IT worked than his colleagues. 'That would be a financially sound move. The forest area—now, that is a piece of prime land with development opportunity written all over it. Obviously the eco lobby would have a fit, but I've never encountered a protection order that wasn't breakable, and the land on the southern boundary...'

His enthusiasm became genuine as he warmed to his theme.

Out of nowhere images of a cool green oasis…the dappled light, the silence, the tall swaying trees, an encounter with a deer or a wild boar…began to slide slowly through Theo's head.

His jaw clenched. He was determined to divest himself of any reminder of his past, and he prided himself on not being sentimental, but the idea of that green oasis being destroyed made nameless things tighten in his chest.

'You're talking about the forest on the northern slopes?' Theo pinned the man with an obsidian stare that made the guy shift uneasily in his seat and consult the blank screen of the tablet on the desk beside him.

'Northern—I think so. All mountain. Yes, not suitable for— But a holiday village would—'

Theo pushed away the image of denuded forest slopes and the sound of machinery. 'A non-starter,' he said coolly. 'It is a protected area, and there are clauses in the deeds of the palazzo.'

'Of course. Palazzo della Stellato…such an evocative name.'

Theo responded to the man's exaggerated Italian pronunciation with a stony look.

'There are other sections that we have already had tentative enquiries about—from several developers who have made it known they would be interested. Let me see… The Wenger Group…'

As one man, all the legal team began to desperately scroll through their assorted devices.

'I have the details here. They approached your father last year, I believe, but he was never… Not a criticism, of course—he was old school, which was understandable, given the historic nature of the estate…'

'I'm not interested in history.' *Only escaping it.* 'And, no, I do not want to sell *some land.*'

The hand Theo ran across the dark surface of his dark hair suggested impatience that they couldn't keep up with him.

'The lot. The palazzo, the contents, the land—just get rid of it all. I want nothing.'

Just the portrait that had hung in his father's study. Was it still there? he wondered. Had his father kept it there to remind himself of his guilt? Or had he rewritten the past to make it easier to live with?

He could feel shocked eyes following him as he left the room. Not that he cared, but all the same he was glad he had bitten back the unspoken rejoinder that had hovered on the tip of his tongue.

I want nothing that reminds me of that bastard.

It would have been sharing too much.

'Half?' Grace echoed. 'You mean half the books?'

She glanced around the shelves of the library they were sitting in. The lawyer was sitting in the chair that Salvatore had sat in when she'd read to him, and it made his absence more of a stark reality than the funeral had.

'Oh, how kind. But I couldn't break up the collection… it's far too valuable. One or two books, maybe?'

'Miss Stewart, I don't think you quite understand…' the man said slowly. 'When I say "half", I mean half of *everything*: the palazzo, the estate, the money. It has been left jointly to you both.'

Grace stared at him blankly for a moment, and then

laughed, although this wasn't funny. It was crazy. Which was most likely the way her laugh sounded too.

'He's left me—?' She had to have the wrong end of the stick. 'Why—no, that can't be right—go back and check. I think you'll find—' She half rose in her seat and collapsed weakly back again as her voice faded.

'Would you like a glass of water?'

The man whose neatly trimmed beard was flecked with white smiled kindly at her.

Grace shook her head, thinking she wouldn't have said no to a brandy. She held her clasped hands tight in her lap—not that it disguised the fact she was shaking. A few deep breaths and the volume of the buzzing in her head lessened, her temporary numbness melting away leaving shock and disbelief.

'You're not joking?' She almost immediately dismissed the idea. 'Sorry, no…no, of course not.'

Could lawyers joke?

Observation of her own immediate family—her brother was a member of that profession—suggested not, but then her other brother, the psychiatrist, never laughed at her jokes either. Nor her ecologist sister, whose TV series had just been sold to the States.

They were a gifted bunch, her family, and they tried to be kind about Grace's deficiencies—the fact that Grace was not the most academically gifted of the Stewart clan. But she knew that her parents—her Oxford professor dad and historian mother, both acknowledged experts and bestselling authors in their fields—had been gutted when Grace had, to everyone's surprise, including her own, got the grades to secure a coveted Oxford place but had chosen instead to embark on a nursing degree.

'You are a very wealthy young woman.'

Grace dragged herself back to the very surreal present. 'Wealthy? I think you've made a mistake. I'm going home today. I have a week's holiday before I start my next—' She stopped and dragged in a gulping breath. 'That *can't* be right. Why would Salvatore leave me anything? I was only his nurse. I only knew him for a couple of months.'

What will people think or say?

Grace didn't voice the last thought out loud. There was no point asking a question when you already knew the answer.

They would think the worst possible thing. They would say there was no smoke without fire—just as they had the last time.

Her heart took a sickening lurch as those memories escaped the box she had locked them in, marked *I have moved on.*

It had been her second job for the nursing agency. A lovely, grateful family with whom she had been on the best of terms—until an extremely valuable necklace and a pile of cash had vanished.

It had been a nightmare.

Grace had been suspended, because the family who had days earlier been thanking her had suddenly been accusing her of being a thief. The truth had come out almost immediately, and she had been proved totally innocent, but the event had left scars.

This is not the same!

'This is… It feels surreal.'

'I can see this has been a shock…but a pleasant one?' The balding figure smiled benignly at her.

'No…yes… But I only knew him— This just isn't right. Can I give it back?'

'Give what back?'

'Everything… The staff can have it. Marta and…'

A hand was lifted to still halt her spill of anxious words. 'The staff have all been remembered very generously in the will, and tenants have been given lifetime tenure. Let me assure you that no one has been forgotten. I think you should take some time to get used to the idea, and then…'

'No. I was his nurse. I can't benefit financially from someone's death. People will think that I took advantage…'

'Not at all,' the lawyer soothed. But he was avoiding her eyes. Because obviously, human nature being what it was, some people would. He considered her for a moment and then, seeming to some to a decision, said, 'Look, if you do feel that way there is an option—though I advise you not to make any decisions yet…'

'What option?'

An hour later Grace walked into the massive kitchen, with its modern state-of-the-art equipment sitting comfortably on the original flagstone floor, among heavy beams and the original kitchen fireplace. No one would have described it as cosy, but it was the most informal room in the palazzo, which boasted too many bedrooms to count and was, unsurprisingly, designed on a palatial scale.

Marta, the housekeeper, wearing her usual crisp white blouse and tailored trousers, was sitting at the table, tapping into the spreadsheets on her laptop, as she sipped a cup of coffee. She looked up when Grace appeared.

'I know that computers are meant to make life easier, but honestly… This—' She stopped, the smile fading from her narrow face as she took in Grace's expression.

'Oh, my, you look pale.' The older woman tutted. 'It's been a hard few days. I wish you'd let me rearrange your flight for later in the week.'

Grace managed a distracted smile. When she'd arrived ten weeks ago the housekeeper, who had been very protective of her employer, had initially been suspicious of the English nurse suddenly living in the palazzo. She had openly questioned why an agency specialising in palliative end-of-life care had not sent an Italian-speaking nurse.

Grace herself had asked the same thing, and had been told that her patient, who was fluent in several languages, did not have a problem with her not speaking Italian.

'We have an army of nurses on rota here already. What are you? A miracle-worker?' Marta had asked scornfully. 'Are you going to make him live?'

Grace, who had heard grief talking before, had been gentle. 'I hope I'll be able to make him a little more comfortable.'

Marta's attitude had changed when she'd seen the difference the new regime of pain relief that Grace had introduced had made to her employer. And how she'd worked in conjunction with Salvatore's own physician, who was universally adored by the staff at the palazzo.

Grace had seen tears in her eyes the day she'd walked into the kitchen and found the previously bedbound Salvatore sitting at the table they were seated at now.

'He was just surviving,' Marta had said in the emotional aftermath of the funeral. 'Thanks to you, he *lived* his last weeks.'

Grace's protests that she'd just been doing her job had been ignored as she was enfolded in a crushing hug.

'I'm not catching a flight. I'm staying,' Grace said now, dragging out a chair and slumping into it.

'You are?'

'He—Salvatore—he's left me half of everything.'

The older woman clamped a hand to her mouth, her eyes as big as saucers above her fingers, staring at Grace.

'I told him—the lawyer—that I couldn't accept. That it wouldn't be proper. He said that *he*—' her eyes narrowed into contemptuous slits '—the son—Theo—apparently wants to buy me out. He has offered a crazy amount of money. I don't want money, Marta. I don't want anything!' she wailed, her voice shaking with emotion.

'Oh, I know that. Everyone here does. *We* all know you, Grace, but I suppose Theo thinks it's such an ancient place, with so much history, that it should stay in the family?' the older woman suggested apologetically.

Grace nodded her agreement. 'I thought that too, and I said he could have it, obviously. Even though he sounds like—'

She bit her tongue and gave a weak smile, thinking, *Suck it up, Grace*. Inexplicably—or at least it was to her—the palazzo staff never badmouthed the absent son.

Grace had her own opinion when it came to Theo Ranieri, who had never *once* visited his dying father, and not even come to the funeral, but she kept it to herself.

'Theo is not poor. You should not give it away.'

Grace's soft mouth hardened. 'I don't intend to. He wants to buy me out, but only so—' angry tears sprang to her blue eyes '—so that he can sell everything! I can't believe that anyone could be so— It's as if he wants to erase everything his father loved! His heritage!' Her soft lips quivered. 'How can he—?' she began. Then she stopped and, making a supreme effort to contain her surging emotions, shook her head.

The housekeeper had gone pale. 'I was afraid of something like this,' she admitted.

'Don't worry. I won't let him. I can stop him,' Grace gritted, tucking the lint-pale strands of hair she had dislodged behind her ears. 'And I will. If I say no—if I live here—he can't sell. And I do say no.'

The older woman looked doubtful; her hand shook as she poured fresh coffee into her cup. 'Theo could always be very stubborn when he made up his mind...'

'So can I,' Grace promised grimly.

'It is so sad that it has come to this.'

Sad? Grace thought. It was totally *outrageous*! And that was a mild way of expressing her feelings.

She had no idea what had caused the relationship between father and son to break down, and although curious she had never considered it her place to ask. Even now things had changed, still she couldn't make herself ask.

Why does he hate his father so much?

Surely indifference could not explain his behaviour?

'Perhaps Salvatore suspected what his son would do? And the will was his way of...? Well, whatever the reason,' she added, her narrow shoulders lifting as she accepted the cup of coffee Marta pushed her way, 'his son can't sell if I say no and live here.' Her blue eyes sparked with a militant light. 'And I *do* say no. He can't sell! This place, the palazzo, the estate, the *people*,' she declared fiercely. 'It was Salvatore's life, and I won't let his son destroy it! I'm moving in and I'm not budging.'

CHAPTER TWO

STRAIGHT AFTER SHE had handed in her notice to the nursing agency Grace had emailed her parents to let them know that she wouldn't be coming home. She had included the bare bones of the situation and then sat back to wait for her phone to ring. Finally it had, and now she was sitting talking online to her entire family, who were crowded into her parents' booklined sitting room.

So far Simon, her lawyer brother, had suggested that the son might stand a good chance of breaking the will, warning that it could get vicious and asking what drugs Salvatore had been on.

'Could the son say he was—?'

Grace immediately saw where he was going and cut across him. 'He remained as sharp as you or me, right up to the end.'

'All right...no need to get het-up. I'm just covering the possibilities.'

'I'm sure you're a very good lawyer, Simon, but you're also my brother.'

Her psychiatrist brother Rob cut in. 'Exactly. Grace needs a bit of support.' Before she could be grateful, he added, 'Were you sleeping with the old guy? Not that I'm judging... I've seen photos. He was good-looking for an old guy.'

Well, if he wasn't judging he'd be the only one, Grace thought grimly. The manager at the agency had made a couple of very pointed comments concerning vulnerable elderly patients and ethics.

Now it was her sister's turn, and it was almost a relief when Hope seemed mostly interested in this inconvenience to her own social calendar.

Grace leaned back from the computer screen as her sister leaned in so close that if she'd had a blemish it would have showed. It didn't, because there was a reason her sister never argued when people complimented her on her perfect skin—she *did* have perfect skin.

Hope, with her supermodel looks, had perfect everything.

She also had the only man that Grace had ever loved.

Grace sometimes asked herself if she *still* loved George…if that was the reason that she'd not had a proper boyfriend since him?

George hadn't changed at all, except he no longer had the cute floppy fringe that Grace had fallen in love with, or the gap between his front teeth which her sister had insisted on being eliminated for the wedding photographs.

'But you *have* to come home, Grace. George and I are having our weekend in Paris—you know that.'

Behind her, her husband waved and looked apologetic. He had looked apologetic when he'd told her he was in love with her sister, but that he still loved her just *like* a sister. He'd seemed to think this would be some sort of compensation.

It hadn't been.

'I've been so busy with the new series. And in case anyone is interested, I'm exhausted—and George is simply off-the-scale stressed.'

'I'm not really....'

His wife ignored him.

'Grace, you promised to babysit. You know we can't leave Artie with anyone else but you. He's so sensitive. And, well, Aria is being *totally* intransigent,' she said, pouting as she referenced their incredible nanny. 'I'm sure her sister would understand if she wasn't there for the wedding.'

'Sorry.' Grace bit her well-bitten tongue. Artie with his sunny smile was gorgeous, and maybe the *easiest* baby on the planet, but she wasn't going to be budged.

'Hope, not everything is about you.'

This online defence came from a most unexpected direction—her mum.

'This is a massive opportunity for your sister. She doesn't have a career—'

'I do have—'

'She doesn't have a partner. I think that she's being very sensible to stay put and show she's not a pushover. It's a very good tactic to up the price. Try not to be such a people-pleaser, Grace. Stand up for yourself.'

Grace sighed. It was rare that she received approval from either of her parents, and the only reason she was now was because they had mistaken her motives. They really thought that her staying put was some sort of 'possession is nine-tenths of the law' negotiating move.

'Good girl, Grace,' said her father, looking just as distinguished as he did on the cover of his latest bestseller.

Modesty forbade him from mentioning that he had held the number one slot on the non-fiction bestseller list for eight weeks last year—well, not mentioning it often... and then only casually.

'Just don't let this guy intimidate you. I'm looking him

up as we speak. He's brilliant, of course, but he's got a reputation for being pretty ruthless and manipulative. I could come over…back you up…'

'I don't want a better price, Dad. I'm not interested in the money. And Salvatore's death is not an o*pportunity*—'

'Of course not, darling. Take the moral high ground,' her mother interrupted. 'Sincerity is *so* you. But a person has to be practical in life—especially someone with no prospects. You have no idea how much we both worry about you in the future, when we're gone.'

The image of her energetic mother, who rose at five a.m. every day to work out and refused to allow white bread in the house, being on her last legs made Grace bite back a laugh. Her anger faded as her sense of the ridiculousness of the situation reasserted itself. She had decided a long time ago that she loved her family, and that the best way to cope with them and not fall out with them when they tried to be 'encouraging' was to consider them a comedy act: a very tall, good-looking, talented comedy act.

Sometimes she felt like a Shetland pony in a family of thoroughbreds…

'I really don't think that's imminent, Mum. And as for taking care of myself—I left home when I was eighteen.'

The moment the words left her lips she knew it had been a bad move to bring up the still-sensitive subject of her leaving home.

Turning down a place at Oxford in favour of a place on a nursing degree course in London had not quite caused her family to disown her, but it had been close. She loved them dearly, but there was no doubt they were a bunch of high-achieving intellectual snobs. Though she also knew that if she was ever in any real trouble they'd be there for her.

'I'm really not interested in money,' she tacked on quickly. 'Oh, gosh... I think I'm losing you...'

She cut the connection and didn't feel even slightly guilty.

Theo loosened his tie, and a moment later it joined his jacket on the back seat of his car. He had driven direct from the Florence office to the palazzo. Though these days he was based mainly in the States and the UK, he had retained his original Italian base.

It was a journey he had not made since he was an angry eighteen-year-old, and then it had been in the opposite direction, his mode of transport his feet and his thumb, his fuel anger.

He remembered the exhilaration of finally being free. He'd been counting down the days to severing all connections since that fateful day he'd discovered what his father was. Thanks to attending boarding school in England, he had only been home for the holidays. When he could he had spent them with friends, but when forced to return home to the palazzo he had studiously ignored his father. Instead he would head out into the hills every day, either alone or with Nico, the estate manager's son, who hated it there as much as he had.

The anger was still there, but there was no shoe leather involved today. Instead the silent growl of an electric engine that powered the convertible.

Theo had vowed that day he'd never set foot in the place again. He'd told his ashen-faced father that now he was an adult, and had a choice, it was no longer his home.

Yet here he was.

He resented the necessity and the reason for that necessity. One Grace Stewart. When his legal team had told him that she wouldn't sell he had been irritated, and instructed them to find out what she wanted and give it to her.

They had come back with the news that she didn't want anything—which he didn't believe. Everyone had a price, and this woman would be no exception.

The slim file that had landed in his inbox had not suggested she was any different, just possibly slightly more boring. There was certainly nothing that could be used as leverage against her in the file. Though to be certain he had employed Rollo Eden to dig a little deeper.

Theo did not particularly *like* Rollo, but liking was not necessary. It was thanks to the private investigator's digging ability that they had not lost a multimillion-dollar contract. The man had outed the mole in their midst who was passing on information to a rival firm. So what if he got near the line sometimes? While he stayed just the right side of it and produced results Theo would continue to utilise his skills when required, with no qualms.

This task was a little below his pay grade, but when Theo had explained the situation he had agreed to handle it personally and not pass it on.

But Theo was not hanging around waiting for Rollo to deliver. He had put a plan into action. Initially he had thought about speaking directly to the little gold-digger, and then another solution had come to him, brilliant in its simplicity.

If she wouldn't move out, he'd move in—which could cramp her style when it came to entertaining. She probably fancied herself as chatelaine of a castle, he concluded scornfully.

If he couldn't sell up without her agreement, the reverse was also true. If she had any plans that involved the estate she'd have to run them past him, and she would find him not co-operative.

Despite the amused smile that played around his lips at the thought, he felt the tension climb into his shoulders. He knew that once he turned the next bend the palazzo would be in view. He couldn't think of it as home any longer—it had stopped being his home the day of his mother's funeral. He'd been so angry with her for leaving him. And then, quite by accident, he had discovered from his hiding place the reason she had left him, and his anger had shifted to the person responsible.

He found his foot easing off the accelerator, delaying the moment of his first glimpse of the iconic view that was replicated in innumerable books on the architectural gems of Tuscany. Whether approaching by helicopter or car, guests arriving were guaranteed a catch-your-breath moment.

The palazzo was built on the site of the original monastic building that had been the dream of an ancestor of his in the sixteenth century. Its classic proportions still incorporated an old clock tower and the original ecclesiastical buildings, spread around the main palazzo like a village.

In his mind, he visualised the massive Renaissance gates which marked the point when a visitor would be hit by the full spectacle of the place. Driving along the tree-lined avenue and upwards towards the palazzo the visitor would be surrounded by tier after tier of immaculate flower-bedecked manicured gardens, intersected by stone walkways and statuary, rising to the final level that stopped short of a cliff face that opened on to the azure ocean.

Aware of the heavy thud of his heart, and refusing to acknowledge it, he veered the car off the dusty track and pulled up with a screech of brakes and a cloud of dust onto the grassy verge.

He told himself that he had stopped to stretch his legs, but the self-delusion was a single cell thin when he opened the door and was hit by the pungent, warm and earthy signature scent that he had never forgotten. It immediately filled his nostrils as his feet hit the pine-needle-strewn floor.

He didn't want to admit even to himself how the familiarity unsettled him—how being *here* unsettled him. He hadn't been prepared to feel this way, and it was all that damned woman's fault.

He had moved on. The death of the father he had rejected had been the final closure of a chapter—the closure that would be complete when he sold his heritage.

The only thing standing in the way was the woman who had got her claws into his father. Well, like they said, there was no fool like an old fool...

Not that his father had been old, as such—sixty-five was nothing these days, and his father had died three days short of that birthday.

Theo had learnt after the fact of his death, from the lawyers. The cold, clinical words of the email had stared up at him.

Regret to inform...dead...lost his brave fight...

It had taken Theo a while to connect the words—for the clichés to make sense. There had been no forewarning. Had his estranged father considered reaching out when he'd known the end was near?

And if he had...?

Theo gave an internal shrug, pushing away the question. Such speculation was pointless. His father had not reached out—except, perhaps, he mused cynically, to his opportunist nurse, who had been his 'companion' in his dying weeks and months.

No, he would do better focusing on the obstacle in his path than on the emotions that had been shaken loose by his father's death, he decided, his thoughts turning to the gold-digger.

His pride was insulted by the idea of anyone thinking they could shake him down.

Maybe she thought it was a case of like father like son?

If so, she would soon discover this was not the case.

He was retracing his steps when he heard the sound. He paused, frowning as he listened, remembering the encounter he'd once had with a wild boar in almost this exact spot.

It was most likely a deer.

Then he heard it again. Not a deer, or a wild boar. Unless they could swear.

Grace was not lost—just slightly off course.

She knew exactly where she was, and she also knew that her directional miscalculation by the stream after that slip had put an extra mile on her morning hike.

A mile would not be an issue if she hadn't turned her ankle…

At least the headache she had woken up with this morning had cleared. Or maybe she couldn't feel it above the throb from her ankle.

She paused, leaning on the fallen branch that made a useful crutch. Her full lower lip caught between her teeth, she bent forward, her determined optimism faltering as she unwrapped the tee shirt she had dipped in the icy stream and wrapped it around her injured extremity to relieve her ankle. Despite her make-do cold compress her ankle was already puffy, starting to discolour, and three times the size of the other.

'It looks worse than it is,' she told herself, without conviction.

From where he stood in the tree line, Theo scanned the injured ankle with clinical detachment. A detachment that soon evaporated, morphing into something less objective as his glance shifted, travelling upwards over the sinuous length of the woman's legs, reaching the understated feminine flare of hips emphasised by the narrowness of a waist that he estimated he could have spanned with his hands.

At that moment the who she was and the how she'd got here became of secondary importance to the way one strap of the vest she was wearing had slid down over a smooth shoulder, revealing a lot of the sports bra she wore underneath. A trickle of sweat was winding a slow path from the hollow at the base of her throat to the cleavage that without the bra would have been revealed.

He had an impression of the soft sounds of nature around them fading out as his eyes followed the slow progress of that pearl of moisture over her pale skin, its journey resulting in a flash of heat that settled solidly in his groin.

For a self-indulgent moment Theo allowed his libido to flare unchecked, welcoming the distraction, taking in the slim curves, the slender, elegant neck, the pale almost silver hair that stuck to her face and spilled untidily down her back.

'It looks pretty bad.'

At the sound of his voice, the woman started like a deer, her head coming up just in time to witness Theo materialising out of the trees.

The electric blue of those wide, scared eyes lifted to his brought Theo to a dead halt as his body was jolted by a fresh sexual charge.

The adrenaline dumped in Grace's bloodstream screamed fight or flight—only flight was not an option. A fact she didn't fully realise until she had scrambled to her feet.

Crying out in pain, she balanced on one leg, her eyes never leaving the man who towered over her for one second as she raised her branch defensively to warn him off. She maintained her stork-like pose for as long as it took her to snatch a deep breath—before she promptly fell on her bottom.

Between losing her balance and hitting the ground she put a name to the face of the sinister stranger.

This was Theo Ranieri.

There were younger, less threatening versions of the palazzo's joint owner in framed photos throughout the palazzo, but even if there hadn't been she would have recognised him. Long before she'd arrived here she'd seen an interview in which he had memorably verbally eviscerated the cocky reporter who had made the mistake of coming ill prepared when he'd been granted an interview.

The recognition came to her in a lightbulb moment—a little like the way your life was meant to flash before your eyes when you were dying.

Except she wasn't dying—or only of mortification.

On the plus side, she was no longer gut-freezingly terrified. Not that her thundering heart had responded to this information yet. Her breath was still coming far too fast to cope with her raised pulse.

'That must have hurt.'

Grace eased herself onto one hip and lifted her ankle off the floor, raising her chin and aiming for a defiant 'don't mess with me' angle.

Some of the defiance slid into something messier and more confusing as her eyes meshed with his dark stare. Shading her eyes with one protective hand, she shook back her hair, most of which had escaped the loose knot it had been gathered in on the back of her neck.

'I'm fine,' she gritted out through clenched teeth, dragging a hand across her sweaty damp face, oblivious to the dusty smear it left.

In the flesh, Theo Ranieri was more of everything he appeared to be in photographs or on the screen. Looking up at him made her feel quivery, light-headed and hot. But that was the pain, she told herself. That and a reaction to that split-second of visceral fear she had experienced when he had appeared out of nowhere.

Someone that big ought to make more noise, she decided resentfully as her eyes swept upwards from his dusty leather shoes over his long legs. The cut of his tailored trousers did not disguise the strength of his muscular thighs. His hips were narrow in comparison to the width of his powerful shoulders, and through the white of his shirt she could see a faint shadow suggestive of body hair.

She polished her righteous indignation to distract herself from the little sexual quiver in the pit of her belly that was a result of the earthy male image he presented.

Even without the vulnerability factor of the setting, Theo Ranieri possessed a raw physical presence that would intimidate and overpower in an air-conditioned crowded room. But somehow he didn't seem out of place in the raw, natural environment. He seemed part of it.

His features were undeniably perfect. The slant of his high cheekbones, the aquiline blade of his nose, his thickly delineated jet brows and his dark, almost black stare were not softened in any way by the crazily long lashes that framed his deep-set eyes. The fuller curve of his lower lip contrasted with the firmness of the upper, but it did not give his mouth a feminine softness, rather a disturbingly sensual provocation and a hint of cruelty.

He raised one dark brow and she brought her lashes down in a protective sweep. He probably took being stared at as his due, but she was damned if she was going to feed his no doubt massive ego.

Ironically, for weeks she had rehearsed the cutting comments she'd like to deliver to Salvatore's callous son if she ever had the opportunity, knowing that because of her profession she never would. But now professional standards no longer applied to her position, and he was here at the mercy of her tongue. She could confront him with his callous treatment of his dying father. A man who had deserved so much better.

Here was the opportunity to put her emotions into words without bawling her head off. But not, it turned out, the ability. Her feelings had solidified into a painful, inarticulate lump in her throat. If she knew one thing, she knew that this was a man she didn't want to cry in front of.

'I'm fine,' she lied, sounding cranky and slightly breathless.

'Debatable...' he drawled, sounding more amused than concerned. 'You've rung someone?'

'I forgot my phone.' The admission came through clenched teeth.

'Careless.'

She found herself hating his drawl. 'It's fine. I happen to live very close.'

She held his eyes with a pretence of cool composure which, considering she was sitting on the dirt floor, looking and for that matter feeling as though she had been dragged through several hedges backwards, was an achievement that deserved applause.

His right eyebrow joined the left, nearly hitting his hairline, then suddenly levelled as she saw a fractional widening of his dark eyes before the glitter of recognition appeared.

'*You're* Grace Stewart?'

Theo felt a surge of irritation the moment the redundant question left his lips. He considered himself intellectually agile, but he did not make assumptions. And yet he had.

Though if someone had thought to include a photograph in the pathetically thin file he had read, he would not have previously been thinking boring and average. The woman sitting on the forest floor, glaring up at him with eyes so searingly shockingly blue, was neither average nor boring. The skin under the smears of dirt had a pale clarity that seemed to glow in the shaded light.

This discovery required some rapid mental readjustment—which was not easy when his libido kept escaping its leash. Maybe it was like father, like son?

His jaw hardened at the thought as he rejected any and all comparisons with his father. Unlike his late parent, he had never pretended to be a saint and he was not a cheat. He had never promised a woman anything, never made vows and broken them, forcing a woman he claimed to love to the point of utter black despair where she saw no way back.

'What are you doing here anyway?'

The accusing words brought his attention back to the moment and to the figure sitting at his feet. 'Did I need to ask permission?'

His sarcasm pushed colour into her pale cheeks. 'I mean I— We had no idea you were coming. A bit of warning might have been nice.'

It sounded petulant and she felt stupid—especially as she was not exactly operating from a position of authority and was actually on her behind!

'Just checking you haven't stolen the silver.'

His lazy mockery touched a nerve and burnt like acid. Her chin went up. 'Very funny.' Then the very real mortifying possibility that he wasn't joking hit her. 'Half of it is mine,' she countered observing from the flare of his nostrils that he hadn't liked that. Well, good—she was glad.

The glare on glare, blue on black contest went on for what to Grace felt like a lifetime before he broke the silence.

'Are you going to stay there all day, or do you want a lift?'

She blinked. Of course he hadn't just materialised. He had a car.

'Or there is always the option, painful though it might be, of crawling on your hands and knees.' His expressive brows twitched. 'Up to you.'

Her eyes narrowed. He wasn't as bad as she had imagined he was going to be—he was much, *much* worse!

'I'll take the lift.'

But would she take the hand that was extended to her?

As she looked at those long brown square-tipped fingers, suddenly the crawling option did not seem so terrible…

Theo watched her regard his hand with the enthusiasm most people reserved for a striking snake. He could almost see her swallow and choke on her pride as finally she stretched out her hand to meet his.

His amusement faded as he captured her slender, pale and cold fingers in his and the resultant shock of sexual electricity made him catch his breath and clench his jaw against its unexpected intensity. The only comfort was the knowledge that she felt it too. He saw it in the shocked wide opening of her dramatic blue eyes.

Maybe she didn't like the idea of not being in control of a situation any more than he did?

Or maybe she was filing away the information to use to her advantage?

Breaking the connection the second she was able, Grace wiped her hand on the cotton of her light trousers.

'Thanks,' she mumbled, swaying as she tried to balance precariously on one leg, before she tentatively placed the injured foot lightly on the ground. Being on her feet gave her very little extra advantage—she was still staring at his mid chest area.

'How much damage have you done?' he asked, sounding impatient.

'It's just a sprain.' She didn't add that sprains could often be more troublesome than a break.

'You a doctor?'

'No, a nurse.'

'So you are…'

Grace caught the glint of anger in his dark eyes.

'A credit to your profession, I'm sure,' he drawled nastily.

'My *ex*-profession,' she said, to needle him. And it did.

'I am assuming you do want a lift back?'

She sighed, and responded with tight-lipped formality. 'That would be most kind, Mr…'

'I think under the circumstances you'd better make it Theo—'

'Circumstances?' she queried as he began to walk away.

'Well, we will be living together,' he tossed over his shoulder, smiling to himself.

'Live? With you? But I'm staying here—you live in England.'

She must have read his bio online.

'So do you,' he retorted, his sardonic smile fading into exaggeration as he watched her make her way towards him in a combination of clearly painful shuffles and hopping steps.

He swore under his breath.

She didn't register his intention until he strode across to her and swept her up into his arms with a casual display of strength.

'I am more than capable,' she said, holding herself stiff while finding the depth and the intensity of her awareness of the hardness of his body, the warmth of his skin, deeply unsettling.

'I'd like to arrive sometime this year.'

She gave a sigh of relief when he set her down beside a gleaming monster of a car, opened the passenger door and left her to climb in as he walked around the vehicle to the driver's side.

By the time Grace had managed to clamber awkwardly in he was already seated and waiting.

'It's not far,' she said, and immediately felt stupid.

Like he doesn't know the way!

'Directions?' he said, seeming to enjoy her discomfort.

'Are you serious?' she asked as the car drew onto the road.

'About what? Directions? No, I remember the way.'

'You're not really going to be staying here?'

He flashed her a quick malicious smile. 'It's a big house. I'm sure we'll rub along nicely.'

CHAPTER THREE

ONCE THEY DREW up outside the porticoed entrance to the palazzo he unbelted and without looking at her spoke in a brusque voice, his eyes trained on the building.

'I'll send someone out for you.'

As if she was a parcel, Grace thought indignantly.

Before she could respond, he had vanished inside.

Grace had made her own slow and painful way as far as the shallow flight of steps that led to the massive metal-banded oak door when someone appeared. It was Marta, looking more flushed than normal.

'Oh, you poor thing! How lucky that Theo found you.'

Grace's lips tightened. She made it sound as though he'd been looking for her.

'Sure, he's my hero,' she said, accepting the arm the older woman placed around her waist and obeying the instruction to lean on Marta with gratitude.

Marta seemed oblivious to her sarcasm as she supported Grace up the steps and through the open door.

'We have rung the doctor.'

'That really isn't necessary.'

'Theo said we should.'

'I don't care what *Theo* says. I don't want a doctor.' She saw the hurt, shocked expression on the housekeeper's face and stretched her lips into a smile. 'All a doctor would say is use a cold compress, elevate my leg and take painkillers.'

'Theo—'

Oh, give me strength, Grace thought, biting back a retort as thoughts of a lifetime of living with people who thought they knew better came into play.

'Fine.'

The older woman looked approving, then doubtful when Grace grabbed the edge of the banister on the curving dramatic staircase that dominated the massive hall.

'I'll get someone to carry you.'

'Really, no. I'm fine.' Grace gave a cheery smile to show just how fine she was.

'Well…all right. Isn't it marvellous that Theo is finally home?'

The woman was serious, Grace realised, and there were tears in her eyes.

'Marvellous,' Grace echoed drily, thinking it would have been a hell of a lot more marvellous if he'd been home in time to say goodbye to his father.

Once she had hobbled up and around the first curve of the staircase, and was confident she was out of sight, Grace sat down and shuffled on her bottom the rest of the way up to her first-floor room. It wasn't the most elegant way of doing things, but compared with the alternative of being carried…

The memory of the recent occasion was too fresh to run the risk of a repeat.

An almost tactile image of long brown fingers pressed lightly against her back was so vivid that in the act of pulling herself to her feet with the aid of the banister she almost fell back down again.

When he arrived, the doctor approved the treatment

she had prescribed herself and suggested a supportive bandage when she got out and about again.

After he had left Grace resisted the temptation to say *I told you so* to Marta as the woman fussed around. Actually, if she was honest, being fussed over had a certain novelty value, coming as she did from a family who didn't do cosseting. Tea and sympathy wasn't a thing for the Stewart clan—they just sucked it up and got on with it.

'Such a shame,' Marta said when she'd checked for the umpteenth time that Grace had everything she needed, 'that you can't join Theo for dinner on his first night here.'

'Oh, God, no!' Grace exclaimed without thinking, then moderated her response by looking at her elevated foot, swathed in ice packs. 'It would be too painful,' she said.

'Of course,' the other woman agreed, obviously pacified by her explanation, leaving Grace mystified as to why people who had loved Salvatore appeared so happy to see his hateful son.

How could they forgive him?

Mass hypnosis, maybe?

Grace got her first text from Nic, the estate manager, an hour later. She frowned and sent him a quick one back.

I'm sure it's just a misunderstanding.

Two hours and five texts later it was clear even to Grace, who was not on top of the details, that they were not dealing with a simple misunderstanding. The bank was apparently blocking payments to their suppliers.

That would stop work on the new olive press, because the suppliers were refusing to deliver. And the progress on the renovations of some of the buildings intended to become eco-tourist accommodation had been halted because the delivery of marble from the local quarry had been cancelled.

Both had been pet projects that Salvatore had taken her to see, and there were several other similar projects.

'It's almost as if someone is deliberately sabotaging us,' Nic observed, his frustration at the situation obvious.

Grace had gradually become relaxed around Nic and lowered her defences, mentally filing him as one of the good guys. Maybe it was because his mother was English. She didn't self-censor before she closed her eyes and swore.

'Don't worry, I'll sort it—'

'Just leave it with me and call it a day,' she said. The face she saw reflected back from the mirror on the opposite wall was set and grimly unfamiliar. 'Go home to your family.'

Salvatore, she thought, with an emotional little mental gulp, had always remembered Nic's children's names. For the first time she was struck—*really* struck—by the weight of responsibility that her inheritance had placed on her, the trust that Salvatore had placed *in* her.

'It's late. I'll get back to you in the morning.'

Pushing aside the supper tray that she had not touched—she had just moved the food around to make it look as though she had—Grace kicked off the ice packs and eased herself out of bed, muttering to herself. She fought her way into the robe slung across the bottom of the bed and then, grabbing the silver-handled cane that Marta had produced earlier, paused to swallow a couple of the painkillers before making her way out into the corridor.

She half slid down the stairs, leaning on the smooth banister, too angry to register the discomfort in her ankle. As it turned out, anger was the best anti-inflammatory on the market.

Leaning on the cane, she went in search of her quarry, her anger getting hotter with every step.

When she reached Salvatore's study the door was open. She paused, her heart thudding, and then felt angry at her caution in hesitating. She pushed the door wider and stepped inside. The lights above the portrait of Salvatore's late wife illuminated the painting of the beautiful woman and cast shadows around the empty room.

Her search progressed.

The chandeliers in the drawing room were lit, but it was empty too. She hobbled across to look through the French doors, but there was no tall figure outside in the moonlight.

The smaller salon was empty too.

As Grace turned to walk along the adjoining corridor, she wondered what people would say if they saw her—then laughed, because nobody was going ask her what she was doing. She didn't work here. She wasn't a visitor. She belonged. The palazzo was hers and she was not going to let anyone drive her out.

Because that was what he was trying to do.

She felt stupid for not realising it immediately.

The door to the smaller dining room where she normally ate was open, light spilling out, along with the sound of a piano playing a soft, heart-squeezing melody.

She pushed the door further open, taking in at a glance the half-burnt candles on the table, the bottle of wine, half full, an empty glass—this was definitely a half-empty day—and a plate.

The figure seated at the piano in the corner had his eyes closed, his fingers moving across the keys. He seemed oblivious to her presence.

The music was ineffably sad. It made Grace think of the eyes of that portrait in the study. How long had she been dead? Had her son known her? Grace had never asked, and nobody spoke about her or the circumstances of her death.

She started as the music stopped and his fingers came down with a discordant crash on the keys. The stool scraped the floor as Theo got to his feet, tall and elegant, in a black shirt open at the neck and black tailored trousers.

Grace despised herself for the quivering awareness that she felt like a dark itch under her skin. Although, in her defence, she really couldn't see how any woman could not be sexually aware of him.

'Are you looking for me? For food?' One dark brow lifted to a sardonic angle. 'Or are you here to broker a deal?'

'I'm looking for you,' she said, not lowering her gaze and fixing him with a steady blue stare.

'Should you be on your feet?' Theo asked.

They were, he noticed, bare. And the robe she was wearing was long enough to trip her up, and gave the impression she was floating. Cinched in tight at the waist, it was the same blue as her eyes.

He found himself wondering what, if anything, she had on underneath, and thought about running his fingers through the fine strands of blonde hair that fell around her face like a silky curtain, framing the oval of her face.

It was no longer a mystery why his father had left her

a fortune. It was easy to see how an elderly, vulnerable man would have fallen for the combination of wide-eyed, wholesome sincerity with a core of sensuality.

He felt the sharp stab of desire, and wished he hadn't ended things with Cleo so abruptly. He was neither elderly, nor vulnerable, but celibacy didn't suit him. It never had.

He didn't need a companion, he needed sex—but not with this woman.

'Your concern is touching,' she said, making her voice cold and refusing to be distracted by the way he was staring at her.

He pushed his hands into his pockets and sauntered towards her. She wanted to yell, *Stop there!* but didn't. Because that would have meant she was scared of him—which she wasn't.

Not of him…but maybe of the feelings he was shaking free inside her?

Turning a deaf ear to the idea, she stuck out her chin.

'So now you've found me what do you want to do with me?'

The purred question sent a rush of blood to her cheeks. She mentally sidestepped the issue of what she'd like to do with him the same way she would have an unexplored bomb in her path.

'I've had some phone calls from Nic.' Despite her efforts to stay calm her voice now shook with anger.

'You have your boyfriend well trained.'

'Nic is the estate manager,' she bit back.

His brow momentarily furrowed but then smoothed. 'After my time.'

During his time the estate manager had been Luis who,

even though he must have been a nuisance, had allowed him to tag along with him and his son, who coincidentally had been called Nico…

'He's been manager eight years.'

His smile held no humour. 'Like I said, after my time,' he said, watching her full lips attempt to pinch into an expression of disapproval their plump generosity was not constructed for. The thought of what those lips were perfectly constructed for slipped past his mental shield, and his focus blurred as a testosterone hit made itself felt.

'Nic has not had a good day. There have been issues—several issues. Cancelled deliveries, payments not going through… Do you know anything about that?'

'I am not cut out to be a silent partner,' he said.

He hadn't even tried to deny it.

'Neither—' she flung back '—am I!'

She paused and tried to gather the frayed ends of her fast-unravelling temper.

'I don't understand…why would you do this?' she asked, genuinely mystified by this level of malice.

'Why do you care?' he countered.

'The projects you are attempting to sabotage were important to your father.' Scanning his face for any sign that her words had had any impact on him, she saw only a flinty stare for her troubles. 'Everyone is working so hard to make them happen because of your father. I—I promised.'

Biting her quivering lip and blinking hard, she opened her mouth to continue and then stopped, a look of horrified suspicion spreading across her face.

'Is that why you're doing this? Out of spite? He's dead,' she reminded him, deciding she had imagined his flinch.

'You can't hurt him any more. Why did you hate him so much?'

The words were out before she could stop them—not that he appeared to register the question.

'The point isn't why…it's more the fact that I *can* do this.'

It did not escape her notice that he didn't deny her suggestion.

'Just as you can stop me selling off the land,' he continued heavily, '*I* can stop your little projects.'

He paused, watching her face grow pale and her blue eyes fly wide with a display of shock that might have been convincing if he hadn't known that she had smiled his father out of a fortune.

'Have you actually read any of the figures?' he asked her. 'Or did you just sign off on them?'

'Of course I read them. I'm not an idiot!' Grace flared indignantly. 'And if you had bothered to do your research,' she bit back, her scorn equal to his, 'you'd know it makes sound financial sense to pay those so-called *inflated* prices. Yes, I am aware that you can source marble for a quarter of the price we are paying, but it would be an inferior product. And, most importantly—'

Her lips tightened in annoyance as Theo cut across her before she could complete her explanation.

'I suppose you're on top of the projected labour costs for this—what was it?—olive press? Who is it pocketing the money on that rip-off? It isn't even very inventive.'

Grace had now gone paper-white with temper. 'You can cast slurs on me if you want—I don't care. But the people who work here deserve more respect. They deserve more than to be pawns in this childish payback.

You can stamp your foot because you don't get your own way, but don't libel people who are just doing their job.'

She folded her arms across her chest and flung him a look of simmering contempt.

'Do you know how *pathetic* that is?'

Grace saw the shock on his face at her contempt, but the shock of being ripped into that way quickly morphed into anger that turned his dark, flinty eyes into black ice.

'You will not speak to me in that manner!' he grated.

'Wanna bet?' she drawled, too angry to be cautious in the face of his white-lipped fury. 'And how about a few more facts for you? As I was saying about the marble—' she flung the word out like a challenge '—agreed, you *could* get it cheaper. But *this* marble is sourced locally, and it will give the local supplier and in turn local tradesmen jobs. It is authentic to the restoration, there will be no air miles involved getting it on site, and even if *you* don't care about that, other people do. You understand money?' she went on. 'Fine. Then you'll recognise good marketing. Those labour costs you think are too high? Those men you dismiss? They are highly skilled stonemasons…they're artisans, local talent. It's all about using skills that could be lost and the people who will stay in those restored buildings. If even half of them understand that, *like* that, it will be worth it, and long term we will recoup the costs!'

By the end of her tirade his anger had turned into amazement. Not just at her knowledge, but her apparent passion.

Could it be genuine?

He dismissed the possibility. With a woman like her there would always be an angle.

'How the hell do you know all this?' he asked.

* * *

Grace took a deep, steadying breath, feeling shaky in the aftermath of her emotional outburst. A lifetime with her charming, infuriating family had taught her that being confrontational was not a solution, and she prided herself on the fact that these days she reacted to provocation with calm reason.

But then she had never encountered Theo and his sneering until now.

'I'm interested,' she responded, struggling belatedly to lower the emotional temperature of the conversation. 'Because passion can be contagious, and your father was passionate about these projects.'

A slow, sad smile spread across her face.

'He had so much knowledge and enthusiasm. He was so— Oh, God!'

She broke off as her chest heaved and a sob bubbled up. She pressed her hand to her mouth to hold it in.

'He was such a lovely man and I miss him,' she mumbled.

He could have destroyed the idealised image she had apparently built up of his father in one brutal sentence.

So why didn't he?

Because he told himself it didn't matter what this woman's relationship with his father was—or rather had been. It didn't matter if she was genuine or a brilliant actress. He needed to focus on the fact that she was here and she stood in his way. Anything else was a distraction.

'Well, he's not here. But I am. And a few tears and an appeal to my eco-credentials are not going to work on me. If you want my signature you have to give me sound financial reasons.'

At the brutal words her head came up. Eyes still shining with unshed tears, she flicked her hair back and glared at him.

'I thought I had.'

Damn her.

She had.

'You're actually a horrible man!'

Not very original, but indisputably accurate.

How, she wondered, remembering the music she had heard him produce, could someone so cold and cruel play the piano with such emotional intensity?

'You have no idea how wounded I am by that.' He produced another of his uniquely unpleasant smiles from a mouth that was uniquely sensual. 'I thought someone in your job needed professional distance. Do you get broken up every time a patient dies? Or only over the ones who have left you a fortune?'

She regarded him with simmering dislike bright in her blue eyes. 'Actually, yes, I do struggle with retaining my detachment.'

And it did take a toll on her personally, that inability to switch off after a long day when she'd become emotionally invested in a patient.

'But I'm a good nurse despite that.'

Though she knew there had been times when the objectivity that had eluded her would have made her a better nurse and also made her life a lot easier.

Her chest lifted in a silent sigh as she struggled for some of that elusive objectivity now.

'Not that I expect you to be particularly interested. Just as I'm not interested in whether you are naturally unpleasant or you're simply working at it. But I am as-

suming that you believe if you're unpleasant enough…
if you throw enough roadblocks in my way… I'll just
roll over?'

She raised her well-defined feathery brows, despite
the fact that her internal temperature had shot into the
red danger zone, and she forced her blue stare to hold his
for several cool moments before the tug of his mouth got
the better of her.

That sculpted, sensual outline was exerting an un-
healthy and disturbing fascination for her.

'I'm staying put,' she told him. 'You can be as vile
and unpleasant as you like. I won't allow you to destroy
Palazzo della Stellato.'

Theo reared back his dark head in shock as she went
on the offensive. This was not going as he had planned.

The knot of frustration in his chest tightened. There
was not a shred of compromise in the challenging blue
gaze that so coolly held his. The pulse kicking wildly
at the base of her throat and her clenched fists were the
only outward indication that she was not as calm as she
appeared.

'What is your problem, anyway?' she demanded. 'Why
do you want to destroy everything? Your father only ever
said what a marvellous person you are…he was proud
of you!'

He gave a smile of brilliant insincerity as he took a
step towards her…

The equally strong instincts that were urging her to step
towards him and retreat cancelled each other out, and
Grace stayed where she was, her feet glued to the spot,
her heart thudding painfully in her chest…

* * *

'You have no idea how much I am looking forward to more cosy chats like this, *cara*,' he drawled, veiling his eyes with long lashes, concealing the flash of shock in their dark depths as he realised that the long fingers of his right hand seemed to be acting on some automatic setting and had found their way to her jaw.

A frown flickered across his brow. His intention had been to break the contact—drop his hand as if her smooth skin stung—but before he could act on that intention he felt the quiver that ran through her body, felt the heat of her blue stare as she looked up at him, her breath coming in a series of quick, shallow little pants that lifted her breasts against the blue of her thin robe.

Theo prided himself on his logic, and on one level, separate from the sense-numbing streak of testosterone heat that immobilised him, his brain was functioning perfectly logically as it analysed the situation.

Yes, there was sexual attraction, a curiosity that was the elephant in the room. But it was a distraction, and unaddressed it would stay there, getting in the way. The best and most efficient way of dealing with it would be to stop wondering how she tasted and find out.

Kiss her and get it over with.

Kill the curiosity stone-dead and move on.

Startled blue eyes met his the moment before his head dipped...

Grace almost literally fell into his kiss.

The hand that slid to her waist was the only thing keeping her on her feet.

And then there was a slow, sensual, ever-deepening exploration as her lips moved across hers, his tongue probed, his tongue tasted...

Breathing hard, Theo drew back a second before his last shred of sanity was obliterated in the blast of heat that had been generated between them.

Grace forced her eyelids open, her gaze drifting to his face. She glimpsed emotions in his dark eyes that made her stomach muscles tighten painfully.

'Oh, Grace, here you are.'

Marta, oblivious to the atmosphere you could have sliced with a knife, bustled into the room, slim and efficient, her movements as neat as the hair coiled on her head.

Grace was so relieved she could have kissed the woman.

She had kissed the man.

She hadn't known kisses could be like that.

She really wished she still didn't, she decided.

Without looking up at him, she took a careful step away.

'If I'd known you wanted to eat down here I would have—'

'No,' Grace interrupted, in a slightly breathless voice. 'I just wanted to stretch my legs...get a glass of milk.'

Learn a few things about raw sexual attraction I would have been happier staying ignorant of.

'You should have rung down,' the woman chided, like a sleek, elegant mother hen.

'I should,' Grace agreed meekly.

She was thinking, *I should have done lots of things... or rather should* not *have done one specific thing.*

I don't suppose you'd give me a hand back to my room?' She looked down at her foot and didn't have to pretend to feel the throb that was reasserting itself.

'Of course.'

Grace was very aware of the dark eyes that followed her as she accepted Marta's supportive arm.

CHAPTER FOUR

To CLEAR HIS head after a restless night, Theo decided to go for a run. Without considering his route, he found himself on a path he remembered from his youth. It had once been worn down by his own feet. Now it was overgrown. At one point oak saplings had taken root, forcing him to make a short detour.

It would need to be cleared…

He almost immediately deleted this addition to his mental to-do list. It wouldn't need to be cleared because he wasn't staying. There wouldn't be other mornings when he ran to clear his head after a sleepless night.

It had been a mistake to come. But everyone made mistakes. The trick, he told himself, was living in the moment and never looking back, even though the uncomfortable voice in his head pointed out that looking back was what he was guilty of.

He upped his pace, even though the ground underfoot was uneven and the path almost indistinguishable from the wild area it cut through. The mingled scent of the sea and the wild herbs underfoot filled his nostrils as he pushed on, losing the thread of his thought for a moment as he remembered the throaty little rasp deep in her throat as his tongue had encountered hers.

He narrowed his eyes as he began to run into the morning sun, dazzled for a second as he picked up his thought. The thing about mistakes was to own them and not repeat them…not beat yourself up over them.

He had, he told himself, acknowledged that the kiss was a mistake, and not one he was going to repeat.

But, *Dio*, it had been enjoyable!

Grace had not objected when her breakfast had been served in her room—actually, her ankle gave her the perfect excuse to stay there. She was briefly tempted, but then felt ashamed. She was not going to run away. *She* had done nothing wrong.

The implication that he *had*, and she was simply some innocent victim, brought a self-derisory furrow to her brow.

In her defence, Grace had not initiated the kiss. But the helpless plea really didn't work, and it made her impatient with herself. She hadn't exactly fought him off with a stick, she told herself scornfully. When she played the moment out in her head—which she had done more times than she could count—she could not have sworn, hand on heart, that she had not met him halfway.

The reality was he was the most *male* male she had ever encountered—and some part of her had responded to all that maleness. It was a weakness she hadn't known she possessed.

Was she going to hide?

The answer came as she unfolded her legs and pushed aside the breakfast tray balanced on the bed. She headed for the bathroom, noticing as she peeled off her nightdress that her ankle was feeling a lot better this morning. It was stiff, sore and colourful, certainly, but it took her weight without a problem, and she would be able to move around—albeit not with exactly fluid grace.

Her pain, she thought bitterly, was in her head. Where Theo had taken up residence!

The rebellion took her as far as the shower, before her inability to make a mess kicked in. She knew someone might be coming in to clean her room the moment she left, but in Grace's mind you cleared up your own stuff.

The nightdress was placed in the hamper supplied for the purpose and she stepped into the shower—which was hot enough to make her step back before she hastily lowered the temperature.

She rarely applied make-up in the morning, and the fact she even thought about it today annoyed her. She was not out to impress anyone. It was enough to select a pair of cut-off jeans past their best, and a tee shirt that definitely said *I am not trying*.

Salvatore, always immaculately dressed, had breakfasted with her in the small dining room, selecting his breakfast from the silver dome-covered dishes along the sideboard. After one very uncomfortable lonely breakfast there after his death, Grace had opted to take her breakfast in the kitchen, sometimes with Marta.

Maybe, she mused, the old arrangement would be reinstated now Theo was in residence?

Grace had no intention of finding out. She headed for the kitchen, hoping to find Marta there.

She hovered a little around the door when it occurred to her that if Marta was there she might not be alone. God, it was too early to face that smug, supercilious smirk.

Bracing her slender shoulders, she stepped inside and found the room empty. Her shoulders sagged and she despised the fact she was relieved—which was ridiculous.

She didn't have to hide away. This was her house and it was about time she acted like it. There was nothing Theo would enjoy more than seeing her creeping around.

That defiance—or was it nervous apprehension?—gave her an appetite, and despite the light breakfast she had already eaten in her room Grace found herself unable to resist the smell of freshly baked bread.

Just one slice, she told herself, heading for the pantry—a massive slate-shelved space as big as her parents' spacious kitchen.

She took a crusty loaf from the stone jar and smothered it with a generous layer of butter, before spooning some honey on top and heading with her coffee back to the table. She was on her second bite when the door was flung open and a figure dressed in black shorts and a sweat-soaked vest that clung to an impressively muscled torso burst into the room.

Grace's anticipation of that second bite vanished and the honey slid onto the plate.

Standing there, his hands braced on his muscular thighs, it was a couple of moment before Theo straightened up and noticed her. He made a noise in his throat that might have indicated anything from revulsion to pleasure.

Grace deleted the latter possibility.

'Good run?' she asked brightly, trying and failing to ignore her physical reaction to him standing there in a vest, his skin steaming moistly.

In sharp tailoring it had been obvious he had an impressive body. Without it just how impressive became uncomfortably clear.

The muscle definition in his upper body was powerful, without being overly bulky. His legs were impossibly long, his hips narrow, his thighs powerful and dusted very lightly with dark hair that showed against the gleam of his skin.

Her stomach went into a series of painful and shaming somersaults and she let it, without feeling a shred of self-contempt. She was human and female. Even if he was a horrible man, with no redeeming features.

He stood there a moment, taking deep breaths that lifted his chest and sucked in the muscles of his flat belly, perfectly clear beneath the damp, clinging fabric. He might be horrible...but, God, he was hot and then some!

'Coffee?' she said casually, hitching one ankle over the other, hoping he'd say no because her knees were visibly shaking.

Grace was not thinking of anything above her knees—it would be too embarrassing to examine in detail what was happening there.

After slinging her a look that wasn't friendly, but left her heart thudding, even though she didn't know why—a lot of her reactions to this man remained inexplicable—she watched as he walked across to the walk-in fridge, from where he extracted a jug of water. He filled a glass, swallowing the contents as he moved across to the old-fashioned range where a percolator bubbled.

He turned to Grace. 'Did you sleep well?'

'No.'

He sketched something approximating a smile that left his heavily lashed eyes dark and dangerous.

'Me neither.'

Reaching to the shelf above, he took a mug from the row and filled it.

She tried to avert her eyes from the taut, rippling

movement of muscles in his shoulders and back. She was still staring when he turned around.

'Good run?' she asked.

'You already asked me.'

'I was being polite.' She bit back the childish addition that good manners were something he clearly knew nothing about.

'You sound nervous,' he said, watching her form under the sweep of his crazily long lashes.

Rather than deny it, she met his eyes levelly.

'Actually, I'm finding this situation quite…uncomfortable.' She felt the need to take another deep breath before adding, 'You own half the estate, and perhaps, technically,' she conceded, 'I should have consulted you before I made any decisions. Last night we left things unresolved, but to be honest—'

The sports watch he wore on his wrist caught the light, glinting metallically against his golden skin as he interrupted her with a sweeping gesture of one hand. 'By all means, let us be honest.'

Her lips tightened. 'You've not made any contact beyond trying to buy me out, and I didn't think you'd be interested in the day-to-day running of the estate,' she flung back.

'I'm not.'

Annoyance flared in her blue eyes. 'So you decided to be awkward just for the hell of it,' she responded, averting her eyes abruptly.

The rippling motion of the muscles in his brown throat worked as he swallowed the black coffee and created some rippling of her own inside her. He was one of those people who could make the most mundane action fascinating…

'So you want me to sign off on these projects?'

Her eyes narrowed. 'That depends on the price of your co-operation.'

Her eyes had flown to his face. They sank again now, and she felt the heat of shame rise in her cheeks as she thought of that kiss—a price that many women, she was sure, would be happy to pay.

'Hard negotiator...'

Her blue gaze lifted and her long lashes fanned across her cheeks as she loosed a peal of infectious laughter, thinking of what her family would make of that statement. Her family who, with an eye-roll, called her sentimental and a soft touch on all the occasions when it didn't suit them that she was.

'That's funny?'

She had a good laugh, he decided. Surprisingly deep and robust. It was actually bigger than she was.

Her delicacy made him feel like a bully, which he didn't like, and yet he had the impression she would have been offended at the idea he needed to make allowances for her physical fragility or her sex.

More tragic than funny, Grace decided with a noncommittal shrug. Because the truth was she loved her family, and she was more amused by their assumptions than crushed.

It suddenly occurred to her how at home Theo would feel with her family. They were all over-achieving thoroughbreds who would have a lot in common, whereas she was just a—

'Shetland pony.'

Oh, God, I said that out loud!

Her features froze.

'Pardon.'

'I was just—thinking of—breeding Shetland ponies… the miniature ones,' she improvised.

'You ride?'

She knew he did. There was a framed photo of him as a boy: skinny, all scratched legs and thick wild hair, as he sat bareback astride what looked like an excitable grey.

There was still a lot of leg, but nowadays they were muscled columns. She lifted her eyes from the hair-roughened surface she had been staring at, struggling to see the coltish boy with the mop of tangled hair and the cute gaps in his teeth in the man before her, who was the epitome of raw maleness.

'One lesson and I fell off. I didn't get back on.'

'A mistake.'

She shrugged. 'Shetlands are more my size,' she retorted, having almost convinced herself that she wasn't lying. She really was discovering her hidden depths.

'So you're afraid of horses?'

'No, just of heights.'

'Good to know you have your weaknesses.'

She got to her feet, ignoring the gleam of speculation in his dark eyes. Was he wondering how he could exploit her weakness for men who looked like him? Her eyes drifted to his mouth. Men who kissed like him?

Abruptly she veiled her eyes with her lashes and hid behind the wings of her pale hair.

'We have things to discuss,' he said.

She rolled her eyes and shook back her hair. As if he was telling her something she didn't already know. It had actually been a lot better when their conversations had taken place through the intermediary of lawyers.

They did have things to discuss, but it would be a lot more comfortable from her point of view if any discussion took place when he had more clothes on.

She wouldn't have put it past him to have engineered this situation. Actually, she wouldn't put *anything* past him!

'I have plans for this morning,' she said.

His expression was momentarily bemused, as if no one had ever given him the brush-off.

They probably hadn't.

'Plans?'

'I am meeting with Nic, the estate manager, to discuss—'

'Fine. I'll join you.'

Her face fell, alarm widening her eyes and sending her stomach into a sickly dive. He didn't have to say anything or be objectionable. His presence alone would ruin the casual chat over coffee with Nic, who didn't patronise her, or make her feel unqualified, or make her stomach quiver.

'That really won't be—'

She might as well have saved her breath. He was already moving towards the door.

'I can be with you…' A glance at his watch. 'When? Where?' he said casually. 'I'll be there.'

'That r-really isn't—'

He closed down her stuttered protest with a sardonic look. 'What's on the agenda?'

'*Agenda*?' she parroted. 'It's not a board meeting…just a chat and a coffee.'

Although her jangling nerves suggested more coffee would not be a good idea.

He sketched a quick smile and drew a hand down his jaw, drawing her eyes to the dark shadow he hadn't shaved yet.

'Fine. I'll ditch the tie.'

She had *wanted* him to take an interest, and yet now he was the situation seemed more worrying, somehow. But then maybe it was her own antipathy stopping her from viewing this as a good thing, making her suspicious when there was no hidden subtext to read.

She thought there probably was plenty of hidden subtext, but she decided to take a more positive approach. This could be an opportunity to soften Theo's negativity about his inheritance, appeal to his emotional side.

He *must* have had some affection for the place where he had grown up, she reasoned. If she could only reawaken those feelings...

His hand on the wall beside the door, he felt his cynical amusement at the panic written on her face become curiosity as panic faded into resolve.

Catching himself wondering what had put it there, he levered himself off the wall. He was really not interested in her thought processes, or what made her tick...what thoughts were going on in that beautiful head.

He had already admitted that their chemistry—animal attraction, sex, whatever you liked to call it—made total indifference impossible, but he was not about to look beyond the beautiful surface.

Grace arrived at Nic's office before Theo, but only by moments. There was no chance for her to explain to Nic her idea of playing the nostalgia card before Theo walked in, his hair still wet from the shower, his chiselled jaw clean. Along with the chip on his shoulder he seemed to be carrying an almost electrical charge.

Her relief that he was wearing more clothes only lasted

a fraction of a second. He was still more handsome than any man had a right to be. From under the sweep of her lashes she took in the details of his outfit: pale blue poplin shirt and grey jeans, a dark belt securing them over narrow hips. He was minus the tie, as promised, and the small vee of deep gold skin at the base of his throat made her stomach muscles quiver.

Before she could gather herself enough to react, Nic was stepping past her, his hand outstretched and a grin pulling his mouth upwards.

'Nico?' Smiling, Theo was moving forward. 'I thought it couldn't be you... The only Nic I know would be as far away from here as he could get!'

Nic clasped the hand extended to him and responded in a burst of warm, fluid Italian before sliding seamlessly back into English.

Grace's mouth opened as she watched the two men exchange a handshake and a masculine thump on the back. Her indignation grew as she watched them—she had been put the other side of the conspiratorial divide.

'I was going to be a rock star, Theo, but things change—people change.'

'Not everything,' Theo said, his face shuttering.

'When Dad got ill I came back...initially to help out.'

'And you stayed?'

Nic nodded and lifted his shoulders in an expressive Latin shrug. '*Si*. And then, after Dad died, Mum moved back to England to be near her twin sister.'

'You weren't tempted to join her?'

'Salvatore asked me to take the job on a permanent basis and, well... I stayed. Got married, had a baby...or actually two.'

Theo, who had stiffened slightly at his father's name,

smiled in response to this update. 'Congratulations.' Then his smile faded and his eyes twitched into a straight line above his patrician nose. 'I'm sorry about your father.'

'It was his heart. There had been issues for some time.'

'Sorry, I didn't know.'

Grace thought it was about time to remind them she existed. 'You two know one another? Well, obviously you do,' she said, scrolling through her memory. Had she expressed her opinion on Theo's character a little too robustly to Nic? 'You never said?'

She'd addressed the comment to Nic, but it was Theo who responded, his lips quirking at the indignation in her voice.

'When you spoke of "Nic" it didn't occur to me that it was Nico...'

He pushed aside the kick of guilt. Far away, it had been easy for him to forget the people whose lives would change when the palazzo and estate changed hands. Being here...

His eyes narrowed. This was not a reason not to divest himself of the past. There was every chance that the new owners would keep Nic and the other staff on after the sale—in fact, he'd make it a condition of sale.

'Theo and I hung out during the holidays when we were kids. I could tell you some stories,' Nic said.

'A threat that scares me,' Theo drawled, a smile in his voice.

It was the first time she had seen him smile for real, and there was enough charm and warmth to tame a tiger and melt an iceberg.

'But remember I also can tell some stories,' he told Nic.

Watching him, she thought he seemed almost human, almost touchable…

She looked away, banished the thought, and reminded herself that he was hard and callous, and that without her and Marta his father would have died alone.

Lost in her own condemnatory tangle of thoughts, she didn't immediately realise that a chair had been pulled out for her—a courtesy that was Nic's, not Theo's. After a slight hesitation she joined the two men, quickly feeling excluded once more as they began to talk, slipping unconsciously from Italian to English and back.

But not because they were reminiscing. It was all estate business.

Grace had worked hard to get her head around the subject, but a lot of what they were now discussing was way above her.

She was sure that Nic was not deliberately excluding her, but Theo's motives were far less clear-cut, and giving him the benefit of the doubt was a long way off—a distant speck on the horizon.

If Theo was trying to make her feel like an outsider he was succeeding, she decided, resenting the way that he automatically took charge of the discussion and—she had to admit—asked far too knowledgeable questions.

Having slid down in her chair a little, nursing a cup of coffee between her hands, she suddenly pulled herself up, recognising in her muddled thoughts a recurring strand of self-pity.

She was sulking—a fault she thought she had cured.

This wasn't about *them*, it was about *her*, and her lingering sense of inferiority. She might not be as brilliant and beautiful as the rest of her family, and her legs might not be as long, but they worked and so did her brain.

She couldn't blame Nic for being relieved to be talking to someone he didn't have to explain every other sentence to, and Theo was probably enjoying seeing her cold-shouldered out. The way she had been a thousand times before, over the dinner table at home, when everyone got very intellectual or political.

She was playing right into his hands by crawling back in her shell.

'Do you mind running that past me one more time?' she asked. 'I didn't quite...'

Nic flushed and looked guilty. Theo didn't look guilty, but that was no surprise. It was already a given that the man was not capable of feeling guilt.

'Sorry, Grace,' Nic said. 'I was just saying that last year's freak weather affected the olive harvest, but we have great hopes that this year will be a bumper crop.'

'Great—you can put that in your prospectus for potential customers.' She turned to Theo. 'Did Nic tell you we have ambitious plans to expand? Several high-class retail outlets have been showing an interest.'

Theo's brows lifted. 'That detail is good news. As we're selling as a going concern, all details are important.'

A going concern?

That was the first she had heard of it. Her impression had been that the estate would be cut up piecemeal. That getting rid of it quickly was more important than profit. But conscious of Nic, who was looking uncomfortable, she didn't challenge Theo on this.

Instead she responded by simply saying, 'Not *we*.' She blew a feathery wisp of fair hair out of her eyes. '*I'm* not selling.'

Maintaining a smile, even though her cheeks were

aching with the effort, she was happy to see her words grated on the intended recipient as she got to her feet.

'If you'll excuse me? I'll leave you both to catch up.'

Spine like steel, she turned and walked out of the room. Indignation took her clear of the building, leaving behind a silence that for one man she knew would be awkward and for the other…

Remembering the glint in his dark eyes, she shook her head. She couldn't figure out what Theo was thinking—which for her peace of mind was probably for the best.

Despite this silent observation she didn't feel philosophical. She felt frustrated—so frustrated she wanted to scream. Instead she swore softly and fluently under her breath as she walked along the path through the expanse of tall Italian cypress and oak, down the rocky incline towards the beach.

She paused to rest her ankle a few times en route to the horseshoe of sand hemmed in by soft waves that hit the shore with a hiss, dragging fine stones back out as it made its relentless advance and retreat.

The doctor had instructed her to use her ankle and not favour it, but maybe he hadn't meant her to use it quite this much, she decided, wincing as she stepped on a rock half concealed in the sand. The heat was building, but she had been scrupulous about applying her usual factor fifty, so she peeled off her linen shirt and sat down beside it.

She wasn't worried about burning.

CHAPTER FIVE

SHE COULD HAVE yelled aloud now, without anyone coming to rescue her, but the sound of the waves had taken the edge off her jagged feelings as she sat in the sand and focused on the hiss of the waves. Until one wave tickled her toes and she realised that the tide had come in while she had been sitting there.

She got to her feet and slung her folded shirt higher up the sand, then stood hands on hips surveying her surroundings: the turquoise water…the white sand. Despite her claim that she had somewhere else to be, actually Grace didn't. She had grown to love this place with a kind of yearning that went beyond logic, but she couldn't feel it was *hers*. It would take more than words on paper to make that feel real.

She was shocked by how much she *wanted* it to be real…*wanted* to belong to this place. How could Theo want to throw all this away?

The fact remained that she was half owner in name only, and Theo's appearance had pushed that knowledge home. He had rejected the palazzo and all it involved, but he *belonged* here and she didn't. The fact that he didn't want the place seemed irrelevant—certainly to the people who lived and worked on the estate. His absence and his neglect of his father seemed to be forgotten and forgiven.

But then, unlike Nic and Marta, they didn't know he was trying to sell the place out from under them—well, she assumed they didn't. It wasn't information she had shared with anyone else, and she was assuming he wouldn't be taking out a full-page ad any time soon.

No matter what rumours might be floating around, there was no question that his appearance was viewed with approval—a real Ranieri at the helm. His appearance had changed everything. Like Nic had, people would automatically look to him now—but she was prepared for it.

It wasn't as if she didn't have experience of being overlooked. Her family weren't the shy, retiring type. When they walked into a room they immediately became the centre of attention, and they all thrived on it.

Whereas Grace genuinely avoided attention. She was not an 'if you've got it flaunt it' sort of person. Glancing down at her modest breasts, she grinned and thought that was just as well, because in some areas she didn't have much to flaunt!

'Non-threatening', her mother had called them when she had complained. At sixteen, Grace had not found this a selling point, but now she recognised that there were plus points—especially on a day like today. She was able to go comfortably braless without worrying about the bounce factor, which was rather nice.

She gave a soft chuckle. While not being resentful about being overlooked, and even though she knew she'd never have the opportunity, it amused her to imagine Theo walking into a room where her family were being their dazzling selves. For once it would be good to see them ignored. Because while her family were dazzling,

Theo had that extra undefinable factor that took dazzle to a whole other level.

Her smile faded. Theo would always *belong*—and not just here. She was willing to bet that he had never felt like an outsider anywhere...the person who never really fitted, the one who was always a disappointment.

He had rejected his family, not the other way around.

Grace immediately felt a stab of guilt. Her family hadn't rejected her...they'd tried to include her, made excuses for her.

We think she might have dyslexia.

Because a dyslexic child was preferable to one who got a B minus in English and maths.

When had she stopped trying?

She frowned at the question that had popped into her head. She liked to leave the past where it was. Besides, there hadn't been a moment...more a gradual realisation that she was never going to do anything good enough to impress her family. So she had embraced her role as the odd one out and consequently been a lot happier.

Why me?

For the thousandth time she asked herself what Salvatore's motivation had been when he'd divided his estate this way. Had he expected her to—?

She gave a despairing sigh as her head dropped to her chest.

When she lifted it, she wriggled the toes of her injured foot in the water, extending her leg to examine it. The bruising was coming out, but the swelling had almost vanished. It seemed possible to walk a little more before she turned back.

It wasn't until she turned that she realised how far she had walked along the shoreline. This was an area she had not previously explored. She glanced at the unusual rock formation to her right. Curiosity sparked, she began to wade towards the place where the rock protruded from the sea. The fork-like formation brought back Salvatore's voice as he had described a grotto—a magical-sounding cave you could walk into at low tide, with a cavernous crystalline roof that glowed green when the water entered.

She edged along the rock, reaching the point where the rock indented, revealing an entrance, the curved portal of which was exactly the way Salvatore had described it. The water here was only ankle-deep, so she figured there could be no harm in just looking inside. She would explore properly when the tide was out.

Theo did not linger long after Grace had left. The conversation with his old friend had left him feeling restless. Nico belonged to another life—one he had left behind. Yet it had been surprisingly easy to pick up the threads of their shared experiences as though the intervening years had not existed.

But it wasn't this that occupied his thoughts…it was the look of hurt he had seen in Grace's blue eyes when his gaze had drifted her way.

Why should it bother him?

He didn't want her to feel wanted. The whole idea was to isolate her, make her life uncomfortable.

Her expression reminded him of a kid at school—the one who had never fitted in. The one who had been bullied until Theo had made it known he was under this protection.

Her look had made Theo feel as if he was one of the bullies.

Annoyed by his irrational response, he took the cliff path back to the house. He needed to contact his office. Frustration rushed over him. He needed not to be here. He needed not to have old wounds reopened.

At first he thought it was a bird that he could hear, and then he realised it was a phone ringing. After a moment he located the sound to a small, indeterminate pile of clothing on the beach. Rather than following the pathway down, he scaled the cliff, muscle memory kicking in as he found the footholds he remembered from his youth.

As he approached the pile the phone began to ring again, beneath the haphazardly discarded pair of sandals and a white linen shirt. Grace's. He remembered it being open and baggy. Without it her fair skin would burn.

He felt a deep flutter in his belly as he grabbed the shirt almost angrily. Without thinking, he lifted it to his face, inhaling the fragrance clinging to the fabric before he realised what he was doing.

With a curse, he dropped it and scanned the sand and the sea beyond. There was no sign of its sweet-smelling owner. Then his narrowed eyes caught the darker indentations in the sand near the water line. There might have been other footsteps, but the tide was coming in fast.

The phone started ringing again, shrill and insistent, but this time it cut off quickly and a moment later it pinged.

As he picked it up, he could see the words.

Assuming you have seen the scurrilous article...?

He read the name of a tabloid that specialised in the scurrilous.

If you'd planned to come to your sister's awards ceremony next week maybe rethink. This is her night...

The rest of the message was hidden, fading from the screen as Theo, his expression thoughtful, stared at the blank screen.

He had not seen the article referenced, but the name of the tabloid made it hard not to guess the theme: *Young nurse left a fortune by elderly patient.*

His jaw tightened as he swore under his breath. The timing and the leak had Rollo's fingerprints all over.

He could only assume that planting the story was Rollo's idea of helping the cause—showing initiative.

He scored a line in the sand with his foot...a line that Rollo wouldn't have recognised if he'd fallen over it.

If the guy had not gone off-piste this way...if he had run it past him—

Theo blinked, an expression of shock spreading across his lean face as it hit him. If Rollo had run the idea past him twenty-four hours ago he would have likely told him to go ahead.

The furrow in his brow deepened as he realised that during that time his plans had shifted and realigned in his head in a way he wasn't comfortable with. It was as inexplicable as the prickle of guilt that he was experiencing.

He replayed the message in his head, which he presumed must have come from one of Grace's family members. Unless there was a supportive section in the latter portion of the text it would seem that Grace wasn't about to receive any tea and sympathy from her nearest and dearest. Which could mean she was a repeat offender, who had embarrassed them previously, or they were heartless bastards.

Or none of the above, he added, aware that he was guilty of the sort of speculation he usually frowned on.

Either way, it would seem she didn't have a support network to fall back on—which should have made him feel happier than it actually did.

He wandered towards the place where he had spotted the footprints, but they were already being sucked into the swirls of water before vanishing like—*like she had vanished.*

He froze, belatedly aware of where he was standing.

A moment later he was not standing. He had kicked off his trainers and was wading into the water. It felt like tortuously slow progress, and Theo felt a surge of relief when he was able to kick away from the bottom and swim.

Head down, in seconds he'd made it through the iconic arch and surfaced, treading water, thinking perhaps his reaction had been an instinct too far. He searched the cavernous cathedral-like interior that appeared to be lit by a deep, subterranean green reflected off the water.

Almost immediately he saw her, sitting like some sort of stranded mermaid—albeit with pale, slender legs—on a stone shelf.

A stranded mermaid in cut-offs and a clinging vest top.

His relief morphed into anger—the logic-cancelling variety.

Cleaving through the water with a few strong strokes, he brought himself up to her side and floated there, treading water.

Grace blinked at the flood of angry, fluid Italian—which, despite her recent lessons, was utterly incomprehensible. The emotion behind the flow of words from the dark-haired figure floating below her, however, did not need translation.

'Hello.'

It sounded so stupid she began to laugh, the tension and fear of the last few minutes evaporating into a weird euphoria.

The speed with which the water had risen when she had emerged from her awed contemplation of the cave had shocked her, but she hadn't panicked. Instead she had escaped the tug of water that was driving her deeper into the cave by dragging herself up onto a rocky ledge that ran along the side. Of course it had quickly become clear that she'd have been better off panicking and swimming out straight away, hoping for the best, before the swirling water got scarily high.

Now the strong surge of the current made it unlikely she'd even make it through the arch into the open sea.

When Theo had appeared she had almost decided that her best hope—her only hope—would be to swim for it before the opening was totally covered by the incoming tide.

'You think this is funny?'

She totally appreciated his outrage. She also appreciated, even at a moment like this, how incredible he looked. His dark hair was clinging to his skull, to the perfect bones of his perfect face, and the sybaritic angles and planes were defined against his wet, olive-toned skin.

'Not at all,' she soothed.

He didn't seem soothed. He looked hotly furious.

'You—'

She could almost see him bite his tongue, and his next words were spaced evenly and enunciated with elaborate calm.

'Can you swim?'

'Of course I can swim.' Otherwise she'd be…well, dead. 'I'm not a great swimmer, but I don't sink—not straight away,' she admitted.

Theo cleared his throat and crafted his civilised response with the utmost difficulty. There would be plenty of time to tell her what he thought of her later. The present problem was what he needed to focus on.

'Right, you do what you can. Let's get out of here.'

He glanced over his shoulder towards the exit that had grown even smaller while he had wasted precious seconds noticing how her small, pointed breasts with their thrusting nipples looked under the clinging wet fabric.

As if he was judging a wet tee shirt competition.

Silently deriding himself for his distraction, he urged her with an imperative gesture to join him.

Hands pressed to the rocky surface, about to lower herself back into the salty water, she paused. 'Just to check… you can swim quite well?'

She knew it was a silly question even as she voiced it. He would do everything well. He was not a man who screamed mediocrity.

Normally perfect people irritated her, but on this occasion his perfection was comforting.

Theo angled her a look through the drops of water trembling on his dark lashes. '*Very* well,' he said, with no display of false modesty, reaching up a hand to support her as she dropped down.

She was conscious as she did so that she was shaking, fine tremors that rippled through her entire body.

'Right, stay close.'

'I will—' she began, then choked as salty water blocked her airway and she spluttered unattractively.

What is wrong with me? Worrying about looking attractive when I'm about to drown?

But she wasn't. That soon became clear. Theo had not exaggerated his claim to swim very well, though even he struggled to get them both safely through the gap, where their heads were scarily close to the rocky arch of their exit. He literally dragged her out at one point, having flipped her over onto her back, with one iron arm strapped around her middle, and kicked hard before the escape route closed.

'You can open your eyes now,' said a voice very close to her ear.

Grace did, and blinked, dazzled, as she stared up into the blue sky overhead—a blue sky she had not allowed herself to think she'd ever see again.

She turned her head and saw the dark face of her rescuer.

'Thank you.'

Theo found the urge to throttle her fading as those blue eyes met his, glowing with gratitude.

'You didn't panic. Well done.'

'Oh, God, don't be nice to me or I'll start crying.'

'You already are.'

'You are so pedantic,' she sniffed—before a wave washed over her head, leaving her spluttering.

'I'd love to hang around here chatting, but we need to move or the tide will take us back into the grotto.'

Grace realised that the entrance was now totally covered in water. She nodded. But the shore looked a long way off.

'Just do what you can and I'll do the rest,' he said, obviously seeing her fearful look.

She nodded again and set her chin.

It seemed a long time later when he said, 'You can stand up now.'

'Easy for you to say,' she mumbled, stretching down to feel the sandy floor, bobbing on one leg to keep her head above the water.

Watching her pale hair streaming around her face like exotic strands of seaweed, as she breathlessly bounced and quite incredibly joked, Theo felt something nameless shift inside him.

She would have been entitled to milk the drama, but here she was cracking jokes. Whatever else she was, she was no coward. Nor, for that matter, a drama queen.

Grace's legs were shaking as, arms outstretched, she strode towards the strip of sand. There was a lot less of it than there had been the last time she'd seen it.

When she got knee high in the water she stood there, her chest lifting with the laboured breaths that sucked in the muscles of her belly, and pushed both shaking hands over her dripping hair, squeezing the water out of the ends.

She turned her head and saw Theo was watching her. His stare made her painfully conscious that her clothes were clinging like a second skin. She fought the urge to wrap her arms around herself and instead returned his stare steadily.

She could hardly come over all Victorian virgin and tell him to avert his eyes. The man had just saved her life and, while the drenched clothes were revealing, they were less so than a bikini. Besides, he was hardly going to be overcome with lust.

Maybe that's your problem?

Almost stumbling as she caught herself in the insane thought that she *wanted* him to lust after her, she threw herself onto the sand.

Theo watched as she took a couple of steps before falling full-length onto the sand, arms and legs outstretched. For a split second he thought she'd collapsed. And then she turned her head to reveal a cheek coated with sand and began to move her supple limbs.

'A sand angel!' she cried, flipping over and repeating the process on her back, her laughing face turned to the sky.

'How much salt water did you swallow?' he asked, amused despite himself.

Her joy was contagious.

She pulled herself into a sitting position, sand-coated knees drawn up to her chin, and started to dust off the wet sand that adhered to her face, only managing to deposit more from her sand-encrusted hands.

'I'm celebrating being alive,' she said, conscious as she stared up at the impossibly tall man standing there that she must have looked…did still look…ridiculous.

No man should be able to look both authoritative and breathtakingly handsome in soggy clothes, with water literally dripping off his lean body, but Theo managed the impossible. She thought despairingly that he looked as sexy as a dark fallen angel…or even Lucifer himself.

'I was being spontaneous.'

She lowered her eyes and gave a self-conscious half-shrug before reaching for her discarded shirt. The action dislodged her phone from its resting place, and it fell to the sand a couple of feet away. She took a couple of squelchy steps and picked it up, nursing it against her chest as she turned to face him and found his eyes on her, the expression in their dark depths impenetrable.

To fill the lengthening uncomfortable silence and drown out the thundering sound of her heartbeat, Grace rushed into speech.

'Lucky I left it here or it would have been ruined.'

She winced at the chirpy sound of her own voice, but felt a rush of relief when he veiled his eyes.

In Theo's experience, people who always looked on the bright side, even when there wasn't one, fell into two camps: the unintelligent and the irritating.

The former he could forgive. The latter...

Grace was not unintelligent, and despite this he found himself fighting off a smile.

'Oh, yes, that shows great foresight,' he drawled. 'If you're going to drown yourself, the number one thing to remember is to protect your mobile devices.'

Grace scowled, but clearly her heart wasn't in it as she fixed him with her big blue stare.

'I know you probably don't want to make a big thing of it, but you did save my life.'

'By all means make a big thing of it,' encouraged Theo, who usually very much disliked the idea of gushing gratitude. 'I'm gutted you're not telling me I'm your hero.'

'I'm grateful, but let's not go overboard...' She paused, her soft lips quivering slightly, as she brushed more of the drying sand from her upper arms.

Her brush with death was clearly too recent for her

to keep up the facade of flippancy. Despite the sun that was beating down, he could see that her skin beneath the layer of sand was marbled with goosebumps.

'Can you walk?' he asked, his brusqueness disguising an inconvenient stab of concern as he looked down at her.

Utterly mortified by the fact that she must be coming across like some swooning Victorian maiden in a melodrama, who fell at the hero's feet in every scene, Grace lifted her chin.

'Of course I can walk,' she retorted coolly, proving the fact by taking a firm step away from him—too firm for her ankle, but she kept the wince inside.

Her action hadn't taken her clear of his personal raw male, mind-numbing zone, but it was an improvement.

'I don't make a habit of—'

Coming across as a total incapable fool.

She paused to tuck her hair behind her ears in a businesslike fashion. 'Obviously I am very grateful...'

'But you don't want to be?'

'This is very embarrassing for me!' she flung, responding angrily to the mockery in his face. 'This is not me. I'm not a person who needs rescuing. I'm the person who makes other people feel safe.'

Deep frustration pushed the words from her lips... words which were followed by taut silence.

'Is that what you did for my—for Salvatore?'

The hands clenched at her sides relaxed as she shot a questioning glance up at him, but her attempt to read his expression was frustrated by his shuttered expression.

'I hope so. I think I did.'

'Were you there when...?' The question seemed to come almost against his will.

'He wasn't alone.' She offered the information quietly. 'Marta and I were both there with him when he slipped away.'

Theo said nothing as he stood there, his feelings hidden behind an impassive mask. He felt the pain like an exposed nerve as a layer of his emotional isolation was stripped away.

He told himself that it was because of this place he hated...this place his father had loved.

'He really is dead.'

He'd spoken as though the reality had just hit him, and Grace felt an unwilling surge of empathy.

'I'm not, though...thanks to you.'

He looked down as if he had forgotten she was there. 'We need to get you back up to the palazzo.'

She talked tough but she looked so fragile, he thought. So damned vulnerable standing there.

He wanted—wanted...

Instead of analysing what he wanted he growled out, '*Dio*, but you need a keeper.'

She stuck her chin out. 'I don't need to be *got* anywhere. I'm not a parcel. I am more than capable of taking myself. I know they say that if you save someone's life it's your responsibility for ever, but don't take it too literally—I really don't make a habit of needing rescuing.'

It seemed a point worth emphasising, and she already had an entire family who would run her life if she allowed them to.

He gave a faint sardonic smile. 'Do they say that?'

She shrugged. 'I might have got that wrong,' she admitted.

'So you have to save my life now?'

His sardonic smile deepened into a wry grin and she tossed him a look that suggested she might leave him to his fate if the roles were reversed.

'I am assuming you were not one of those little girls who fantasised about being rescued by a handsome prince.'

She lifted her eyebrows as she shrugged on the oversized shirt, which chafed against the sand on her skin but at least offered some protection from the midday sun.

'*Handsome!* My, you do think a lot of yourself,' she came back. But she was thinking, *And not without good cause.*

Not that 'handsome' covered what he was, she decided, as her eyes moved with helpless fascination over the strong, powerful contours of his face before sliding lower over his lean body. A shudder rippled through her body as she remembered the tensile strength of the hard body that had supported her, that had driven them both through the water with sleek efficiency.

'Lucky you're around to keep my ego in check.'

She snorted. It seemed to her that his bulletproof vest ego would survive any natural disaster and several manmade ones.

'My sister and I were encouraged to think of ourselves as the ones who should be doing the rescuing.'

He fell into step beside her as she moved towards the path, the rocks they trod on worn smooth from years of use.

'So you have a sister?' he said casually, although he

already knew the answer from that brief file he had
scanned.

She nodded. 'A sister and two brothers.'

She started, as the phone she was clutching beeped.
She glanced at the screen automatically and then paused,
gnawing down on her full lower lip as she threw out a
hurried, 'Sorry, I should check…'

There were three messages and a heap of missed calls.

Scanning the first message, she felt her heart take a
lurching journey to her feet. Apparently a tabloid had run
the story of her inheritance, and had produced a piece that
was a mix of truth, lies and smutty innuendo.

Her parents were asking her, under the circumstances,
not to come to an awards ceremony for her sister the next
week. Her presence would be 'a distraction'.

Grace correctly translated that as an *embarrassment*.
But you could see their point.

Things did not get better.

The second message said that a hastily called family
conference had decided it would be best for her to sell
up and make a sizeable donation to charity with the pro-
ceeds, to mitigate the bad publicity. In other words she
was not to fight the fact she had been found guilty in the
court of public opinion.

The last message told her not to worry—they had put
the case in the hands of Uncle Charlie, known to the
world as Sir Charles Taverner KC, a lawyer who litigated
for the great, the good and the famous. He would sort it
all out for her.

They would all be pleased to see her, of course but
actually it might be better for her to stay where she was,
sit tight until things had died down, because two news

channels had already picked up the story and dug out a picture of her in a bikini from somewhere...

Oh, well, a *bikini*... That really made her a scarlet woman.

A one-line postscript telling her that maybe she should beef up her security made her glance over her shoulder nervously.

Theo watched her scroll through the messages, her face partially shielded by the wings of her lint-pale wet hair.

But even without being able to see the play of emotion across her face he could read her body language, the tension in her shoulders, and the white knuckles on her free hand made it clear that what she was reading was not good news.

'A problem?' he asked.

She compressed her lips over a snarled response. 'Not one that would interest you,' she replied tightly—and then thought it probably would, as seeing her reputation trashed in the tabloid press would only...

What...?

Would it help him?

She had no idea, but she knew that the idea of her life being trawled through made her feel sick, even though it would make pretty boring reading.

'If you're contacted by a lawyer claiming to work for me, don't believe him,' she told him grimly. 'He doesn't speak for me.'

Her parents, who had been unusually hands-off so far, had clearly reverted to type in response to the tabloid threat to the family name. They were staging a takeover bid.

In the past she had often given in for a quiet life, saving her resistance for the times when it really mattered to her.

This mattered to her.

'Is that likely?' he asked.

'Oh, yes,' she replied grimly, gently swatting away a bee disturbed when she'd brushed against the wild herbs growing along the pathway.

'This person is not a lawyer?'

Her eyes widened as she responded bitterly. 'He's a very *expensive* lawyer, but not *my* lawyer. He's my parents' best friend and my godfather. However, even though I have no doubt he'll say things you want to hear, he does not speak for me.'

'So you intend to say things I do not want to hear?'

'Yes…that is, no. I'm not selling.'

She threw him a sideways look, expecting him to react, but he didn't.

His expression was—

She frowned, unable to read his expression…

CHAPTER SIX

'YOU'RE NOT ON good terms with your family? Maybe it's time to cut your losses and dump them.'

His words broke into the mental list of home truths she wanted to deliver at the next family meeting.

She stared at him.

'Cut my losses?' she echoed. 'This is not a financial deal—this is my family!'

He shrugged. 'Therefore a million times more toxic.'

'You don't cut yourself off from your family just because they're impossible sometimes. Families disagree, but they— I *love* my family,' she gritted out through clenched teeth, before giving a little laugh.

He frowned at her laugh, and as she scanned his beautiful, austere, *implacable* face, she could see that he hadn't understood a word she had said.

'If I let them, my family would run my life. They would…*suffocate* me. They are beautiful, talented, and not at all like me. They're like you,' she added, flicking a critical look up at his lean face before wondering why she was telling him this, when she knew there was zero chance of him getting it.

'I'm assuming that is not a compliment,' he said.

Grace had started walking as they spoke, and as they

reached the lower tier of the manicured terraces he noticed she was limping.

'It seems to me sentimental and self-destructive to maintain contact with people who make you unhappy, who manipulate you, manipulate the truth…'

'I can't believe that Salvatore manipulated you!' she exclaimed, without thinking.

He froze, and so did his expression. 'We are not talking about my family. We are talking about yours.'

The sardonic lift of her feathery brow made him grind his teeth, but it was the knowing sympathy in her blue eyes that sent his temper surging into the red zone.

'Maybe,' she said quietly, 'we should not talk at all.'

She slung the words over her shoulder as she began to trudge ahead—no, not trudge, *limp*, he corrected, watching her through narrowed eyes.

After a moment of watching her, he gave a sigh.

It took him seconds to overtake her.

'You have hurt your foot again?' he accused.

Grace, her face set, attempted to sidestep around him.

He mirrored her.

Teeth gritted, she stopped.

As much as she would have liked to try, he wasn't the sort of person you could nudge out of the way or walk through.

'No, the other one.' She knew she must sound like some sort of accident-prone idiot. 'It's nothing, really… Just sand in my sandal and it's rubbing.'

She lifted the painful foot off the ground.

He sighed and looked exasperated and bored at the same time. 'Then getting the sand out would seem like a solution.'

Childishly, she wanted to refuse. But his suggestion, even if it was couched as an order, made common sense.

'You don't have to wait,' she said as she lowered herself onto a large smooth rock, taking care not to crush the alpine plant with its spikes of orange flowers that was crawling over it. 'I'll catch you up.'

She added a silent postscript—*Not!*

She was curling up her leg to loosen the buckle across her foot when he dropped into a casual squat beside her. She felt a flare of alarm as his dark face came level with her own and thought, *What do you not understand about 'I'll catch you up'?*

How, she wondered, casting him a look through her lashes, could anyone look so elegant when they had to be squelching?

After a moment she reacted to his imperative gesture and his look of impatience and extended her foot, reluctance etched into her face and the action.

She sat immobile, breathing shallowly as he took the sandal by the heel and drew it over her narrow foot. Dropping it, he held her foot, turning it lightly from side to side, seeing the red inflamed area under the crusting of damp and drying sand.

The clicking sound of his tongue suggested to Grace that he thought she had done it on purpose, just to irritate him, but nothing could have been more gentle or clinical than his touch as he brushed the sand away, exposing a small blister below the protrusion of her ankle and a wider reddened area on the pale blue veined skin.

His job was done, but he didn't release her foot, and neither did Grace withdraw it. She was experiencing a strange, not-quite-there, drugged dreamy sensation as his long square-tipped fingers moved over the delicate bones of her foot almost as though he was memorising them.

Grace's breath came in short, shallow, staccato gasps. She was unable to see his face so she stared at the top of his dark head. The sun was already starting to dry the glossy raven strands, but she felt sure that had she sunk her hands into the abundant growth it would have been wet against his scalp.

She wouldn't, obviously.

Her flexing fingertips didn't seem to hear the message. She had actually half extended her hand when he dropped her foot abruptly and sank back on his heels, grabbing her sandal and handing it to her.

As if released from a spell, Grace started to breathe again, the heat that had expanded in her belly putting colour in her pale cheeks.

She snatched the sandal from his hand, reacting to some inbuilt protective instinct and taking care not to make contact with his fingers.

'I have some plasters in my room…fast healing for blisters,' she babbled inanely as she thrust her foot back into her sandal. And then, in case he thought she was asking him to help, she added far too brightly, 'I'm quite a dab hand with plasters…medical training and all…'

She was addressing her flow of words to her feet and not the man beside her.

She began to struggle to her feet, pretending she had not seen the hand extended to her, which was quickly dropped as its owner stood back to watch her.

Stubborn, hard-headed little witch.

'I hope you are not expecting me to carry you?' he said.

His hooded gaze slid down her slim, supple curves,

moulded by saturated clothing, and he made the mistake of allowing the memory of how she had felt warm and soft in his arms to surface and taunt him.

Seven and a half stone wet and encrusted with sand… An image formed in his head of removing not just the sand on her slender foot but from her entire body…the smooth supple expanses and the secret crevices.

He dropped his hand and rose abruptly to his feet. He knew there was no water available that would cool the heat that hardened his body.

'I think I'll manage,' she said, addressing her dry retort to the left side of shoulder.

But somehow she encountered his eyes, dark and—

The expression in them and the damped-down heat in their darkness made her stomach muscles quiver violently.

It was not one of the search parties that Marta had sent out that found them but Marta herself, and she listened to the story of the grotto delivered by Theo with an expression of horror on her face.

Grace stood passively listening to the interchange and shot him a fulminating glare. He might have played down his own heroism, but he had definitely played up her helplessness and stupidity.

The older woman looked white with shock as she took Grace's arm, and Grace experienced a spasm of guilt.

'Oh—you must be—let me…'

'I'm fine,' Grace insisted, but was not actually believed by any of the four members of the house staff who had materialised and were now listening to her protests.

Story of my life.

By the time she had been ushered tenderly into the palazzo, as though she was made of glass, through the double doors that led to the kitchen and its associated utility rooms, Theo had vanished.

She envied and resented his vanishing act.

Theo had taken the call out of idle curiosity, he told himself. The man had been urbane, witty and warm—presumably to make him, the recipient of his honeyed tone, lower his defences before he got to the actual subject of his call.

'A lovely girl, little Grace… And I have to own to a personal interest here. She's actually my favourite god-daughter, but stubborn…you have to know how to handle her—'

Theo, without knowing why, cut across this flow of confidences. 'No.'

'I beg your pardon?'

'I said, no. Has Grace appointed you as her spokesperson? Do you speak on her behalf?'

'Not exactly. But her family… The thing is, dear chap, we both want the same thing here. And if we were to combine…'

Taking exception to the conspiratorial tone, Theo stiffened. 'So that's a no. I have to say, Sir Charles, I find your attitude a tad…*unprofessional*.'

There was an audible indignant inhalation on the other end of the phone, but also, when he responded, Theo noted a defensive undertone to his response that hadn't been there previously.

'We— Her family— I am looking out for Grace's interests.'

'You have the advantage,' said Theo. 'I do not know

Grace. But what I have seen of her so far does not suggest to me that she needs anyone to look after her interests. She is a remarkably capable woman.'

If accident-prone and bloody infuriating, he tacked on silently.

'Well, yes, of course. But—'

'Sorry, but I have another call. Feel free to contact my assistant at any time.'

His phone rang almost immediately.

It was his assistant, which made him smile.

'I know you're going to be angry and yell…'

'I never yell.'

'You yell quietly,' she retorted.

'Loren…?'

'All right. Look, I'm sorry… I know you asked me to clear your schedule, and I did. Except I forgot something. And I know it's just a courtesy, but you cancelled your game the last few times, and—'

'Leonard! *Damn!'*

Leonard Morris, who had refused a knighthood, was a legend. Theo had conned his way into his office when he was a kid, with big ideas and not much of a clue, and the other man had had his security team throw him out.

Theo had gone back the next day, when Leonard had not given him a job, or advice, but he hadn't thrown him out either. Instead he had offered to play him at chess. Leonard had won and Theo had learnt.

He thought that he had learnt more from their chess games and post-game analysis than he would have at the best university.

Their games had since become a bi-monthly event. Once it had been Leonard who had made time for him.

Since Leonard's retirement it had been Theo who made time for Leonard.

It wasn't a good deed. He found the older man's mind as sharp as ever, and fascinating, and hoped that one day, if he was lucky, he might be in Leonard's position.

'Don't cancel.'

The trip would give him an opportunity to tell Rollo in person just how far he had overstepped the mark with that press leak.

The new file he had submitted still lay unopened on his laptop. Theo did not delve too deeply into the reason for his lack of urgency in opening it. Perhaps he liked the idea that life still offered some surprises, he mused, thinking of cobalt blue eyes.

Theo strolled into the library. 'Are you ready?'

Grace dropped the book she had picked up and all the kinks that had vanished from her spine returned, along with the beginnings of a headache.

'I thought you'd left.'

But silently and without an explanation here he was, looking…

Her eyes made a veiled sweep of his tall frame, from his feet to his glossy dark head.

He was not dressed for the office, more the beach, in khaki swimming shorts and a black tee shirt that exposed his muscular biceps.

Her sensitive stomach muscles quivered.

She smiled and dismissed the physical response. Eye candy, she told herself dismissively, and immediately experienced an inner cringe moment. It was a lazy analogy, and maybe showed the level of chaos he created in her head.

Grace knew that there was a lot more to the man than the body of a Greek god.

'I'm back. Did you miss me?'

She wanted to say, *I barely noticed*, but she was basically an honest person.

Instead she snorted, but didn't quite meet his eyes. 'It has been quiet and peaceful. Ready for what?' she added, thinking, *I knew it was too good to be true.*

He produced a megawatt smile, all perfect teeth and hidden meaning. 'Getting back on the horse.'

'I don't ride.'

'The grotto.'

She tensed, images of the event flashing through her head. 'What about it?'

'You're scared, and there is no shame in that.'

Her chin went up, and then up a little more, because he was smiling. 'I'm *not* scared.'

'I've had a tedious flight—a drunk decided he wanted to exit at thirty thousand feet. This is what you get for being conscious of your carbon footprint. First class is overrated when compared to a private jet. But let's not go there. I was going to go for a swim to loosen up, and I thought of my last swim...'

His expression was impassive, the words innocuous, but his honey-toned delivery made her skin prickle—and not with suspicion.

The fact was she *had* been relieved when he had vanished with no word, no explanation—so typical of his arrogance!

It had been the not knowing if or when he would return that had bothered her...not his absence. The fact she hadn't been able to let her defences down completely.

Missing him would be like missing the absence of a pain in the rear.

But had things felt a little flat with him not around?

She pushed away the laughable idea. She liked a quiet life and it had been very quiet—and peaceful. Twenty-four hours without being constantly on edge.

Boring?

She ignored the silent intervention in her head.

'Enjoy your swim,' she said flashing him a brilliantly insincere smile.

'So have you resisted the scene of the crime?'

'I have been to the beach several times and stayed in the shallows.'

'You need to face your fears.'

'I really don't need advice from you. If I want my head examined, my brother is a psychiatrist.'

'Interesting family…'

He'd know just how interesting, he assumed, when he got around to reading Rollo's file, which he had been promised held some 'juicy stuff'. The man's ebullient confidence seemed undimmed by his tongue-lashing from Theo.

Though Theo had not immediately made the connection, he now realised that he'd once met Grace's sister. She had seemed to him at the time brittle and driven—which were no bad things—but also a little insecure… the sort of insecure that made her show off.

In retrospect, he could feel more sympathy for her—at the time he'd just been irritated when she'd spoken over people and missed every social cue.

It had to be hard for any woman, having a sister like

Grace, who was not only beautiful, but natural, with a quirky charm and smartness that couldn't be learnt.

'*Fascinating,*' Grace said waspishly, clearly not focusing on her inner charm.

'Look, the offer stands,' he told her. 'Come and explore the grotto and it won't be the scary place it has become in your head. It's low tide and perfectly safe. We can wade in and walk out—job done.'

'Is this a trick? Why are you being so nice?'

'Not nice…'

His mind slid back to yesterday's chess game. He had lost, and when he'd said ruefully he wasn't sure why, Leonard had asked him if he actually wanted to know.

Amused, Theo had said yes. 'I am not afraid of a hard truth,' he had joked.

'You have a tendency to take a fixed position before examining the evidence,' Leonard had said. 'That inflexibility, it makes you vulnerable, Theo. You miss opportunities.'

He knew the old man could not see into his head, but it sometimes seemed awfully like it.

He was not about to change his mind, but he was also not about to prejudge Grace. He would get to know her.

'It won't be deep?' she asked.

He shrugged off his light-hearted attitude. 'I have been afraid of things in my life. Believe me, it is better to face your devils and laugh at them.'

Half an hour later Grace found herself standing on the beach, trembling as though the temperature was sub-zero and not a balmy twenty-three. She had no idea why, but knew it must have seemed like a good idea at the time.

She welcomed the distraction when Theo stripped off

his top, revealing the slabbed perfection of his flat belly and the definition of his bronzed chest.

'The first step is always the hardest,' he said.

'I'm not scared.'

'I know.'

She was gripping his hand and she didn't really know how or why. The ankle-deep ripples were innocuous and warm against her bare skin. Then the water reached above her ankles and her stomach muscles clenched.

'Nice swimsuit.'

It was plain black, high on the leg and scooped at the back and front, quite low, but secure. She was not afraid of anything falling out because she didn't have that much there. If she had, his comment would have made her very nervous. As it was, it just provided a useful distraction.

'You're doing great.'

She smiled and stopped looking at her feet. 'I am… I really am!' she agreed fervently, and then, as their eyes clashed, she added a soft, 'Thanks for this.'

She didn't care if he had an ulterior motive. He was doing her a massive favour, and she had never been one to hold a grudge.

She released his hand as they entered the grotto.

'It is so beautiful…' she breathed, turning full circle as she gazed around the echoey chamber. The nightmare images in her head were losing their grip…she could almost hear them receding into the distance. 'It feels I should whisper—like in a church.'

'So, not scary?' he asked, watching the look of wonder on her face as she tilted her head back and spun around, her silver-blonde hair spilling down her back.

He felt the years peel away as he saw the place fresh

through her eyes, remembered how it had used to feel this way to him once, before everything had become poisoned in his head.

'No, just beautiful…*awesome*.' She took a deep breath and smiled up at him sunnily. 'You saved me twice.'

The warmth and uncomplicated gratitude in her face as she smiled into his face took his breath away.

She didn't appear to register his sharp intake of breath as, with a slight furrow in her brow, she looked around the space, struggling to get her bearings. He knew all her recollections would be through the filter of fear.

'I sat up there?' Her eye lifted to the ledge where she had sought refuge.

It was a long way up.

'The tide here is so—' She stopped as her eyes went fearfully to the arched stone entrance.

'We are quite safe.'

She nodded and instinctively moved in closer to his side. 'It all looks so different.'

And the outcome, she realised, could have been very different indeed.

'I am grateful, you know—I'm very glad you were here and you didn't walk away.'

His expression froze. 'Is that who you think I am? Someone who walks away?'

Aware she had struck a nerve, and surprised by it, she responded evenly. 'I don't know you well enough to make any judgement. I don't know who you are. But I do know for *sure*,' she emphasised, 'that without you I would not be here. That's all I'm trying to say. I'm not normally so reckless.'

Some of the stiffness left his face.

'This was my playground when I was a child,' he said. His expansive gesture took in the incredible glittering ceiling above their head. 'You wouldn't be the first person to be caught out by the tides. There was a camera crew in the eighties, apparently, that barely escaped. They lost a fortune's worth of photographic gear, so the story goes. Nature is not something that adapts to you—you have to do the adapting.'

She nodded, looking up at him and wondering if she was seeing the real Theo, before lowering her eyes, but not her defences. That *would* be reckless. Seeing something she wanted to see, something that wasn't there, was a trap she was not about to blunder into.

'It was stupid...careless of me,' she said.

And it would be even more stupid to believe that there was more to this man than met the eye—that she had some sort of unique insight. Women had been thinking they would be the one who saw the good in a bad boy—they would be the one to reform him—from time immemorial.

'Don't beat yourself up,' he told her.

Good advice, she thought.

'I won't.' A wave lapped at her feet and she shivered. 'Should we be going back?' she asked nervously.

'You're safe with me.'

The crazy thing was, she realised, replaying his words in her head, she believed it. At that moment he made her feel safe—and yet he was the most dangerous man she had ever met.

Like the man himself, her feelings were totally contradictory.

They walked back to the beach in silence—not comfortable, but not innately confrontational either. For once he wasn't goading her. He seemed lost in his own thoughts.

Standing on the beach, she felt unease return. He was not staring, but she was suddenly conscious that she was in a swimsuit. She replaced her oversized sunglasses on her nose. A tent to hide behind would have been nice, but they were at least something.

'Perhaps we should talk,' he said.

She tensed. The charm offensive seemed to be over. 'About what?'

'Our situation. This doesn't have to be a war of attrition, you know.'

She stared at him warily and ran a hand over the low ponytail that confined her silvery hair.

'Doesn't it?'

'There has to be some middle ground,' he began, feeling his way.

He was not surprised she looked confused. He wasn't even sure himself what he was suggesting. In his head, compromise had always equated with weakness.

Was he thinking about a compromise?

Had he gone soft? Or was he reacting to the tug of those blue eyes now hidden behind the dark lenses? Or was he simply asking himself the wrong questions?

He felt a surge of self-irritation. This wasn't complicated. It was sex. The fact was he had never wanted a woman the way he wanted Grace Stewart. The hunger was just eating him up. And it wasn't just sex he needed—which had been his first assumption—it was her. A fact that had been brought home to him when he'd bumped into an ex-lover at the airport and found himself refusing her offer to spend the night with him.

'I belonged here once,' he said, his gaze sweeping over the panorama, the scene soaking into him, awakening memories that were not all bad.

Or possibly he had started seeing the place through Grace's eyes…her rose-tinted spectacles.

He had no idea if it was feasible, sharing this place with her, but he did know he wanted to share a bed with her. For the sake of his sanity, that was non-negotiable. The sexual charge between them was tangible, but she seemed reluctant to acknowledge it—an attitude that seemed strange to him in someone who seemed so up-front in every other way.

'When did that change?' she asked.

His dark eyes levelled on her face, and after a tense second stretched into a minute he shrugged and said abruptly, 'My mother died.'

Her blue eyes shone with compassion. 'How old were you?'

'Thirteen.'

Grace took a deep breath and came to a decision. A person had to eat, and it would be good to break the deadlock. Also, she was now immune—or very nearly immune—to his smile.

'All right.'

The glitter in his eyes made her stomach dip, but a moment later it was gone as he nodded casually.

'Later, then.'

Was this some sort of trap? she wondered, watching him stride away, excitement quivering through her. If so, it was a trap she had jumped into blindly. But it was so far out of her comfort zone that Mars would have felt safer and more familiar than the path she was walking.

Just dinner, cautioned a voice in her head.

And, being a realist, Grace listened to it.

CHAPTER SEVEN

GRACE WAS FIVE-THREE, and she wore heels whenever the opportunity arose.

However, although her ankle was better, it was not *that* much better, and it was deeply frustrating to have that option taken off the table when she was about to share a table—was that the right phrase?—with a man who made her feel like a hobbit.

She had selected, quite accidentally, her sexiest dress. A short, silky teal shift with a slight gather and a side tie at the waist, designed to hide any thickening around the waist area. She cinched in the defining sash absently, without looking at her reflection.

Grace had no added inches to disguise—she would have actually welcomed a few extra pounds—but when it came to clothes and her appearance Grace dealt with reality and not wishful thinking. Wishing did not give you six extra inches in height, or hair that wasn't baby-fine and didn't frizz in the rain.

Grace shook back her freshly blow-dried hair so that it fell river-straight and silky around her shoulders and down her narrow back. There was a hint of defiance in her face as she stared at her reflection in the full-length mirror.

She was not dressing for Theo, she told herself firmly.

'I'm dressing for myself, and this is not a date,' she announced to the room.

Which was probably just as well. She'd never been very good at dates—perhaps through her inability to read the room, or maybe just men. She had dressed up for George and had thought he was attracted to her, and look how well that had turned out.

She pushed away those thoughts and told herself that looking good was about confidence and feeling good about herself. She focused on her reflection, smoothing down the dress, and feeling quite pleased with what she saw.

She might not be a clothes horse, but she always felt good in this dress, because it made her look as if she actually had hips and elongated her legs.

It looked way better with heels, obviously, but that was not an option. So Grace embraced her vertical challenge in a slim pair of slingbacks, butter-soft, with a barely-there kitten heel, which were beautiful and kind to her ankle.

Giving her reflection one last critical look, she tried a swish of her blonde hair and stopped dead.

Why is your stomach cramped in knots, Grace? Why are you even joining Theo for supper?

Because he had asked.

Which in itself was strange—the asking part, at least. To her mind he was more of an ultimatum man, she decided. An image of his tall dark personage floated through her head, accompanied by an upping of the intensity in the uncomfortable shivery feeling in the pit of her belly.

The man had saved her life, so she reasoned it would have been churlish, under the circumstances, not to agree to eat with him. And today he had seemed less confrontational—less *dangerous*.

The word slipped into her head unbidden, and she shivered. If there was a way to break this standoff that didn't involve her giving in, obviously, she was not going to allow her antipathy to get in the way.

To be honest, if antipathy had been the only gut reaction she had towards Theo there wouldn't have been so much of a problem—but it wasn't.

There was no point in pretending that she was immune to his aura of sheer raw masculinity. The way he had of making a glance feel like a caress. And his sensuous mouth was…

She inhaled and closed down this dangerous line of thought. She intended to keep it closed this evening—it was just a casual dinner.

She glanced down, a frown pleating her brow. So maybe she was going overboard with the dress?

She dismissed the idea. It didn't matter what she was wearing—this was about listening. Ultra-wary of his apparent change of attitude, she was quite prepared not to like what she heard. And there was still a big question mark over his motivation. But there was only one way to find out.

She didn't want to be early and appear eager—which she really *wasn't*—so she took her time and an indirect route, which took her past Salvatore's study.

The door was ajar.

The eyes of the portrait on the wall seemed to follow her as she stepped into the room and over to the desk, where the papers she had started sorting at the start of the week were still stacked in piles. She ran a hand over the chair where Salvatore had sat and felt a deep welling of sadness that the man had gone but his paperwork remained.

When Marta had tentatively suggested that she begin to go through his papers Grace had been reluctant. It had felt like an intrusion. But she could see the logic of the request. If she didn't, who would?

Well, now maybe his son would. It was one of the things she would ask this evening.

She sat down—not in Salvatore's chair, but in a smaller, straight-backed version—with her back to the portrait and her elbows on the desk. She glanced at the clock on the wall opposite and one of her elbows slipped on the shiny polished surface of the desk, sending a stack of the assorted papers awaiting her attention sliding to the floor.

She swore softly and pushed her chair back. Then, anchoring the curtain of her hair away from her face with one forearm, she began to gather them up and return them to the desk.

The last item she retrieved was a slim leatherbound book. As she picked it up a scrap of paper that appeared to have been used as a bookmark fluttered out of it. After retrieving that too, she saw that it was not a piece of paper at all, but a snapshot, its glossy finish faded and dulled with years of handling.

Leaning back in her chair, Grace looked at it.

How old would Theo have been when it was taken? Eight or nine, maybe? He was dressed up in a shirt and tie, his youthful face shiny and scrubbed, and the woman whose hand he was holding was waving at the camera. Theo was not looking at the camera. He was looking up at the woman. His mother.

The expression on his youthful face made her throat

thicken with emotion. She could not even begin to imagine the empty space that losing a mother at such an early age would leave in a child's life—the empty space where a mother should be.

It was so unfair, she reflected with a deep sigh. She might complain about her parents, but she knew how lucky she was to have them.

As she took hold of the book, to slide the photo back inside, it fell open at a page crowded with close-spaced writing in a hand she recognised as Salvatore's.

She paused, a sentence leaping out at her from the page.

Have I done the right thing?

She half closed the book. She already knew from the papers she had begun to sort out that Salvatore had used English in his private papers—the ones he presumably hadn't wanted any of the staff to catch a glimpse of.

She fingered the tooled leather and then opened it again, impelled by the tug of Pandora's box.

A word or two, she decided, maybe a sentence.

She ignored the guilty twinge as she bent over the open book.

Half an hour later she turned a page and saw that it was empty. Flicking through the pages, she saw that the rest of the book was too.

She turned back to the first page and saw the smudges where her tears had fallen. She glanced at the snapshot before sliding it back inside, her heart aching for every person involved in the real-life drama she had just been given a glimpse into.

Salvatore's love for his son had leapt from the page, as had his love for his wife, who came across as fragile and damaged. Clearly Salvatore had made a choice that had tortured him. Had he been right? Who was she to say, standing here years in the future? But it was hard not to think that had he not tried to protect his son from the truth things might be very different now... Theo might be very different.

'What are you doing?'

So engrossed in the tragedy of the past, Grace had lost all sense of place and time, and she jumped a mile. Looking, she knew, the picture of guilt, she turned to face the hostile figure looming in the doorway.

For a second his eyes were on the portrait on the wall, and she glimpsed a world of pain in them before it was gone, and then he was looking at her, his brow lightly furrowed, the suspicion in his eyes hardening.

She reacted to an instinctive impulse and tried to conceal the book clumsily behind her back.

'What is that?' he said, looking dark and dangerous and deeply suspicious as he stalked, lean and panther-like, into the room.

There was something buried beneath the compassion she felt for him that reacted in an irrational or maybe simply a hormonal level to the aura of maleness he projected.

She stretched her stiff lips into a smile and got to her feet, disarranging the papers with a casual sweep of her hand and burying the book beneath the pile.

As he walked forward, casting her a stare of smouldering contempt, Grace's sinking heart told her that her sleight of hand was no good, and she was only delaying the inevitable.

And not for long.

His brown fingers went unerringly to the leatherbound diary, which he extracted.

His thumb flicked at the gold-edged pages. 'What is this?'

'A diary,' she said.

'A diary?' he echoed. His eyes went to her pale face and some of the tension left his own. 'Yours?'

He reached to hand it back to her—then dropped it when she shook her head.

'Your father's...' she whispered.

'And what sort of incriminating evidence does it hold, *cara*, that you are so anxious for me not to read it? What did Salvatore write about you?' he asked, feeling a surge of self-contempt.

He had almost relaxed his guard, due to his interest in what lay under that blue silk. It had caused him to forget that the owner of the big blue eyes and the supple seductive curves was the woman who had caused Salvatore—who worshipped at the altar of family and heritage—to split his estate.

That was quite a power, and it required a degree of cunning that it would be a mistake for him to overlook—*his* mistake, and one he was not about to repeat. Sex made some men blind, but not him.

Grace closed her eyes and sighed. 'It's not about me. It's an old diary, and I don't think you should read it, Theo,' she said, and she was almost pleading now as she watched him.

His upper lip curled. 'I had noticed that,' he drawled nastily.

She heaved a big sigh, as if recognising the inevitable, and as she looked at him with big compassionate eyes, bright with unshed tears, she nodded to the big French doors that opened onto the lawn.

'I'll wait outside for you. I'll be just there.'

He didn't respond beyond flinging her a frigid look of seething contempt. He had already taken his father's chair at the desk.

CHAPTER EIGHT

THE NIGHT WAS WARM, but Grace was shivering as she stared out at the distant gleam of the sea, her nerves too strung out to find the soft murmur of the wind in the pine trees soothing.

The ratcheting tension made her unable to keep still. She moved with restless energy across the grass, back and forth, starting at the slightest sound, turning intermittently to look at the illuminated fairy tale facade of the palazzo with the starlit sky backdrop that gave it its name.

She almost leapt out of her skin when she heard a loud crashing sound from inside the room. She took an impulsive step and then hesitated, before deciding to stay where she was. He would probably tell her to go away—probably not in polite terms, she reflected with a rueful half-smile.

But he was making a life-changing discovery, and no one should be alone at such a moment—even a man like Theo, who came across as someone so self-contained. Which, considering the number of women's names that had come up when she had typed his name into a search engine, might seem an odd description, but it was one that fitted.

Well, now she knew the closely guarded secret—she

knew what had caused the rift between father and son, and it was a tragic story.

She now knew, from reading the diary entries, that she was not the only person at the palazzo who was aware of the full story. But they had been sworn to silence by Salvatore. It was a measure of their loyalty and respect for the man that no one had breathed a word after his death.

They had protected Salvatore's secret.

His pain had leapt off the page as he'd described the moment when he'd decided to conceal the truth. They were words that Grace knew she would never forget.

Theo is hurting. I could see the hate in his eyes. I opened my mouth to defend myself, to tell him I would never cheat on his mother, and then I realised what that would mean.

Better he hates me than his mother. I couldn't protect her in life, but I can protect her in death. A child can never understand that a parent is human, has weaknesses.

If only I had realised what was in her mind...

I cannot risk the suicide note being discovered. I will burn it.

I have asked Marta never to mention it. I know she won't.

It broke Grace's heart to think of father and son both hurting.

Salvatore's instinct to protect his wife's memory and the love his young son had meant that he had lied when the young Theo—traumatised after his mother had taken her life—had put his own interpretation on the snatches of a conversation he'd overheard.

'*She just couldn't live with the shame of the affair.*'

It had never crossed his mind that his mother was living with the shame of her *own* affair.

The diary entry had explained that being unable even to go to the funeral of her married lover had sent the emotionally fragile woman into a deep spiral of depression that she had never pulled out of.

Salvatore could have told the truth when confronted by his young son. Instead he had taken on the burden of guilt as his own.

She couldn't begin to imagine what Theo would be feeling as he read his father's thoughts, found the tenets he had built his adult life upon being deconstructed. It had to leave a person who dealt in certainties—indeed *any* person—feel adrift.

She walked some more, back and forth, wearing a groove in the neatly trimmed grass, and then the French doors opened. His hands on the double doors, he stood for a moment in the white light, curtains blowing behind him, a tall, broad-shouldered silhouette.

Then he saw her…paused before surging forward. It seemed at first as if he'd walk straight past her, but then at the last moment he stopped and turned to face her.

His face, normally lit by a vibrant glow, was tinged with grey, strain written into every line. At a moment like this she knew that he needed someone not involved… someone objective… Sadly Grace didn't feel objective at all. Her heart was aching for him.

'Did you know?' he asked abruptly, his voice a low growl as he stepped back.

Grace saw that since she had left the room he had discarded his jacket. His dark, normally sleek hair stood in spiky disarray around his face, as though he had run his fingers through it multiple times, and several of the buttons on his shirt had come adrift, enough to reveal a section of his muscled chest.

'No, not until just now, when I read what your father had written. But, Theo…' His head turned from his brooding contemplation of the starlit sky. 'I did know how much your father loved you.'

He suddenly raised clenched hands to his temples, and his laugh sounded like glass breaking. 'Well, that makes it all right, then. Sorry…' he ground out, clenching his jaw.

'It's fine,' she said, in her best objective observer voice, seeing through his anger to the pain beneath.

'I can't believe this. All these years… Why the hell would he do that?' He swung back to her once more. 'He stood in that room when I was kid and I told him I hated him. I called him— The things I said— And he just stood there and took it. *Why?*'

He groaned, and the sound was almost one of animalistic pain that made her want to cover her ears.

'Why didn't he just say that it was *her* affair…*her* shame? She had to have been cheating on him for years. He *lived* with her. He *knew* about her infidelity. And yet he— Why did he let me think that he—?'

He was shaking his head, and she could see him digging deep for control, gathering his considerable resources before he turned back.

'This has nothing to do with you. I'm sorry. It's not your problem. It's just that you were…here…'

'Salvatore made it my problem when for his own reasons—which we might never know—he named me in his will,' Grace reminded him quietly. 'So, you see, I am now involved.'

'You had no part in the lie I have been living most of

my life…hating the man. He was right you know,' he added.

'Right…?'

A muscle clenched in his jaw. 'I would have hated her.' He flung the words at her almost like a challenge.

'You were a child, Theo.' Her heart ached for his pain. 'And your mother was not well.'

'Is that what you call cheating on your husband?'

'She was in love.'

'Are you defending her?'

'Parents are just people…like you and me. They're not perfect. I'm sure your mother loved your father too, in a different way, and she *did* love you,' she added sadly, thinking of the tragic figure in the portrait. 'I suppose you can't pick who you love.'

He was staring at her with an intensity that was hard to bear but she didn't look away. Her heart twisted painfully in her chest when she tried to imagine what he must be feeling at this moment.

'She didn't love him *or* me.'

The words seemed wrenched from him against his will.

'Oh, no!' she exclaimed stepping forward.

She hesitated a moment before reaching up to place her hand palm flat against the rigid muscles of his upper arm, letting it lie there.

She doubted he even registered it.

'I've seen the photos. She *adored* you. And your father… Well, maybe they drifted apart, or she couldn't love him in the way he loved her. It happens.'

Something in her voice seemed to penetrate his black mood and made him look at her sharply. 'It's happened to you?'

She thought about lying, or not saying anything more, but decided that if focusing on her messed-up life took his mind off his own she could live with having her privacy invaded.

She nodded. 'I thought he loved me, but he didn't…' She swallowed. 'Except as a sister,' she added.

'And now?'

'We're friends now. He married my sister.'

'And you are all right with that?' he asked incredulously.

'I don't have a lot of choice.'

'What a bastard!'

She gave a light laugh. 'Now, that *would* make it easier,' she admitted wryly, beginning to feel embarrassed that she had shared something so private. 'But actually George is awfully nice. And she's my sister. It's not like I could—' She stopped, a self-conscious expression drifting across her face.

'Not like you could cut her out of your life? You'd be surprised how easy it is,' he drawled. 'I'm the expert.'

'I didn't mean that.'

Theo inhaled, his chest lifting as he stared blankly straight ahead, and then he said abruptly, 'Salvatore…' He paused. 'My father…'

It was as if not even in the privacy of his own thoughts had he used the word for a very long time.

'He's dead, and I will never— We will never be able to— I was a child, but now— He took that choice away from me.'

'I know,' she said, every cell in her body aching at the suffering etched in his face. 'But your father loved you.'

Her soft, calm voice seemed to be getting through the maelstrom of emotions that must be gripping him.

'And he knew that deep down you loved him. I'm sure of it. I can't judge his choice. I think he judged himself. But he thought he was doing the right thing. He struggled with it, but in the end he didn't want to tarnish the love you had for her mother. He wanted to protect your memories of her.'

She felt some of the tension in his bulging biceps relax a notch.

'I understand that you're angry.'

'Understand?'

She winced at the snarled response.

'No, you're right,' she admitted. 'I have no idea how you're feeling—how could I?'

His expression softened fractionally as he looked down at her face. 'I don't know how I'm feeling,' he admitted with a wry twist of his lips as he lifted his gaze, looking out into the distance towards the sea. 'He went to his grave letting me think that he killed my mother—that the shame that drove her to take her life was the fact that *he* was unfaithful.'

Grace didn't respond. She didn't think he expected her to.

'It's such a bloody unholy mess…' He jabbed his long fingers into his dark pelt of hair, leaving a few extra sexy spikes when he lowered them. 'The times I have thought of this place…'

'You love it, don't you?' she said, not realising she had voiced her discovery out loud until he tipped his head sharply to stare down at her.

'I have a Welsh friend… They have a word for it: *hiraeth*—there's no translation in English,' he added, turning his gaze to the dark outline of the distant mountains against the night sky. 'But it means a tug…a *yearning* for a place or a feeling that is lost. Something that can never be revisited—a kind of deep longing…homesickness tinged with sorrow.'

She felt tears prick her eyes. She suspected this was the first time he had admitted, even to himself, his emotional connection to this place.

'And now you're home,' she said softly.

His home—not hers, she reminded herself as he glanced down at her, looking startled by her comment, as though the idea had not occurred to him. But it would. If not now, then soon, she was sure.

He might not realise it yet, but there was no reason for Theo to reject his birthright any longer—which meant there was no reason for her to be here.

And when she had left—when this was all a memory and she was back nursing, which she loved—would she feel a sense of what he was describing? This…*hiraeth*? Could a person grow that close to somewhere in such a short space of time?

People fell in love in a short space of time, or so she had heard.

She had known George for a year before she'd decided her warm feelings for him were love.

These days she wondered if that 'love' hadn't just been having someone who listened to what she was saying and looked interested. As a person who came from a family where everyone was more knowledgeable than she was, Grace was used to having her opinion drowned out in any conversation. It had been quite intoxicating to have someone hear what she was saying.

But when she'd looked at George she had never felt the sort of sexual hunger that she did when she looked at Theo.

'We haven't eaten,' he said.

She blinked and shook her head, admitting, 'I'd forgotten.'

Getting dressed that evening, knowing there was only one person she was trying to impress, feeling that little illicit thrill of excitement in the pit of her belly that she wouldn't acknowledge but enjoyed, seemed a lifetime ago.

'I'm not really hungry now.'

He didn't force it, and she reasoned he probably wanted to be alone. He had a lot to process.

'I— Well— Goodnight,' she said suddenly unable to meet his eyes.

It hadn't been easy, but she had been able to fight her powerful attraction to his dark, brooding looks. Glimpsing his vulnerability had cut through all her defences.

'I'm glad he had you for those last weeks.'

Theo looked as surprised to hear himself delivering the comment as Grace felt receiving it.

'He was not in pain,' she said, hoping that made him feel better.

'Good. But I meant that you… I think your company must have made his last days… I'm glad he was not alone.'

His eyes were drawn to her mouth, and he felt a quiver of lust as his glance lingered on the lush, quivering outline.

'I enjoyed his company—*just* his company,' she said, flushing. An antagonistic glitter appeared in her electric blue eyes as she lifted her chin. 'No matter what the tabloids say. I suppose you've read the article?'

'I don't read tabloids,' he said, not adding that he didn't have to.

There were people in his employ who did it for him—people, in this instance, who planted the stories to begin with.

'Shame not everyone follows your example,' she said.

'Their numbers are falling all the time, and nobody believes what they read,' he said, finding himself unable to meet her eyes.

She smiled, appreciating his attempt to make her feel better.

'I wish that were true—' she began, then promptly lost her thread as their glances collided and held.

It was as if some invisible force had her in its grip.

Grace had never felt anything like it.

The air quivered as the elusive attraction between them flared and grew hot.

If only life was as simple and uncomplicated as lust, Theo mused, feeling its tug. For once he didn't push back against it. He let it envelop him, heat his blood, awaken his senses and fill his head.

Looking at her mouth, he didn't have to think…he didn't have to sift through the maze of emotions that today's discovery had shaken free.

In the space of time it had taken for him to read those handwritten pages everything Theo had believed had slipped away. He felt as though he was walking through quicksand. For years when he'd thought of his father it had been with a flat, cold anger—anger that was still there. He felt cheated…mortified… And the first scratches of guilt were like nails on a blackboard.

His jaw clenched as he tried to block the emotional gut-punch.

Staring at her mouth was, he discovered, a way of silencing the angry buzz of thoughts swirling in his head.

Grace was no longer trying to break eye contact with Theo. He was still staring at her. With an expression in his dark eyes that made her heart rate quicken and her knees shake a little.

'It must be a lot to take in,' she said, feeling impelled to say something, even if it did sound trite.

She had to cut through this new tension that buzzed in the air between them.

'Tomorrow,' he said. 'I don't want to take it in tonight.'

Tonight he wanted to bury himself in her soft body and experience the uncomplicated, mind-numbing pleasure of sex.

Grace wanted to look away, but she couldn't. Her throat was dry, her heart was hammering, and the fist of desire in her chest was making it hard for her to breathe as she looked up at him with eyes that were feverishly jewel-bright.

'What do you want to do tonight?'

Hearing the words that fell from her lips…hearing a voice she barely recognised as her own…she suddenly experienced a moment's panic.

What if she was reading this wrong?

'The same thing as you.'

She gave him a long, level look. 'You don't know what I want.'

'I like a challenge.'

He smiled, then. It was not a gentle smile—it was dark and dangerous and it made her shake.

'I'm open to instruction.'

His fingers were gentle as they cupped her chin, drawing her face up to his, one hand stroking her hair as he bent down and fitted his mouth to hers.

There was a desperation and a terrifying need in his kiss that lit something inside her. With a half-moan, half-sob, Grace fell into him, grabbing at his shirt, hooking her fingers into the nape of his neck, to drag herself close. She pressed her body against his hard, muscular chest, revelling in the exciting solidity of his lean body.

He answered her aggression by increasing the pressure of his thrusting tongue, opening her mouth wider, until she felt as though he would consume her.

Then he found her breast, his hand curving across the small mound, moulding it, while softening the kiss until it was a slow, aching, gentle torment.

By this point Grace's brain had stopped functioning. Instinct and blind hunger were in charge. She was just along for the ride. Her knees had buckled and she was floating…holding on for dear life.

He drew his head back for a moment and looked down at her face, his glazed eyes half closed, his face flushed, his delicious lips parted against her mouth.

'You are perfect,' he breathed, tracing a slow and not quite steady path with one finger down her jaw. 'I need you. I need *this*…' he groaned.

'I need this too,' she said, breathing as hard as he was.

His dark eyes flared with a primitive satisfaction as he picked her up.

She didn't protest. She just linked her arms around his neck as he strode towards the illuminated building.

CHAPTER NINE

'YOUR PLACE OR MINE?' he said as he turned and, still carrying her, shouldered his way through a side door and then a small corridor that was dimly lit by a row of shaded wall lights.

'Whichever is nearer.'

'Good thinking,' he said, with a fierce smile that melted her bones. 'Then yours it is. I want to kiss you some more, but if I do we won't get to your bedroom. And I don't think our first time should be on a back staircase. But please know,' he added, taking the stairs in question two at a time, 'that I am thinking about kissing you. I am thinking about kissing every inch of you.'

When they got there her room was just the way she'd left it. But she was very different.

She was about to take a lover!

And not before time, said the voice in her head.

Theo walked over to the four-poster bed and haphazardly pulled back the pretty quilt, before laying her on her back across the bed and kneeling above her, his hands either side of her face.

'Now...' he said, trailing a series of butterfly kisses along her jaw. 'Those kisses I owe you, *cara...*'

Neck extended, back arched, her head pushed deep into the mattress, she lay there with her eyes closed. And above her head her fingers curled while he kissed his way down the swanlike column of her throat, along her jaw. He paused as he reached her mouth, staring down at her before he claimed it, tasting and teasing, tugging sensuously, as if filling his mouth with the taste of her and letting her taste him.

Grace felt the flames inside her getting hotter as the kiss deepened. She lowered her arms in order to slide them around his ribcage, locking them against his spine as she kissed him back, meeting his exploring tongue and opening her mouth wide to deepen the penetration.

She strained upwards, pressing her aching breasts against his chest as they rolled over, locked together, his hands in her hair, then on her body. She was on fire.

She gave a murmur of protest as his mouth pulled away.

His eyes were smoky and hot. 'Just let me…'

She watched as he fought his way out of his shirt, finally flinging it aside. She sucked in a breath through her flared nostrils and arched up to lay her hands flat against his hard, ridged belly, feeling the illusion of control as the muscles there contracted.

She knew it was an illusion because she had never felt less in control in her life.

It was an incredible feeling.

'You are totally beautiful,' she told him throatily. 'I bet you get told that a lot… You *feel* beautiful.'

One hand braced on the mattress, she raised herself upwards to press her mouth to his belly, allowing her tongue to move across his skin.

'You taste…' She tilted her head back to direct a sultry look up at him through her lashes. 'Salty.'

Her head dipped forward once more, but his hands

tangling in her hair pulled her away. Ignoring her growl of discontent, he pushed her back to the mattress.

She fell and lay there, breathing hard. Sitting astride her, he looked down into her hectically flushed face.

'My turn, I think,' he said, laying one hand flat on the blue silk that covered her belly. 'Nice dress...but you look hot.'

She nodded fervently, then let out a low moan when he covered one breast with his hand, rubbing the engorged nipple with his thumb.

He peeled the straps down her shoulders and gave a low, feral groan. There was a husky reverence in his tone as he pulled her body up against his, hunger in his face, and rasped, 'Just perfect.'

Her quivering insides liquefied as she wound her arms around his neck, and she was so involved in being excited by the skin-to-skin contact that she had no idea how she ended up lying on her side, face to face with him... thigh to thigh.

Her body moved urgently against his as his hands slid down between them to touch her through the silk, while the clever pull of his lips against her mouth, the stroke of his tongue, made her moan and whimper, then guide his hand back to a place that she liked.

Theo felt his control, his sanity, slipping from his grip. She was more responsive to his touch than any woman he had ever been with. Her sensuality was innate, and her sensitivity to his lightest touch sent hunger roaring through him like an out-of-control forest fire, burning him up.

He was aware of a growing possessiveness in him as he looked at her. Something that he had never felt with a woman before. It was an almost primeval need to claim her as his own, and he knew the feeling was linked not just to the beautiful body that drove him insane but the whole person she was.

'My beautiful...' his hand slid to her deliciously rounded little bottom, kneading the firm flesh '...wanton...' he watched the rapid rise and fall of her small, perfect, quivering breasts as he located the zip of her dress and tugged it smoothly down '...angel,' he rasped, punctuating each word with a deep, downing kiss.

Her eyes fluttered open as he pulled the dress down in one smooth motion.

'Just cooling you down.'

Except of course he wasn't.

Grace was not cool at all.

She was burning up with a need that was like nothing she had ever imagined.

In addition to the dark prickles under the surface of her ultra-sensitised skin, she felt her core temperature shifting several degrees higher.

She watched him, her head propped on her elbow, her breathing shallow and uneven, as he held her eyes and freed himself of his tailored trousers, only dropping her gaze when the zipper got stuck as he dragged it over his erection.

The bulging outline in his boxers suggested why there had been some issues. Her cheeks were stinging pink as he dragged her towards him, his expression tense. She didn't want to say anything or do anything to break the spell. She just stared back. Words had little meaning anyway. She didn't have the vocabulary to describe what she was feeling and the total, absolute and earth-shattering *rightness* of it.

He stroked her hair, the tenderness in his touch in stark contrast to the ferocity drawn in his hard-boned dark face. She felt the tension of being in the eye of a storm, the false calm before all hell broke loose—or in this case all *heaven*.

Then, as his glance drifted to her mouth, he began to kiss her again, stroking into the warm recesses of her mouth, dragging her into him, sealing their bodies at the hip while he kissed her, trailing kisses down her throat until he reached her breast.

Ignoring, actually enjoying, the abrasive rasp of his stubble against her skin, she slid her fingers into his hair and held him there. She tried to press in harder and, sensing her frustration, he stopped, pulling her thigh across his so that, without thinking, she rubbed the aching damp core of her sex against him, feeling the desperation build inside her as they lay there in a tangle of sweet, slick limbs and gasps and moans.

She was so involved in what she was feeling that she barely registered her silk panties were gone until he slid a finger into her wet heat.

'You are so tight,' he murmured against her mouth.

'Am I?' she whispered dragging her foot down the back of his leg as she breathed in the warm, earthy smell of his arousal.

'It's been a long time for you?'

The idea that she had not got over this George person filled him with a fierce, savage determination that he would make her forget the man ever existed.

'Sort of…'

She nodded, closing her eyes as he curved his hand over one breast, making a sound of throaty appreciation when he discovered it fitted perfectly in his hand.

His appreciation had apparently given her confidence, because she admitted in a rush, 'Actually, not a long time…more never.'

It took a few seconds for her meaning to penetrate, at which point he froze and lifted his head to look at her, the dark ridges along his cheekbones emphasising the sybaritic cast of his sculpted features.

'You're saying…?'

Grace nodded, thinking that if he rejected her now—

She found herself unable even to think that far ahead—but she could almost taste the desolation she would feel. It would be nothing remotely like the way she had felt when George had rejected her—that would be like comparing a flickering candle flame to a full-blown forest fire…

'Oh, *cara*…' he crooned throatily, stroking her face with a tenderness that was in stark contrast to the smoky passion in his eyes. 'Are you sure you want this now… with me…?'

The answer came easily to her.

She wanted him—all of him, only him—here and now. 'Very sure.'

'I will make it good for you, I promise.'

She watched through her lashes as he divested himself of his boxers, drinking in the sight of his body, which was an essay in male perfection—not an ounce of surplus flesh to disguise the muscular ripples that defined every muscle and sinew of his long greyhound-lean body.

When he rolled towards her again, bringing himself

closer, he traced the dip of her waist and the gentle female flare of her hip with a finger.

He stared at her, wanting to lose himself in her, the need so strong that he hesitated.

She was so small, so fragile…

He kissed her collar bone, her mouth…

He was afraid that he would break her.

But her passion was bigger than her frame, and the knowledge darkened his eyes with passion.

She made him think of a sleek and supple little cat…

Her breath quickened in anticipation as she saw his eyes darken.

'I need you,' he said.

'Please, yes…'

Her breath left her body in a long, soundless gasp as he slid into her. Her eyes squeezed closed, blanking out everything, including the expressive series of shadows that moved across his clenched features.

Everything but the exquisite sensation of him filling her slowly, slowly, until she had all of him.

She could fill the tension inside her build as he moved, his strokes faster and deeper. She could not match his technique, nor his powers of seduction, so she just held on for the ride. And then she arrived with an explosion of sensation so intense she didn't know where she began and he ended…it was just one pulsing explosion of pleasure that made them one.

Her sex-soaked brain came lazily back to life as she drifted down to earth, her body racked by pleasurable little aftershocks.

She kept her eyes closed. She knew she had to be careful not to project her feelings onto Theo. But it wasn't easy. She wanted to scream…yell it from the rooftops. Everything felt so good and so special, so utterly perfect, that she wanted to share—though in this case she knew it would be an overshare.

'Are you asleep, Grace?'

'Yes.'

She almost was—and anyhow, she definitely wasn't awake enough for a post-coital post-mortem over why he was her first lover.

If she hadn't told him, would he have noticed? He might not have. She thought for a beginner she had not been bad, and hopefully what she'd lacked in technique she had made up for in enthusiasm.

'B plus,' she mumbled.

'What was that?'

'I didn't say anything.'

Theo laughed and stared down at her face, stroking her soft cheek for a while before sliding down the bed, pressing her face into his shoulder and adjusting his body as she curled into him.

This was not an intimacy he had ever allowed himself—it was not a tenderness that he had wanted—but it felt *right*.

He was too tired to analyse its rightness…

When Grace woke it was still dark, and Theo was wide awake, looking down at her.

'You're leaving?' she asked.

'Do you want me to?'

She shook her head.

'Good.'

He kissed her—a long, dreamy kiss that she felt all the way down to her curling toes. Then, to her annoyance he pulled away, propping himself on one elbow.

'So—before you distract me—what,' he asked, 'was wrong with your George?'

She didn't misunderstand his meaning. 'Maybe I should have mentioned before—?'

He rolled his eyes. 'That you were a virgin? *Maybe?* Seriously, Grace?'

The shock still hadn't worn off. Nor had the knowledge that he had found it arousing to be her first lover—arousing and incomprehensible, considering her innate sensuality.

'Last night you needed sex,' Grace said.

And she had been handy, she knew.

'And I needed to— Well, I needed— You get to a certain age and it's— People think there's something wrong with you if you've not had a lover. And there's the whole "do you mention it on the first date or—?" Look,' she said touching her hot cheeks. 'I'm blushing and I've seen you naked.'

He still was, she assumed, her glance sliding to the sheet that was gathered around his narrow waist.

'Last night with you…it didn't feel awkward.'

Something flashed in his eyes, but Grace almost missed the moment as her eyes closed in concentration while she tried to find the right words.

'I didn't overthink, and it just felt…well, really perfect.'

'I can see that you overthink things sometimes.'

Anxious that this was his way of telling her not to read

anything deep and meaningful into last night, she agreed quickly. 'Absolutely.'

'And before George?'

'Men say I'm too nice. They think of me as a sister. And I'm not very highly sexed.'

His lips quirked as they slid to her breasts above the covers. 'Believe me, Grace, they do *not* think of you like a sister and we both know there is nothing wrong with your sex drive. I think your problem is more common than you might think. Men are daunted by beautiful, smart women. You intimidate them.'

Grace stared at him, waiting for the punchline—it didn't come.

Theo Ranieri, the most gorgeous man on the planet, thought she was beautiful, smart and also sexy?

She lowered her lashes, hugging this extraordinary knowledge to herself.

'This George of yours...' He shook his head.

'George respected me,' she said primly.

'George sounds like a loser. Does he have sex with your sister? Or is theirs a pure and elevated love? A meeting of minds such that they only read poetry to one another?'

'They have a child,' she retorted.

'Immaculate conception?'

She swatted at him and found it amazing that she was naked, laughing with Theo Ranieri, and it felt normal.

'George does write poetry though.' She couldn't keep her laughter in. 'Very bad poetry. But seriously, I don't think George ever actually fancied me.'

'The man is a loser.'

'Will you stop saying that? We were waiting...'

'For what? He sounds like a loser to me.'

'He slept with my sister the first night they met.'

She spoke matter-of-factly, even managed a soft laugh, but at the time the discovery had been devastating and had sent her confidence to an all-time low.

'He had come home with me to meet my parents. He gave her a lift home and they made out in the back seat.'

'Oh, very classy!' Theo sneered, adding, 'He *told* you this?'

'She told me. George just didn't fancy me.'

Now she knew that the feeling had been mutual— what she had felt for George had been friendship, though she hadn't known it at the time. Back then, she hadn't known what passion was…what the need to lose yourself in someone could feel like…that surrender could feel so powerful.

That you could feel a never-ending fascination for a man's body.

And the discovery was still all new and wonderful.

She ran her hand down his flank, letting it rest possessively on his behind, loving the fact that he was all sinew and muscle.

He blew out a heavy breath. 'It sounds like a match made in heaven.'

'My sister is very beautiful, successful—and scarily smart.'

'I'm sure she would agree with that assessment. I met her once.'

Grace tensed. 'Did you sleep with her?'

The question was out of her mouth before her self-censoring facility had kicked in.

'Sleep with her?' He laughed. 'I can't honestly remember what the woman looked like,' he admitted. 'But what struck me most was her pig-headed confidence that she was right about—I think—everything. It must be nice to be so utterly convinced of your own infallibility.'

She was struck with how right he was about Hope, who never suffered a moment's doubt. Though, considering its source, the comment struck Grace as uniquely funny.

'You should know!'

She stopped, a look of horror spreading across her face, as she realised how after this evening's events that was the wrong joke to make on so many levels.

'Relax,' he soothed.

'If I hadn't found that diary and read it you wouldn't know.'

And we might not be in bed.

Actually, strike the *might*. He had reached out last night because he'd wanted to forget, and she had been handy.

Ready and willing, mocked the voice in her head.

'I'm glad you did. I'm glad I know.'

Grace wasn't sure she believed him—she had witnessed his devastation last night.

He read the doubt in her face. 'Everyone deserves the truth, no matter how painful that truth is. Without the truth you can't make an informed decision. I have based all my decisions on a lie. Oh, I know why he—my father—lied, but it was wrong.'

She reached out and touched his shoulder.

'For a billionaire workaholic, you sound very grounded,' she added naughtily.

His eyes crinkling at the corners, he threw back his head and laughed.

She watched with approval. 'Maybe laughter isn't *the* best medicine,' she said. 'But it's up there…just underneath wild, head-banging sex.'

She felt his eyes on her face. He wasn't smiling or laughing. He was looking tense—she could almost see the tension radiating out of his warm body.

'Did I say that out loud?'

'I happen to be in complete agreement with you on the subject,' he purred, rolling over on one elbow as he pushed her fair hair back from her face. 'They say abstinence is character-building, but I'm willing to take the risk if you are.'

He leaned forward, but Grace held her hand against his, preventing him from kissing her, knowing that once he did she'd be toast and she'd never ask.

'I hope you don't mind me asking, Theo,' she began hesitantly, 'but last night…things are a bit…well, blurry. And I was a bit focused on— Well, the thing is, did you take precautions?'

The expressions flickering across his face settled into tenderness. 'I did use a condom. I would never be so selfish as to risk an unwanted pregnancy. You can relax. I will look after you. Will you trust me to do that, *cara*?'

'Of course!' It was not something she even needed to think about.

For some reason she couldn't fathom, her response made him scowl and look severe. 'You are safe with me, but you shouldn't be so trusting—not all men are so careful with their partners.'

She started to sit up. 'Can I wait until you kick me out of the bed before I go looking for your replacement?' she enquired acidly. 'Do you want to vet him or run a security check?'

'Calm down,' he said, placing a restraining hand on her breast. 'No insult intended. I know you can look after

yourself. I've been on the receiving end of your inciner-
ate-at-fifty-paces stare.'

He veiled his eyes so that the lingering effects of a
stab of jealousy so intense it had felt like a blade sliding
between his ribs might not show in his face.

A stab of jealousy that had spurred him into unhelpful speech.

That, and the image of some faceless future lover enjoying the passion *he* had unlocked made him feel physically sick.

The militant light faded from Grace's eyes as she realised
the lie in his words.

*If I could look after myself I wouldn't have allowed
myself to have feelings for my enemy...to sleep with him
and to want to do it again.*

She had never been in this situation before, but she
was pretty sure that at some point there was going to be
pain and regret involved.

The really scary part was that she didn't care.

The bittersweet knowledge added another layer to her
emotions as they made love again, and this time it was
less frantic. It was still passionate, but tender, and Theo
was considerate of her body, which ached in places she
hadn't known could ache.

This time he fulfilled his unrealistic intention of kissing every inch of her body and then some, and coached
her in how to touch him, to drive him to edge and then
back again, building her confidence and increasing her
fascination with his hard, lean body.

He seemed reluctant to leave the heat of her body after
they had both climaxed, and Grace had no issue with the
way his heavy body felt against hers. Sliding in and out

of an exhausted sleep, she had no idea how long they stayed that way.

When Grace woke up fully, she was alone and it was daytime.

Talk about the cold light of day, she thought, feeling the mattress that bore the imprint and scent of him, but no Theo.

It was cold.

He was long gone.

CHAPTER TEN

SHE HAD WASHED, dressed, and donned a steely resolve not to be clingy along with double denim—which was probably a mistake. If last night had been a one-off, she told herself, embracing a 'laughing in the face of disaster' mentality was totally fine.

It was twelve thirty-one when Theo entered her room. She knew because she had been glancing at the time roughly every minute.

'Hello,' she said her smile extra-bright.

'I was just talking to Marta.'

'Oh?' Grace murmured vaguely, adopting an expression she hoped made it clear that she didn't think she was owed any explanation of his whereabouts, and she definitely *wasn't* keeping tabs on him.

She continued to line up her nail varnishes on the dressing table.

'I told her about the diary and asked her to fill in any blanks she was able to.'

'Oh!'

Grace abandoned her neat, geometrically precise line, and walked quickly over to him. 'How did it go?'

'She was upset, and things got pretty emotional. She was put in an impossible position by my father, and she imagined I would be angry—'

'But you weren't?' she cut in quickly.

'Hell, of course not! It seems that there were only six people who knew about the suicide note—it seems the affair was only ever believed to be a rumour. They were very discreet, apparently, and everyone knew that my mother had a history of mental health issues. This was a long time ago, and such things were spoken of in hushed whispers. Three of those staff who were in the know are dead, one has retired and gone to live with his son in Rome, my father's old butler has had a stroke and is in a care home, and that leaves Marta.'

'Is that good?'

'Not for the dead people or the old butler.'

She threw him a look. 'So that's it, then?'

'Marta is as much in the dark about the will as we are, but she has a theory. She thinks that he left you half the estate to bring me back here. Apparently he never stopped believing I belonged here. She tells me that he always believed that if I returned—even once—I would never leave.'

Grace swallowed past the emotional lump in her throat. 'And he was right, wasn't he?' she said quietly. 'You do belong here.'

'Maybe...' he said cautiously. 'I have a very different life now.'

'I don't believe you were ever going to sell. I think there would have come a point—'

'You're a romantic!' he accused.

'No!' she protested.

He flopped down with careless long-limbed elegance on a straight-backed chintzy sofa, winced, and surged back to his feet. 'That thing is like sitting on a concrete doorstep,' he complained.

'Well, you can get rid of it—make the place over to your liking. I'll sign whatever you want. Obviously, your father never really wanted the estate to go out of the family or be split. And I don't want to profit from it.'

Theo shook his head and wondered how he had ever thought this woman was a hustler. With her warm heart and generosity she was much more likely to be taken advantage of…to be a victim of some unscrupulous bastard.

'You're never going to be rich,' he told her.

She shrugged. 'I don't particularly want to be.'

'You love it here, don't you?'

'It's not my home,' she said, dodging his eyes.

'But it could be. Look, for the moment, why don't we just leave things as they are? It's never a good idea to make hasty decisions,' he said—the man who had once been quoted as saying that instinct won, hesitation lost. 'I have a life away from here. And the day-to-day running of the palazzo—'

'Nic,' she interrupted, 'is very capable.'

'Nic is expecting—well, his wife is expecting a new baby. He's already asked for a temporary reduction in hours.'

Theo still found it hard to think of his rebellious old friend as a hands-on dad.

'And according to him there is no one on his team who is at the stage of stepping up. He was telling me how relieved he is that you're around to take up the slack. As he pointed out, you don't mind hard work.'

She hesitated.

'So you're thinking I could be some sort of manager?' she said, and paused, flicking her low ponytail around her finger and letting it uncoil.

'You're not a manager—you are the co-owner.'

'Salvatore never really intended that,' she fretted.

'You can't know that. Look, let's call this a holding position until we both settle into the arrangement...play it by ear?'

And play by night, he thought, looking at her through the screen of his jet lashes.

'Think of it as a co-operative—that would suit your egalitarian principles.'

In the act of nudging a nail varnish bottle into line she spun around. 'How do you know I have egalitarian principles?'

'You're trying to give away a fortune. That is kind of a clue, *cara*.'

She needed protecting from herself, he decided, his eyes flickering to the bed, neatly made up with clean linen.

She slung him a cranky look and then pushed all the nail varnish bottles into a wastepaper bin with a sweep of her hand.

'I'm confused,' she snapped, and he half wondered if that wasn't the idea.

'All right, then. Let's get down to basics: stay until you get bored with screwing me.'

'Or you get bored with screwing me,' she returned, struggling to match his flippancy, and refusing to be fazed by the crudity.

The reality was she was shamefully aroused. She shifted her weight casually from one foot to the other, but it did nothing to relieve the ache between her legs.

A voice in her head was telling her that the time was fast approaching when she would not be able to disguise her emerging feelings. She took a deep breath. She just had to stay in control and enjoy every moment, savour them to think back on when she left.

'I think we have some time to go before that happens,' he said drily. 'Sex with you is the best sex I have ever experienced. I love it that you can blush after what we did last night. You have nothing to compare last night with, but let me tell you I have. And we're great in bed together. Or,' he added, with a wicked devil-on-steroids grin, 'just about anywhere. We could actually do it in all the rooms in the building. Have you been in the attics? It's a rabbit warren. But I draw a line at the cellars—they're creepy,' he admitted, his eyes dancing.

'Theo!' she gasped, thinking of all the rooms in the palazzo and getting hot and bothered.

'Grace...' he mocked. 'You're going to say yes—we both know it. You want me now, don't you?' he purred. 'You like it when I talk dirty...'

She said yes.

Luca Ferrara was one of Theo's oldest friends and also a bestselling author. Theo, it seemed, had introduced him to his wife, the American actress Sophia Halton.

The photogenic pair were so famous that they were known by a joint name: *Luphia*.

Tonight was to be a small 'intimate' gathering of a hundred or so of their 'closest' friends—their inner circle—to celebrate the actress's birthday. Sophia, who really did have everything, had requested donations to her favourite worthy cause rather than gifts.

The security was to be very tight. But although there would be no press or cameras allowed inside, the couple were allowing selected press to take photos of their guests arriving and leaving.

Mobile phones would be left at the door.

A big announcement was rumoured, and speculation had reached fever pitch that it would be the news of an imminent birth. It was no secret that the couple had been trying for a baby for years, and had been through several rounds of IVF with no good news at the end. So maybe Sophia didn't have it all?

Grace was one of the few people who knew the truth.

The announcement *was* about a baby—or rather two— and they were eighteen months old, twins, one born with a learning disability. The adoption had gone through the previous month, and the couple wanted to announce how happy they were with their new family.

All the pleasure Grace had felt when Theo had shared the secret with her had vanished when he had returned later that day specifically to remind her that the information was confidential, and his friends were relying on discretion from the few in the know.

As if he thought she was about to blab on social media!

She had swallowed the hurt, held her tongue, and despised herself for the careful restraint she displayed as she told him she understood. Which was true. She understood that Theo didn't really trust her, and this wasn't the first time the issue had shown itself in other ways over the past month.

Not big things, but they had a cumulative effect.

There'd been occasions when he had closed his laptop to prevent her seeing the screen when she walked into room, and she'd pretended not to notice. He could vanish for twenty-four hours without any explanation, and it never seemed to occur to him that she might want to know where he was—or maybe it did, and his not telling her was his way of saying that she didn't have the right to know.

She might be seeing things that weren't there, but if he didn't communicate what else could she do? It made it incredibly difficult to develop a really intimate connection—but maybe that was the point. He didn't want intimacy outside the bedroom, and she—

Grace had stopped fighting the knowledge that she had fallen in love with him and had decided to simply live in the moment and deal with the inevitable pain when it arrived.

Tonight, the future did not lie heavy on her mind. Tonight it was occupied with big things, like whether to wear her hair up or down…

The decision was delayed when her mobile phone rang.

Glancing at the caller ID, she answered.

Her sister Hope got straight to the point. 'Is it true that you have been invited to the Luphia birthday bash?'

The jealous indignation in her sister's voice brought home to Grace just what a big deal it was, and sent her stomach muscles nervously fluttering all over again.

'Hardly a *bash*…it's just a meal. Salvatore left their charity a sizeable bequest in his will. I think it's a sort of thank-you,' Grace said, attempting to downplay the entire event, and mostly her part in it.

Her sister allowed herself to be mollified, and spent the next five minutes lecturing her sister on what to wear and how to behave at such an event.

'I know,' she ended comfortingly, 'that no one is going to be looking at *you*, but slipping under the radar might be a good thing. I know how you hate these sorts of things and they'll mostly be couples there. Oh, did the gorgeous Theo get an invitation too?'

Grace smothered an inappropriate laugh before responding. 'Well, Salvatore was his father, so I'm assuming…' she said, feigning ignorance and not feeling as guilty as she suspected she should.

Their relationship was never likely to reach the public eye—it might not even reach next week, she reminded herself, thinking it was not good to build castles in the air when you were standing on quicksand. But even if things had been different she would still have kept Theo clear of her family for as long as humanly possible.

It wasn't just George who had fallen under the spell of her family—virtually every person she had ever taken home had been charmed by them. She had always been philosophical about the situation. But this was different. Theo was hers and she didn't want to share him—especially with her family.

Except, of course, he wasn't hers. But that thought she locked away behind closed doors in her head, for study and tears at a later date.

Grace was living in the present and for once she was not planning sensibly for the future. She now knew that you couldn't plan for anything—including who you fell in love with.

George, bless him, had been right about that.

'You must see something of the man,' said Hope. 'He owns half your palazzo, or whatever it's called.'

'It's a big place.'

'Maybe I'll get to see it one day,' Hope said pointedly.

Grace gave a noncommittal grunt.

'Well, I expect some juicy gossip—so do make an effort, Grace. I can't believe you don't even know who Theo is dating. There must be some clues if you bother looking. There's a lot of speculation… He's not been seen in the usual places for a month now. Anyway, enjoy yourself,' she finished generously. 'Oh, and George sends his love…' There was a slight pause before she added drily, 'As always.'

Grace put her phone down, congratulating herself on dodging a bullet and thinking about that cryptic little *'as always'*. It took her only two seconds to dismiss the idea that her sister was jealous of her.

She felt like a coward, because her family knew nothing about her and Theo and Grace had every intention of maintaining total radio silence on the subject. She was salving her conscience by telling herself that, realistically speaking, there was not much point, and that the likelihood of them finding out before there was nothing to tell was low to zero.

Grace tried not to focus on the 'nothing to tell' eventuality and focused on her determination to extract every last ounce of pleasure out of being Theo's lover—to store up as many memories for what she saw as a pretty bleak future for her love-life as possible.

She knew now that any future that didn't have Theo in it would be bleak. Because for better or worse she had fallen in love with him, and he was definitely a hard act to follow!

She tried to bury her feelings, terrified that he might guess. But the truth was that ever since the first time they had made love, when she had floated back down to earth and stroked his hair as he fell asleep, his head against her breasts, she had known that she was in love and that this would all end in tears.

But in the meantime she was going to enjoy it, she told her mirror image defiantly, before turning away to carefully pull up the invisible zip of the dress that fitted her as if it had been made for her—which it had.

If Hope knew, she'd be wild with jealousy.

When a team from the couturier had arrived earlier in the week Grace had been utterly gobsmacked, looking to Theo for an explanation. He hadn't seemed to think one was necessary—which was probably to be expected of a man who had never bought a suit off the peg in his life.

'You must see something of the man!'

Her sister's words came back to her as an image of the last time she had seen 'the man' slipped through Grace's head. He had been rolling out of bed when it was still dark, the golden flesh of his broad sculpted back gleaming in the half-light. She had reached out and trailed her fingers down his warm skin and he had turned his beautiful head, a blur in the dark, caught her hand and lifted her palm to his lips before apologising for waking her.

'Any time, big boy,' she had joked, in an exaggerated husky purr, and he had laughed.

Even the memory of the warm sound made her shiver.

'I need to make a few calls,' he'd told her.

She had sighed. He was on Los Angeles time at the moment—apparently there was a big merger in the pipeline there. Grace didn't know the details, but it did seem to her that it would surely have been easier for him to travel to the States rather than come to bed in the early hours, having retreated to his office after dinner and worked straight through. Or, like today, got up around one or two a.m. to conduct business.

One thing she had learnt about Theo was that he functioned on very little sleep—which from her point of view was a plus! No matter what his schedule, he did not neglect their shared bed—which was her bed. Though he never once referred to it as *their* room, even if it was littered with his belongings. Maybe because there was no 'we' in his head…only in her heart.

Oh, God, if I carry on thinking like that I'll cry and ruin my make-up.

Grace had refused to have someone come in and do it for her tonight—she had to draw the line somewhere. Though she had agreed to a lesson from a well-known make-up artist. There had barely been time for her to catch her breath after he'd left, leaving behind what felt like a lifetime's supply of designer make-up for Grace—who was a 'smudge of gloss and sweep of a mascara' sort of girl—before the designer had turned up for her second dress fitting.

They never mentioned in the stories how intensive and boring it was being Cinderella, or how much effort went into looking groomed and glossy.

Which she did, she decided now, looking into the mirror.

'Should I wear my hair loose?' she asked her reflection, her lips twisted into a grimace of indecision.

She wanted to get it right.

She wanted Theo's eyes to darken with desire when he saw her.

Her lips tugged in a secret little smile at the prospect as she walked across to her dressing table and picked up a sapphire collar necklace from its velvet bed.

Theo had said the sapphires were the same colour as her eyes. She had shivered at the touch of his fingers on her skin as he had fastened them and declared them perfect—declared *her* perfect.

The shine in her eyes had dimmed slightly when he had prosaically pointed out, in response to her protests of it being too much, that it was half hers anyway, and that it was better she wear it than it sit in a bank vault somewhere.

'There are other things you might like too,' he'd told her.

She fastened the sapphires herself now, compressing her lower lip with her pearly teeth as she struggled with the clasp. The gems felt cool against her skin as she walked back across the room to look at the results of her efforts in the mirrors that lined one wall.

The dress that had been made for her was of bias-cut black silk, deceptively simple in style. The sleeveless bodice was modest in the front, moulding her small high breasts, and fell into a dramatic low vee at the back, almost to her waist—which was why she had chosen to put her hair in an up-do, the chignon softened by the tendrils she had artfully arranged to frame her face.

The style did make her appear taller—an effect aided by the spiky pointed heels held on to her slender feet by wide, gem-encrusted cushiony velvet straps.

She knew she looked good, and knowing it was a confidence boost—not that she fooled herself that anyone was going to be looking at her with a glamorous Hollywood actress in attendance. The truth was that Grace didn't *want* to be the centre of attention—she wanted to be the centre of *Theo's* attention.

Moving restlessly across the room once more, she bent over the dressing table and applied a fresh coat of lipstick she didn't need, then promptly smudged it. She regarded her extended hand, visibly shaking, with a mixture of exasperation and dismay. Luckily the butterflies in her belly were less obvious—at least to anyone but her.

She was nervous. Not because of her famous hosts or the prestigious names on the guest list at the black-tie dinner, but because this was a first, of sorts. The irony was, of course, that she really did not know if she was attending as Theo's date or, as she had told Hope, as joint beneficiary of Salvatore's will.

It would not have been difficult to find out—she could have just opened her mouth and asked.

She closed her eyes and felt her stomach quiver—this time not with excitement or nerves but with self-disgust. When had she started avoiding asking questions when there was a chance that she wouldn't like the answer?

Sometimes she felt as if all those unvoiced questions would explode out of her—after all, what would she learn that she didn't already know? She was crazily, madly in love with Theo, and he just wanted sex.

Her mouth firmed. No, there *had* to be more. His love-making could not be so heart-racingly tender if he didn't feel *something* for her.

She gave a small sigh and reached for her lipstick again. This was a conversation she had had with herself a dozen times, and it had never reached a point where she'd put her optimistic theory to the test.

She redid her lipstick and walked across to the marble mantelpiece, where the gold-embossed invitation was propped behind an art deco statuette.

She was not going as an anonymous 'plus one'.

Her name was there, alongside Theo's.

It felt…official. Like the next step. They were a couple on the invitation and Theo didn't seem to object.

Of course she could just be reading too much into it. Though that morning it had been Theo who had suggested inviting her family for a visit.

'Seriously?' she'd said.

He'd searched her face. 'You don't want them here?' he'd asked.

And have you fall under their spell?

She veiled her eyes. 'Of course I do. Just maybe not yet…'

'You're afraid I will embarrass you?'

'I'm afraid *they'll* embarrass me!' she retorted.

'I will be on my best behaviour.'

She had thrown him a look of pouting challenge and affected disappointment. 'Not *too* well-behaved, I hope.'

'Seriously, though,' he'd said, his wicked grin fading as he'd put aside his empty coffee cup. 'There will be ground rules. I won't let them bully you.'

'They don't! I have never said that they bully me. I am not a *victim*.' The idea that she had come across that way had horrified her.

He'd shrugged. 'I happen to be excellent at reading between the lines. So, all right, they disrespect and ride roughshod over you. It amounts to the same unacceptable behaviour.'

Her smile had a smugness to it now, as she recalled this earlier unexpected declaration of war on her behalf. But the smile faded as her memory moved on to recall what had happened next. Its power made her feel warm—almost as if he were still inside her.

His throaty response to her saying, 'Anyone could come in!' had been a growled, 'Let them!'

Shocking. But not as shocking as the fact that she had allowed him to make love to her right there in the morning room, all the while knowing that if she'd wanted to, she could have stopped him at any moment.

Some days Grace hardly recognised herself…

The chime of the clock on the wall made her frown. Theo had reminded her to be ready for the helicopter transfer at seven before he'd vanished. It was a quarter to and where was he?

CHAPTER ELEVEN

THEO WAS IN the office—not his father's study which, even without the painful connections, was not large enough for his needs. Instead, he had kitted out a book-lined room for the purpose of—

Of what? Becoming a home worker?

He pushed away the question. It was one of a few others he had been dodging for the past few weeks.

He held in his hand the envelope that contained a hard copy of the file that still lay unopened on his computer. For the past week Theo had thought about coming clean and revealing the truth to Grace. The truth that he was indirectly—actually, not so indirectly—responsible for the story leaked to the tabloids. The story responsible for her family treating her as though she was an embarrassment. The story that had been the subject only yesterday of some misogynist podcast investigation that went under the guise of 'public interest'.

He took a deep breath, and tried not to recognise the fear that swelled in him like a balloon when he imagined her reaction.

It could end everything.

The truth was overrated, he decided—and then thought fiercely, *I do not want this to be over yet.*

It would be one day, quite obviously—nothing lasted for ever.

His father's love for his wife had lasted for ever, the voice in his head reminded him. She had been his one and only love.

With a growl of frustration, he pushed the thought away. He had tonight's party to worry about, and the fact they were about to be seen together—something he had so far avoided. Grace seemed oblivious to the spin the press might put on them being perceived as a couple.

A flicker of shock moved like a wave across Theo's face as he realised that that was the way *he* thought about them.

He felt a fresh kick of guilt as he thought of Grace being fresh meat for the tabloids.

The headlines almost wrote themselves: *She jumped out of the father's bed into the son's!*

The idea sent his protective instincts into full war mode. Still, tonight he would be able to control the story to some degree. The press attending were a select few, and their access strictly limited. If they shoved microphones in the guests' faces they knew that they would never get the gig again. And at least she would be facing them under his protection.

It was only when she saw the expressive flare in his dark hooded eyes that Grace knew she had not achieved the effortlessly elegant and chic finish she had been aiming for.

That look said she had instead landed on sensual, sleek and sizzling hot.

Her earrings swung as she tossed her head, enjoying the dizzying sense of power the knowledge gave her. 'You like?'

He growled and sighed. 'You are a provocative little witch—you know that, don't you?'

'You look very beautiful too,' she offered generously.

It was an understatement. In a formal dinner suit he looked exclusive, and nothing short of heart-stoppingly spectacular.

He held out a crooked arm and after a moment she laid her hand on it, feeling the sinewed strength beneath her fingers.

'Your carriage awaits.'

He set his teeth in a smile that she knew hid his struggle to control his raging libido.

'Actually, your helicopter. The press will be there when we arrive.'

Grace hitched up her skirt as they stepped out onto the protective carpet of fake grass that had been thrown across the lawn, making a path to the helicopter. Her heels said thank you for the thought.

'I know...you said.'

'You know that it is unlikely anyone will ask you any questions?'

'But if they do I won't say anything. I'll be fine, Theo,' she said soothingly. She couldn't really blame him for worrying that she would put her foot in it and embarrass him.

'That damned story,' he gritted. 'I am so sorry.'

Grace was touched, but gave a philosophical shrug. 'It's not your fault,' she said, and saw something flash in his eyes before he looked away.

At the other end of their transfer, where they parked up alongside three other helicopters, there was eco matting to protect her heels, and they were greeted by a

uniformed team of concierges to guide them to the illuminated Palladian villa.

It was a massive edifice. The columns and steps leading up to a wide central entrance were guarded by what
appeared to be statues of gods which were interspersed
with ornamental fountains.

They came to a halt as a couple up ahead paused at the
base of the villa steps to pose for photographs. She was
aware of the pressure of Theo's hand in the small of her
back, making its presence felt.

'This is pretty wow…' she said.

If she had not spent the last few months of her life living at the palazzo Grace would have found her surroundings utterly overwhelming, but instead she was able to
look around curiously.

'Are you all right?' he said from behind clenched teeth
when it was their turn to pose.

Grace nodded, and glanced up at the tall, handsome
man beside her, thinking it was more than could be said
for her escort. She hadn't realised how much Theo disliked the press till now. Despite his fixed smile, his black
eyes sent laser rays of loathing at the faces behind the
cameras. It was a surprise to her that they didn't all immediately shrivel up and die, so great was the venom in
his stare.

She felt some of the tension leave him as they moved
ahead towards their hosts, who were waiting to greet
them.

Grace had seen Sophia Halton on the screen, of course,
but the flesh-and-blood version was even more stunning. Topping six feet even without the four-inch heels
she was wearing, the woman was wrapped in a beaded

gold gown that clung to her voluptuous curves. She was breathtaking.

'Theo!' Her smile as she stepped forward, hands outstretched to Theo, oozed warmth. 'And this must be Grace…oh, you are so lovely.'

Bemused, Grace knew her smile was a little dazed. It was weird to be told you were lovely by a glowing goddess.

'So happy you could join us…' said Luca Ferrara.

With his neatly trimmed greying beard, he was a good couple of inches shorter than his statuesque wife. He appeared more restrained, but Grace liked the ironic twinkle in his eyes that suggested he had seen the effect his wife had on unsuspecting onlookers many a time before and he still got a kick out of it.

He opened his mouth, but Grace never got to hear what he was about to say as a figure in uniform, with a tray in one hand and a phone in the other, emerged to their right from behind one of the statues.

'So, Grace… You enjoy a Ranieri—?'

He didn't get any farther, and the slimy smile soon slid off his face. One minute he was standing there…the next he was up against one of the columns with Theo's hand on his collar. There was an expression on his face that she had never seen before. His features were contorted into a primitive mask of fury.

'Theo… Theo! *Theo*…' Luca's voice, low and calm, finally appeared to penetrate. 'Let the guy breathe…just a little.'

Theo relaxed his grip enough for the man to open his mouth. 'Do not say a word,' he told him.

The guy closed his mouth, and Grace heard the sound of his phone being thrown on the floor and shattering before she found herself smoothly ushered into a side room by her hostess.

'Are you all right?' asked Sophia.

Grace shook her head woodenly, aware that her legs were shaking.

A moment later Theo and Luca joined them. They were talking in Italian—well, Theo was talking—and the way he spat out his words suggested he had not calmed down yet.

'No harm done,' Sophia said with a shimmering golden calm as she ignored Theo's snort. 'Drink up,' she advised Grace, who now looked at the glass of champagne in her hand, having no knowledge as to how it had actually got there.

She saw that Theo was holding a glass of something amber, and Luca was talking to him in low tones.

A moment later he patted Theo's shoulder and turned to Grace. 'We are so sorry that that happened, Grace.'

She shook her head. 'It's not your fault,' she said embarrassed about all the fuss. It was not the intruding reporter who had spooked her—it was Theo's reaction to him.

'Theo might not agree,' Luca said, glancing at his friend.

'We have to get back to meet and greet,' Sophia said apologetically as she grabbed her husband's arm. 'When you two are ready take the secret staircase.'

She moved a book in one of the bookshelves that lined the room and a door swung open, revealing a lit staircase.

'I'm sorry,' Theo said, when the room had emptied.

'I wasn't going to say anything to him. You know I'm not stupid. I wouldn't have embarrassed you,' said Grace earnestly.

'Embarrassed me?' he echoed. 'I wasn't embarrassed. I just...' He paused and shook his head, as if not only had he not protected her, but he was also the cause of the harassment.

She looked at him feeling frustration at his silence, his seeming distance from her. He remained closed off, while she was laying her soul out for him.

He put down his untouched glass. 'I might have over-reacted slightly.'

She compressed her lips over the words, *You think?* This really was not a moment for irony.

'You've had a bad day?' she asked.

'I've had a bad *month*!' he exploded, and Grace flinched.

She'd been in his life for a month—it was not hard to read the message there.

'Shall we go upstairs?' she asked in a frigid, controlled little voice as she glanced towards the hidden stairway.

After a moment, he nodded.

They emerged into a space that made Grace blink. The room was lit by chandeliers and lined with frescoes and a series of niches in between arched windows that were open to the warm evening air. A string quartet played softly on a dais at the far end, directly next to an area that held tables loaded with silver, crystal and flowers.

People were mingling at this end.

Grace had never seen so much glittering jewellery and over-the-top glitz in one place in her life. She unconsciously fingered the sapphires round her neck...they no longer seemed like overkill.

'Hope would love this,' she said.

'Do you love it?' he asked.

She sensed his eyes on her face, but didn't look up.

'It's a bit like the zoo…fascinating, but I wouldn't want to visit every week. Although I'm not thinking I'd prefer to see the exhibits in their own habitat, because this *is* their habitat.'

But not mine, she added silently.

'Grace, let me introduce you to someone who is dying to meet you.'

Sophia, an irresistible force if ever there was one, swooped in to carry her away. And as she smiled and looked interested, she watched through her lashes as Theo worked the room with effortless ease, not amused when she saw there were often three or four females jostling for his attention.

At the dinner table she was seated opposite Theo, too far away for her to speak to him, but she was beside Luca, who was charming and attentive.

After the meal he left her side to join Sophia at the head of the table as they made their big announcement, and there was not a dry eye in the room including Grace's. They didn't produce their babies, who were tucked up and fast asleep. They just said that they'd wanted to share their news with their friends before the rest of the world.

'You look exhausted,' Theo said to Grace when they took their seats in the helicopter at last.

'I'm OK,' she said, meeting his dark eyes with a blue-eyed stare. 'But I think we need to talk.'

This only saying the right thing to keep going as long as possible was no longer working for her. It was too exhausting. She owed it to herself to tell him how she really felt, even if the truth put an end to what they had.

He nodded. 'I agree. There are some things I need to tell you, too.'

CHAPTER TWELVE

THEO WAS SPLITTING open the envelope when his personal phone rang. He was not surprised to see the caller ID.

'How is Grace?' Luca asked.

'We're just about to share a nightcap.'

And some home truths, he didn't add.

Instead he said sincerely, 'I'm sorry if we were a distraction.'

'No one noticed—and if we're talking fault it was my security's failure. Sophia is with the girls, but she wanted me to pass on a message for Grace. If Grace wants to meet up she is always available to a friend, and if there's anyone who knows what it feels like to have lies written about her it is my Sophia, the original tall poppy.'

Theo thanked his friend and hung up, promising to pass on the message.

He tipped the contents of the envelope on the table and let them fall—his version of coming clean. The paper that lay on top caught his eye: it was a photocopy of an old newspaper report.

He scanned it and felt his gut freeze. He knew that lightning did, in fact, strike in the same place twice. But this was not lightning. This was a woman being accused of theft...of using her position for financial gain not once but twice—*what were the odds?*

And what were the odds that he wouldn't have accepted her word without question if he hadn't been… well, *obsessed* with her? A woman had never made him feel this way before—not just his hunger for her, which was insatiable, but this dangerous need to reach out to her.

A snarl of frustration left his lips, no one could be as good and fine and *perfect* as she appeared.

He took a deep breath and told himself he wasn't judging. He'd give her a chance to explain herself—he could not be any more reasonable than that.

The disclaimer didn't lessen the irrational feeling of guilt he was experiencing. For that he could blame the fact there might be a small part of him that would be relieved if the stories were true.

It would mean he didn't have to think about this being more than just sex and work out where they went from here. Words like *commitment* made him uncomfortable.

'Hello,' Grace said, walking into the room and interrupting his dark train of thought. 'What's happened? You look—'

She shook her head worriedly, scanning his face.

For several moments Theo said nothing. She took his breath away, quite literally, standing there with her skin glowing, a pearlescent sheen against the stark black of the dress.

He imagined seeing her without the dress, still in those killer heels, with only the sapphires and him against her silky skin.

He sucked in a breath and ignored the instincts that were telling him to throw her on the floor and make love to her.

'You tell me,' he said.

'No wonder you coped so well with the tabloid stuff. You've been there…done that before…' he said, watching her face as held out the incriminating clipping to her.

She looked down but didn't read it. Instead she said quietly, 'This is an article about a police report saying that a nurse stole a necklace and a pile of cash.' Her face hardened. 'This didn't just appear by magic.'

She walked over to the table and moved her hand across the pile of papers lying there before she looked back.

'None of this did. You really don't trust me, do you, Theo? Or maybe you're just looking for a back door to escape through because you're too gutless to commit to anything. Yes, you had a tough break as a child, but so do lots of people. That doesn't make them emotional cowards! Is this is what you wanted to talk about?' she yelled, bashing the heel of her hand on the papers.

'Oh, no. I wanted to apologise.' The irony of his need to clear his conscience drew a bitter laugh from his throat. 'I felt guilty. Because the guy I asked to collate this information on you went off-piste and leaked the story.'

If she had been pale before, now she was snow-white, her eyes deep blue pools of accusing hurt as she stared up at him.

'You leaked the story to that—? *You*?'

'I did not authorise it, but, yes. Essentially, the man was working for me.'

'And you let me think—? I was so worried I'd embarrassed you! Well, you came here to confess, and funnily enough so did I. No, not to this,' she added, screwing up the clipping in her fingers and throwing it on the floor. 'I wanted to confess that I love you. I was fed up with pretending.'

* * *

Without waiting for him to react to this revelation, Grace pushed grimly on.

'The Quants—Mr Quant was a lovely man...'

His family had been too, and they had been so complimentary about her work—until a necklace and some money had gone missing. She had been accused for about five minutes—until their grandson had been blue-lighted to Accident and Emergency with an overdose, and the missing money that hadn't already gone to his dealer had been found in his flat and the necklace hidden in a teapot.

'So you know what I'm talking about?' demanded Theo. 'This happened?'

She looked at his face and read the eager condemnation there, and suddenly she went cold. It was as if her entire body had been immersed in ice water.

'Yes, there was an accusation about five years ago... my second job.' Amazingly her voice was calm and steady, despite the sensation that the walls of the room closing in on her.

'Am I permitted to know the details?'

She searched his face and felt like a total and complete idiot for allowing herself to believe that she meant anything to him beyond good sex on tap.

'What would you like? Eye witnesses who can vouch for me? Some CCTV footage of the real culprit? Or will a sworn statement signed in blood do?'

She'd heard it said that hearing was the last faculty to be lost when a person was dying... Well, it turned out that sarcasm was the last thing to go when your heart was breaking. Who knew?

She knew now. Because hers was.

She could imagine it lying in a million shards at her feet, and a lump of ice in the empty space left by the vital organ.

'You're being ridiculous—and childish,' he snapped back, feeling sweat break out on his brow as something close to panic beat a tattoo in his blood, pounding at his temples.

He only knew about neat, passionless endings to liaisons. This was not neat, and this was not passionless! And they hadn't had a liaison… They had had—or so he'd thought—a relationship! And the irony was he had wanted more.

Grace was looking at him as though he were the biggest disappointment in her life. She was looking at him as though she hated him.

'I have to tell you that this sort of reaction does not suggest someone as innocent as the driven snow,' he said.

'Thanks to you, I'm not innocent any more,' she retorted. 'Sorry, that was wrong. I don't regret sleeping with you. Just falling in love with you!' she bellowed.

'Just stop the drama and tell me what happened, and then we can go back to the way we were,' he snapped out, frustrated.

She took a deep breath and willed herself to stop shaking, unable to believe he thought it was that simple.

'The way we were?' she echoed. 'What if I don't want to go back to "the way we were"? What if I want *more*? But you can't give more, can you? Well, being your sex on tap is not my idea of a fulfilling future—it's the sort of thing you can pay for!'

'Why don't you just give me an explanation and cut the drama?'

'I could explain what happened…and you could believe me or allow yourself to be convinced. But what then?'

She would never forget that look of doubt in his eyes. The shadow of it would always be between them.

'This is rubbish!' he charged. 'You're overreacting. If I am to protect you, I need to know the facts.'

'*Protect* me?' she scorned.

She wanted to scream. *I don't want protecting. I want to be loved!*

But there could be no love without trust.

'You decided I was guilty before I even walked into this room!'

The accusation vibrated in the air between them like a silent echo. He didn't deny it. He didn't even look at her. She turned away for a moment, afraid for a split second that she was actually going to throw up, and not turning back until she had regained control.

'This will probably make you laugh, but I'd fooled myself that we might have some sort of future together. I know—a joke or what? It's not even as though I can blame my parents. They never allowed me to read any happy-ever-after stories as a kid, so there's no excuse. This is all on me.'

She moved her hands in a slashing gesture down her body, as if to emphasise her culpability.

'There is no reason that we cannot carry on as we are,' he said.

She looked at him pityingly. 'If you really think that then you are an idiot. This is about trust. It doesn't matter how much you want to rip my clothes off—and if it's any comfort I really want to rip yours off too—without trust…'

She pursed her lips and emitted a whistling sound, and with it went all the nervous energy from her body. Suddenly the fire was gone and she felt empty.

If she had managed to unfasten the clasp on her necklace and throw it at him it would have been the dramatic flourish she wanted. But she hadn't, so instead she dropped her hands and picked up a pile of the papers that were neatly folded on the table, glared at him and hissed, 'You want childish? Now, *this* is childish.'

She snarled, throwing them at him.

He stared from the trail of papers leading like a yellow brick road and ending at his feet to her face. Her fierce— no, her sad, beautiful face.

He felt he had no control over the tightness in his chest.

She gave a slightly wild laugh, letting it escape her parched throat, then turned on her heel and left the room.

She made it as far as her en suite bathroom, where she bolted the door and, shoulders pressed to the wood, slid slowly down the wall.

She sobbed for something she had never had.

She didn't know for how long.

It was a knock on the door that broke her free of her miasma of misery.

She slowly pulled herself onto her knees, then to her feet, feeling like an old woman as she shot the latch.

Marta looked at her, and the warmth and compassion in the other woman's face made her dissolve into tears all over again.

Several minutes later she lifted her face off the other woman's shoulder and straightened her shoulders.

'Sorry about that.'

Then she told the other woman what she wanted to happen next.

Marta cautioned her to pause and think—even produced some crazy story about a weather front into the argument—but Grace smiled and closed her ears. She'd had years of practice at resisting people who were convinced they were talking sense…people who thought they knew better than her.

'I'll be fine,' she said, amused by Marta's hysterical reaction to the prospect of a little bit of rain. 'I'm British—we know about rain,' she told the woman, who was wringing her hands in anxiety as Grace remained adamant.

Exactly an hour later she and her minimal baggage were in a car—not one of the fleet of shiny, high-end expensive vehicles that sat in the garages at the palazzo, but the housekeeper's own Mini, which was much less daunting.

Grace's escape plan was split into small, manageable sections. She would complete one and then worry about the next. The trick was not to pause too long to think about it.

She wasn't thinking—she was acting. And she wasn't looking back. Although the not looking back might be a mistake, she thought with a wince, as she put the car into reverse and narrowly missed a branch that the wind had brought down in the courtyard.

It soon became clear that Marta had not invented the weather front. It was now windy and raining—a fact that was much more obvious away from the shelter offered by the palazzo buildings. She drove through the big gates and wondered if she would ever return.

It was doubtful.

She drove past the spot where she had first seen Theo and felt the tears begin to seep from her eyes and run silently down her cheeks. How could anything feel so right and end up so wrong?

She sniffed and told herself firmly that this happening now was actually a good thing. It could have gone on for weeks with her hoping and wishing…seeing things that weren't there.

It was now raining so heavily that the windscreen wipers couldn't cope. She pressed her face as near to the screen as possible. She screwed up her eyes as she tried to see the narrow road ahead. Then quite suddenly there was no road.

She gasped and threw the steering wheel to one side. The wild movement saved the car from launching out into space, but sent it into an uncontrolled skid.

Grace closed her eyes. It didn't make much difference. The windscreen was completely covered in a thick, dark coating of muddy sludge. The car hit something—and Grace's scream was drowned out by the screech of metal.

'Yes, I will be in the office tomorrow. I want to see all the team.'

Theo ignored the knock on the door as he continued to reel off a list of instructions to his PA. He paused to listen to an interjection she made.

'I don't give a damn where he is,' he snapped. 'I expect him in the meeting tomorrow and I will want a full run of the progress made.'

The door opened and he turned. If this was Grace, come crawling back with an apology for her behaviour, he'd make her wait.

It was Marta. He took one look at her face and put the phone down.

'What's wrong?'

'Grace asked me not to tell you, and I promised I wouldn't, but I'm very worried. There's been a mud slide and—and I lent her my car. You know she is not actually the best driver, and—'

'Stop and start again from the beginning. What has Grace done?' he asked with forced calm. Marta was not a woman who panicked.

'She has left.'

'Left?' he echoed in stunned outrage.

She was not leaving—he *was*.

'In my car. And now…' Marta took a deep, shuddering breath. 'Now Marco—he has just returned from his—well, that is unimportant—he says there has been a landslide on the north road and it is blocked.'

'And Grace went that way?'

The housekeeper nodded.

Theo fought his way through a rush of icy, gut-clenching, paralysing fear that was like nothing he had ever experienced before. He walked blindly across the room and pressed both hands on the desk, leaning forward and inhaling, struggling to clear his head of the image of Grace alone, afraid, hurt. Screaming for help. Screaming for him.

He shook his head. He needed to think.

'When did she leave?'

'I think two hours ago…maybe a little more, I tried hard to dissuade her, but she—'

'Is as stubborn as a mule. I know.' He touched the older woman's shoulder. 'You tried to ring her mobile?'

She nodded. 'No answer. Oh, I should have stopped her!'

'It's not your fault.' He gave a thin, bleak smile. 'It's mine.' As he spoke, he was already moving towards the door. 'Ring me on my mobile if you have any news, and get Nic to send some men down the east road towards the river, in case she changed her mind or doubled back. Let me know if they see *anything*. I am assuming that the helicopters are grounded?'

'Oh, I didn't— I don't—'

'Well, confirm it. And let them know that when the weather breaks we'll need a search party.'

Marta nodded. 'Be careful, and please—'

Theo, halfway out through the door, turned.

'Bring her back to us. We all love her.'

Something flickered in Theo's eyes.

'I will,' he promised.

Theo arrived at the garages just as Nic was pulling up in a Land Rover. The other man climbed out and began peeling off his waterproof. He stopped when he saw Theo approaching and moved towards him, hand outstretched.

His hand fell when he saw Theo's face.

Nic stayed silent while Theo explained the situation, and when he had finished tossed Theo the keys for the four-wheel drive.

'This is the toughest car we have for that terrain. Stay in touch—and don't worry. We'll have no shortage of volunteers.'

He had barely taken two steps before Theo had pulled away in the four-wheel drive with an agonised screech of tyres.

Theo kept the accelerator floored until he reached a point where the track was virtually washed away. He weaved his own path, negotiating the worst of the craters and rocks, though not all. The four-wheel drive bumped and jolted, rocking from side to side on the worst sections.

His teeth clenched in frustration he drove on and the windscreen wipers screeched in protest—and she was in a Mini.

'Typical Grace! Damn you, woman!'

Over the next couple of miles the rain lessened, and the going was easier, and Theo made better time—until he reached the end of the trail. Literally. His heart froze as he stopped the car and surveyed the devastation. A section of the hillside had slipped, leaving a raw wound. The road ahead was completely blocked with mud, rocks and uprooted trees.

Theo reached into the back of seat where he had flung a rucksack full of emergency supplies: basic first aid stuff, a foil survival blanket, some high-calorie energy food. The flask with a hot drink handed to him by Marta was on top, with his own addition of brandy. He fastened the straps, zipped up his waterproof and shrugged the rucksack on as he stepped out.

The wind appeared to have dropped, but the rain was relentless again—a physical assault. There was no sign of the sunny spells that had been promised to follow the storm, and no sign of a red Mini.

Had she made it through before this section had become blocked?

Theo would not—*could* not—allow himself to believe that she had not. She was too stubborn to die...too hard-headed to give up.

'Damn you... *Damn you!*' he gritted, wiping away the moisture running down his face and tasting salt.

He hadn't asked to fall in love—he hadn't *wanted* to fall in love. How many people had their lives ruined by love? How many people ended up disillusioned and bitter when they were betrayed by the person they had entrusted their life to?

For years his father had symbolised the betrayal associated with love—a betrayal which had become inevitable in Theo's head. Now he knew the truth. That his father had been a victim of love too.

The problem was that people persisted in thinking that there were winners in this race to the bottom of common sense. It was not a race he had had any intention of competing in. But the idea that Grace was out here lost... hurt... His arrogance suddenly seemed astounding, his cowardice contemptible.

He had spent the last few weeks fighting the truth, not willing to relinquish control, but wasn't that what love was? You put your future happiness and well-being— your *sanity*—into the hands of another person.

He had built his protective walls so damned high that he had become smugly confident that no one would get inside. And then there was Grace... Those walls had crumbled the first time he'd looked into her blue eyes. Trust, he thought, feeling ashamed. Her total integrity had been there in her beautiful eyes.

He had let her go without a fight because he was a coward. And now he was going to find her and let her decide his future—because without her he didn't have one.

'Grace!'

Cupping his hands over his mouth he paused every few steps and called her name, his eyes constantly searching for any sign, dreading what he might see, hoping that she was tucked up cosily in a warm, dry room somewhere, nursing a glass of wine and cursing him.

He had taken a route through the debris and come out the other side as he tried to formulate a plan for what to do next when he saw it. His heart froze. The image of the twisted metal in the valley, deposited within the mud and debris of the slide, imprinted itself on his retina—a nightmare to relive for the rest of his life.

'Oh, Grace… Grace!'

He wanted to stand there and wail, but he locked the feral cry in his throat and scanned the incline below, visualising a path, picking out potential footholds and storing the information as he prepared to climb down.

Grace had thought she was dreaming when she heard her name—and his voice.

She was hearing what she wanted to hear, she told herself, her heart thudding as she scrambled over a small mountain of rubble and branches, negotiating a fallen tree with its roots exposed by sitting astride it and swinging her legs over.

And then she saw him.

'My God, Theo! Get away from there! It's dangerous! What on earth are you doing?'

On the edge of the dizzying drop, Theo turned, the abrupt action sending loose rubble skittering down the ravine.

Grace's eyes went wide with fear. 'Come away, you idiot! You're going to kill yourself.'

Theo did not step away. He stepped towards her.

He intended to spend the rest of his life stepping towards her.

Towards Grace.

There were any number of things that he wanted to say, but the obvious one came out of his mouth.

'You're alive!'

'Of course…'

She stopped, her eyes widening, then going from his grey face to the remnants of the car below.

'You thought…?' Remorse filled her face. 'The car got carried towards the edge.' She bit her quivering lip in an effort to steady her voice and pulled a stray twig out of her hair. 'But it got caught on a tree. I think the impetus I think must have turned us around. The car continued to slide nearer the edge, but more slowly, and I knew I had to get out. But the door was jammed,' she said.

Theo saw her eyes, dark with the memory of that moment when she must have thought she was trapped… thought it was the end.

He swore, choking on the unshed tears that filled his throat.

'You weren't there to save me, so I had to save myself. I tried to smash the window, but couldn't. Stupidly, it didn't occur to me straight off that all I had to do was open it. Lucky I'm skinny… Although even so I had to take off my sweater and—'

'Shut up!'

It was hard to talk when you were being kissed.

He kissed her as though he'd drain her—as though she was the last drop of water in a desert. He was fierce—desperate, even—but so amazingly tender that her eyes started leaking again.

When his head lifted it took her several moments before she opened her eyes.

'I saved you. Now we're even,' she said, staring up at his beautiful face and telling herself not to read too much into a kiss.

Although that was one kiss it was very hard not to read a lot into…

* * *

A laugh was dragged from his throat, which was raw from yelling her name. His eyes darkened with the memory of those last minutes, the like of which he never wanted to live again.

He would never, he decided, let her out of his sight again.

In the act of brushing mud from her wet cheek, he paused.

'*You* saved *me*?'

He left that for later and ran his hands, palm flat, down her body.

'You're not hurt anywhere…?'

'I'm fine. Just cold and—' She looked at her coated hands and grimaced. 'A bit dirty.'

His hands slid to her shoulders, then moved down her body as though he was convincing himself that she was really there, that everything was where it should be. It was at that point that he took in what she was wearing— or not. Because she stood there shivering, her shoulders hunched in a pitiable attempt to retain some heat, in a sleeveless white vest that sagged under the weight of rainwater. Her engorged nipples were pressing hard against the almost transparent fabric.

'Why are you wearing a vest?'

'I t-told you—I couldn't fit through the window with my sweater on,' she said, continuing to shake with a combination of cold and shock.

Cursing, Theo shrugged off his backpack and unzipped his waterproof, draping it around her shoulders and pulling the zip up firmly to her chin.

She looked up at him from under the hood. 'You'll get wet.'

'I'll live,' he said drily as he located the foil thermal sheet and shook it out, adding the additional layer.

'I must look ridiculous… I was wearing haute couture two hours ago.'

She swallowed down what sounded like a bubble of hysteria and he saw her try to control the chattering of her teeth.

He shrugged on the backpack and turned to her, his expression fierce. 'You looked stunning…but now you look *beautiful*,' he ground out rawly. 'And you look *alive*. I thought—' His voice broke.

Grace watched as he fought to regain control, his chest heaving with the effort.

'You thought I'd gone over? Oh, Theo, I am so, so sorry to put you through that.' Another thought came to her, and her eyes popped wider. 'Oh, gosh! I do hope Marta's car is insured with me driving. I did sort of bully her a bit to let me have it…'

'That I do not doubt for one moment,' he intoned grimly. 'Come—we cannot stand here. We need shelter and I need—' He took her arm. 'Can you walk?'

'I have been walking for—I don't know long. It felt like an age. And then,' she revealed with a bleak little laugh, 'I discovered I was back where I started. I was almost giv—'

She shook her head. She was not about to admit that, to her shame, she had almost given in to sheer despair.

'Then I heard your voice, and I thought it was a dream, because I'd been praying so hard that you would come and… Oh, Theo, I was so afraid…'

She sighed as his arms circled around her, feeling warm and safe—well, safe and a little less freezing—as he drew her into his lean body.

Then he scooped her up.

'Before you say it, I know you are quite capable of walking, but right now we need to get into some shelter—and I need to ring the palazzo so that they can call the search parties off.'

Grace, who hadn't been going to protest, was quite pleased that he thought she was that tough, and she just pressed her face into his shoulder and hung on.

A short time later he put her back on her feet. She stood there, feeling bereft, but glad they were standing on solid ground, and watched as he extracted his phone from his pocket.

'This won't take long.'

Raising his phone to his ear, he punched in a number and she heard the call picked up almost instantly.

'I have her, Nic, and she's uninjured.'

For where she stood Grace could hear shouting at the other end—more than one voice, as though the news was being shared with a crowd.

Theo grinned and held the phone away from him until the noise subsided. 'Thanks, I will. I thought we'd head—'

There was a short pause as someone—presumably Nic—spoke over Theo, who nodded while he listened. 'You read my mind. And it's still got a roof?'

Another pause gave Grace an opportunity to study his face hungrily, loving every hollow and line.

'Impressive… Thanks for that. Ring me when the chopper is free. Yes, the evacuation should definitely take priority. We will just sit tight.'

'I've been an enormous amount of trouble, haven't I?' Grace remarked guiltily.

Theo looked at her. 'You've been trouble since the moment you arrived.'

She swallowed the hurt. Though it was harsh, it was hard to dispute under the circumstances.

He approached, one hand extended. There was tension still in his face, but the haggard look had vanished and he was exuding an almost indecent amount of vitality. He took her hand in his and led her to a pathway that was only revealed when he stomped down some brambles with his boot.

She looked at his brown fingers covering hers. Only a few moments ago she had felt unable to put one foot in front of the other, but it was almost as if he had transmitted some of his energy to her, she mused, as she followed his instruction to be careful where she trod.

'Almost there,' he said, studying her as he paused to allow her to catch her breath.

She suspected that she was running on adrenalin and sheer determination.

'Most people seem to think that having you around is worth the trouble you bring,' he said.

Her eyes flickered upwards, a question in them.

'Not all?' she asked.

He shrugged. 'I can only speak for myself.'

Before she had time to react to this revelation they were moving again. She had suspected he was humouring her with the 'almost there', but he lifted an overhanging branch and suddenly there it was: a small square building, its walls clad in silvered larch wood, the roof red corrugated metal, and the window frames painted turquoise.

It looked as if it belonged in a picture book, she decided.

Inside, most surprisingly, there was no dust. The

wooden floor was neatly scrubbed and brushed clean. There were no pictures on the wall, just maps marked with walking trails and posters picturing native animal and bird life. There was a cupboard, marked *Take what you need* in several languages, and an honesty box underneath.

There was also a wood-burning stove ready laid with kindling beside a basket of dry logs, two folding camp beds stood against one wall, while the opposite wall contained a built-in old-fashioned bed frame that would be cosy when the curtain that hung across it was pulled.

Theo, who seemed to be taking in their surroundings too, put the rucksack on the table that stood in the centre of the room and looked at her.

'It seems that we have several of these across the estate. Walkers and bird watchers use them for free, on a "one-night-only-and-move-on" basis. A good innovation… We could expand on this idea, I think.'

Did that mean he was staying? How was she to interpret that 'we'? Was he speaking for himself?

So many questions… Her head buzzed with them.

It was fear of the answers that kept her silent as she watched him walk to the cast-iron wood-burner, ignite the paper and close the door before he straightened up.

'It won't take long to warm up,' he said, nodding to the flames already dancing behind the glass door.

'What was this place?'

'An old hunter's cabin. Nic and I used to camp here when we were kids. I thought it might have fallen down by now—I didn't know about this initiative.'

She nodded, surprised when, instead of walking over to the two-ring hob beside a deep old-fashioned sink set on bricks, he walked across to the table.

'Marta,' he said, opening a flask and filling a cup. 'Me,' he added, producing a smaller flask and adding a generous amount of the amber liquid it contained into the hot drink.

'Thanks,' she said, feeling unaccountably shy as she took it from him.

She took a sip of the scalding liquid, cooled by the additional generous shot of brandy which made her blink.

'We might be here a while now they know you're safe,' he said. 'The rescue chopper is evacuating a village where the river broke its banks.'

'Is anyone hurt?'

'Not seriously, luckily. The new flood defences didn't hold, but they lessened the damage. When we were children it was a different story. A flood could take several lives. I remember news clips of people being lifted off roofs. And there was once a landslide in almost exactly the same spot as the one today that took a truck with it. The driver left a widow and two children.'

Had Theo remembered that tragedy when he was searching for her? And not just Theo but all the others who had gone out in this weather to find her?

Grace realised the enormity of what she had done... what had nearly happened...and drained her cup in one gulp.

'I'm not normally so reckless.' She recognised now that she had been.

'Define "normally" for you.'

'I was just desperate to escape.'

Theo was tempted to lift the flask to his own lips, for Dutch courage, but he wanted his wits about him to say what he needed to.

'There is no escape for me—not from you. We were always going end up here. Your actions just speeded it up. Not here as in this cabin. Here as in this moment.'

He paused, the effort of lowering his guard almost physical, and then pushed on.

'I might have spent another week, another month, arguing with myself, debating, hating you, loving you... but I would have reached this point eventually and come running after you. I refuse to believe, Grace, that fate would have robbed us of this chance.'

Grace's breath caught as their eyes connected, and the message in his sent her heart thudding. The silver sheet fell to the floor and pooled at her feet as she took a tentative step towards him, arms outstretched like a sleepwalker, eyes wide, but wary.

'Before you say anything—' he continued, in the same driven tone.

She tipped her head vaguely in encouragement. Even if she had been going to say anything she doubted she could have—her throat was tight with a hard knot of emotion.

'Let me try and explain.' He dragged a hand across his wet hair and gave a hard laugh. 'Explain? I hardly understand myself! But I'll try. When my mother died I think I associated all emotion—love—with pain. Being lonely was my strength...it was safety. And then you exploded into my life and started walking around in my head, taking up residence there, challenging my entire belief system, making me question everything, making me... making me not lonely. I never doubted you. I doubted me,' he admitted, his voice filled with self-disgust. 'I couldn't believe that I was lucky enough to have someone like you in my life, Grace. I was waiting for it all to fall apart. I could not bear to lose you, *tesoro mio*!'

He grabbed hold of the hand extended to him and reeled her in until she stood in the shelter of his arms.

'Oh, Theo, I love you.'

He looked into her face and released her hands, but only to frame her face and look down with wondering disbelief into her beautiful glowing eyes.

He held her as though she was something precious that might break, and she felt warm, safe, and loved by the most incredible man on the planet.

'If you're leaving I will too,' he told her.

She pulled back to look into his face, amazed by his declaration. 'I'm not going anywhere. I can help manage the estate.'

He laughed then. 'I don't want a manager, Grace. I want a wife.'

Her eyes flew wide, her jaw dropped. 'Marry you?'

'Surely you don't think I will settle for anything less?' he said, the hauteur back in his voice. 'Besides, don't you think it's a good idea if I'm around to rescue you the next time you decide to dice with death.'

'I think that would be a very good idea. Not that I am going to do anything so daft. Oh, Theo, I love you so much!' she cried, throwing herself at him. 'Thank you for rescuing me!'

'You rescued *me*, *cara*. You rescued me from a barren, empty life. You gave me life when you gifted me your love—'

He suddenly broke off his loving contemplation of her features and lifted his head, an expression of disgust etched on his handsome face.

'What's wrong?' she asked.

'Unless I'm mistaken, we're about to be *rescued*,' he said raising his voice above the whirr of helicopter blades low above their heads. 'Talk about bad timing!'

She laughed. 'Oh, I think it's a good thing to get back. We have another hundred rooms at least to tick off our list.'

He gave her a loving smile that melted her bones.

'I like the way you think. In fact I like everything about you—except your tendency to rush headlong into danger.'

Stretching up on her tiptoes to plant a long, lingering kiss on his mouth, before lowering herself back to terra firma, she flashed him a serious look.

'Now I can rush headlong into you, I think I'll be safe,' she said, and smiled confidently.

EPILOGUE

GRACE WALKED INTO her wardrobe and stopped.

Beside her, Marta said nothing.

'What the—? What has happened? Where are my—?'

She went to the shelf where her most used items were kept. It was empty. She looked around in bewilderment—nothing was where she usually put it. Her clothes had not vanished, but they were hung in neat, colour-co-ordinated rows marked *Summer*, *Winter*, *Autumn*…

Marta cleared her throat. 'Apparently the person your sister brought with her thinks you are not a spring person, and also that your shoes are out of balance with the natural world—something to do with the way they were facing. I put them in the bedroom closet. I will return them when the guests have left.'

Grace let out a little scream of sheer frustration. 'I will kill her—I really will.'

'It seemed simpler not to argue. Everything can be put back,' Marta pointed out placidly. 'And your sister was enjoying herself.'

Grace's ready sense of humour reasserted itself and she began to laugh—until Marta pointed out that she would need her make-up done again.

'Hope had her first internship at an office in a law firm,' she told Marta. 'Her second day the clerk was out of the office and she rearranged the entire filing system. Luckily it was all backed up. She really couldn't understand why people were so upset, because—'

'Her system was much more efficient?'

Grace spun around to see Theo. 'You shouldn't be here. It's bad luck to see the bride's dress before the wedding.'

'You're not wearing your dress—unless that delightful little number is what you intend to walk down the aisle in. I have no objections, but I'm thinking of the heart attack risk. There are several guests who might well need medical attention. Garters and stockings…now, why don't women wear them more often?'

'Because they are so damned uncomfortable, maybe?' she suggested, deciding that she might bring them out on special occasions if Theo liked them so much. 'You really shouldn't be here Theo,' she added in a softer voice. And then, realising that her husband-to-be was wearing jeans and tee shirt, she let out a small shriek. 'You're not dressed!'

'Neither are you,' he pointed out.

Her chest, which was squeezed into a corset, swelled. 'I have endured two hours of being primped and polished. There's been an army of people in here. We've only just got rid of them—haven't we, Marta?' She looked around. 'Where is Marta?'

'Marta tactfully withdrew to give us a private moment.'

'We'll have a lifetime of private moments. Oh, Theo, you do want this, don't you? You're not having second thoughts?'

He held her gaze steadily. 'Never,' he said simply. 'For me this is just a formality. I committed myself to you months ago.'

She nodded, loving him. 'I feel that way too,' she said huskily. 'Why has it taken so long to organise our wedding?'

'Because we have tried to please too many people.'

She sighed. 'You mean me? I know. It's just—'

'You can allow people this day and then we will have the life that suits me—' He broke off as there was a tap on the door.

'If that's my mother or my sister, tell them I'm dead.'

'Relax…it won't be. They're trying to sober up your brother, using some quite brutal methods.'

'Oh, God, which one? No, don't tell me!' she added, shaking her head as she walked past him to the door.

Her shoulders relaxed when she saw Sophia standing there. In the past months she and Grace had grown close, and last month Grace had become godmother to one of Sophia's twin daughters.

'Do you want me to go away?' Sophia said, glancing humorously at Theo.

'I have already been given my marching orders,' Theo said, brushing past the two women. 'Lovely as always, Sophia,' he called, turning in the doorway and bowing to both women.

'I don't know how he can be so relaxed,' said Grace. 'I'm a bag of nerves.'

'It's a front. Luca was a wreck. I just came to say don't forget to enjoy yourself. I'll leave you…'

'No, Sophia, don't go. They'll all be back soon, and it will be bedlam. Do you mind helping me get into my dress before they descend?'

'Of course.'

At least her sister had not rearranged her wedding dress. It was still hung in layers of tissue inside a polythene bag emblazoned with the name of the couturier who had designed it.

'Right…careful with your hair—we don't want to… Perfect,' Sophia said as Grace held her arms out. 'And let's not get make-up on the fabric… Oh, yes, that is gorgeous,' she said, admiring the silk column with its sheer lace overlay and the floating train of exquisitely embroidered satin with delicately frayed edges. 'Very vintage.'

'My grandmother wore a dress very similar, but when we got it out the moths had been at it. The designer tried to recreate it with some modern twists.'

Grace stood impassive as her friend arranged the folds of fabric and fastened the tiny silk-covered buttons in their loops, then rearranged the embroidered train and stood back.

'Oh, my, Grace… You look just— There are going to be a lot of tears when you walk down that aisle,' she predicted, kissing Grace's cheek. 'Are you wearing a veil? No, don't tell me! Let it be a surprise. See you in there, girl.'

As Grace paused outside the door her tearful sister, who was her maid of honour, took her arm.

'You're beautiful, Grace…just so beautiful. You're going knock him out.' Then, rather to her surprise, her sister echoed Sophia. 'Don't forget to enjoy it. I was so terrified that I don't remember my wedding day at all.'

Impulsively Grace kissed her sister, who squealed.

'You'll crush your flowers! Trust you to choose wild-flowers… They are beautiful, though—everything is.'

Originally the service had been going to take place in the small chapel on the estate, but when the guest list had grown it had been decided to use the ballroom.

As the music started and she stepped inside, Grace was bombarded with a myriad of sensations: the scent of the flowers that filled the room, the sight of all the heads turned her way… She felt a moment's panic, and then relaxed her face into a smile as she met the eyes of the man who was already her husband in her heart.

She began to walk towards him, her steps quickening as she processed through the room. Halfway there she suddenly started to run, not afraid of falling because she knew he would catch her.

There were a few gasps, and then ripples of laughter, and then, when she reached Theo, several piercing whistles, a lot of foot-stamping and a deafening clapping as people got to their feet, the order of service forgotten in the joy of the moment.

Theo caught his bride's hand, his eyes glowing. 'Wow, you look like an angel! And, future wife of mine, do you know how to make an entrance!'

The priest cleared his throat. 'If we're ready?'

'Thank you, Father. Yes, I'm ready for the rest of my life with this incredible woman.'

When the congregation had subsided into their seats the priest began—and so did the rest of Grace's life.

* * * * *

COMING SOON!

We really hope you enjoyed reading this book.
If you're looking for more romance
be sure to head to the shops when
new books are available on

Thursday 14th March

To see which titles are coming soon, please visit
millsandboon.co.uk/nextmonth

MILLS & BOON

MILLS & BOON ®

Coming next month

THE KING'S HIDDEN HEIR
Sharon Kendrick

'Look... I should have told you sooner.' Emmy swallowed.

She was biting her lip in a way which was making warning bells ring loudly inside his head when suddenly she sat up, all that hair streaming down over her shoulders, like liquid gold. She looked like a goddess, he thought achingly when her next words drove every other thought from his head.

'You have a son, Kostandin.'

What she said didn't compute. In fact, she'd taken him so completely by surprise that Kostandin almost told her the truth. That he'd never had a child, nor wanted one. His determination never to procreate was his get-out-of-jail-free card. He felt the beat of a pulse at his temple. Because what good was a king, without an heir?

Continue reading
THE KING'S HIDDEN HEIR
Sharon Kendrick

Available next month
millsandboon.co.uk

afterglow BOOKS

Introducing our newest series, Afterglow.

From showing up to glowing up, Afterglow characters are on the path to leading their best lives and finding romance along the way – with a dash of sizzling spice!

Follow characters from all walks of life as they chase their dreams and find that true love is only the beginning...

OUT NOW

millsandboon.co.uk

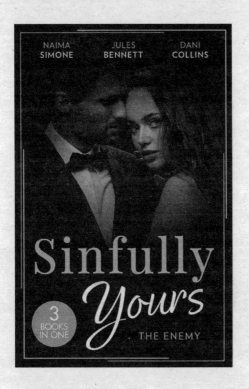

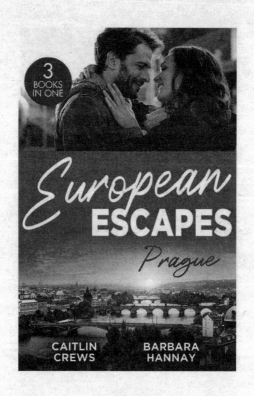

LET'S TALK
Romance

For exclusive extracts, competitions and special offers, find us online:

- **f** MillsandBoon
- **X** @MillsandBoon
- **◎** @MillsandBoonUK
- **♪** @MillsandBoonUK

Get in touch on 01413 063 232

MILLS & BOON

THE HEART OF ROMANCE

A ROMANCE FOR EVERY READER

MODERN

Prepare to be swept off your feet by sophisticated, sexy and seductive heroes, in some of the world's most glamourous and romantic locations, where power and passion collide.

HISTORICAL

Escape with historical heroes from time gone by. Whether your passion is for wicked Regency Rakes, muscled Vikings or rugge Highlanders, awaken the romance of the past.

MEDICAL

Set your pulse racing with dedicated, delectable doctors in the high-pressure world of medicine, where emotions run high and passion, comfort and love are the best medicine.

True Love

Celebrate true love with tender stories of heartfelt romance, from the rush of falling in love to the joy a new baby can bring, and a focus on the emotional heart of a relationship.

HEROES

The excitement of a gripping thriller, with intense romance at its heart. Resourceful, true-to-life women and strong, fearless men face danger and desire - a killer combination!

From showing up to glowing up, these characters are on the path to leading their best lives and finding romance along the way – with plenty of sizzling spice!

To see which titles are coming soon, please visit

millsandboon.co.uk/nextmonth

GET YOUR ROMANCE FIX!

Get the latest romance news, exclusive author interviews, story extracts and much more!

blog.millsandboon.co.uk